"Do you want to stay warm tonight?"

✳

"Make room," he then said, lifting the furs and sliding his long, lithe body in beside hers. She flinched as his hard thigh touched hers.

"You intended this all along," she accused him softly, "from the moment you started building this shelter."

"Yes." He didn't question what she meant. There was no shame in his voice.

Now he was touching her. And his touch was doing more than thawing her cold flesh. It was melting her resolve as well.

His hand moved from her foot to her calf, and the chafing had become a soft caress.

"Are you getting warmer?"

"Yes." Indeed, her blood had begun to run like a hot river running through her veins, and an insidious warmth was spreading out from the pit of her belly. A most improper reaction. Ladies did not enjoy a man's touch. But then, Miri was beginning to suspect that she was no lady.

Jordan lay back down beside her. He lowered his mouth to hers.

———————— ✳ ————————

Also by
Emily Carmichael

•   •   •

Autumnfire
Surrender
Touch of Fire

Published by
WARNER BOOKS

EMILY CARMICHAEL
VISIONS OF THE HEART

WARNER BOOKS

A Time Warner Company

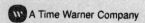

✳ **1** ✳

Miriam Sutcliffe's midnight blue eyes had been known to make mush of male hearts. One suitor had uncharitably claimed those eyes were the only part of her that showed the least bit of warmth, but even that disillusioned gentleman was forced to admit that they alone were capable of setting a man afire, even if the lady's unfeeling heart did promptly douse the flame. But the young man seated in Miriam's London parlor on this March day of 1813 could detect nothing but frost in those fabled blue depths. In fact, he was being treated to an indignant glare that was every bit as cold as a blast of January air.

"If this is a jest, Hamilton Greer, then it is in very poor taste."

The young man replied in somber tones. "I only wish it were a jest."

"How can you be leaving for America when our wedding is in three weeks' time? The invitations have been delivered, the musicians engaged. Are you saying we should postpone the ceremony?"

"No. My darling Miri, that's not what I'm saying." Hamilton lowered his head to his hands and rubbed wearily at his brow. "As I said, I'm in a spot of trouble. I have to leave. I really can't say how long I'll be gone."

"A spot of trouble, cousin? How could you be so irresponsible? And now, of all times!" Miri huffed and rose from her chair, regarding her fiancé with a frown. She could well believe her distant cousin was in trouble. His clothing, usually groomed to dandyish perfection, was a mess— Wellington boots scuffed and spattered with droplets of mud, skintight buckskin pantaloons grass-stained on one knee, cutaway coat rumpled, and painstakingly tied cravat askew. Even the fashionable collar that nudged his earlobes had lost its customary stiffness. "What kind of trouble is it this time, Ham? A gambling debt? Is that it? I don't know why they still let you in the door to White's, the way—"

"No, no." Hamilton sighed. "It's nothing you would understand, my love. I'm sorry. I really am sorry."

"Nothing I would understand? Ridiculous. We've been friends since we were children together in this house, and I'm soon to be your wife. Hamilton, no one understands you the way I do."

Hamilton shook his head, eyeing Miri's small, pert face; outthrust, stubborn chin; and bright auburn curls with a glance of mild regret. "You really are something, Miri. No doubt you would have turned me into a proper Christian husband. No gaming, no cursing, no smoking in the parlor." He sighed. "Yes, no doubt you would have. If we'd married a year ago, when I first proposed, none of this would have happened."

"Hamilton!" Miri sat down again, her voice steely with determination not to panic. "I insist that you tell me what is happening. I think I have the right to know. Do you realize that you are as good as leaving me at the altar? Think of my reputation! It will be damaged beyond repair. That awful Mrs. Pelham will be absolutely delighted to spread a new Sutcliffe scandal throughout all of society."

"I'm sorry, Miri—I really am." Hamilton was beginning

to look somewhat less sorry as Miri's tone grew sharper, but he made a manful attempt to hide it. "I vow no man has ever anticipated his nuptials with more joy than I. But Miri, my love, if I stay in London for three more weeks, I'll be dead rather than wed. I must leave immediately."

Miri's eyes narrowed slightly. "And you won't tell me why?"

"Believe me. It's best that you don't know."

"Well, then, we must simply announce a postponement."

"I'm afraid that won't do, my love. I have no idea when I can return."

"An indefinite postponement, then."

Hamilton rubbed his brow again. "I'm sorry, Miriam. But I refuse to involve you in this. Much as it breaks my heart, I release you from your vows. You can have it put about that you learned what a cad I really am and wisely gave me a boot out the door. You'll be the toast of the season, I assure you."

Miri looked at her cousin in thoughtful silence. He really was in a dreadful state. She had a perfect right to be outraged, of course. Being jilted was no small thing. But perhaps Hamilton really was in trouble this time. And in that case, it was her duty to give him whatever help she could. After all, he was not only her fiancé, he was family.

"If you're actually in danger, Ham, I suppose I must wish you well and try to understand."

Hamilton smiled weakly. "That's very good of you, Miri."

He did look as though the devil himself had him by the ear. Miri supposed she was so accustomed to Hamilton's little scrapes that she wasn't assigning this one the significance it deserved. His passion for gentlemanly gambling had led to trouble in the past. She had always wondered how his position at the Foreign Office, prestigious as it was, afforded him the means to indulge himself so. But, of course, all that would have ended when they married and she took him in hand. Unlike most of her other suitors, Hamilton shared her enthusiasm for right and proper behavior, and had showed every willingness to overcome his lamentable weakness.

"And Hamilton . . ." Her eyes softened as they roved over his fatigued face. The usually immaculate wavy black hair was rumpled and his eyes looked tired. "You must tell me if there is anything I can do to help you."

"There's nothing you can do, dear." He managed a fond smile. "I'm sorry, Miri. I'm giving you a dreadful time. I've always been a trial to you."

"At least tell me where you are going."

He looked away guiltily. "I'm going to America, as I told you. I thought perhaps . . . perhaps your father might hide me until all this passes over."

"My father?" Miri's voice took on a new edge.

"I know I haven't seen him since he left—since we were children. But he's the only person I know who might help. And America must be a perfect place to hide, you know. It is the remotest part of the world that I can think of."

"Yes," Miri's fingers drummed in distressed rhythm on the Bible lying on the table beside her chair. "It certainly is. But you'll at least spend the night with us and get some rest and a good meal."

"No. I can't, Miri. I've stayed much too long already. If you would fetch Aunt Eliza so that I may say my farewells, I would appreciate it. Time is slipping away from me."

Tight-lipped, Miri rose to do his bidding. His words stopped her at the door.

"I do love you, Miri. God knows I do. And . . . I'm sorry."

"I know you are, Ham. And I wish you Godspeed."

A quarter of an hour later Miri paced back and forth across the length of her chamber and glared out the window into the foggy night. "Can you imagine?" she asked of the birdlike little woman who perched on her bed. "Would you have believed that Hamilton could do such a thing to me?"

"Oh, yes, my dear," Eliza Edwards chirped. She had listened to her niece's indignant recital of Hamilton's perfidies and nodded knowingly through the whole thing.

"Handsome is as handsome does, you know. I always have suspected that Hamilton is just like his mother. Flighty, that woman was. No sense of family, or loyalty. Did you know that Cousin Charlotte did not acknowledge your mother or me once—not even once!—after that silly furor about your father?"

"Yes, Aunt, you told me." *Many times*, Miri added silently.

"He's the very image of his mother, that boy—a pretty face but not an ounce of backbone to go with it."

Miri flounced down on the bed beside her aunt. "There will be a scandal." She sighed. "Just what this family needs—another scandal. Absolutely everyone will be pointing and whispering their nasty little speculations. Oh, Aunt Eliza!"

"Now, now, dear." The little woman patted Miri's slumped shoulder and handed her a handkerchief to mop the tears. "Engagements are broken every day. Well, at least every month or so. It's not such a disaster. You're much too good for a dull fellow like Hamilton anyway."

"That's not true," Miri insisted. "Hamilton is perfect for me—polished, refined, gentle. And I'm very properly fond of him, without any danger of becoming . . . well . . . too involved."

"Too involved!" Eliza tittered. "I should hope not, with that dandy! I vow, if Hamilton Greer were a pudding, he would be vanilla, or maybe tapioca. You deserve something much more interesting."

Miri sniffed huffily and dabbed at her eyes. "Interesting! Like my father, I suppose you mean."

"He was interesting," Eliza admitted with a little smile.

"Yes," Miri said. She pushed herself off the bed and resumed her angry pacing. "My father was very interesting. It was just fascinating the way he broke my mother's heart and blackened her name because of his lack of mature responsibility. I'll take vanilla pudding, thank you! Spicy foods so often curdle in the stomach."

"Now, dear. You really shouldn't talk that way. Your

father loved your mother very much, you know. But he just never fit into the stuffy parlors and silly rules we have here in London. He was too accustomed to his forests, or lakes, or whatever it is they have over there in the colonies. You really should try to be more understanding of human foibles, my love. We all have one or two, you know.''

''Pooh! How you can condemn Hamilton with one breath and defend my father with the next is beyond understanding.'' Miri gave her aunt a sharp look. She had always suspected that Eliza was half in love with her sister's husband, and that was why she pardoned him so easily. One would have to be blind with love to excuse the actions of a man who would leave a loving wife and a seven-year-old daughter just because he was homesick for his cursed American forests. If he'd longed so for a silly forest, he could have found one right outside London.

''I want to forget about my father, not talk about him,'' Miri said testily. But how could she forget her mother's grief and humiliation, and the melancholy on her face when she had died? Aunt Eliza was wrong. A woman should offer prayers of thanks to be wed to a bland Hamilton Greer rather than a man of her father's stripe. ''Besides, we have problems more pressing. Lord! I wish I knew what to do.''

Eliza bounced spryly off the big four-poster bed and yawned. ''You'll think of something, dear. You always do.'' She gave Miri's arm a little pat of comfort. ''After all, the scandal was—what was it?—sixteen years ago. No one's going to remember after all this time. And you can just tell those nosy old biddies that you booted Hamilton down the road. No one can say a thing against you, dear.''

''Yes. I'll think of something. Good night, Aunt Eliza.''

I will think of something, Miri vowed as she donned a prim dressing robe and wandered down to the parlor. She sat in her favorite chair and spent several distressing minutes thinking about the exact wording she should use for the announcement that must go into the *Times*. Sparing a thought or two for Hamilton and his problem, she almost wished that whomever he owed money, or had insulted, would this time catch up with him. It would serve him right for continuing such childish behavior when he knew better. Then she chastised herself for lack of charity. Whatever had sent her cousin fleeing all the way to America, and to her father, of all people, must be truly awful indeed.

The mantel clock struck midnight, and Miri wearily rested her head back on the chair. She should be in bed, but she would never sleep with her mind in such turmoil. With a sigh she picked up the Bible that lay on the table beside her and opened the well-worn book to Psalms. Thirty minutes later, calmer by far, she climbed the stairs and went to bed.

Captain Gerald Michaels stiffened into a martial stance and nodded for his sergeant to knock on the door in front of them. Then he glanced around him at the well-tended grounds, the carefully trimmed trees, the clean-swept walk bordered by neat little hedges. A tidy little place, he thought, in a neighborhood that only the well-heeled could afford. The house wasn't ostentatious, but a host of fine details whispered of wealth. One would need to have a modest fortune to live here. Why did people never appreciate what they had? Why were they always messing up their lives, dabbling in mischief to acquire just a little more wealth, or fame, or power?

The door was opened by a sleepy-eyed housekeeper who had obviously dressed in a hurry. Her cap was askew and several of her buttons were still unfastened. It was before the time of day that even a housekeeper could be expected to be alert. Captain Michaels smiled at her discomposure. He liked to get this sort of duty done first thing. Most people, including blackguards, thieves, and traitors, were less nimble thinkers in the very early morning, he had discovered.

"Is this the residence of the Misses Eliza Edwards and Miriam Sutcliffe?" the sergeant droned.

The housekeeper squinted suspiciously. "An' 'oo wants ta know, might I ask?"

The sergeant frowned, but his retort was forestalled by

Michaels' raised hand. "I am Captain Gerald Michaels, madam, and I have official business with Miss Sutcliffe and her aunt. May I ask whom I am addressing?"

"Mrs. Simmons," the woman said with a sniff. " 'Ousekeeper. It's a bit early for callin', gents."

"This is not a social call, Mrs. Simmons." Michaels politely but firmly led his sergeant and two troopers through the door, ignoring the housekeepers's indignant sputtering.

" 'Ere now! Don't get pushy!" Mrs. Simmons plucked indignantly at her generous bosom, where a trooper had accidentally brushed by her. "The misses 'aven't yet risen. If ye'll leave yer card I'll see they gets it."

"That won't be necessary," Michaels insisted. "If you would be so kind as to rouse your mistresses? I fear my business is of the utmost urgency."

The doughty Mrs. Simmons seemed ready to refuse, but a look from the captain convinced her otherwise. She contented herself with a backward glance of indignation as she climbed the stairs to the bedchambers.

Twenty minutes later Miriam swept down the stairs. She acknowledged Captain Michaels' introduction with a coldly civil nod, ushered him and his men into the small front parlor, and sent Mrs. Simmons off to fetch tea.

"What urgent mission has set you to rouse my household at this early hour, Captain? Might I have an explanation?"

Michaels smiled blandly. "I believe you know the explanation as well as I, Miss Sutcliffe."

"Indeed I do not."

"You are very convincing as the outraged innocent, but I assure you that you waste your effort. I know everything."

For a moment Miri looked confused, then an irritated frown puckered her brows. "How extraordinary. You know everything. That's certainly more than I can boast—especially at this moment. Would you care to be a bit more precise?"

Michaels stifled a rare impulse to chuckle. She was a pert little saucebox, this Miriam Sutcliffe—not at all the milksop spinster he had expected. He had to give Greer credit for good taste in women, at least. It was a shame the girl had allowed herself to be used by that cheap hustler.

"Then I will be more precise, Miss Sutcliffe, if that will please you. I have come for the document that Mr. Hamilton Greer left with you last evening. It will go much more easily for you if you simply give it over without wasting my time on denials."

"Document? I haven't the slightest idea what you're talking about, Captain. Mr. Greer called last evening. I certainly won't deny that. But he said nothing of any document, nor did he leave anything with me."

The little minx is going to be tiresome, Michaels thought with regret. *What a shame*. She was a pretty thing, and got prettier as anger sparked a fire in those incredibly large eyes and painted a high color on her face. Even her hair seemed to be aflame, gleaming like burnished copper in a ray of the early morning sun. Michaels was almost moved to pity. Unmarried females were always easy prey for cads like Greer.

"Miss Sutcliffe, I really have no time for this. I am not without sympathy, and I understand how an unmarried lady such as yourself might be easily influenced by . . ."

"I am not easily influenced by anyone, Captain, I can assure you. Nor am I easily intimidated." Miri's chin lifted another notch.

Michaels sighed. "One of my men followed Hamilton Greer to this house last evening."

"I didn't deny that he was here."

"Let me finish, Miss Sutcliffe. I know he had a certain document with him when he arrived here, and he didn't have it when he left."

Mrs. Simmons pushed through the parlor door with a tray of hot tea and scones. Eyeing the military contingent with open dislike, she cleared the books and the Bible from the table beside Miri's chair and set the tray down.

"Tea, Captain?" Miri invited in a chilly voice.

"Thank you, no. As I was saying, Mr. Greer was apprehended leaving your house . . ." Michaels noted Miri's start of surprise with satisfaction. "He didn't have the document with him."

"Then why don't you ask Mr. Greer what he did with it, instead of harassing an innocent woman?"

"He escaped," Michaels admitted, giving his sergeant a brief look of displeasure. "But the obvious conclusion is that he left it with you."

"Then you should look for a less obvious conclusion, Captain, for Mr. Greer gave me nothing last evening. Might I trouble you to tell me just what this precious document is that I am supposedly harboring?"

Michaels sighed impatiently. As if the little witch didn't know. What kind of game did she think she was playing, sitting in her prim parlor, drinking her morning tea, as though she weren't involved in the worst sort of traitorous activity and caught out at it? It was going to be a damned long morning.

"If we must continue to play this game, miss, then I will explain. Mr. Greer used his position in the Foreign Office to gain access to quite sensitive information. He compiled, among other things, a list of British informants in the American government and military. His plan to sell this information to the Americans was disrupted when I apprehended his contact. Upon learning of the American's arrest, Mr. Greer fled. And since he is aware that we cannot condemn him without concrete evidence, I am positive he is trying to hide the documents in a safe place."

Miri's face had turned a shade paler. "That's outrageous. If what you say is true, he could simply have thrown his dashed list into the river."

"Your fiancé is a greedy man, Miss Sutcliffe. He would not have destroyed his chance for such a tidy fortune." He gave her a knowing look. "What better place to hide the documents than with an adoring fiancée who seems above reproach?"

Miri set her teacup on the table with an uncharacteristically clumsy rattle. She got up, paced the length of the parlor, glanced at the captain, then paced some more. "Perhaps what you say of Hamilton is true—though I find it hard to credit that he was actually involved in this plot. More than likely it is simply a misunderstanding. Did the American give you Hamilton's name?''

''No. He refuses to give us anything, no matter what the persuasion. But we have other lines of evidence, Miss Sutcliffe. This is no misunderstanding.''

Miri glared at the captain out of those alarmingly blue eyes, and met a determined hazel gaze that was just as steady as her own. Finally, she sighed and looked away. ''Perhaps,'' she allowed. ''Hamilton was . . . is . . . sometimes greedy and unwise. But he knows that I would never consent to participate in such behavior. I don't have what you're seeking, Captain Michaels.''

''You don't have what, child?'' Aunt Eliza, whose hair was frazzled into a graying halo and whose eyes were still puffy from sleep, tottered groggily into the parlor with a worried-looking Mrs. Simmons trailing behind. ''What are these rude men doing here, Miri? Why, the sun is scarcely up, I vow!''

''Aunt Eliza, you needn't have come down.''

''Needn't have come down, you say! And how is a body to sleep with all this chitchat going on down here?'' She turned an irritable eye on Captain Michaels. ''And who are these fellows, eh?''

''Captain Gerald Michaels, madam.'' Michaels sketched a perfunctory bow in Eliza's direction. ''I am . . .''

''Captain Michaels is chasing after Cousin Hamilton, Aunt. He believes Ham has absconded with some information that he shouldn't have.''

''Tch! Nothing but trouble, that boy. Just like his mother. Still, that's no reason to rouse two God-fearing, decent women at this unholy hour. I thought the king's officers were supposed to be gentlemen, but no gentleman would . . .''

''Aunt,'' Miri interrupted. ''The captain is convinced that Ham left a certain document here. Do you know anything of this?''

''Certainly not! We said the briefest of good-byes. And if

I'd known then what he'd done to you, I wouldn't even have allowed him a good-bye kiss.''

Michaels was instantly suspicious. ''What did he do to you, Miss Sutcliffe?''

''If you must pry, Captain,'' Miri said with a certain reluctance, ''my cousin came here last night to break off our engagement. He said he was in a spot of trouble and had to leave. He wouldn't tell me what the trouble was or . . . or where he was going.''

Michaels caught the flush of guilt that colored Miri's face. At least part of that little story was a lie—probably all of it.

''And he left nothing with you?''

''No.''

''Then you won't mind if my men conduct a search of the house.''

''We certainly do!'' Eliza protested. ''It's indecent, and I won't have it! Miriam, tell these rude fellows to leave!''

Miri calmed her aunt with an arm around her tiny waist. ''Go ahead and search, Captain. Why should I mind?''

Michaels' men were efficient, Miri had to admit. Cupboards and drawers were opened, closets scrutinized, bed covers turned back, and mattresses overturned. By now the entire household was in a frenzy. The cook screeched about the disruption of her kitchen; Mrs. Simmons's face got redder with every linen that was turned out; and Miri's maid Lucy was brought to tears at the shambles made of her mistress's fine things. Miri herself declined to follow in the path of Michaels' juggernauts. She sat in the parlor with her tearful aunt and put on a calm face, finished the tea and scones, and tried to keep her teeth from grinding with indignation.

That cursed Hamilton! She hoped they caught him and stewed him in his own juice! A spot of trouble, indeed! No wonder he was fleeing all the way to the savage wilderness. The least he could have done was warn her. And if he had left a shred of evidence in this house to implicate her or

Eliza, she hoped the American savages roasted him over a hot fire and had him for tea!

"Well, Miss Sutcliffe, it appears you have hidden Mr. Greer's list very well." Michaels stood at the parlor door, looking sterner than ever. His ramrod-straight posture made him look taller than he really was, and the official garishness of his scarlet and white uniform endowed him with an air of menace.

"I haven't hidden anything at all, Captain." Miri schooled her face to innocent calm, but she saw disbelief in the set of Michaels's face.

"I am sorry that I cannot take you at your word, miss. It distresses me to discommode a lady, but I must insist that you surrender Mr. Greer's list within twenty-four hours, or I will be forced to charge you with treason."

"Treason!" Miri sputtered indignantly. "You wouldn't dare! You have no proof—not a shred of evidence other than your own vile suppositions! You said yourself you need concrete evidence!"

"I'm sure it will be found in time, Miss Sutcliffe. And I don't think you will enjoy the waiting—in prison. So I beg you to be reasonable."

The captain's eyes caught Miri's for a long moment, and in them she read implacable determination and absolute belief that he was right. There would be no swaying this man with pretty pleadings, or even desperate entreaties.

"Twenty-four hours, then. I will call first thing tomorrow morning to save you the inconvenience of searching me out at my headquarters." With the briefest of polite bows, he left.

Miri and Eliza enlisted the aid of the entire household staff to turn the house inside out. At first Miri insisted that the treasonous document could not possibly be on the premises. Hamilton had ventured only as far as the back parlor, and someone had been with him all during his visit. Then she remembered that she had left to fetch her aunt for good-byes, and it had been fully ten minutes before Eliza had descended the stairs to the parlor—plenty of time for

Hamilton to dash to any of the numerous nooks and crannies that they had used in their childish games so many years ago.

As Miri searched one potential hiding place after another, old memories of her and Hamilton as children together floated to the surface of her mind. Hamilton hadn't actually lived in the same house, but he might as well have, for he and his family were such frequent visitors that Miri had felt for a time that Ham was a brother rather than a distant cousin. They had been very close in those young, innocent days. At that time Miri's family had spent much of the year at a country house in Kent. Young as Miri was, Ham had dragged her all over the countryside on horseback whenever he and his family had visited there. But when they were at the London house, they had to content themselves with supervised runs in the park and games of hide-and-seek in the closets and storerooms and old tunnels that they had called their secret passages. The house dated from the time of Cromwell and was built with hiding places in mind. Hamilton knew every one of them.

The daylong search was fruitless, and as the grumbling servants put things back in order, Miri and Eliza sat morosely in the parlor.

"It's hopeless," Miri moaned. "If Hamilton left that list here we'll never find it. We've searched all the places I know. Lord! What am I to do? That wretched captain will be back in the morning to cart me off to prison."

Eliza looked thoughtful. "I suppose we could appeal to Cousin Harold. After all, he is the head of the family, and a belted earl, at that. He should have some influence, even though he was most rude last time I called."

"Cousin Harold doesn't want his precious social standing to be tainted with the Sutcliffe family cloud," Miri said woefully. "Besides, I can't imagine a hidebound autocrat like Captain Michaels being terribly impressed by a minor earl."

"Well," Eliza sighed. "Perhaps prison is not that bad a place. I understand if you're willing to put forth a bit of money you can have quite a decent place to stay. And I could have fruit delivered, and fresh bread . . ." She trailed off at the astonishment in her niece's stare. "Well, dear, as you say, there's nothing we can do. Unless, of course, you want to ask Hamilton where he put his little list."

Miri did not trust her aunt's innocent smile. "What do you mean, ask Hamilton? Knowing my precious cousin, he's already sailing off on some illegal blockade runner bound for America. When he runs away from something, he doesn't waste time."

"Yes, dear. But there are other ships sailing for America. You could follow."

Her aunt had finally crossed the boundary from eccentric to mad, Miri decided. Go to America. What a ridiculous idea—a frightening idea.

"We're at war with America," Miri objected.

"Hmph! That piddling little war? Tempest in a teapot! Besides, you shall sail across to Canada. Yes, that's the very thing. We're not at war with them."

"Impossible. Aunt Eliza, you don't know what you're talking about. I won't consider it."

Of course it was impossible. America was a dreadfully uncivilized place. Her mother had raised Miri to be a genteel lady, not to go traipsing off into the wilderness in pursuit of her misguided cousin. Besides, she had promised her mother that she would never speak or write to her father again. And Hamilton was headed straight to him. If she wanted to find Hamilton, she would have to talk to her father first. Unthinkable! "No," Miri repeated vigorously. "I won't consider it."

Eliza's round little eyes shone with a sly gleam. "Of course you won't, dear. It was silly of me to suggest it. Prison would be much preferable, I'm sure. Although I absolutely shudder to think of how we shall save your reputation when it becomes known that you've been carted off to Newgate."

"Traveling alone to America would shred my reputation just as thoroughly."

"Of course, you're right. Except that your little maid Lucy could go with you as companion, and we could have it put about that you are merely paying a visit to your father. Society might forgive that sooner than your living in a prison with . . . well . . . all sorts of unmentionable people."

Miri sent her aunt a narrow-eyed look. The old lady was fond of Miri's father, and she had always insisted that Miri needed to meet someone who was more "interesting" than London's "weak-kneed dandies." Was her aunt taking advantage of this horrible situation to push her toward an adventure she didn't want and certainly wasn't up to? Well, Miri wouldn't have it. It wasn't that she was afraid to go. Not at all. She simply held the entire continent in utter disdain. And she disliked ships intensely. There were other solutions to the problem. She would . . . she would . . . Lord! What would she do? There was nowhere to turn, no one would help her. Her mother's family—except for dear Aunt Eliza—had done their best to forget she existed, just as they had tried to forget her father, and the divorce. They would certainly not be anxious to leap to her defense now.

Watching the flow of expressions across her niece's face, Eliza smiled. "Don't be too upset, dear. I'm sure that Cousin Harold will manage to get you out in a few months' time—no matter how he feels about us. And I will send fresh fruit every week."

Miri's face was bleak. The American wilderness or a London jail—what a choice to make. She sighed in unhappy resignation. At least in the wilderness she would not have to endure Mrs. Pelham's inevitable comments on her broken engagement. "You won't have to bother with the fruit, Aunt. I shall follow Hamilton to America."

The rest of the evening was spent in preparation. Lucy was dismayed to learn that she was to accompany her mistress, and wailed of savages and wilderness while carefully packing the gowns, petticoats, gloves, slippers, and pantalets she thought were appropriate for an expedition into the wilderness.

"We can't take too much," Miri mused aloud, "seeing

that we have to carry everything through the underground tunnel and out through the storeroom into the woods. Captain Michaels would leave that dreadful sergeant to watch the house!''

"Oh, miss,'' Lucy sniffed. "Are ye sure ye want to do this? My sister's 'usband was in America once. 'E says there's savages that rip the 'air right off people's 'eads over there.''

"We're not going to meet any savages, Lucy, so stop your whining. My father lives in a great fur trading center— quite civilized, I imagine. We are simply going to find my cousin and then come right back to England. We'll be home before summer is done.''

The packing was finished by midnight. Miri's chest and Lucy's small bag were carried down to the kitchen pantry, where a wall of shelves rotated to give access to an old tunnel that had once been used to hustle Royalists to safety. The tunnel exited into a storeroom that was detached from the main house and backed up against the woods behind the garden. They would have to walk through the woods until they were out of sight of Michaels' watchdog, then regain the road. The gardener's son Henry would escort them to a hotel were they could await passage to the colonies. He had even managed to procure them transportation, in the form of an obliging friend with a horse-drawn cart. It was not the style in which Miri was accustomed to travel, but under the circumstances, it would have to do.

As the luggage was carried from her bedchamber, followed by Aunt Eliza and a woeful Lucy, Miri hung back. She crossed to the window and looked out upon the starlit garden. It would be her last look upon that familiar scene for many months. Miri comforted herself by the thought that when she returned, the browns and grays of winter would have given way to softly blooming colors of late summer. Then there would be no more threat from Captain Michaels, and life could return to normal. Then she could forget about Hamilton and his cursed list—and about America.

Miri's mind still rang with Lucy's wails. America—untamed

land of savages and uncivilized ruffians. She felt her heart sink as she stared out into the cold, unfeeling night, wondering which saint or angel she had offended to merit such a grim fate.

✳ 2 ✳

Miri shivered and pulled her shawl more tightly around her. It was cool for the beginning of June, and a brisk breeze riffled the blue water of Lake Huron's North Channel. One more day, Miri told herself—two, at most—and this dreadful journey would be over.

The birchbark canoe in which Miri traveled carried eight men—voyageurs, they were called—who made a profession of transporting goods from Montreal to the trading centers in the west and returning with bundles of beaver, rabbit, otter, and muskrat pelts to sell to the clothiers in England and Europe. It was a most uncomfortable way to travel, Miri thought. But it was the fastest route from the eastern coast of America to her father's holdings on Michilimackinac Island. She had studied all her father's letters with great care before they had left London, and he seemed quite definite in saying that the Ottawa River route was the shortest and most efficient way to travel. Speed is what Miri was interested in right now, not comfort. The sooner this misadventure was over, the sooner she could return to the comforts of London.

And a misadventure it had been from the very beginning. She and Lucy had been forced to spend three weeks in barely adequate accommodations while awaiting passage to Canada, then endure an Atlantic crossing that had kept her stomach in a constant uproar. Then at Montreal—which was hardly a town at all, by Miri's standards—officials of the Northwest Company had been less impressed by her father's name than Miri expected. Yes, David Sutcliffe was a partner of the company, but they didn't seem to think that being his daughter entitled her to any particular courtesy. When she finally convinced them to provide her passage to Michili-mackinac in one of their canoe brigades, Miri was distressed to discover that she was treated with a deal less ceremony than the cargo, and since her presence aboard the canoe meant harder work for the voyageurs, she had met with nothing but grumbling and truculence the entire voyage.

Miri looked up from her reverie to see Lucy waving to her from another canoe. She waved back halfheartedly, not understanding how her maid, who had quailed so at the idea of coming to America, had conceived such an enthusiasm for this benighted wilderness. And it was much more of a wilderness than Miri had imagined. She had promised Lucy they would meet no savages, but they had encountered them at every turn—Iroquois and Algonquin at the beginning of their journey, and more recently, Maskegons, Missisakies, and Chippewa. They had even spent a night in a village of friendly Algonquin, and Miri had been both fascinated and horrified at their primitive and uninhibited way of life.

Lucy, who had been so timid in London, seemed to regard the whole misadventure as though she were a child who suddenly and unexpectedly had found herself in fairyland. She struck up friendly conversations with the savages—English and sign language on Lucy's part, and sign language and grunts on the part of the Indians. She endured the heat, the cold, the rapids, long portages, and even the horrid mosquitoes and black flies without complaint. The voyageurs in Lucy's canoe laughed and talked and joked with their passenger, while Miri's comrades seemed to regard her, with her fashionable gown, soft slippers, and frilly parasol, as a particularly odious piece of useless cargo.

It was now a month to the day since the brigade of four trade canoes had set out from Lachine, the embarkation point on the St. Lawrence River below Montreal. As few days later they had left the St. Lawrence and paddled up the Ottawa, or the Des Outaouais River, as the voyageurs called it. They had made steady progress, stopping occasionally for canoe repairs and more frequently to portage their goods around unnavigable rapids. Finally, they had reached the mouth of the Matawan River and had ascended the waterway to the calm waters of Lake Nipissing. From the lake they made the perilous descent down the French River to Lake Huron, and now, at last, they were paddling steadily toward their destination, which was only a day away.

Fort Michilimackinac, Miri understood from her father's letters, stood on a small island in the Straits of Mackinac, which was the narrow body of water connecting Lake Huron and Lake Michigan. It had been turned over to the upstart United States at the end of their revolution, but in July of 1812 had been recaptured by the British under the command of a Captain Roberts. But as far as the fur trade was concerned, her father had written, it mattered little who claimed the island. The British Canadians had always made it their headquarters for sending trade goods out to the West and collecting incoming peltries from the Indians. Miri didn't care a bit about the fur trade, but it was a comfort to know that her destination was ruled by her countrymen. The British could be depended upon to be civilized, at least. She had her doubts about the Americans.

One of the voyageurs in the stern of the canoe started gabbling in rapid-fire French. Many of the men who plied the rivers were French Canadians, and Miri had been distressed to learn that though she spoke passable drawing-room French, she could seldom understand the voyageurs unless they made an effort to be understood, which was almost never. Miri suspected that she was often the subject of their more jocular conversations.

But the tone of the urgent conversation that followed was anything but jocular. Soon, the man in the bow of the canoe shouted to the rest of the brigade. They waved back, and Miri's canoe angled away toward the shore.

"What are we doing?" Miri asked nervously.

"We have sprung a leak, mademoiselle. We will stay here tonight and repair it. The others, they do not wish to stay. We are so close to Michilimackinac. You understand?"

Miri frowned. "I thought the canoes of the brigade always traveled together, for safety."

The voyageur smiled. *"Oui*, mademoiselle. That is how it is done. But there is no danger now. The difficulties of the journey are over. We will only be delayed by a day."

"I see." Miri saw, but scarcely approved. The other canoes of the brigade, Lucy with them, were rapidly becoming mere dots on the horizon, and she did not look forward to making camp with only these eight rough men for company. In their own way, these burly French Canadians seemed more dangerous than the savages they had met along the passage. A curse on the stupid canoe for springing a leak now, of all times.

In only a few moments they had reached the rocky shore. Miri suffered through the indignity of being carried to land in the arms of a grinning voyageur, a ritual she had been forced to endure every time the canoe had beached. A cargo-laden canoe was never allowed to actually touch the shore for fear of injuring its delicate birchbark skin, and the first day of the voyage, Miri had decided that being carried ashore was preferable to stumbling through the water and letting her skirts, pantalets, stockings, and slippers be soaked through with water, mud, and sand. Even so, it was definitely the lesser of two evils.

The canoe had sprung more than one leak. In truth, it had been taking on water since their run down the last white water of the French River. While Miri watched impatiently from her perch on a dried-out driftwood log, the men stood waist deep in the freezing water and unloaded the boxes of trade goods, passing each from man to man until it reached the safety of the beach. There were sixty hundred-pound boxes in all, each carefully labeled as to its contents. Blankets, coats, calicos, linens, shirts, leggings, ribbons, beads, gunpowder, steel flints, gun screws, brandy and rum, cutlery, kettles, guns, combs, mirrors, tobacco, shot, and ball—all goods that would end up in Indian lodges in return for the fine peltries they brought back from their winter encampments.

It took two hours' work to unload the cargo boxes and pull the canoe up onto the beach for repair. Only then did the men turn to other pressing needs. The sun was resting on the horizon by the time camp was made. Two of the voyageurs set out to bring in fresh meat for the evening meal while the others started soaking the birchbark and heating the pine gum that would make their vessel watertight once again.

Miri watched in helpless boredom as camp was set up and a rabbit stew set to boiling over the fire. Early in the voyage she had somewhat doubtfully offered to do her share of the work, but once the men had tasted her cooking, she had promptly been relegated to the role of onlooker. So she spent the evening feeling useless and longing for Lucy's company. Finally, while the men still squatted around the fire and chatted in their incomprehensible French, Miri retired to her bed of pine boughs and blankets, knowing that no one had noticed her leave.

The next morning was the coldest since they had set out from Montreal. The air was heavy with moisture and the sun invisible behind a sullen veil of low-hanging clouds. If Miri hadn't known better, she would have thought it was midwinter, not late spring. The men were in a chipper mood, though, for one more day's hard paddling would land them at Michilimackinac Island, where waited rum, women, and the comforts of a warm, dry bed. For both Miri and her companions, a long and tedious journey was finally coming to an end.

As the morning progressed the sky seemed to drop lower and lower, and the clouds at times almost touched the gray water. Miri's gauzy muslin gown and silk tunic were the height of fashion in London, but provided very little protection from the elements. She wished desperately for the redingote packed in with her clothes, but her chest was buried under a layer of cargo boxes. To make matters worse, they had abandoned their shore-hugging course and set out across the body of Lake Huron. Even the large islands that had been visible in the early morning were disappearing into the shroud of mist and cloud. To Miri this so-called lake seemed every bit as threatening as the ocean, and the thought that a fragile birchbark canoe was her only protection on this vast expanse of water made her shiver with something other than the cold.

Soon Miri's straining eyes could find no land at all. If it was within the range of her eyes, it was hidden in the cold mist. The choppy swells that passed under the canoe seemed to get larger with every passing minute. They were shorter, higher, and more vicious than the smooth swells of the ocean, or perhaps the small size of the canoe just made them seem so. In any case, the uncomfortable rolling of the canoe was making Miri's stomach lurch in a way reminiscent of her unpleasant Atlantic crossing. She clutched her shawl around her and hoped with all her might that the elusive Michilimackinac Island would appear soon on the horizon.

At noon Miri refused her ration of dried corn mashed into prepared fat. This standard fare of the rivermen had always been unappetizing, but with her stomach about to stage a rebellion, it was even more so. Much to her surprise, several of the voyageurs also passed up their midday meal. They looked almost as bad as she felt, Miri noted uneasily. Were these conditions so unusual then, that even the men were becoming ill?

As the day grew older the wind rose with an alarming force. The unease in the voyageurs' faces was now plain to see. Their destination island had been spotted an hour before, but was now almost invisible in a thickening mist that was rapidly becoming rain. The wind-driven waves regularly washed over the gunwales, and two of the men had stopped paddling to bail full-time. Miri could no longer deny to herself that they were in real danger. The men had stopped talking and joking hours ago, and the tense set of their jaws and desperate straining of their muscles visible under their wet shirts told Miri more than she wanted to know. She pulled her shawl more tightly around her and clutched at the small Bible that Eliza had pressed upon her just as she had left their house. She had carried it close to her person throughout this entire disastrous journey, often deriving comfort from its mere proximity. Now it brought her no comfort at all. She could think of only how cold she was, how mountainous the waves had grown, and how small and fragile she and the men seemed in their tiny canoe.

The boat seemed to be wallowing more uncertainly with every wave that rolled beneath them. Two more of the voyageurs had joined in the bailing, leaving only four to manuever the canoe. With an unusually vicious lurch the bow rose on the steep slope of a wave, then dipped awkwardly down as the crest rolled under them. Another, larger wave was waiting, but instead of rising, the canoe plunged its bow into the heaving mound of water. One of the men uttered a string of French that Miri recognized as a prayer, crossed himself, then paddled desperately forward. Too late.

A smaller canoe bobbed in the swells just off Michilimackinac Island. Two Chippewa brothers, one stocky and barrel-chested, the other tall and lean, sat at ease with fishing lines trailing from their hands into the water.

"It has been a good morning," the tall one said. He referred to the fishing rather than the weather, because the wind was rising sharply and even this close to shore the chop was growing uncomfortable.

"A good morning for you," the stocky Indian scoffed. "I taught you too well, Eyes of a Ghost. For one who started so slowly you became a fast learner. But I never thought I would see the day when you were a better fisherman than I."

Eyes of a Ghost grinned, softening the lean, hawkish features of his face. Most of the fish at the bottom of the canoe had been procured with his long spear, not a line. Spearfishing required a quick eye and a quicker hand, and was a particular proficiency of his. Only now, when there were enough fish for two good meals, with plenty left over to smoke, did he relax with a fishing line in his hand.

"My brother Rides the Waves should remember that a good student is a credit to the teacher." His teasing smile belied the humility of his words.

Rides the Waves grunted. "This student is trying to show up his teacher. Lake Dancer will be stoking the fires for a week just to smoke what you have caught. Otherwise, I would show you how a master of a skill works and bring in twice the catch that you have speared."

Eyes of a Ghost grunted in good-natured disbelief. "But to be considerate of your sweet sister, you won't. And, of course"—he grinned tauntingly—"the weather grows worse. The fish are all hiding on the bottom to escape the storm." There were not many things the tall Chippewa could do better than his brother, and when he found one, he liked to rub it in. It kept Rides the Waves properly humble.

"That is truth," Rides the Waves replied blandly. "I'm glad you understand." He glanced at the lowering sky and wiped the first cold drops of rain from his face. "I think winter has returned for a short while, my brother. The waters are beginning to churn uncomfortably, and if my bones tell me true, this rain will shortly become snow."

"A true Chippewa is not deterred by the raging of the elements," his brother replied with mock solemnity.

Rides the Waves picked up his paddle and pointed the canoe toward the shore. "A smart Chippewa sits inside his lodge and warms his hands by the fire when the cold wind howls through the forest."

The two men were unloading their fish onto the shore, backs hunched against the driving rain, when Eyes of a Ghost noticed the trade canoe battling against the wind and waves. He touched his brother's shoulder and pointed.

"The foolish whites will never make it," Rides the Waves commented. "Even a child should know better than to be so far out on the lake with the wind this high."

"Most likely they came from the north shore. A brigade arrived yesterday that had left one of its canoes a day behind. They should have known to stay where they were until the weather cleared.''

Rides the Waves nodded agreement. The two of them watched grimly as the trade canoe bobbed like a water-logged cork on the waves. Its buoyancy seemed to diminish even as they watched. Then the inevitable happened. The canoe was close enough to the island for the two Indians to hear the voyageurs' shouts as the boat rolled slowly to one side, dumpling its cargo into the lake. The cries were carried to shore on the wind, along with a terrified scream that could only have come from a woman. Without a word, Rides the Waves trotted up the shore to get help, while Eyes of a Ghost plunged into the heaving water.

Too late. All the voyageurs' efforts were too late. The canoe had taken on too much water, and the troughs between the towering waves were not wide enough to give the boat time to recover from its downward plunge on the back of the passing swell. The canoe plowed into the wave ahead. Freezing water washed from bow to stern, filling the canoe to the gunwales. Slowly it rolled to one side, and continued to roll. The men shouted and cursed. Miri screamed.

The lake reached up and grabbed her. Only for a second did Miri feel the cold. Then she was numb, and helplessly sinking. The cargo boxes sank with her, oscillating gently to the rhythm of the storm.

Miri spent only a second regretting that she had never learned to swim. It had never been necessary. Always a trifle uneasy around water, she had never felt the beckoning of millponds and streams that other children of her acquaintance had seemed to feel. But now the lake was beckoning, and demanding, and could not be refused. Death seemed to laugh at her from the dark, freezing depths.

Spots were floating before Miri's eyes and her lungs screamed at her in burning agony. Her arms and legs felt almost detached from her body. Still, she wouldn't surrender to the encroaching darkness. She struck out with heavy arms and kicked with rubbery legs, the way she had seen Hamilton do in the pond by their country house. Again and again, kick after kick, she clawed her way upward. The sinking boxes battered and scraped against her as she fought to rise, but her body was too numb to feel the damage.

An eternity passed, then her head broke the surface. With a great gasp she filled her lungs with air, then choked as a wave rolled over her head and filled her mouth and nose with water. She struck out again, only this time her skirts tangled in her flailing legs. She struggled briefly, then sank, too weary to fight the inevitable.

She hardly felt it when a hand grabbed her arm and pulled upward. When her head broke the surface, a few seconds passed before Miri realized she was still alive, and someone was struggling with only partial success to hold her head above the waves. Water splashed into her nose and mouth, and for the first time she panicked. Her arms flailed as she struggled to grab hold of her rescuer, desperate to secure a grip that neither the surging waves nor her savior's own will could break. Breathing became the center of her existence, and nothing—not the fury of the storm nor the tossing chaos of Lake Huron—was going to drag her down into the depths again. Miri lunged and grabbed, feeling her fingers close around skin and hard muscle that struggled to throw her off. She clawed for a firmer hold, pulling them both under the surface. An ear bent beneath her desperate grip. Hair tangled in her fingers.

They broke the surface together. Miri had time only for a brief gulp of air before her savior's fist exploded against her jaw. As with the other batterings she had endured, Miri scarcely felt the blow, but fireworks rocketed through her head and her fingers loosened their grasp. Before she could regain her senses she was twisted around and secured helplessly against the wall of a hard chest. A brawny arm passed over her shoulder and crossed her breasts, holding her a helpless prisoner as her rescuer laboriously fought against the waves and current to bring them both to safety.

Miri was half drowned by the time her legs scraped against the rocks of the beach. But even then the struggle wasn't over. The lake that had been so determined to keep them now seemed anxious to spit them out, but not without first taunting them cruelly. Like helpless bits of flotsam they were flung forward onto the rocks. Foaming waves rolled them over and over, dragging them mercilessly against jagged stones and then sucking them back before their feet could find a secure hold. They struggled forward, only to have the same thing happen again. Through it all the steely arm clasped Miri tightly against a rock-hard body. Her savior refused to let her go, and with the limited sensibility left to her, Miri realized that if he had released his hold she would have been sucked helplessly back to a watery grave.

When it was finally over, Miri was almost too numb to realize she was safe. It seemed no easier to breathe on the land than in the lake, and her mind registered only mild surprise that the rain and snow pelting down from the sky seemed every bit as able to drown her as the tossing waves.

"Turn over, damn you!"

The rough voice failed to bring her to her senses, and from what seemed an enormous distance Miri saw her limp body picked up, dragged farther up the beach, and flopped down again in a prone position. She was most certainly dead, Miri thought. Otherwise, she would be horrified to see a half-naked man climb astride her helpless body and brutally pummel her unresponding flesh. As it was, she felt only mild curiosity about what the fellow was doing, and gratitude that she was not forced to be in her body while he was doing it.

"Breathe, dammit! Breathe!"

This time, Miri heard the words from an uncomfortably close distance as the misery of her continued existence crashed down upon her. She choked, gasped, inhaled sand, and choked again. Her lungs were on fire, and the flames reached out to lick every quivering nerve in her body.

"That's it! Breathe, woman!"

She breathed. Her body convulsed and ejected an enormous quantity of sour-tasting water. She breathed again, her lungs taking their rhythm from the painful weight that pressed in regular cadence upon her back. Stones ate agonizingly into her hips where her rescuer straddled her and into her breasts and shoulders with every press of his hands.

"St . . . stop!" she gasped, trying feebly to dislodge his painful weight. "Please!"

Apparently satisfied that he had pumped enough of Lake Huron from her lungs, the man rolled off her, collapsing to the ground himself to lay spread-eagled, taking in great gulps of air, seeming heedless of the rain and snow. Presently he raised himself on one elbow to regard the bedraggled creature he had hauled ashore.

Feeling was slowly returning to Miri's body, and as merciful numbness faded, she realized how very cold she was. Her muscles seemed frozen in position, unable to move her from the spot where her rescuer had left her. She huddled there shivering, miserable, and uncertain even that she was glad to be alive.

"Come on." The man had risen to his feet, and was now urging her to do the same. When she didn't respond, he grasped her arm and pulled upward. "Let's get those wet clothes off you before you freeze."

"What?" Miri's teeth had begun to chatter, and she was sure she was turning blue. She lurched to her feet, but her legs refused to function as ordered and sent her stumbling forward into the man's wet embrace.

With an impatient grunt, he lifted her in his arms and carried her up the beach. Just beyond the edge of the trees a small canoe was overturned. He set her on her feet in a spot where thickly woven branches provided some protection from the wind and sleet.

"Can you stand?"

"Of course," Miri gritted through chattering teeth. "If you'll just . . ."

"Take off those wet clothes." He squatted and peered under the canoe. "The blanket under here should still be dry."

Miri stared at him, uncomprehending.

"Go ahead. Take them off."

The idiot really wanted her to take off her clothes? Here? In the out-of-doors, in the middle of a raging storm, and in front of his very eyes? What did he think she was?

"If you'll just take me to the nearest dwelling, sir, I'll . . ."

"Oh, for Christ's sake! Don't be such a stubborn little bitch! Do you want to freeze? Or catch your death of pneumonia?"

"Just take me someplace where I can get warm, Mr. . . ."

"Eyes of a Ghost." He stood, and his towering height was suddenly very intimidating. The top of Miri's head reached no higher than his shoulder.

"Mr. . . . Eyes of a Ghost." Ghost indeed! He looked distressingly carnal to have a name like that.

Miri backed away and nervously pushed back a hank of wet, sand-encrusted hair. Her shivering was almost convulsive, and she could barely move her lips to form words. Her gown clung to her in an icy mantle that seemed to suck out what little heat was left in her body, but under no circumstances would she be persuaded to peel it off. She was a civilized woman of proper moral fiber, and if she had to freeze to preserve her decency, then so be it.

The Indian stepped forward as Miri continued to ease back. In the uncertain light he looked like a bulky, featureless shadow with the broad-shouldered shape of a man— truly a monster plucked out of her childhood nightmares.

"I didn't pull you out of the lake just to have you freeze to death once I got you on shore, you senseless female. Now, take off those wet clothes and wrap yourself in that blanket under the canoe. Then I'll take you someplace where you can be cared for."

"I prefer to . . ."

"I don't give a damn what you prefer!"

He was upon her before Miri could move. One hand grasped her arm in an unbreakable grip while the other yanked at the sash that was tied under her high-waisted bodice. His knuckle brushed the wet silk covering her breasts, starting shivers of a different kind racing up her spine.

Miri screeched in outrage. "Unhand me, you uncouth barbarian! What do you think you . . . oh!"

The silk tunic was yanked unceremoniously over her head and discarded to the whims of the wind. Next his hands plunged inside her bodice and ripped it asunder.

Miri's screams rose above the wind as she felt rough male skin grazing her cold flesh and hardened hands touching where no man's hands had the right to be. She was being peeled like a a ripe plum, and all her twisting, convulsing, scratching, clawing, and kicking seemed to have no effect whatsoever on her attacker. She wailed in agony as he yanked her icy pantalets down over her hips, past her knees, and finally free of her ankles and feet. Her bare legs—and unthinkably more—were exposed to the open air, and to the eyes of the detestable male animal who was doling out this dose of humiliation. The final piece to go was her chemise, ripped apart in the cad's ice-cold hands. Miri was as bare as a newborn babe, and just as howlingly indignant.

"Don't know what you're so fired up about, silly woman. You'll be glad enough when . . . Yowwwl!"

Miri's struggles finally landed a knee in a most sensitive male area. She was instantly released. Stunned by her unexpected reprieve, she whimpered in indecision, then made a dive for the blanket under the canoe. Wrapping it around her, she headed for the trees and ignored the angry demands coming from behind her.

"Come back here, you ungrateful she-cat! Do you know where the hell you're going?"

Miri didn't. She stopped uncertainly. There could be wild savages worse than the one pursuing her lurking in those dark woods ahead. And the surge of strength that had accompanied her anger was fading fast. Her legs were turning to rubber again, and the woods were starting a slow, dizzy spin.

"Vicious little wildcat! You very nearly unmanned me!" The savage's hand on her shoulder whirled her around and started Miri's heart jumping in alarm. She had hesitated one second too long.

"Touch me again and I'll . . ."

"You'll what, woman? I think you've already done your worst."

The rain and snow were slowing to a mere drizzle. The clouds were beginning to lift, and watery light stabbed tentatively through the gloom. For the first time Miri looked the Indian full in the face, and what she saw held her momentarily spellbound. He was a sight that no proper lady should be forced to behold, for delicate sensibilities were not schooled to accept raw primitiveness in such a natural state. Tall, broad-shouldered, with lean muscle moving like bands of steel beneath coppery skin, Eyes of a Ghost was a magnificent display of savage masculinity. Miri's heart skipped more than one beat, but she couldn't tear her eyes from the form revealed to such advantage by his scandalously scanty attire of leggings and breechclout. She understood now where he got his name, for the eyes that stared back at her were a ghostly silver-gray. Prominent brows and high, well-defined cheekbones gave his face the look of a hawk, saved from unrelenting masculine severity only by a wide and generously curved mouth.

The intimidating maleness of him took Miri's breath away, but it was what topped off the picture that sent her senses tottering. The savage's head was neatly shaven around a scalp lock—a style Miri had already observed among the Indians encountered by their canoe brigade. But this head was different. This savage standing before her in raw and primitive splendor sported a thick scalp lock that was undeniably, irrefutably, and most unreasonably a golden, tawny blond.

For the first time in her life Miri gave up her senses in a ladylike swoon.

✻ 3 ✻

The feather bed had to be the best invention since man discovered sleep, Miri thought comfortably. She felt as though she were floating, surrounded by soft, warm clouds that pillowed her weary body and tempted her to sink back into blissful slumber. How long had it been since she had slept so well, since she had felt such luxurious comfort as a . . . feather bed?!

Miri opened her eyes, then shut them quickly, not believing the scene that met her brief peek. Whitewashed walls, window curtains of gay cotton print? She opened her eyes again and squinted against the bright sunlight streaming through the window. For weeks the damp ground had been her bed and threadbare woolen blankets her only protection from the cold. How was she lying on such softness, with pillows, quilts, and comforters? A lace doily covered the table beside the bed, and across the room, an ornate china pitcher and basin sat on a carved oak dresser. Beside the pitcher was folded a spotless white linen towel. Had she died and gone to heaven?

"Where am I?" Miri whispered. Definitely not in heaven, she decided quickly. Only in the mortal world was there such discomfort. Her voice rasped, her throat burned, and when she stirred from her lethargy, every muscle in her body felt as though it had been twisted into knots. The pain brought memory to the fore—the storm, the mountainous waves, the rescue. . . .

"Oh, my Lord!" The sudden recollection of the half-naked savage who had pulled her from the lake made Miri sit straight up in her bed. She gasped at the pain, and then a fit of coughing tried to tear her lungs from her chest. Every cough felt like a knife cutting into her body. She heard the door open and then close again, but she couldn't turn her head to see who had come in.

"There, there. Easy now, my girl." A plump hand patted Miri on the back while another supported her head. Slowly the hacking eased and she sank gratefully back onto the pillows. "That's right. Just lie back and sip at this."

A cup of water was offered. Miri drank slowly, then lifted her eyes to regard her benefactor. A comfortably plump woman in early middle years stood regarding her with sympathetic eyes. "Poor thing. You must be terribly confused."

Miri nodded, afraid to force words through her burning throat.

"You're safe as can be, dear, so don't worry about a thing. I'm the Widow Peavey, and you're at my farm on Michilimackinac Island. Jordan Scott brought you here yesterday evening. Limp as a rag doll you were, poor dear, and you've been out ever since."

"Jordan . . . who?" Miri croaked.

"I can see he didn't properly introduce himself. I vow, that man has got the manners of a mule, and he's twice as contrary."

"The . . . the yellow-haired Indian."

"That's him." The widow smiled, and Miri noted that the smile gave her plump, pretty face an aspect of true beauty. "I suppose your mind is just brimming with questions, isn't it? It's quite an introduction you've had to our little island. But I think you should just try to rest now." She fluffed Miri's pillows and smoothed the rumpled quilt. "You've taken quite a beating, you know, and have a congestion of the lungs to top it all off. You just lie there while I fetch you some nice soup. We'll have plenty of time to talk when you're feeling better."

Suddenly Miri felt more secure than she had in weeks. She settled back and closed her eyes as the widow woman bustled off with a soft flurry of voluminous skirts. It was hard to imagine. She was alive and safe, though a bit the worse for wear. And most miraculous of all, she had reached her destination. Now all she had to do was find her father and Hamilton, pry the whereabouts of that troublesome list from her cousin, and go back home to London. Then she could forget all about this disastrous journey—the terrifying rapids, arduous portages, irritating insects, and rude rivermen. She could forget that America even existed. And, oh, yes. That brutal, uncivilized savage who called himself Eyes of a Ghost, and who was really Jordan . . . who? —she could forget him, too.

"Here we are." Widow Peavey swept back into the room with a bowl trailing fragrant steam. Her mouth lifted in a motherly smile. "Beef barley soup—'little eye soup,' my daughters call it. Put some of this in your stomach, Miss Sutcliffe, and you'll feel right as rain."

Miri cocked a questioning eye toward her hostess.

"Oh, yes, dear," Widow Peavey said, spreading a napkin on Miri's lap and setting the bowl atop. "Everyone knew you were coming. Your little Lucy arrived with the rest of your brigade the day before the storm. News spreads fast on an island like this, you know. Everyone was expecting your arrival."

Everyone? Miri thought. Then why wasn't her father here? Perhaps he was. Perhaps even now he was waiting in the next room, until she should have strength enough to receive him. But if that was so, wouldn't the widow have said something?

Miri closed her eyes and gave up that particular fantasy. It was more likely that David Sutcliffe didn't care to meet the daughter he had deserted sixteen years ago, in spite of the many letters he had sent her.

"And I expect you're wondering about your sweet little maid," the widow said in a cheerful voice. "Lucy is staying here also and is as fine as she can be. I must say, for a city girl, she weathered your journey quite well."

Miri scarcely did the soup justice before giving up the effort. It was delicious, and the warmth in her stomach was migrating out into the rest of her sorely abused body. But a weariness was spreading over her that made even swallowing a difficult feat.

"The men in my canoe?" she asked hoarsely.

"I'm afraid they're at the bottom of the lake, dear, and all your things with them. You're very fortunate that Jordan saw your boat overturn and was able to pull you out." The widow shook her head. "It's a miracle that you weren't both drowned in that tempest."

Miri was silent, wondering at the sorrow she felt for those strange rough men who had been her constant companions for the last weeks. Then she gathered the courage to ask the question she dreaded.

"Has . . . has my father been notified that I'm here?" The look that came to Widow Peavey's face seemed to confirm her worst fears. He didn't want to see her.

"Your father . . ." The widow hesitated, and the look of sympathy in her eyes made Miri's heart contract with dread. "There's no easy way to say it, child. Your good father, beloved by us all, died of pneumonia this past winter. Father Carroll wrote you, but I suppose the letter must have gone astray."

"My father . . . died?" It had never occurred to Miri that her father might someday die. In her thoughts he had been larger than life, if only because she hated him so. And now he was dead. Gone. It was almost too much to believe.

"He was such a good man, Miss Sutcliffe. All of us share your grief."

A good man. No. Never. Unexpected tears filled Miri's eyes and overflowed onto her cheeks. "I . . . I haven't seen him since I was seven," was the only thing she could think to say.

Widow Peavey patted her hand with awkward tenderness. "I know, dear. Your father used to tell all his friends what a beautiful little girl he had back in England. He would have been so pleased to see what a fine young lady you grew to be. Sometimes God's will is a mite hard to understand."

Tears ran down Miri's face in hot streams, though she didn't know why she was crying.

"I expect you'd like to be alone, my dear. There's a Bible in the drawer there"—she pointed to the bedside table—"if you'd care to look for comfort. You call if you need a shoulder to cry on. This shoulder of mine has seen a lot of tears in its time."

The widow closed the door softly behind her, and Miri's tears became a full-scale flood. Why was she crying? Her father had been a cad, a toad, a monster of callousness. He hadn't deserved to live to old age. He had broken her poor mother's heart, deserted his only child, made her family an object of derision and gossip throughout all of London society. Hell was too good for an uncivilized, unfeeling, irresponsible blackguard like David Sutcliffe.

Miri dabbed at her wet cheeks with the snowy white bedsheets. She thought of the bundle of her father's letters she had brought with her from London. She had refused to answer any of them, but for some reason had read them through again and again and carefully saved them in a little box on her dressing table. Now they were at the bottom of Lake Huron, together with all her belongings, Aunt Eliza's Bible, and eight rough but vital men. Gone forever, just like her father.

Another flood of tears set Miri's eyes to swimming. She pictured her father as she had last seen him. To a seven-year-old girl he had appeared huge—big knobby hands, a whiskery face, a booming voice, and a raucous laugh that had turned everyone's head in his direction. He had been wearing buckskins the day he left England—flaunting them like some badge of honor. Miri remembered distinctly how ridiculous he had looked. Everyone had eyed him with contempt, but her father had ignored them.

Miri had never seen anyone look so happy and so sad at the same time. But mostly she remembered him looking happy, standing on the dock in those uncivilized clothes and smiling at the ship that would take him away. He had tried to explain why he was leaving, but the seven-year-old Miri had not understood. At the ripe age of three-and-twenty she still didn't understand why her father had abandoned everything—family, comfort, civilization itself—to return to a land filled with wild savages and crude log huts. Her mother had not understood, either. It had been Aunt Eliza who had held Miri's hand as her father walked up the gangplank. Her mother had refused to see him off. Two years later their divorce was finally granted.

Miri sniffed back the last of her tears. Now both her parents were gone. She wondered if they would meet in the hereafter and reconcile the differences that had kept them apart in life. Probably not, Miri mused bitterly. More likely her father would like heaven no more than he had liked London. His ghost would no doubt return to this nasty wilderness to haunt the lakes and streams, along with the black flies.

Weariness was dragging Miri down toward sleep as the thought of ghosts and hauntings brought the image of her rescuer back into her mind. Eyes of a Ghost. Ridiculous name. But she could see where he had gotten it. Those silver-gray eyes of his did give the impression they were looking out from some other world. It was enough to send shivers down her spine just thinking about them—and him. The savage's disturbing image stayed in her mind as she drifted into sleep.

When Miri woke the sun was still streaming through the windows, but now the light had the rosy glow of early morning, rather than the brightness of midafternoon. She had slept the day and night through.

"Hello."

Miri turned her head at the voice. Her eyes were greeted by three girlish faces arranged in a stairstep from tallest to smallest.

"I'm Margaret Peavey," the tallest informed her with ladylike solemnity. "And . . ."

"I can do it, Mags!" The middle sister gave Margaret a little push. "I'm Mary Beth. And this is Martha." She poked at the smallest sister, who conceded to courtesy by taking her finger from her mouth, but would not go so far as to smile. "You're English, aren't you? Just like those lobsterbacks up at the fort. Ma said so."

"Mary Beth!" Margaret objected. "You're being rude.

Mother has never called anyone a lobsterback. And Miss Sutcliffe is a guest.''

"Yes, she is," the widow's voice chided from the open doorway. "And I told you three that she was not to be disturbed. What are you doing in here?"

"It's all right," Miri said softly. Her throat felt better, but her voice was still a husky whisper. "I was awake."

"Good," Widow Peavey bustled in, shooing her daughters away from the bed as a mother hen might scatter bothersome chicks. "Are you feeling better, dear? Do you think you might eat something?"

At the mention of food, Miri's stomach rumbled. "Yes, I think I might eat a bit." Like a whole cow, if one were available. She was truly ravenous.

"And a bath might make you feel more the thing. Your Miss Lucy has kept the water heated in anticipation of your waking, and you just have time before breakfast."

Bless dear Lucy! Miri felt as though the mud and sand of Lake Huron was chafing every crevice of her body. "Thank you, Mrs. Peavey."

"Please call me Grace, my dear. We're not very formal over here, you know. Now, let me send the girls for the tub."

Lucy burst into tears when she saw her mistress sitting shakily on the edge of her bed. Her sentiment almost caused her to drop the steaming kettle she was carrying. Hastily she set the kettle down and rushed over to take Miri's hands.

"Oh, miss! I thought ye was dead for certain when we 'eard yer canoe 'ad overturned. I cried me eyes out before that Indian chap came up the road with ye slung over 'is shoulder."

"Slung over his shoulder?" Miri croaked.

"An' ye so pale. I thought ye were gone, miss. That I did! An' look at ye now." The maid started weeping once again, giving Miri a clue that her present appearance was not all that good either.

"I'm sure I will look a good deal better once I have had a bath and a meal, Lucy, so . . ."

"Right away, miss."

Grace came in with a bundle of clothes under her arm. "Here, let me help you up. That's it."

Miri tottered on stiff legs toward the tub. Halfway there she caught a glimpse of herself in the dressing table mirror. It took a moment for her to realize that the bloated mess of black and blue was really her face.

Grace's eyes met Miri's in the looking glass. "Don't you be concerned, Miriam—you don't mind if I call you Miriam, do you? You'll be looking fine again in a couple of weeks."

The rest of her body, Miri noted as she lowered herself painfully into the tub, looked no better. But Grace assured her that there were no breaks—just nasty bruises where the cargo boxes had battered and scraped. And one of the purple swellings on her face was from a man's hard fist. Many things about her near drowning and rescue were a merciful blur, but Miri remembered that particular detail with bitter clarity.

All the long weeks of her journey Miri had looked forward to a real bath—to the luxury of lying in warm, fragant water and watching drowsily as tendrils of steam curled up into the air. But she was denied the luxury of a leisurely soak, for her scrapes and bruises protested painfully the moment she lowered herself into the hot water. She tolerated it only long enough to wash the worst of the dirt from her skin and squeeze soap through her hair.

"Oh, your hair," Lucy sighed as she gave the tangled mass a final rinse. "Your poor hair, miss. Whatever are we to do with it?"

Grace helped Miri from the tub and wrapped her in a voluminous towel. Then she ran plump fingers through the dripping mass of auburn mats that hung almost to Miri's waist. "I'm afraid there's no help for this. We'll just have to cut it."

That was the last straw. Miri had never considered herself a vain woman, but the thought of losing her hair, on top of losing her looks, was simply too much. Short hair was actually in vogue back in London, but Miri had always taken pride in the mass of waves that cascaded down her back like a waterfall of silk.

"Noooo!" she wailed. "I'll comb it out. Lucy will help me."

Lucy looked doubtful, and Grace just shook her head. "You'll never get the knots out, love. Now, don't get missish on us. Nobody expects a girl to look like a queen after having plowed up the bottom of Lake Huron with her face. Even a lady like yourself, dear."

Miri wept openly as the mats were cut from her head. She hadn't known until now that she was afflicted with such vanity. Lucy tried to comfort her as the auburn pile on the floor grew larger and larger, but Miri couldn't bear to look in the mirror. She remembered Lucy's comment in London about the Indian savages ripping the scalp right off a person's head. No doubt if Miri met any scalp-crazy savages, they would simply put away their knives and laugh.

"That doesn't look bad at all," Grace commented, stepping back to view her handiwork. "If I do say so myself, it looks rather nice."

Nice is not the word that came to Miri's mind. Her hair curled around her face in a halo of soft red-brown. She looked like a ten-year-old moppet, Miri decided gloomily, or worse yet, like a swollen and discolored image from a particularly vivid nightmare.

"It's pretty," Lucy insisted.

Miri grunted noncommittally.

"And look here," Grace offered. "Here are some underthings and a dress of Margaret's. Small as you are, I think you two are about the same size. You can wear these for now, then, when you're feeling better, we can start to work making you some clothes. The dry goods store in town has some of the prettiest cottons and woolens you can imagine."

Miri tried to smile. It hurt her face. She let herself be combed and dressed and fussed over, then led down to breakfast looking like a curly topped, purple- and blue-faced clown wearing the cast-off dress of an adolescent farm girl. If she ever found Hamilton Greer and his stupid list, she vowed, she was going to strangle the blackguard with his own cravat for getting her into this.

Miri spent the next three days sleeping, fending off the huge meals that Grace Peavey placed before her, and submitting herself to the poultices that Lucy swore would drive the pain from her body and the swelling from her face.

On the fourth day, her conscience began to give her more pain than her injuries. In spite of being accustomed to the ministrations of servants, Miri was aware that this was a simple farmhouse where pampering was not an everyday occurrence. She had no claim on Grace Peavey's hospitality other than the fact that she had been dumped on her doorstep by that silver-eyed Indian. Miri had no desire to become a burden on the farm widow's resources, which might be slim. Indeed, she had no desire other than to find her cousin, extract from him the information she needed— along with a little revenge, if possible—and return to the sane world of civilization. But as long as she was accepting Grace's hospitality, she should try to contribute the worth of her keep.

"I don't know if that's a good idea, miss, if you'll pardon my saying so." Lucy was exercising great patience in tutoring her mistress in the craft of sewing straight seams and neat stitches. Grace had returned from town the day before laden with cottons, muslins, and wool meant to clothe her guest. Firmly refusing any offer of payment, she had piled scissors, patterns, pins, and thread in front of Miri and bustled about her own chores. Ashamed of admitting that her sewing skill was limited to useless samplers, Miri had enlisted Lucy's aid.

"You're doing your part around the household, Lucy. I believe that I should do the same. I'm sure Grace will not accept payment for our keep, and I see no other way to repay her kindness."

"But miss! I'm used to farm work. I was raised on a farm, you know, in Cornwall. The land's 'ard there. 'Arder than it is 'ere. This sort o' work isn't new to me. In fact, it makes me feel at 'ome some'ow. I allus did miss the farm."

Odd that she had never known that Lucy was a farm girl, Miri thought. But she supposed that like the other servants in the London house, Lucy had been more a fixture than a person with feelings. "It will only be for a little while, Lucy. And I think you're not giving me credit. I can be a very competent sort when I wish."

Grace chuckled and shook her head when Miri expressed her desire to do her share. But on her guest's continued insistence, she assigned a delighted Mary Beth to show her around the farm. It was a good-sized plot of land by British standards, and Miri was surprised to learn that all the work was done by Grace and her three daughters.

"It's not so bad," Mary Beth assured her with eleven-year-old pride. "We grow most of what we use—corn, onions, potatoes, turnips." She made a wry face at the last. "Not a lot of livestock. Just the pigs and chickens, and the four goats."

"No cows?" Miri asked.

"Naw. Just goats. Three does and a buck. Come meet them. It's time to milk, and they'll be mighty displeased if I don't get to them soon."

Miri was not entirely happy with the knowledge that all the delicious milk and butter she had been eating these last few days derived from goats. When she met the creatures, she was even less happy. Grace had decided that one of the chores she could help with was the milking. Miri's images of milking involved rosy-cheeked milkmaids and fat, benign dairy cows. But these animals were neither fat nor cows. And they had a decidely undocile look in their eyes.

"Let me show you what to do," Mary Beth offered with a twinkle.

Only her ill-timed boast to Lucy kept Miri from pleading a relapse of illness. She gingerly obeyed as Mary Beth instructed her to loop a rope around the first goat's neck and coax it onto the milk stand.

"This is Petunia," Mary Beth said by way of introduction. "She's a good milker, but sometimes she's a little shy of strangers."

Miri seated herself tentatively on the milk stand and Petunia gave her a jaundiced look out of the corner of her eye. The goat didn't look a bit shy to Miri. She looked downright hostile.

"She's got nice big teats." Mary Beth ignored the color that rushed to Miri's face. "You grab with these two fingers here, and then . . ." She demonstrated a downward rolling motion with her fingers.

Miri blinked. The little imp really expected her to do this? Wasn't there something else she could help with, like dusting furniture or chasing the birds out of the garden?

The milking did not go well. Miri's hands stubbornly refused to roll in the required motion, and Petunia had a distressing habit of trying to put her rear foot in the milk pail. When Mary Beth finally shook her head in disgust and took over, Miri was amazed to see how easily the youngster coaxed a steady stream of milk from goat to pail.

"Did you see Jordan when he came calling this morning?" Mary Beth asked unexpectedly. A mischievous smile quirked the corner of her mouth.

"Mr. Scott came . . . calling?

"Early this morning. I expect you were still abed."

Miri reluctantly acknowledged that with a twinge of guilt. No matter that the man had been brutal and totally uncivil, he had saved her life at considerable risk to his own. She should have made an effort by now to thank him personally.

"Was he looking for me?" Miri asked.

"Oh, no. He comes to see us a lot. My father and he were good friends, and ever since Pa died, Jordan always makes sure we have enough to eat."

Oh, my! And here she was, another mouth to feed, and Lucy, as well. Miri's misgivings returned with a vengeance. "I didn't know food was a problem."

The girl shrugged. "Only during the winter. The lake freezes up, you know, and the snow makes it hard to get fresh game. But we're always fine. Jordan taught Ma how to smoke fish the way the Chippewa ladies do. He always makes sure we have enough for the winter." Mary Beth pursed her lips in distaste. "Sure get tired of smoked fish around about March." Petunia kicked at a fly, narrowly missing the bucket with her foot. "Just be patient, you ol' biddy. We're almost through."

After the goats were milked, the pigs had to be fed and eggs collected from the henhouse. "Egging" the chickens without getting pecked, Mary Beth insisted, was an art that Miri would surely learn in a few days' time, just as she would learn never to turn her back on an unhappy goat and keep her distance from the pig wallow. Miri was not convinced, and by the end of the day she felt she had been pecked at, grunted at, clucked at, and butted in a measure sufficient to last a lifetime. If she had ever had yearnings toward the simple life of the farm, they were put to rest forever.

Jordan Scott's name came up again at dinner, thanks to Mary Beth. The youngster seemed convinced she had found a sensitive spot in Miri's composure, and her impish nature demanded that she poke at it.

"You should meet Lake Dancer," Mary Beth insisted.

"Yes," little Martha chimed in. "Lake Dancer's beautiful." The words were thrown out in the manner of a challenge, drawing a glare of warning from her mother.

"Who is Lake Dancer?" Miri asked.

It was Grace who answered. "Lake Dancer is the Chippewa woman who pulled Jordan out of the rapids at Sault Ste. Marie." She smiled, remembering. "It's difficult to believe, seeing him now, but when Jordan first came to this area— oh, it must be ten years ago—he and his partner were green as grass. Jordan was straight from some fancy school in Boston, and the other fellow was some sort of sea captain friend of his. They tried to shoot the sault when the water was too high and got themselves a dunking for their foolishness. Lake Dancer was scarcely more than a child at the time, but she managed to get Jordan up onto the shore. The other man was drowned. Jordan has been living with the Chippewa ever since."

"Lake Dancer's his wife," Mary Beth threw out tauntingly.

Miri's brows rose. "Mr. Scott married an Indian girl?"

"Yes," Grace admitted. "Though the Chippewa are very casual about such relationships. When a man wants a woman, he simply moves into her wigwam. If they want to end the marriage, one of them moves out. It is not at all the solemn union that civilized people make it, and divorce is not considered the social anathema that we . . ." She stopped at the sight of Miri's reddening face. "I'm sorry, Miriam. It was thoughtless of me to say something like that."

"That's quite all right," Miri replied stiffly, a flush crawling up her cheeks. Of course these people would know about the scandal, since they were her father's acquaintances.

"Yes, well," the widow hurried to continue, "Jordan has been with Lake Dancer a good long while now. He seems very fond of her, in his own way."

"Do they live here on the island?"

"No," Grace told her, "The summer village is right across the straits. And in the winter, each household in the village goes to its own separate winter hunting grounds."

"Lake Dancer taught me how to put beads on my moccasins," Martha said proudly. "Jordan said they were the prettiest moccasins he'd ever seen."

Grace smiled apologetically. "I'm afraid the girls have rather adopted Jordan as a substitute father. They'll talk about him incessantly if given a chance."

"That's quite all right," Miri said. "I find Mr. Scott an . . . interesting subject. And I certainly owe him a debt of gratitude. I'm sorry I didn't get the chance to thank him when he was here this morning."

"You could go see him at the village," Mary Beth proposed eagerly. "I could go with you!"

"Now, Mary Beth!" Grace chided. "Leave Miriam be. I'm sure she doesn't need to go traipsing among the savages. Likely, Jordan doesn't think what he did is anything extraordinary."

Miri squirmed uncomfortably. Common courtesy did demand that she express her thanks to her rescuer, even if he was an uncivilized brute. He might have forgotten the meaning of civilized behavior, but that was no reason for her to do the same. Lord! How could a white man who had been raised with the benefits of Christian civilization—and an educated man, at that, according to Grace—let himself sink so low as to embrace a life of primitive savagery? Whatever the man's upbringing had been, he was certainly a discredit to his race.

"Of course, if you wanted to go, Miriam, it is no great task to paddle across the straits in good weather. And I'm sure Margaret would be happy to take you." Grace quelled Mary Beth's objection with a sharp look. "Margaret is the eldest, Mary Beth. Remember your manners, young lady. Besides, Margaret needs to pick up those rabbit skins that Little Dog promised her."

Miri sighed and tried to put on a brave smile. She was trapped by her own conscience and her hostess's overly accommodating nature.

The very next morning, Miri and Margaret set out across the straits. A lively breeze was blowing, and most of the crossing was accomplished with the help of a sail. It was a fast trip, to Miri's relief, for from the moment she set foot in the canoe she was assaulted by uncomfortable visions from her last experience with this unpredictable lake.

The Chippewa village was every bit as bad as Miri had expected. Thin, mangy-looking dogs raised a raucous clamor, and near-naked children chattered and ran about in a completely undisciplined manner. They greeted the girls' canoe with little jumps and hoots of joy, reminding Miri of a pack of little brown monkeys. The braves that helped pull the canoe onto the beach were little better. They greeted young Margaret with a complete lack of the decorum that was due a girl emerging into womanhood, and Margaret accepted their overly familiar manner with nary a ladylike blush.

Miri told herself sternly that she was in a frontier wilderness, and naturally, things were not the same here as in London society. But it was still very difficult to accept. When one of the braves took her hand to help her from the boat, she thanked him politely and tried to avert her eyes from his entirely too exposed anatomy. As a result of her distraction, she tripped, stumbled forward, and ended up caught in the man's arms, her eyes not two inches away from puckered male nipples. Face flaming, she pulled abruptly away. The Indian's eyes crinkled in amusement. He spoke a few guttural words, then reached out and fingered the short auburn strands of her hair.

"What did he say?" Miri asked as a grinning Margaret led her away from the beach.

"He said your face is the same color as the fire in your hair." The girl chuckled. "Even your bruises turned red, Miriam."

Miri felt her face flame even hotter. Oh, to have this whole adventure over with and return to London, where people were decently covered and a woman's sensibilities were admired, not ridiculed!

"That is Jordan's wigwam." Margaret pointed to a hut constructed from bent sapling poles and crudely woven rush mats. It was identical to the other twenty or so huts that were scattered in seemingly haphazard manner around the clearing. "I'm going to Little Dog's wigwam, over there." The girl pointed in the opposite direction. "Just give a call when you want to leave."

"You mean . . . go up there alone?" Miri stammered.

Margaret just smiled—somewhat maliciously, Miri thought. "You've already been introduced, haven't you?" With a casual wave she walked away.

Miri took her courage in her hands and walked over to the hut that Margaret had pointed out. A blanket covered the door. How did one knock on a blanket? This had not been a good idea at all, Miri admitted. Good manners be dashed!

"Are you looking for me?"

Miri whirled with a squeak of alarm. "Mr. Scott! You startled me, coming up so quietly like that."

He stood for a moment in silence, regarding her with an impassive stare. If he was surprised to see her standing in front of his wigwam, looking like a ragamuffin refugee from an alehouse brawl, he didn't show it. Finally, he nodded. "Miss Sutcliffe."

He was bigger than Miri remembered, and just as indecently clad as the other braves in the village. Muscles ripped beneath bronzed skin in places where no civilized man would have muscles, and the directness of his silver-gray regard both irritated and discomfited her. After all, some of her unsightly bruises were due to his uncivilized brutality.

"I . . . I thought it only . . . that is . . ."

"Yes?"

Miri's tongue twisted around her mouth in a futile attempt at coherent speech. Sudden impressions of the last time she had met this man—the tactile sensation of his cold skin against hers, his fingers brushing against her as he ripped off her clothes, the hardness of his thighs as he straddled her on the beach—all flooded her brain and robbed her of the ability to think. She stood and stared at him, her heart thudding so loudly in her chest that she was sure the wretch could hear it.

"I came . . . I thought it only right to . . . pay a call and thank you for my life, sir." Sanity was returning, prompted by the hint of amusement she saw in his eyes. He was laughing at her embarrassment, the cad! Or perhaps at her still-distorted face, the ridiculous cropped hair, the ill-fitting, borrowed gown. "It seems I owe you a great deal."

"It was nothing, Miss Sutcliffe."

Miri bristled. "I don't regard my life as nothing, Mr. Scott."

His eyes crinkled, and again Miri saw the glint of laughter in the silver-gray depths. He lifted the doorway blanket, and Miri's attention was unwillingly drawn to the ripple of lean muscle in his arm.

"Would you care to come in?" he asked.

"Thank you."

Tight-lipped and determined, Miri ducked inside the entrance. What was waiting in the smoky interior left no doubt in her mind that this visit had been a very poor idea, indeed.

✳ 4 ✳

It took Miri's eyes a moment to adjust to the dim light inside the wigwam, but when she could discern the outline of the woman who sat against the far wall, she backed toward the door in dismay. Only the barrier of Jordan's broad-shouldered body kept her from making a hasty exit out the opening.

"Dancer," Jordan said, "this is the woman I pulled out of the lake."

The Chippewa woman smiled and with difficulty heaved herself to her feet for a formal greeting. "You are welcome to my wigwam." She did not seem at all shy about her unmentionable condition.

"This is Lake Dancer," Jordan told Miri from uncomfortably close behind her. She could hear the amusement in his voice. The insensitive clod was laughing at her discomfiture, no doubt thinking a woman's sensibilities were naught but fuel for his rude diversion. She longed to spin around and give the cad a hard slap. Just see how entertained he was then!

"I take it that Lake Dancer is your . . . wife," Miri ventured, turning to give Jordan a quelling look.

The brute's only answer was a jackass grin. Miri felt the blood rush to her face. It was all too much—the half-naked man with his knowing, supercilious smile, and the woman, earthy and sensual in a way that only a pregnant woman can be.

"Won't you please sit down?" Lake Dancer said in perfect English.

Miri sat, her back ramrod straight, a stiff little smile pasted on her face. Jordan crossed the little room and helped

Dancer ease herself back to the floor while the Indian woman looked at him with adoration in her eyes. The silence stretched very thin.

"I don't want to intrude," Miri said awkwardly. Lord! What could she say that would be polite? No decent woman would think of receiving callers in such an advanced and delicate condition. While a primitive could hardly be expected to have the sensibilities of a civilized gentlewoman, the girl could at least show some modesty! The tunic she wore emphasized, rather than concealed her condition, and her face was flushed with pride, rather than a proper measure of embarrassment. But Miri had come for propriety's sake, and she was determined to remain polite. "I simply came to . . . to express my gratitude for Mr. Scott's efforts in saving my life. I am greatly in his debt."

Lake Dancer smiled kindly at Miri, then gave her husband another adoring look. "There is no debt. It is good for the strong to help the weak."

"Yes . . . Well, I am grateful all the same." Weak, indeed! Miri might be weaker physically, but she certainly had stronger moral fiber than Mr. Jordan Scott. There he sat, squatting in a primitive hut, flaunting this poor Indian woman and taking obvious male pride in what he had done to her. What could possibly move a civilized, educated white man to so abandon every advantage of his upbringing? Was he running from the law? Or was it simply a basic, venal weakness in himself that made him prefer the raw and unenlightened life of a savage?

"You must have some tea," Lake Dancer said. She took a wooden cup from a shelf along the wigwam wall, poured an aromatic liquid from the kettle steaming on the fire, and handed the cup to Miri.

Miri took a cautious sip, wrinkled her nose, then instantly regretted the unthinking grimace as she saw Lake Dancer's face fall. "It's nice," she managed to choke out. "Very nice."

"Made from wild cherry twigs," Jordan said with a grin.

Miri took another sip, prompted by the malicious humor

she saw in his face. The ill-mannered brute was laughing at her again, and there was a glint in those cynical eyes that made something inside her want to cringe away. But she would be damned if she would let such a man upset her composure. After a second sip and then a third, she found herself becoming accustomed to the taste of the tea.

The silence grew strained, and Miri groped for something polite and neutral for conversation. "You speak English very well," she finally said, looking at the Indian girl and pointedly ignoring her husband.

Lake Dancer beamed. Her smile of open friendliness was hard to resist. "Everybody in the village speaks English. English traders brought their language many years ago. But Jordan taught me proper... proper..."

"Grammar," Jordan supplied.

"Grammar," the girl parroted.

How like a child she was—an innocent child with no notion that the man she obviously worshiped was probably taking advantage of her simple nature.

"Well, you speak beautifully." Duty done, Miri hastened to unfold herself from her awkward position on the floor. "I'm afraid I must go now. As I said, I only came to say my thanks. No need to get up," she told Lake Dancer, who had started to heave herself once again to her feet. "I shall find my own way out. It's been lovely talking with you, uh... Mrs. Scott. And thank you very much for the tea."

Jordan followed Miri out of the wigwam and stopped beside her as she frantically waved to Margaret that she was finished. Margaret, sitting with distressing familiarity in front of a wigwam and chatting with an Indian couple, waved back and nodded, but made no move to leave.

"Would you like to see the rest of the village?" Jordan asked in a bland voice.

"No, thank you," Miri answered. "I've seen quite enough. That is, it isn't necessary for you to trouble yourself to entertain me. Miss Peavey and I will be leaving any moment." She began walking toward the canoe, attracting the attention of curious children and dogs. Jordan stayed at her side.

"I take it you don't much approve of what you see," he said.

"Does it matter?"

"No. But if you're going to be here for any length of time, Miss Sutcliffe, I suggest you don't show your disapproval so openly. The Indians along the Great Lakes are proud people, and they don't take well to whites who look down their noses at them. In the past, it's led to some fairly nasty incidents."

"I have not expressed disapproval of anything or anyone, Mr. Scott."

"Haven't you? In the wigwam a few minutes ago the air fairly reeked with your scorn. It had Lake Dancer worried, and I don't like to see her upset."

Miri gave him a cool look. "I would not think of upsetting your wife, Mr. Scott. For that sweet girl I have only sympathy."

"Really?" His mouth curled in the hint of a smile. It did nothing to soften his harshly masculine face. "Then I assume the scorn was directed my way."

"And if it was, do you care?"

"Not in the least."

"I thought not." Miri's voice was airy with unconcern, but her eyes slid away before his unwavering silver gaze.

They reached the canoe, and the herd of children and dogs became distracted by a noisy game of chase along the water's edge. Miri wished desperately that Margaret would stop her gabbing and come to her rescue. She was feeling more uncomfortable by the moment. All the men of her acquaintance were well-mannered, civilized, and, most important, decently clothed. Not at all like this man, who deliberately flaunted all conventions of proper behavior and seemed to enjoy testing her composure by his blatant lack of decency. Even now, as he bent over to inspect Grace's canoe, he was leaning disconcertingly close. She couldn't help but notice the ripple of heavy muscle beneath his smooth bronzed skin, the faint masculine scent of sweat and smoke and sunlight.

Miri cleared her throat and moved a step back. The silence between them was becoming too heavy to bear.

"Lake Dancer seems a very sweet sort of girl," she began, choosing the safest subject that she could.

"She is," Jordan agreed, straightening.

"How long ago were you married?"

Jordan gave her a chilly look. "We've been living together eight years. It is not the Chippewa custom to hold ceremonies about such things."

"But Grace mentioned that Lake Dancer was your wife, so you've surely. . ." Miri's eyes grew wide as she suddenly realized that most probably he hadn't. The desire for a safe subject of conversation gave way before righteous indignation. "Surely you've married the girl in a Christian ceremony!"

"As I said," Jordan answered coldly, "the Chippewa do not rely on such ceremonies."

"But you are a white man. Don't you want your child to have the advantage of a proper name? It may not be my place to speak, but . . ."

"It's not your place to speak." Jordan's voice was sharp with hostility. "Lake Dancer is my wife in the eyes of God and the Chippewa. That's good enough for me, and her."

Miri rose to the challenge, his cold arrogance simply provoking her stubbornness. "I wonder if your poor child will agree, when he's old enough to understand."

"I think he'll find it doesn't hurt him. Being a bastard hasn't made me any less a man."

Caught off guard, Miri was effectively silenced.

"Do you find that shocking, Miss Sutcliffe?" Jordan lifted a cynical brow. "Did Grace fail to inform you that Scott was my mother's name? Only God, or perhaps the devil, knows my father's."

She stared at him as if he had grown horns. Bad blood would always tell, her Aunt Eliza always said. But this was the first concrete example of that old adage that Miri had ever seen.

"Are you ready to go?"

Margaret's sudden appearance on the scene took Miri by surprise. She sent Jordan a silencing frown, cautioning him that such an inappropriate subject should not be discussed before an innocent child. He shook his head and laughed, and Miri couldn't help but notice how the laughter suddenly transformed the harsh planes of his face and softened the metallic glitter of his eyes. She caught herself staring again, only for a different reason, and pulled her gaze away as though she had been burned.

"Yes," she replied in a clipped voice. "I'm ready to go." Giving Jordan her back, she helped Margaret push the canoe into the water, then settled into the boat with a flounce of her skirts and a barely concealed sigh of relief.

As Jordan stood watching the canoe pull steadily away, Lake Dancer slipped her arm through his. She had come up silently, and he looked down at her in surprise.

"She is very pretty," the Indian girl commented, reverting to her comfortable Chippewa.

"Pretty?" Jordan snorted. "She looks like a tart who's been in a barroom brawl. I'd hardly call her pretty."

"You are unkind, my husband. Underneath those bruises there is beauty. Just as there is courage and a woman's heart under all that pompous primness. You will see someday— when you know her better."

"And you know her so well?" Jordan patted his wife's hand and shook his head. He had no intention of pursuing further acquaintance with the priggish Miss Sutcliffe. He knew her quite well enough, thank you. Like a specter from his past, she breathed life into memories that were best left to die. If he'd had a brain in his head, he would have thrown her back into the lake to drown the first time he had seen her.

The next week at the Peavey farm improved Miri's spirits considerably. She learned that she could milk a goat if she set her mind to it, although it took her twice the time it took Mary Beth. And she began to feel a certain pride of accomplishment in eating an egg that she herself had plucked from beneath the indignantly fluffed feathers of a hen. Better still, the swelling of her face disappeared, and the ugly discoloration of bruises and scrapes faded to nothing. A bit of artful trimming by Grace made Miri's hair fluff into a mass of curls that was really quite attractive, and she now possessed two reasonably fashionable muslin gowns that Lucy and she had managed to finish. A more complete wardrobe was in the works.

Miri was beginning to feel quite human again. And with strength and health came the renewed determination to find her cousin and set her world to rights.

"Oh, my!" Grace exclaimed. "Don't you look every bit the fine lady!"

Miri pirouetted for the widow's inspection. The gown had cost her mightily in frustration and pricked fingers, but the results were almost worth the price. The muslin draped gracefully around her hips and legs. A high waistline and gathered bodice made her look sweetly feminine, and the square-cut neckline was flattering to her curves while still being suitably modest.

"You'll be the envy of every female on the island. Why, if I had such a figure I'd ... I'd ... Well, I don't know what I'd do."

Miri didn't care about being an object of feminine envy. Respectability was what she was after—enough respectability to be admitted for an interview with the commanding officer of Fort Michilimackinac. She didn't know where else to turn for information about Hamilton. No one else seemed to know anything about a young man who would have been seeking her father several weeks ago.

"Do you think he will see me?" she asked anxiously, pausing before the farmhouse's one looking glass to give her hair a final pat.

"He's ten kinds of a fool if he doesn't." Grace ran an assessing eye over her guest. "Who would've thought that the drenched and bedraggled little kitten Jordan hauled from the lake would turn out to be such a beauty?''

"Oh, no," Miri denied with a blush. "Not a beauty. Not with this snub nose and these round cheeks. And this hair." She shook her head ruefully, making her curls bounce. "But maybe good enough to charm Captain—what did you say his name was? Captain Roberts?—into giving me some information."

"Well, dear, if anyone knows about your cousin, it's the British captain. Not much escapes that man's eye, and I imagine he'd know of any Britisher who passed though the island."

As Grace predicted, the British troops at the fort were enough impressed by Miri's British accent and refinement to pass her immediately through the guarded gates and into the presence of the second in command, a Lieutenant Renquist, who promptly petitioned the commander in her behalf.

"Captain Roberts will see you in just a few minutes," the lieutenant said as he emerged from the commander's office. "If you would care to be seated . . . ?"

Miri gave him her most charming smile and seated herself on the crudely carved chair that was the room's only piece of furniture other than a large desk. Fort Michilimackinac was not what she had expected of a British installation in a frontier wilderness. She had thought it would be an outpost of civilization that set an example for the savage Indians and rustic Americans who lived within its influence.

Instead, she found nothing but a walled enclosure of crude buildings occupied by troops every bit as ragtag as the Americans who lived outside the walls.

The only imposing quality of the fort was the steep limestone cliff that set it above the town, and the only touch of gentility was the young officer who stood gazing at her with polite but obvious curiosity. The brass on his scarlet uniform shone with a well-rubbed luster; his boots were spotless and shiny black; and his cravat and breeches were a blinding white. The lieutenant's brown hair, though somewhat creased by his hat, was worn in a fashionably tousled manner. All in all, he was the first hint of refinement and civilization Miri had seen since she had left London.

Apparently, the lieutenant was thinking the same about her.

"Please pardon me for staring so rudely, Miss Sutcliffe, but you are the first lady of delicacy and sensibility that I have encountered in this benighted wilderness. The sight of you reminds my soul that beauty and refinement still exist."

Miri responded with a ladylike blush. "You flatter me, Lieutenant. And I'm afraid you do not catch me at my best. I've had a rather harrowing two weeks on your island."

"I heard of your father's untimely death," the lieutenant sympathized. "And your dreadful accident. But I must admit my selfishness in being glad that you are here, Miss Sutcliffe, for you are certainly a sight that refreshes the weary spirit. Dare I hope that you will be staying for some time?"

"I'm staying only long enough to locate my cousin, who came to visit my father before my arrival. I hope that with the help of Captain Roberts I shall soon be on my way back to England."

Renquist smiled wistfully. "I can fully appreciate your haste to leave. The wild forests, the wilder Indians and Americans"—he grimaced—"it's all rather overwhelming for those of us who appreciate the advantages of civilization. But your departure will certainly be my very great loss."

Miri was just beginning to thoroughly enjoy the lieutenant's flowery compliments when the door to the inner office opened and Captain Roberts motioned her to enter. She smiled a charming good-bye to her admirer and followed the commander into his office, which was every bit as spartan as the anteroom had been.

Like the fort, the commander was not what Miri had expected. Captain Roberts was an old man. Wheezing breath and an ashen face told of his failing health, and it was hard to imagine that this was the clever warrior who had ousted the Americans from their strategic island stronghold without so much as a shot being fired. But his mind was as sharp as ever, and he listened attentively while Miri described Hamilton and spun him an innocent and competely untruthful account of why her cousin must be found. She was practiced at the false tale, for it was the same one she had given Grace and her family.

The captain was silent for a moment after she finished, eyeing her thoughtfully and drumming his fingers on the top of the desk. For a moment Miri feared that the news of Hamilton's treason had traveled all the way to America, but then Roberts smiled.

"Well, now, Miss Sutcliffe, it seems I remember a chap like the one you describe, except his name wasn't Hamilton Greer, it was Kenneth Shelby. This fellow was tall and had black hair, as you say, and he did inquire after your father." The captain gave her a piercing look. "Any reason your cousin might be using another name?"

"I . . . well . . . not that I know of. I haven't seen Hamilton in several years." Another lie. Lord! Where would it end?

"This Shelby chap seemed a bit upset when he learned your father had died, but he seemed determined to carry on with his business. I believe he bought a canoe load of trade goods and started out for the West with a guide by the name of Gage Delacroix."

"Do you know precisely where they were headed?"

Captain Roberts chuckled. "I don't think even the young man knew exactly where he was headed, miss. He was rather inexperienced where this country is concerned, and seemed in a hurry to be on his way. I wouldn't worry too much about him, though, if this is your cousin. Gage is a reliable guide. He's half Iroquois, and he knows this country better than most of the Indians hereabouts."

Miri tried to hide her disappointment. "Yes, well . . . Thank you, Captain. You've been a great help."

"No trouble," he assured her. "I try to keep an eye on what's happening in this area, you understand. Particularly when my countrymen are involved."

"You've been very kind to take the time to see me."

"My pleasure, miss. You're a sight for an old man's eyes." He sighed. "After a time one gets bored with talking only to Indians, fur traders, and farmers. It's a shame your cousin isn't still around. Perhaps the two of you could have been persuaded to stay on the island for a while and enlighten us with the latest news from London. But as it is, I suppose you'll be wanting to arrange return passage as soon as possible."

"I . . . I haven't decided yet what to do."

The commander rose, his mind obviously already moving to other concerns. "Well, if I can be of any help, miss, just let me or the lieutenant out there know."

"I certainly will." She smiled as he sketched a brief bow over her hand. "And thank you again for your help."

It was not quite true that Miri had not yet decided what to do, for the moment she learned that Hamilton had indeed passed this way, she knew she could not give up the search. And she knew just who she could employ to sniff out her elusive cousin—or, at least, she thought she knew.

The very next morning she rose with the sun and asked Grace's permission to use the canoe. Upon hearing that Miri was headed for the village across the straits, Mary Beth pleaded to go, offering to paddle the entire way, but Miri insisted she could handle the canoe by herself.

"Besides," she said as Mary Beth's lower lip slipped out into a pout, "who would milk the goats?"

"Mags could milk them. All she ever does is sit around and sew and help Ma cook. It's about time she did some real work."

"I don't know how long I'll be, Mary Beth. And your mother can't spare you all day."

"She would if you asked her. You goin' to visit Jordan and Lake Dancer? I bet if you asked him, Jordan would show you his scalps. He won't show me. But if you asked him, he might show both of us."

Miri grimaced. "Don't be ridiculous. Mr. Scott doesn't have any scalps."

Mary Beth's eyes grew wide and an impish smile lit her

face. "Yes, he does. Margaret told me. All the braves in the village have scalps from when they make war on the Sioux, and he has more than just about anybody. He's a war chief, and they have to be better at fighting than just about anybody."

"You're spinning me a tale, Mary Beth. If you think to scare me into taking you with me, you're quite mistaken. I have business with Mr. Scott and I need to speak with him in private."

"Well," the girl said with a resigned shrug. "Don't make him mad. Or anybody else over there, either." She gauged the effect of her warning out of the corner of her eye, then smirked in satisfaction. "Margaret said those braves were surely impressed by the color of your hair when the sun hits it. I'd be careful if I was you."

"Oh, pooh!" Miri grabbed the milk bucket from its peg on the wall and shoved it into Mary Beth's hand. "Go see about the chores and put the lid on that imagination of yours. Scalps, indeed!"

Mary Beth was a mischievous little storyteller that any sensible adult would ignore, Miri told herself. But good sense was not sufficient to keep her own imagination from churning as she painfully paddled her way across the straits. Grace had told her the chilling story of the massacre of 1763, when the Chippewa had slaughtered the British at the old fort on the mainland to the south, torn out their victims' hearts, and bathed themselves in their blood. And the Chippewa and Sioux had periodically attacked each other for generations. Could part of what the little imp said be true? Could Jordan Scott—a white man with a civilized upbringing and education—really have sunk to such savagery? And if so, was such a man trustworthy to send after her cousin?

Miri stoutheartedly quelled her doubts. Jordan Scott was the only man she knew who might possibly find her cousin. If Hamilton didn't like the sort of fellow she sent after him, then he could just blame himself for creating the necessity.

The sun was almost at its zenith when Miri finally

reached the village. Paddling a canoe was much more taxing than it looked. Her arms and shoulders were on fire, and her cotton dress was unpleasantly damp with sweat—not the state in which she would have chosen to present herself to Jordan and his wife. But there was nothing to be done about it.

Children, dogs, and insufficiently clad braves greeted her as they had before, with friendly smiles and raucous shouts. She smiled and nodded at their broken English, and, not wanting to offend, accepted a brave's offer of escort to Lake Dancer's wigwam.

The doorway blanket was fastened to one side, and Miri called hesitantly through the dim opening. In a short moment Lake Dancer appeared at the door with a surprised smile on her face.

"Miss Sutcliffe. I am honored that you come to visit. Come in. Sit down, I will fetch tea."

Miri ducked through the doorway and stood awkwardly as Lake Dancer busied herself with the kettle. "I . . . I came to talk to Mr. Scott. I . . . is he here?"

"Ah." Lake Dancer nodded her head. "My husband will return shortly. He helps one of the young men repair a canoe. Please sit down and drink some tea."

Miri sat and accepted the proffered cup. The cherry twig tea tasted less bitter this time. Perhaps she was simply becoming accustomed to the primitive brew. Lake Dancer poured herself a cup and settled herself heavily across the low fire.

"I am told you seek your man," the Indian girl said with disconcerting directness.

Miri sputtered into her tea. "I beg your pardon?"

"Your—what is the word?—betrothed. One of our men heard it from a white man in the town."

News certainly spreads fast, Miri thought. She had solicited information from Captain Roberts, the Catholic and Anglican priests, and a few traders she had met in town, and now the story had spread all the way to the Chippewa village.

"Yes," Miri replied. "I am looking for my cousin. That is the reason I traveled to this country."

Lake Dancer looked doubtful. "You would marry your cousin? That I do not understand. We Chippewa are forbidden to marry within our own clan. Eyes of a Ghost is of the Wolf Clan, even though he was adopted by our family, and I am of the Catfish."

"Hamilton is a very distant cousin," Miri explained. "He's not really of my . . . my clan. And right now I am not at all certain that we will marry. I think I've decided that life would be entirely more pleasant without men."

"Then it is good that you wait," Lake Dancer said with a sage nod. "But it is not good for a woman to live alone. You are beautiful and have courage and kindness. A strong man would be fortunate to have you for a wife."

Lake Dancer's voice was friendly, even affectionate, but her eyes were sad. Miri felt she had suddenly started reading a story in the middle of the book. Something in this conversation was eluding her.

"I am flattered by your compliments, Mrs. Scott. But you don't even know me."

The Chippewa girl smiled. "Your face is well-known to me. And your nature, also. Someday soon I will tell you where it was we met. Until then, know that I am your friend, your sister of the heart. It will be that you will come to visit me often and tell me of my husband's people, and I will teach you the ways of the Chippewa. We will both learn what we need before the gods take us in their grasp."

Miri would have demanded an explanation, but Jordan chose that moment to return. Lake Dancer gave her husband a brief greeting, then rose and left the wigwam without another word. Miri was startled to see a sheen of moisture on the Indian girl's cheeks as she stepped out into the sunlight.

Jordan turned a thunderous frown on Miri. "I told you once before that I don't like seeing my wife upset. What did you say to her?"

"I assure you, Mr. Scott, I said nothing to offend your

wife. She made some very odd comments, though. Are you sure she is well?''

"She is well enough." He stared after his wife with a doubtful frown that belied his easy words. "Indian women do not posture and carry on about having a baby as white women do. They are more sensible. What did she say?"

Miri balked at the difficulty of explaining Lake Dancer's peculiar words, or the strange feelings they had induced. "It's not important. Besides, I came here to speak with you, not your wife." She set down her cup and rose with determination. "Could we talk outside? It's much too stuffy in here." Especially with Jordan's broad shoulders blocking the light from the doorway and his hard-muscled bulk making the hut seem so very small.

Once outside, with the fresh breeze on her face, Miri found the courage to state her proposition. And Jordan had the temerity to laugh.

"Why should I find your cousin for you? I have no interest in you or your man."

"He is not 'my man,'" Miri denied. "And you should do it for money, of course. I have none with me presently—it was all lost in the lake. But I have only to send to London for a draft upon my bank. I assure you that I can pay very well, indeed."

Jordan's expression held a certain amount of malice. "No doubt you can pay very well, Miss Sutcliffe. But I am no more interested in your money than in any other part of your proposition. And even if I were, I could hardly leave right now, with my wife expecting to deliver in a few weeks."

Miri had not expected Jordan to be so concerned with such things. Most gentlemen of her acquaintance would gladly be absent during the "female busines" of confinement and delivery. "I respect your concern for your wife, Mr. Scott, but . . ."

"No buts. I'm not interested."

"But you're my only hope of finding him."

"You're a stubborn woman, Miss Sutcliffe. You should learn to listen when a man says no."

"You're the one who's being stubborn," Miri tossed back with a frown. "Hamilton only left two weeks ago. With luck you could find them and be back before Lake Dancer delivers."

"I said no."

"I could pay you . . ."

"No."

The metallic glitter of those silver-gray eyes made Miri bite back her next words. The man was as stubborn as a granite block, and just as immovable.

"Very well," she conceded with a lift of her small chin. "I shall do without your help. I'm sure there are others who would be willing to undertake the task."

"You might find that in these parts, your money and ladylike airs won't always guarantee that you get your way, Miss Sutcliffe."

Miri's eyes narrowed as she fixed Jordan with a cold glare. "I'm sure not everyone here lacks your manners, Mr. Scott. There will be someone willing to help a lady in need."

Jordan just smiled in reply. Miri returned the smile with a frosty "Good day to you, sir," then turned and flounced off toward her canoe, where Lake Dancer joined her.

The Indian girl's brow creased in worry when she saw Miri's expression. "You are not happy with my husband?"

Miri softened her frown, reminding herself that it was not Lake Dancer who deserved her ire. "Your husband can be a most irritating man."

"You will still come back to visit me?"

Miri hesitated. The girl seemed so eager for her company. And could she, in good conscience, refuse to enlighten the poor innocent about the advantages of civilized ways? "I'll come visit you, Lake Dancer, if your husband permits."

"He will permit." The girl nodded happily and motioned to Jordan, who had been watching their conversation with a scowl darkening his already forbidding face. "He will paddle you across to the island. You are tired, are you not? You are not used to such work."

"I wouldn't dream of imposing upon him," Miri replied acidly.

"It is no imposition. My husband," she said as Jordan walked up, "you will help Miss Sutcliffe across the straits, will you not? And pick me up a new kettle at the trading house?"

"As you wish." Jordan gave his wife a look of distinct displeasure. Miri he did not condescend to look at.

They paddled across the straits in Jordan's canoe with Miri's trailing behind. The trip was silent and awkward. Miri stared at the bottom of the boat, at the quiet water rippling off their hull, at the receding mainland, at the sky—anywhere but at the man sitting opposite her in the canoe. But her eyes were drawn in spite of her determination. And when they finally came to rest on Jordan, she was distressed to discover the intensity of the silver-gray gaze that was fastened upon her. Her eyes quickly bounced away, unwilling to acknowledge that she had seen. He looked to her mind every bit as savage as the mischievous Mary Beth had made him out to be—a man perfectly capable of carrying his enemies' scalps around on his belt and thinking it a display to be proud of. At this moment, in fact, Jordan looked as though he were contemplating adding a cropped, curly auburn scalp to his collection.

What had she done or said to earn such animosity? She had admitted herself to be in his debt for saving her life, she had been very properly polite in spite of the irregular nature of his circumstances, and he answered her mannerly conduct with cruel barbs and outrageous disrespect.

Poor Lake Dancer. How could such a sweet girl tolerate the man as husband, constantly subject to the blackguard's temper, and hurtfulness—and lusts? Miri stole another glance toward her companion, noting the roll of hard muscle under his bronzed skin, the harsh masculinity of his face. His stern features were softened only by a beautifully curved mouth that even the most ominous frown couldn't disguise. Her imagination abandoned its usual discipline and tried to conceive how it would be to endure the embraces of such a frightening man. Unwelcome images of Jordan taking brutal possession of his wife crept into her mind, making her shiver convulsively. With horrified determination she drove the images away, telling herself that the shiver was from outraged delicacy—nothing more.

"Are you cold?"

Miri looked up to find Jordan's eyes still upon her. They seemed to look through her to the heart of her turmoil, reading the very indecent turn of her mind. At that moment she could well believe that Jordan Scott was one of those much-talked-about Chippewa sorcerers who could summon supernatural forces to their aid. She shivered again and dropped her eyes to the bottom of the canoe. "No, I'm not cold."

God help her if she weren't becoming as licentious and superstitious as these primitive savages. With or without Hamilton's list, she had to return to civilization soon.

✳ 5 ✳

"That's really very pretty," Margaret commented, appreciatively eyeing the just-completed gown that Miri held up for her inspection.

"It is!" Grace agreed. "You've become a very clever seamstress, my dear. And to think that just three weeks ago you could scarcely thread a needle! Those drooping puffed sleeves are very smart. Wherever did you get the idea?"

"The ladies in Montreal were wearing gowns similar to this one," Miri told them. She didn't add that no matter how impressed she was with her new talent, she wouldn't think of wearing such an amateurish creation if she were in London.

"Petunia would like that bit of lace on the bodice," Mary Beth smirked. "You better not wear it around her."

Margaret regarded her younger sister with all the disdain of her two years of seniority. "One does not wear a fashionable gown to milk goats, Mary Beth. Even you should know that."

"How do you know what a body wears to milk goats?" Mary Beth huffed. "You hardly ever go into the barn, much less get your hands dirty by helping with the chores. At least Miri helps me with the goats and chickens and pigs!"

Margaret's nose went higher into the air. "I have plenty to do without the goats and chickens and pigs. That's because you leave all the dusting,"—she began counting chores on her fingers—"the scrubbing, the sweeping, the bed-making, the sewing, and the cooking to me, you little lump. You'll be sorry when you grow up and find out what a *woman's* work is really like."

Mary Beth was out of her chair to attack when Grace's firm voice intervened. "Leave off, you two. If you can't act like ladies, then go and live with the savages, where you belong. I don't think either one of you is overworked. And instead of complaining, I think you should try to follow little Lucy's example. Now, there's a lass who can work hard and still be a lady while she's doing it. And Miriam also," she added as an afterthought. "You never see those two ladies scrapping like barnyard cats, do you?"

Grace's words gave Miri a little start. She had never before been classed as an equal with a servant like Lucy, though in this primitive culture it was true that the boundaries between classes were somewhat blurred, and in the last weeks she had worked as hard as Lucy did—harder, perhaps, for she had been forced to learn skills that Lucy already had. In truth, she was inordinately pleased with her small accomplishments of menial labor. It was certainly nothing she would want to tell her London friends about. But it gave her a feeling of satisfying competence, just the same.

Mary Beth sniffed. "I'd like to see Lucy's face when

Jordan brings us a heaping catch this fall and we start cleaning and smoking the fish! And Miri's, too. Ladies!'' She sniffed again. ''They'll be just like Mags. She won't go near the fish pile!''

Glad to be able to get Mary Beth back with a bit of her own sauciness, Miri smiled maliciously. ''You'll have that chore all to yourself, Mary Beth. By that time Lucy and I will be on our way back to London. We're only waiting for Mr. Delacroix to return with word of my cousin.''

Mary Beth struck back. ''Jordan says that Gage Delacroix is lucky if he can find his . . .''

''Mary Beth!'' Grace warned. ''Don't pay the scamp any mind, Miri. Jordan and Gage have been friendly rivals for years. Sometimes those two don't realize their joking isn't suitable for little girls' ears.''

''I'm not a little girl!'' Mary Beth countered. ''And if Miri really wanted to find her cousin, she'd ask Jordan. He can track anything.''

Miri was silent. She hadn't told the Peavey family that she had done that very thing, and been curtly and most definitely refused. They had assumed that her visit to the village that day had been to see Lake Dancer, just as her subsequent visits had been.

Knowing that Grace and her daughters were fond of Jordan, Miri had borne the girls' talk about the renegade with a bland face and declined to comment on their misguided hero worship. Even Grace seemed ridiculously fond of the fellow, and over the last weeks she had filled Miri's head with stories of Jordan's escapades with her late husband. The widow had nothing but praise for his character. Grace obviously didn't know the true man, Miri thought. She excused the widow's lack of perception on the grounds that Grace had lived her entire life in the uncivilized American wilderness.

Grace found excuses for the renegade's behavior in his supposed mistreatment at the hands of Boston society. His mother was Jane Scott, she'd explained, a gently raised girl who had had the misfortune to conceive a child out of wedlock and was consequently driven from her family in disgrace. The woman had become a wealthy courtesan, and her death had left Jordan very comfortably fixed. The money had bought the whore's bastard an education at Harvard, but had been unable to purchase respectability. Grace thought it was an unsuitable romantic alliance that finally had made Jordan Scott flee Boston to lose himself in the Northwest frontier. But her husband had been unwilling to reveal Jordan's confidences on that particular subject.

Miri had listened to Grace's account with both pity and disgust. Jordan's background, as far as she was concerned, explained much, but it excused nothing. People should be able to rise above the disadvantages of their beginnings. And Jordan Scott had only degenerated. Grace herself admitted that many of the white settlers of the area regarded Jordan with a wary eye, but the widow attributed that to ignorance and prejudice directed toward the Indians. The savages were not so terrible, Grace insisted. Though it was true they had massacred a number of British some fifty years ago—she looked at Miri with a hint of apology—the British had probably deserved it. And the constant fighting with the Sioux (while she admitted that Jordan did participate in these forays, she denied that he would sink so low as to take scalps) was really no worse than the frequent bloody squabbles of white men. Grace theorized that the white settlers around the Straits of Mackinac found Jordan an unhappy reminder that for all their civilized ways, white men were really not so far removed from primitive savagery.

Miri mouthed polite agreement whenever her hostess argued in this vein, but she privately thought that Jordan Scott deserved every bit of disdain he got from his fellow white men.

Lake Dancer, on the other hand, was as lovely a girl as one could ever hope to meet, though of course her primitive culture had to be taken into account when assessing her virtues. Miri had intended to return to the village only once, in order to keep her promise to visit Jordan's wife. But after the first visit, a growing friendship with Lake Dancer had made her return. The Indian girl's strangeness had disappeared. She made no more baffling comments about having met Miri before, and her natural grace and gentility were so charming that Miri found herself truly enjoying her visits. They talked of the cities to the east, and London, and Miri read to her aloud from a book of poetry that the Indian girl said belonged to her husband. Jordan would not read to her from the white man's book, Lake Dancer complained, or tell her stories of his life before he came to live with her people. She was eager to discover all she could of the world to which her husband had been born.

In return, Lake Dancer told Miri stories and legends of her people, whom she called Anishanabe, or "first man," and whom their Indian neighbors had named the Ojibwa. She spun tales of the great totems; of Gitchimanido, the great spirit; and of the lesser guardian spirits that granted mortal men and women visions of knowledge and power. She told stories of great battles, sorcerers, great evil, sweet love, stalwart courage.

Miri was so fascinated that she sometimes stayed for hours. In spite of their vast differences, a strange comradeship grew up between the two women. Miri found that she could open her heart to Lake Dancer as she never could even to dear Aunt Eliza. She could talk of her parents, her childhood, and her ideals without fear of judgment. In her turn, she listened with sympathy to Lake Dancer's hopes for her child—a long-hoped-for blessing after eight years of barrenness. The strange sadness that Miri had noted when she first met Lake Dancer had disappeared, and Miri credited her visits with the change. All the girl had needed was a sympathetic ear to listen to her concerns, she reasoned.

It was a warm July afternoon when Miri stopped in town on her way back from a visit to the Chippewa village. She didn't notice the beauty of the day or the greetings from the few others who walked through the streets. Her mind was full of Lake Dancer. The Indian girl had been a bit strange again today, and also somewhat melancholy. Miri had wanted to stay longer and assure herself that her friend was not ill, but Jordan had returned unexpectedly and she had been forced to leave.

Miri was grateful that she did not often have to endure Jordan's presence during her visits to Lake Dancer's wigwam. At first sight of her he would take himself off on some errand or chore. And if he returned before she left, Miri would cut her visit short. The moment he walked into the wigwam she could feel those silver-gray eyes upon her, making something inside her squirm for release. Miri didn't know what sort of an imp Jordan Scott had planted in her soul. She didn't want to know, either. With enough neglect, the imp would surely die.

The afternoon shadows were growing long as Miri walked up the town's main street toward the Anglican church. Grace had asked her to stop by the rectory—a mere log cabin roofed by bark and enclosed by a tall cedar picket fence—to invite Father Carroll to dinner on Sunday. The poor man had few enough friends on the island, for most of the traders and the British troops on Michilimackinac frequented taverns more often than churches, and the more religious-minded French Canadians attended the big stone Catholic church at the other end of town.

Miri's thoughts were so occupied that she didn't hear the footsteps behind her.

"Nice afternoon, Miss Sutcliffe." The words were slightly slurred, but the voice was still cultured and gentlemanly.

"What?" she asked, startled out of her reverie. "Oh, yes, it is very nice, isn't it?" Miri halted and let Lieutenant Renquist draw even with her. She instantly regretted it, for a strong odor of liquor assaulted her the minute he drew near. Not one for mincing words, Miri accosted him with the fact immediately. "Lieutenant, have you been drinking?"

"My lady," he said with a woozy smile, "I have, indeed. Who would not resort to strong spirits when informed they must spend yet another year on this little mudhole of an island? Even if one must stoop to the rotgut rum that passes for liquor in this primitive village."

Miri felt a twinge of sympathy. She could understand his

desire to flee this wilderness and once again enjoy the refinements of civilization. Did she not feel the same need? But certainly his predicament was no excuse for over-indulgence.

"Lieutenant," she said primly, "rum will not make your tenure here any easier."

He laughed unsteadily. "Perhaps you're right, lovely lady. But the company of one as beautiful as you would surely ease my lot. May I accompany you on your way? The sight of your face and the sound of your voice are surely a"—he stopped momentarily, then hiccuped—"a balm for my . . . my battered soul."

Wrinkling her nose in disgust, Miri backed away. "I think not, Lieutenant. My errand is brief, and I must return home before the sun sets."

"Why?" he slurred. "When the night falls do you . . . you turn into a pumpkin? Or a bumpkin?" He laughed. "Turn into a bumpkin, like the rest of the bumpkins on this island. How appropriate."

Miri had had enough. Lieutenant Renquist had seemed such a gentleman. Did this terrible country cause all men to degenerate into scoundrels? She turned to proceed on her way, but Renquist's arm flashed out to detain her.

"Don't leave, lovely lady. You're the first bit of refinement I've seen in . . . how long? A year or more."

"Let go, Lieutenant."

"I'd give my right arm for a kind word." He aimed a wet kiss at her hand and instead hit her lower arm. "I'd die for a kiss."

Miri struggled in vain to loose her arm from his grip. "Lieutenant Renquist! Really!"

"Yes, really, Lieutenant Renquist." A new voice brought them both around to stare at the tall half-clad figure standing, arms crossed over his broad chest and feet spread, in the roadway behind them. "My guess is that you'd have to marry this particular lady to get that kiss, and I doubt it would be worth your while. So why don't you just leave her be and go on your way?"

Renquist stiffened, looking unsure about just which of them had been insulted—he or Miri. "The lady is not your business," he finally said in a belligerent tone.

"Nor is she yours," Jordan replied calmly. "Why don't you just go somewhere to sleep off your little celebration?" Jordan's eyes narrowed to a dangerous sliver of ice as Renquist's hand move toward the pistol in his belt. "I wouldn't," he warned. "Not unless you want your stay on this island shortened in a very unpleasant manner."

Renquist's lips tightened, and for a moment his fingers jerked as though they would grip the pistol of their own accord. Then he hiccuped, and his hand went back to his side. "Filthy savage!" He spat in the dirt at Jordan's feet. Without a word he spun on his heel, stumbled, shakily recovered his balance, and weaved off in the direction of the fort.

Miri heaved a sigh of relief and regarded Jordan cautiously. "I suppose I must thank you once again, Mr. Scott. You do seem to happen along when I am in need of assistance."

His mouth lifted in an unpleasant smile. "Is that your idea of a civilized gentleman, Miss Sutcliffe? Perhaps I should take note of his behavior and take lessons."

"The lieutenant is not himself. All the same, he was being most unpleasant, and I owe you . . ."

"Not now, Miss Sutcliffe. You can tell me of your gratitude as we walk to the farm. I'm in a hurry to talk to Grace."

"What is it?" Miri was struck with an instant's foreboding. "I just left you at the village. Is . . . ?"

"Lake Dancer is in labor. I came over to fetch the post surgeon, but he can't be bothered with a mere Indian girl. Grace will have to play at midwife."

"But, but," Miri stammered as she tried to match his long strides. The invitation to the lonely priest was completely forgotten. "Is everything all right?"

"I don't know. Chippewa women generally have very easy deliveries. But Lake Dancer has been trying for years to have a child, and I'll feel better having someone in attendance other than the village women.''

Miri heard the genuine concern in his voice, and for a moment her heart softened toward him. Then she reminded herself that it was because of him that poor Lake Dancer was in this delicate condition, and all without the benefit of Christian marriage.

When Grace heard the news she gathered a sharp knife, a set of ugly forceps, a rope, clean linen, and a shawl. Brusquely she told Miri and Jordan to follow as she bustled out the farmhouse door. ''Don't look so worried,'' she threw at Jordan. ''Do you think this is the first baby that's been born into the world? Dancer will be fine.''

But Dancer was not fine. She had been removed to a small wigwam that the village women had built especially for the coming delivery. There on a pallet of cedar boughs, woven rush mats, and tanned hides she lay, listless and pale, gripping the supportive hands of two attendant women whenever the pain took her in its grip.

''We'll have an end to this!'' Grace declared as she surveyed the situation. ''Smiles at Sunrise!'' she pointed to one of the women. ''Take those filthy hides out of here. And those mats are none too clean. Get rid of them. I don't care what your cursed traditions say!''

When the offensive items were removed, Grace instructed the women to bring in clean hides for the pallet. Over these she spread the clean linen she had brought from the farm.

''Miri,'' Grace ordered, ''you help Dancer to get up. That's right. Now, just have her walk slowly around the hut. It will help with the pain. And you two''—she nodded at the Indian women, who were regarding her with mixed amazement and resentment— ''get some water boiling over that fire outside. At least two kettles full. Now get moving! Both of you!''

The Chippewa women scurried out, muttering in their own language. Miri encouraged Lake Dancer to lean on her as they proceeded slowly around the wigwam, stopping every few minutes as the Indian girl's body doubled up with pain.

Lake Dancer paid Miri and Grace no mind. She did as she was told, but uttered no word—just the whimpers and groans that were wrenched from her throat as the pain tore through her. It seemed to Miri that her friend had turned every ounce of strength and every bit of concentration inward. She was totally absorbed in the drama of her own body.

Two hours had passed when a stocky Indian pushed his way into the hut. Miri's eyes widened in shock and she hastily covered Lake Dancer, who was now lying on the pallet.

"It's all right," Grace told her. "This is Dancer's brother. Rides the Waves, meet Miriam Sutcliffe."

Rides the Waves nodded briefly. His face was grave as he handed a cup to Grace. Grace's mouth tightened in disgust. "I suppose Smiles sent you after I shooed her out of here. For a smart woman, she certainly does set store by a lot of heathen hocus-pocus!"

Nevertheless, she handed the cup down to Miri, who was sitting on the ground beside the pallet. "Give her a few swallows of this," Grace instructed.

Miri looked at the pinkish liquid in the cup. "What is it?"

"Snake's blood mixed with water. The Indians believe it's a foolproof remedy for difficult childbirth."

Miri's stomach lurched. She looked at Grace in disbelief.

"Go ahead. It won't do her any harm, and you can be sure that Rides the Waves won't leave until she's downed it all."

The foolproof Chippewa remedy did not relieve Dancer's distress, however. As the midnight hour approached, there was still no sign of the baby, and the village resounded with Lake Dancer's screams. At one point Jordan, face white and eyes desperate, burst into the wigwam to demand that someone do something—anything—to help his wife. But there was nothing that anyone could do. It had taken two strong Indian men to remove him, for the sight of him had pulled Lake Dancer from her inner world and sharpened her distress.

As the morning sun rose above the horizon, Lake Dancer was delivered of a daughter who made her entrance into the world rump-first. Blue-tinged and listless, the baby took a full two minutes to gasp her first breath. And that was merely a quiet, tentative inhalation, as if the newborn was unsure she wanted to make the effort. She was too weak to cry.

Miri thought the baby was possibly the ugliest thing she had ever seen. The whole process of birth had repelled her, and it had only been Grace's stern looks that kept her from fleeing the wigwam during the last stages of labor. But the look on Dancer's face as the weak little baby was placed in her arms put a new and bright patina on what had just occurred. Miri had never seen anyone look quite so radiant as Lake Dancer when she looked at her new daughter. Lake Dancer herself looked almost as bad as the child—her eyes great black pools in an ashy-gray face—but her smile made her beautiful.

Grace motioned for Miri to follow her out of the wigwam. Immediately outside the door, they confronted a ravaged-looking Jordan.

"I'll tell you straight, my friend." Grace fixed Jordan with a level gaze. "Your wife and daughter are alive, but they won't be on this earth another hour. The baby was in the wrong position, and Dancer was too small. She's torn to pieces inside, Jordan, and I can't stop the bleeding. And the babe is so weak I'm surprised it was born with any life in its little body."

Miri felt her stomach drop. She hadn't realized it was so bad. She saw a muscle twitch in Jordan's jaw, and his broad shoulders hunched as though a great weight had been laid upon them.

"You go in there and say good-bye to your wife," Grace ordered. "You send her out of this world happy, you hear? That little girl is the bravest, sweetest soul I ever did know."

Jordan regarded them both out of a face carved from granite. Anger and grief melted together in the hot cauldron of his eyes, and Miri wondered if the anger was directed at cruel fate, or at the two women who had failed to save Dancer's life. Without a word he ducked into the wigwam.

Miri collapsed onto a nearby log and hid her face in her hands. Every muscle in her body trembled with exhaustion, and every corner of her mind was panting with horror and grief. Sweet, kind, beautiful Lake Dancer. How unjust that she should die in such misery, bearing an illegitimate child for a bastard scoundrel like Jordan Scott. Tears stung her eyes and overflowed in a hot flood.

It was not long before Jordan emerged from the wigwam looking grimmer than ever. He advanced on Miri, and the look on his face made her flinch away.

"Lake Dancer wants to see you."

At first Miri wanted to shout no, she couldn't bear it. She wanted nothing so much as to run and hide and forget this entire night. But Jordan's gaze dragged her off her seat and compelled her to obey. Those silver-gray eyes had lost their luster and were now dull as stone, and just as hard.

The wigwam was silent when Miri entered. There were no more screams to set the village on edge. All that was finished now. For Lake Dancer, almost everything was finished. Grace was moving quietly around the hut, gathering up bloody linen and setting things straight. As Miri entered she looked up with a weary smile. She came over to Miri and gave her an encouraging pat on the shoulder. "Good child," she said. "Now put a smile on your face. For Dancer."

Lake Dancer lay quietly on her pallet, her pitiful child held tightly in her arms, her eyelids drooping over dull eyes. But a spark of life lit her face when she heard Miri's voice.

"Lake Dancer." Miri knelt awkwardly beside the pallet. What did one say to a friend who was at death's threshold?

"Miriam." Dancer's cold hand groped out and caught hers. Slowly the Indian girl's head turned her way and the eyes focused. "I am happy that you are here."

"I am here, Dancer. But . . . should your husband not be with you?"

"Jordan . . . Jordan has said his good-byes." Dancer smiled weakly. "He was the best of husbands. His heart was only half mine, but that was enough." Her eyes focused on Miri's face. "I am . . . so glad that you are beautiful. And kind." Dancer paused as a great shudder rolled through her slight body. "I see the lake spirit. My guardian has come for me."

"Dancer," Miri said in a shaky voice. "Do you want me to fetch Jordan?"

"No. I must tell you of my vision." Dancer smiled, and her voice seemed to gain in strength. "I had a dream many months ago. My guardian spirit came to me and showed me what would be before the year had passed. He showed me your face, and said you would be mother to my child and wife to my husband, so I should not be concerned for them. He said . . . he said I must come with him to where the ghosts dance together with the gods."

"Dancer, don't say that."

Lake Dancer tightened her hand around Miri's. "Do you think I do not know that I die? I have known of my fate for months. Dreams do not lie." She looked into Miri's face. "There are tears in your eyes, Miriam. Do not cry for me. I am content to go where I go. And you will care for my daughter and make my husband happy—as my vision promised."

Miri could think of nothing to say. The tears were out of control and spilling over onto her cheeks.

"Will you?"

"I will care for your daughter."

Dancer smiled and closed her eyes. Her body seemed to relax. "I have named her Bright Spirit. She will bring you joy, as she has brought me."

The Chippewa girl did not draw another breath. Through the blur of her tears, Miri could see the peace that had settled upon Dancer's face. With a strange sense of reverence and awe, she reached out and took the infant from its mother's arms.

The noon sun blazed down upon the shimmering lake and touched the sand, rocks, trees, and grasses with its warmth. The day showed summer at its best. Birds caroled their songs to a brilliant blue sky, and the trees sang a soft melody of their own as the breeze rustled through the needles and leaves.

All Jordan could think about was the injustice that Lake Dancer should die on such a day. She could not hear the birds or feel the sun's warmth on her face, or smell the fresh scent of the breeze. She was beyond such joy—cold and stiff and hidden from the eyes of those who loved her by a birchbark shroud.

The little group of Chippewa—Lake Dancer's parents and cousins and friends—chanted softly as Rides the Waves danced with solemn dignity around the freshly dug grave. Jordan did not join in the chanting. He stood still and silent as a statue, remembering all the years, all the happy times that Lake Dancer had given him. She had saved his life back when he was young and foolish and sure that he was stronger than anything nature could throw in his path. Her brother had become his brother, her father and mother had become the loving parents he had never had. It had been only natural that they join their lives together, and Lake Dancer had been the sweetest and most undemanding of wives. She had given him everything. And what had he given her in return?

He had given her a husband who couldn't love her as she deserved to be loved; he had given her days of loneliness when he had uncaringly spent weeks away on hunting and war expeditions; he had returned her love with a casual affection that was little better than indifference; and finally, he had planted inside her the child who had killed her. And now she was gone—sweet Dancer who had laughed away his foul moods, washed away his bitterness, and finally taught him that love was more than passion and more, perhaps, than he was capable of giving to anyone. Always laughing and happy, delighting in each day of life, Lake Dancer had seemed well content with what Jordan could give. But now that she was gone, the memory that she had been happy was not enough for his conscience. He should have given her more.

Rides the Waves' dance had stopped. The group around the grave fell silent as he began his eulogy.

"Your feet are now on the road of souls, my sister. You were with us such a short while, and we will miss you, those of us who loved you. You were a virtuous woman, a faithful wife, a loving daughter, a sister dear to my heart."

Jordan looked up to see Miri standing on the edge of the mourners. Rides the Waves' praises of Lake Dancer's virtues faded into the background, and for a moment, the little Englishwoman seemed to be the only thing in the world that was in sharp focus. Jordan's conscience jolted with remorse. He had barely spoken to the girl since he had first pulled her out of the lake a month ago. And he had certainly never laid a hand upon her. So why did he feel that he had somehow betrayed his faithful Lake Dancer with that cold and prim little bitch? Her face had been in his dreams and had haunted his waking hours as well. Why? It was not a beautiful face—not like Elizabeth's face, which had outshone every beauty in Boston so many years ago. The nose was too snub, like a child's. The chin was too pointed and stubborn, the eyes too big, the cheeks too round. And she was a priggish little hypocrite, just as Elizabeth had been, convinced that her prudish ways and moral platitudes put her on the same level with God and the saints.

But whenever she was in sight his eyes jerked in her direction, his heart beat a bit faster, and unwelcome heat flooded his loins—an uncontrollable animal reaction, and one he had ignored as best he could. But still he felt a wave of guilt. He had let Miriam Sutcliffe, with her enormous blue eyes and her ridiculous mop of auburn curls, get under his skin. Lake Dancer had deserved better of her husband.

The eulogy was over. Two men moved to Lake Dancer's

body, which was encased in sheets of birchback fastened with basswood cord, and gently lowered it into the shallow grave with the feet pointing west, the direction of the spirit's journey to the hereafter. On top of the birchbark shroud were placed Dancer's favorite packstrap, a little kettle, and a knife and a spoon to serve her on her four-day journey to the land of spirits. Then each mourner went to the grave to say good-bye. Confident that Lake Dancer's spirit still hovered near her body, they gave advice as a parting gift.

As the crowd shifted, Jordan saw that Miri was holding a small bundle in her arms. A thin wail told him that the bundle was his newborn daughter. He had no feeling for the child, and had not given it a thought since Lake Dancer had died. It was a hideous thing that had taken the life of his wife. It was a reminder of his guilt in the careless, passionate planting of his seed that had resulted in a sweet girl's death. Grace had told him the infant would die, and Jordan thought it best that it happen that way. Why was the cursed girl stepping in where she wasn't wanted?

Lake Dancer's mother, Smiles at Sunrise, was taking a long time at the grave side talking to the spirit of her departed daughter. She was reciting the names of spirits her daughter could trust to help her on her journey, and more spirits that she should shun. Jordan felt his heart contract. How much more could he stand? How long could he stand here with the semblance of dignity that was expected of a man and not give way to the flood of his grief? His eyes met the gaze of Rides the Waves over the bent head of his friend's mother. Their sorrow met and joined, suddenly more than either man could bear. They tore their eyes away from each other.

Smiles at Sunrise moved on, her face streaming with tears. Slowly the grave was filled and smoothed over. Jordan lifted grim eyes from the ground where they had been fastened while his wife's body was covered with dirt. Lake Dancer was gone, covered by the warm soil, part of the earth once again. Gone forever.

As if drawn by a magnet, his gaze was pulled to the spot

where the Englishwoman had stood with his daughter only moments before. They, too, were gone.

✳ 6 ✳

"Miriam, child, you must get some rest. What am I to do if you fall ill?" Grace brushed errant curls from Miri's face with a loving hand. "Look at you, dear. You look like a ghost. You haven't slept, and you've eaten only enough to keep a bird alive. I will tend the child while you sleep for a while."

Miri raised her head wearily and caught a glimpse of herself in the large parlor mirror. Her eyes looked larger than ever against her pale skin, and the rounded, rosy cheeks were now stretched taut over the fine bones of her face. For the last two days it seemed she had not moved from the rocking chair that sat between kitchen and parlor. "She must eat, Grace. She must eat or she'll die, poor babe."

Grace dropped heavily into a chair at the kitchen table, where Mary Beth and little Martha also sat, eating their lunch. She regarded the wailing bundle in Miri's arms with resigned sadness. "Has she taken anything at all?"

"Nothing," Miri answered. "No milk, no water. I don't know what to do, Grace. Nothing I try seems to work."

The thin, pitiful wailing hadn't stopped from the moment Miri had taken the baby from its mother's arms. Bright Spirit did not squirm or kick or wave her arms like a normal, vigorous baby. She simply lay listlessly in Miri's arms, wrinkled up her little bluish face, and cried. Even the cry was not a healthy thing. It was wavering and tired—a pathetic sound that had everyone in the household on edge.

Miri had tried everything she could think of. Grace and Margaret had helped her devise a nipple from the finger of a glove, but the baby refused to close her mouth to suck in the warm goat's milk that was offered. Likewise did she refuse water.

"Could I try to feed her?" Mary Beth asked. "I'm good at feeding baby goats."

"Not now," Grace said with a tired smile. "Maybe later, when she's bigger."

Little Martha watched the infant solemnly between nibbles of bread and cheese. "I think she's ugly," she pronounced. "She's purple. And she's got all those wrinkles."

"She's sick and hungry," Miri said, instantly defensive.

Martha stuck her finger in her mouth and looked thoughtful. Then she pushed her own cup of milk toward Miri. "She can have mine."

A little sob escaped Miri's throat, and a tear dribbled from the corner of her eye.

"Don't you two have chores to do?" Grace hinted at her daughters.

Mary Beth grimaced and took her younger sister's arm. "Come on, Martha. Ma wants to talk and doesn't want us to hear what she says. You can help me clean the chicken coop."

When the girls were gone, Grace fixed Miri with a stern eye. "You go to bed right now, young lady. I'll tend the baby, or Lucy will."

"She's going to die," Miri sobbed, her control eroded by exhaustion. She had let no one else tend the baby since she had brought it home.

"Maybe it's best that she die, then, Miriam. She won't eat or sleep. All she does is lie there and cry. Maybe it's best that she join her mother."

"No," Miri whispered miserably. "I promised Lake Dancer I would look after her."

Grace rose wearily from her chair and stepped over to look at the infant. "She's not right, dear. The birthing was too long, and Dancer wasn't the only one damaged. What kindness is it to fight for the baby's life, when that life will only be a few months of misery? Anyone who looks at this child can tell she'll not live out her first year, and if she did, she would never be like a normal child.''

''I can't accept that. If she would only eat. I know if we could get her to eat, she would be fine.''

Grace sighed and folded her arms. ''Well, you'll never get her to eat if you collapse from a fever, and you're just asking to take sick. Give me the baby, and I'll promise to wake you if anything changes.''

Miri reluctantly rose from the rocker and placed her precious bundle in Grace's arms.

''Go on with you now, dear. I'll call you. I promise.''

In spite of Miri's intentions of taking only a brief nap, she slept a full ten hours, and even then she did not wake easily. But Margaret's vigorous shaking finally brought her eyes open.

''Jordan is here,'' Margaret said without preliminary.

Miri blinked groggily. Jordan. Why was he here? The baby. Of course, the baby. Panic drove the last cobwebs of sleep from her mind.

''How is the baby?''

''The same,'' Margaret said. ''Still crying. Ma couldn't get her to eat, either. She looks pretty bad, I guess. Jordan looked a bit shaken when he saw her. He didn't say anything. Just stood there and looked at her like she was an ugly toad or something.''

''You let Jordan see the baby?'' Miri cried.

Margaret shrugged. ''He is the father, after all.''

''Yes. Yes, of course.'' Miri climbed out of the bed, smoothed her chemise, and hurried to put on stockings, pantalets, and a gown. She ran her fingers hastily through the mass of curls on her head and then rushed out the door.

Jordan turned his eyes toward Miri the moment she stepped into the kitchen. It struck her then how aptly he was named. Eyes of a Ghost. Those silver-gray orbs certainly looked now as though they belonged to a haunted spirit. The hollows under his prominent cheekbones were more pro-

nounced than when last she had seen him, and his entire
face had a gaunt and desperate appearance that made him
look meaner than a wolf and twice as dangerous.

Miri tore her eyes away from him and tried to focus her
attention on Grace, who was sitting in the rocker trying to
offer the makeshift nipple to the baby, just as Miri had
done.

"Has she eaten?"

"Not a drop, poor babe."

Miri retrieved the infant from Grace's arms and cooed
gently to soothe the sudden distressed squall. "Maybe we
should try a smaller nipple."

"Why do you try?" Jordan asked in a hoarse voice. "It
was not meant to live."

Miri whirled upon him, eyes snapping in anger. "Bright
Spirit is not an *it*. She is your daughter. How can you come
in here and say that she wasn't meant to live!" She had
been afraid that Jordan had come to take the baby from her,
but now she could see that the odious blackguard had no
care at all for his child. Eyes shuttered and face stony, he
looked at the baby as though it were a lifeless lump of clay.
It angered Miri past all reason. "Why have you come? After
two days did you suddenly remember that you have a
daughter? Did you remember that Lake Dancer gave her life
to bring this child into the world? Or did you just come to
see for yourself that she is dying and won't be a burden on
your life much longer?"

"Miriam," Grace warned with a shake of her head. She
knew Jordan well enough to fear the sudden glint that came
to his eyes.

"Give me the baby," Jordan commanded quietly.

Miri flinched back and clasped the infant protectively to
her breast.

"He has the right, Miriam," Grace reminded her. "He is
the father."

"But I promised Lake Dancer I would care for her."

Jordan held out his arms, and Miri reluctantly placed the
little bundle in them. The baby wailed up into his face, and

for a moment life seemed to come back into his silver-gray eyes. But it was for a moment only. When he looked back up at Miri, his face was even more rigid than before. "Why are you torturing this little creature? It cannot live."

Miri's hands curled into tight fists by her side. She longed to slam them into his stony face again and again and again, until she saw some emotion there. The baby was his daughter. How could he not care? How could he hold the baby in his arms and not feel the warmth, the need, the helplessness, and not be moved to fight for her life? "She is not a creature. She's your daughter. And she will live." She held out her arms. "Give her back and I will feed her."

"No. I am taking her back to the village."

"But you can't do that. You have no goats. She must have milk, and warmth, and . . . !"

"She is too weak to live. Even a baby should have the right to die in dignity and peace, without a gaggle of women poking and prodding her to do what she cannot."

He turned to leave, the baby firmly wedged in the crook of one muscular arm.

"No!" Miri detained him with a hand on his bare shoulder, causing them both to pull back as though each had burned the other. Miri's face flushed with shame at her forwardness, but she refused to give up. "You can't do this, Mr. Scott. She can live. I promise you. Just give me one more day to make her eat. Please! One more day."

Jordan turned and gave her a dark look. "You are a stubborn woman, Miss Sutcliffe. But the baby is my daughter. You said it yourself."

"Yes. She's your daughter." Miri swallowed, then lifted her chin in determination. "You have the right to take her. But Lake Dancer asked most particularly for me to care for the baby. And I think it is too early to give up. One more day is all I ask."

The tense silence between them was broken only by the infant's piteous wails. Miri held her breath. Jordan glared at her from under ominously lowered brows, and Grace watched them both with a thoughtful look upon her face. When Miri felt she would collapse from the weight of his gaze, Jordan finally spoke.

"One more day is all you get." Without looking at the infant, he placed it in Miri's eagerly outstretched arms and left without another word.

"One more day," Miri repeated with a sigh, then looked down at the little bluish face and smiled.

Grace laid a sympathetic hand on her shoulder. "You're setting yourself up for heartbreak, dear. Much as I hate to say it, Jordan was right. You should have let her go now, before you become any more involved."

Miri scarcely listened. "She will eat," she declared. "I know she will."

But the afternoon and night passed and the baby still would take neither milk nor water. Miri gave up on the nipple and finally tried dripping milk slowly onto the infant's tongue, but the baby seemed not to know how to swallow, and the milk simply dribbled out the corners of her mouth and ran down her wrinkled little cheeks. By the morning the wailing had stopped. Little Bright Spirit was too weak to make any sound other than an occasional mewl.

The entire household moved about doing morning chores in subdued silence while Miri sat in the little parlor that joined the kitchen. The infant lay unmoving upon her lap. The curtains were closed and the room was dim, but not as dim as Miri's spirits. She was ready to give up hope. Jordan had been right. She had only prolonged everyone's agony by insisting that the baby could live. Miri herself couldn't explain why the life of a half-breed infant had become so important to her. Perhaps because Lake Dancer had reached across the chasm of their different backgrounds and touched her in a way she hadn't been touched before. Or perhaps the baby itself—helpless, weak, and without a mother to shield it from the world's harshness—had gotten a hold on her heart that defied both reason and good sense. But whatever Miri's reason for entering the struggle, she had failed— failed Lake Dancer, failed poor little Bright Spirit.

When Grace ushered Jordan into the parlor, it seemed to

Miri that the baby was barely breathing. She said not a word, knowing the infant's appearance spoke for itself. Jordan quietly knelt by her chair and touched the baby's face with his finger. Miri wished she knew what he was feeling, but his face was as unchanging as ever. Only the spasmodic twitch of a muscle in his jaw gave her a clue that he felt anything at all in seeing his daughter lying at death's threshold.

"She is alive?"

It wasn't Jordan who asked. Startled, Miri looked up to see that a Chippewa man had entered the room with Jordan. She recognized Rides the Waves, Lake Dancer's brother.

"Barely alive," Jordan answered, wearily rising from his knees.

"Then we must try," Waves said. "I will inform my father."

"What . . . what are you going to do?" she asked Jordan as the Indian left the room.

"She will be given a name," he said.

"She has a name. Dancer named her Bright Spirit."

"That is a pet name only. It means nothing. Rides the Waves has brought his father to give her a name of power. Smoke Catcher is a Midewiwin shaman of high degree."

"A what?"

"The Midewiwin is the Grand Medicine Society. Its members are healers and sorcerers. The naming ceremony is usually not performed until a child is old enough to know the meaning of what is done. But the . . . my daughter needs the power now."

Miri rose, picking the baby up from her lap and clasping her protectively. "Do you mean that you would subject this poor child, whose soul is about to return to her Maker, to some heathen ceremony? And you accused me of torturing her! I've never heard of such a ridiculous notion!"

"The ceremony will often heal the sick. The name of power will give her a guardian spirit who will preserve her from evil." Jordan rose to his feet. In the dim confines of the little parlor, he seemed bigger than Miri remembered, but she refused to be intimidated.

"So much rubbish! How can you, a white man, believe in such heathenish sorcery! If anything, you should have summoned Father Carroll to baptize the poor thing and give her a Christian name."

Jordan sighed, and Miri heard the concern in the sigh that she couldn't see in his face. "I don't hold much with Christian ceremonies, Miss Sutcliffe. I doubt that God does, either. And in truth, I don't think that anything will make a difference now. But Waves wants to try, and the baby is his sister's daughter, so I will respect his wishes."

"If you must do this, then at least give the baby a Christian name, as well. She's a child of both worlds. If she is to have a heathen name, then she should have a Christian name, too."

Jordan's eyes shifted from Miri to the baby. He regarded the infant with a blank stare that could have hidden anything from hatred to adoration. "Very well. I will name her Jane. Jane Scott." His mouth curved in a sad smile as he reached out to take the infant from Miri's desperate grip. "Jane Scott," he said more gently, looking down at the baby with hooded eyes. "May you be more fortunate than your namesake."

Jane Scott. Miri remembered Grace telling her that Jordan was the son of a woman named Jane Scott, who had been a courtesan of some sort. Fine name for an innocent babe! But what could one expect from a man who regarded morals and propriety as a joke?

Miri had no chance to comment upon Jordan's choice of names, however, for just then Rides the Waves came back into the room with a tall Indian at his side. The man stood at a height rivaling Jordan's, a half head taller than his son. Age had whitened his hair and seamed his face, but he stood as straight and proud as a man in his prime, and his dark eyes hinted at a wisdom that comes only with many years of living. Miri had seen him in the village during several of her visits to Lake Dancer, but she hadn't guessed he was

Dancer's father. He certainly didn't look like Miri's idea of a sorcerer.

The tall Indian walked into the room as though he owned it and made straight for Miri. He stopped in front of her and gave her an assessing look that ended in the hint of a smile. Then he addressed her in flawless English.

"You are the white woman who befriended my daughter and has cared for my grandchild. Lake Dancer spoke to me of her affection for you, and I, Smoke Catcher, am grateful for what you have done."

Miri gestured helplessly toward the infant in Jordan's arms. "I have done nothing," she said softly.

Smoke Catcher turned toward Jordan and regarded little Bright Spirit with a penetrating gaze that made Miri want to squirm, even though the look was not directed at her. If she didn't have the benefit of an enlightened, civilized education, even she might believe that this dignified old man was a sorcerer.

"Do you truly want this child to live, Eyes of a Ghost, husband of my daughter?"

Jordan hesitated. He looked at Miri, and for a moment she thought she could see past the hard glitter of his eyes to the turmoil of his feelings. Did he hate the baby because it had taken Dancer's life? Did he despise its pitiful weakness? Did he have any feelings at all for the tiny morsel of his own flesh and blood? Miri could not define just what it was she saw in that brief lowering of his defenses, but she was relieved somehow that the man was not as cold and uncaring as she had believed.

Jordan turned his eyes back to Smoke Catcher. "I do want her to live, my father."

"Then let us begin."

The babe was placed on a blanket in the middle of the floor. As Grace, the three girls, Jordan, Waves, and Miri all gathered around, Smoke Catcher began to chant in Chippewa.

"What's he saying?" Miri whispered to Margaret.

"He's telling about a dream vision—how he decided

upon a name. The name gives her power to call upon a guardian spirit.''

"Nonsense," Miri whispered. "You don't really believe this rubbish, do you?"

Margaret shrugged and motioned her to silence. Smoke Catcher had picked up little Bright Spirit and was talking to her softly. Then he raised his eyes toward the ceiling and began to chant loudly. The chant went on and on, then ended abruptly, leaving a heavy silence in its wake.

Smoke Catcher handed the infant to Jordan, addressing him solemnly in Chippewa.

Margaret quietly translated for Miri. "He named her Wren. He says that the wren is a plain little bird who is with us only for a season. When summer is gone she flies off to . . . I don't know that word. But she brings joy to those who listen for her song.''

Some name of power, Miri thought. Poor Bright Spirit. She had only been in the world for three short days, and already she had collected three names—an ugly little bird, a Boston whore, and the name bestowed by a dying mother. It seemed she could perish from the weight of her names alone.

But little Jane did not suffer under the weight of all her names. Even as Smoke Catcher pronounced the name of power, her distressed mewling ceased. By the time the ceremony had ended she was fast asleep in her father's arms.

"You will keep her here until she is strong?" Smoke Catcher asked, turning to Miri.

Miri looked at Jordan. He said nothing, leaving the decision up to her. "Yes, I will keep her." *Until she dies*, Miri thought silently. These last few hours of her life, she would see that nothing disturbed the baby.

Smoke Catcher smiled. "You have been given more than you know."

Without a word, Jordan handed the infant to Miri and left the room. Nodding solemnly to Grace and her daughters, Smoke Catcher and Rides the Waves both followed.

Smoke Catcher was as batty as his daughter had been, Miri mused. Like father, like daughter. And considering what kind of a father Jane had, perhaps it would be a kindness if she didn't grow up.

Little Jane slept for the rest of the day. She did not wake when night fell, nor did she stir when Miri gently laid her in the crib Grace had brought down from the attic and set beside Miri's bed. Miri no longer tried to give her milk or water. The child was dying. Miri had resigned herself. Even though her breathing seemed a bit stronger and her color slightly more normal, little Jane had set her tiny feet on the same road that Lake Dancer had taken.

The morning was still dark when Miri was awakened by the sound of Jane crying. She hadn't intended to sleep, but sometime in the quiet of the night, exhaustion had claimed her. Now she opened her eyes to a sound that was quite different from the thin wailing that had tortured her ears for the past three days. This cry, while not exactly lusty, was certainly indignant, and above all, hungry.

Acting on an intuition that she knew was illogical, Miri allowed her heart to swell with hope. Scarcely taking the time to pull on a robe, she hurried to the kitchen and, with shaking hands, started a fire in the wood stove to warm the milk. The task seemed to take forever, and Jane's cries brought both Grace and Mary Beth padding into the kitchen to see what was afoot. Without a word they followed Miri into her bedroom and watched as she picked up the crying infant and placed the nipple into its wide-open mouth. Instantly the baby latched on and sucked. Half the milk was gone before she stopped, her little mouth releasing the nipple as she fell back to sleep.

"She's still ugly," Mary Beth commented.

"All new babies are ugly." Grace smiled and ran her hand over the black fuzz on Jane's little head. "But now there might be a chance that she'll grow out of it."

The next weeks were a unique experience for Miri. Jane continued to eat and gain weight, but her skin retained a worrisome bluish tinge and her eyes lacked the bright curiosity of a growing baby. Miri frequently recalled Grace's warning that if the baby lived, she would never grow to be a normal, healthy child, but she didn't let it bother her overmuch. It was enough for her that the baby was out of danger and seemed to fill a void in her life that she hadn't known existed.

Jordan was a frequent visitor to the Peavey farm, and each time he came, Miri steeled herself for the worst. But he didn't again mention taking his daughter from her care. He couldn't, Miri realized in her calmer moments, when Jordan was nowhere near. The infant would take only goat's milk, and while it might be possible to find a wet nurse in the Chippewa village, Grace had told her that soon the village would disband into individual family units, each of which would travel to its own winter hunting grounds. If Jordan were traveling with his wife's family, then it would be unlikely he could find care for an infant in that group.

In spite of her reasoning, Jordan's visits made her nervous. He spoke scarcely at all, and spent all his time simply sitting and looking at his tiny daughter. When he did look at Miri, it seemed to her that he regarded her with wary dislike, but there was something in those silver-gray eyes that reminded her uncomfortably of the horrible day they had met and the humiliating and brutal intimacy of his actions. Then he would turn his eyes back on his daughter, and Miri would tell herself she was imagining things.

For all that Jordan made her uncomfortable, Miri could not deny that it was impossible to maintain a decent level of loathing for the man. Irresponsible scoundrel he might be, but there were not many men of her acquaintance who would allow a slobbering infant to use their fingers as a sugar tit, or let it spit up on a bare arm or shoulder without a single offended grimace. Miri could see, during those rare moments when his face lost its impassive mask, that Jordan was a man at war within himself. What the battle concerned Miri didn't know. She only knew that Jordan Scott was not quite the uncaring blackguard she had thought him. And for some reason, that realization made her even more uncomfortable than before.

Jordan Scott was merely a tiny part of Miri's concerns, however. As the weeks passed, she became more and more concerned about the mission that had brought her to this wilderness. Gage Delacroix should have returned by now, it seemed to Miri, even if he had taken Hamilton to the very ends of the earth. She couldn't help but worry about Aunt Eliza, who might very well have the vindictive Captain Michaels making her life miserable. And there was always the chance that word of Hamilton's treason—and Miri's supposed involvement—might get from London to the British commanders in America, who would no doubt forward the information directly on to Captain Roberts at Fort Michilimackinac.

Every night Miri would lie on her feather bed, close her eyes, and try to picture London as it had looked when she had left it. Then, the flowers in the garden had scarcely begun to show signs of life. Now they would be a riot of color and sweet fragrance. Aunt Eliza would cut blossoms every day for the table, just as she did each summer.

But fond as the memories were, they did not stir a violent longing to be home in England where she belonged, and that disturbed Miri. She had allowed herself to become too involved with the people in this uncivilized, insignificant corner of the world. Grace and her daughters—Margaret, with her attempts at grown-up dignity; Mary Beth, with her hoyden impishness; and even little Martha and her awkward shyness—had come to be like the family she had never had. It was going to be a wrench to leave them. Worse still, how could she bear to leave little Jane? She had warned herself time and again that Jane was not hers, that any day Jordan would come and take his daughter away, and even if he didn't, Miri would have to give her over into Grace's care when she left to find Hamilton. But the warnings had no effect on her heart. Leaving baby Jane was going to be the hardest thing of all.

When August passed and the cool winds of September

blew across the lake, Miri decided she'd had enough of patient waiting. She had been so occupied with the baby, with sewing an adequate wardrobe, and with helping around the farm, that she hadn't been to town in weeks. Captain Roberts had no doubt forgotten that he had promised to tell her when he heard of the guide's return, and it had been much too long since she had checked with the town's merchants. Delacroix might have returned weeks ago and even now might be lounging in the tavern or haggling with the fur merchants. Donning her bonnet and a lightweight cloak, she set her chin at a determined angle and headed for town.

Fort Michilimackinac stood atop a limestone cliff above the island's only town. To one who was accustomed to Britain's old castles it was a less than imposing structure, even with its stout wall and glowering blockhouses. And Miri thought the troops walking the ramparts and guarding the gate looked somewhat scruffier than they had in June, when she had seen them last.

She had stopped and talked with several merchants in the town, seeking information about the half-breed guide, and had heard rumors that British supplies were running short. Already the commander had negotiated to buy foodstuffs from the civilian merchants—both for his own men and the Indian allies who were drifting in from the west. It was common speculation that the British did not have supplies to survive the harsh winter. Miri hoped it wasn't so. The British had the most splendid army in the world, and for them to retreat from such a backwater stronghold would be humiliation, indeed.

Lieutenant Renquist greeted Miri in the commander's anteroom. She had hoped that perhaps the man had been granted his wish to be posted back to England, but it was a vain hope. For here he was, and the look on his face told Miri he had in no way forgotten their last meeting.

"Miss Sutcliffe," he greeted her with a cold smile. "How may I help you?"

Miri sighed. Gentlemen freely made fools of themselves

while in their cups, but they would seldom forgive a lady who witnessed such a display. Not that she craved the man's admiring attention. He was not to her taste at all. But neither did she feel comfortable with his animosity.

"I have come to see Captain Roberts. He is extremely busy, I know, but I shall take only a moment of his time."

Renquist's mouth tightened to a bitter line. "I also would like to see Captain Roberts, for he is on his way to England, where I should be."

"I beg your pardon?"

"Captain Roberts left a week ago, relieved because of health problems."

"I see." Miri frowned in agitation toward the commander's office. "Then perhaps I could see the new commanding officer. Captain Roberts had told me . . . you see . . . Well, I won't trouble you, Lieutenant. Might I talk to him?"

"Suit yourself. He left for the parade ground a few minutes ago, to drill our"—he laughed unpleasantly—"our crack troops. A real stickler for form, this fellow is."

"Perhaps you would be so good to point him out to me."

"As you wish." He rose and escorted her to the anteroom's one window. "There he is." He pointed toward a man standing at attention not thirty feet from the window. "He'll be out drilling them for hours if I know the fellow. And I doubt he'll welcome a distraction—even one as tempting as you—but you're welcome to try."

Miri did not reply to Renquist's rude remarks. The cold chill running up her spine had left her quite speechless. There could be no doubt about it—no doubt at all. The man Renquist had indicated was none other than Gerald Michaels.

✳ 7 ✳

"Margaret, that neckline is entirely too low for a young girl your age. I want to see at least another inch of lace at the neck before you wear it again."

"Maaa!" Margaret turned from the parlor mirror and scowled into the kitchen at her mother, whose eyes were on Margaret's newly completed garment rather than the bread dough she was kneading. "Not fair, Ma! Didn't you see the dress that Miri's sewing up? She says this style is the latest . . .!"

"Miriam is a grown woman," Grace replied with pursed lips, "not a thirteen-year-old miss who's still in the schoolroom."

"I'm not a child anymore! Caroline Fraser's ma was married at thirteen, and Lake Dancer told me that when a girl starts her monthlies she's a woman grown!"

"Don't you take that tone with me, miss! You're not so old I can't turn you over my knee and . . . what's this?"

The door to the farmhouse swung abruptly open as a red-faced Miri stumbled through, then closed with a bang as she fell back against it, gasping for breath and closing her eyes.

"Miriam, child! What in heaven's name . . .?" Grace set aside the bread dough she was kneading and rushed into the parlor. "Are you ill? Are you hurt?"

Miri allowed herself to be led to a chair. "I'm fine," she gasped. "I'm fine. I ran all the way from town. Lord! I would never have guessed that I was able!"

"What's wrong, child? You look as if the devil himself is at your heels."

"He is." Miri breathed deeply and brushed back the sweat-dampened curls that fell in her face. "The very devil himself! Who could've thought that this would happen?"

"What, Miri?" Margaret drew a chair close to Miri's and sat on the edge, her eyes alight with eager interest. "Did you hear something at the fort? Are the Americans going to attack? Is that it?"

"Hush, girl!" Grace admonished. "Don't be absurd! Go fetch Miriam a cup of water. Now child"—she turned her attention back to Miri—"tell us what the trouble is before both Margaret and I collapse from worry."

Miri drew a deep breath and tried to steady her trembling hands as she reached out for the cup Margaret handed her. "I don't believe this is happening. But I suppose I must tell it all and hope you will find it in your hearts to understand. I told you that I was looking for my cousin Hamilton because of a family problem. That's true, as far as it goes, but . . . oh, my! Where do I start?"

The story of Hamilton, the treasonous list, and Gerald Michaels tumbled out, along with her hopes of finding Hamilton and putting things right.

"So, you see," she concluded, "that's really the reason I came here to find Hamilton. He hid that cursed list somewhere, and unless I can find out where, there's a prison cell waiting for me back in London. I'm sure by now that Captain Michaels has filed charges, and if he sees me here, he'll have me shipped back to England."

"Oh!" Margaret was rapt with excitement. "How dreadful! To think he followed you all the way to this little corner of the world!"

Miri got up and started to pace. Her color was slowly returning to normal. "Michaels wouldn't have followed me here. I'm sure it's all simply an unfortunate coincidence. After all, there is a war going on between Britain and your United States. I suppose it's understandable he should be sent here."

"That's all well and good, Miriam." Grace's brow furrowed in a troubled frown. "But the man is certain to find out you're on the island. All the merchants and traders know you, the troops know you—everyone does. And they all know that you're staying here at the farm.''

"He may already be on his way here," Miri agreed. "Lieutenant Renquist will have mentioned my name to him, I'm sure. I was so shocked when the lieutenant pointed out the new commander, I completely lost my wits.'' She sighed and ran her hair through her cropped curls, leaving them in an unladylike jumble. "I ran from the room in a dreadfully rude way. Lieutenant Renquist looked at me as though I had suddenly gone mad. Lord! Michaels might even have seen me as I left the fort. Oh, Grace! I don't know what I shall do!''

"Now, now! Sit down, Miriam. And stop your babbling.'' Grace got up and firmly guided Miri toward a chair. "We'll think of something. You're almost a part of this family, child. And if some British tin soldier thinks he can just cart you off from right under my nose, he's got a surprise coming. That he does!''

"Oh, Miri!'' Margaret said in a thrilled voice. "Will they try to hang you, do you suppose?''

Miri looked at Margaret and swallowed hard. The possibility had never before occurred to her. But people were commonly hanged for treason, weren't they?

"Now, that's enough of that, young lady!'' Grace scolded her daughter. "You take yourself into the bedroom and check on little Jane. Miriam and I have some thinking to do.''

"No,'' Miri said, waving Margaret back to her chair. "I'll check on Jane. I've probably awakened her with my loud wailing, poor baby.'' She disappeared into the bedroom and emerged a moment later with a fretting baby in her arms. "Did I wake you, my sweet?'' She nuzzled the infant's fuzzy little head. "Well, you're a good one, aren't you? Look at those bright eyes.''

Grace watched as Miri snuggled the baby against her breast. No one in his right mind would ever call Jane's lackluster eyes bright, but Miri seemed to have a mother's blindness toward the baby's imperfections. Even now, with the British army probably nipping at her heels, the girl seemed to enter a separate world when she held that weak little motherless child in her arms. Strange that the infant should provoke such a response in a prim and spinsterish girl, while the natural father grew more remote and withdrawn every time he saw the baby.

A frown creased Grace's brow as she watched the maternal scene a moment longer. An idea was taking form in her mind—one that might be the answer to more than one problem. She motioned Margaret to her side, whispered quiet instructions into her ear, and then smiled in satisfaction as her daughter hurried out of the room.

Two hours later, Miri had nearly worn a path in the bare wood floor with her pacing, and Grace was exhausted just from watching her fret. Lucy had come in from her chores and been told the news, and now she added to the mood by sitting on the parlor settee—Grace's one good piece of furniture—and periodically wailing about returning to England. Little Martha sprawled at her mother's feet and watched Miri and Lucy with wide eyes, while Grace sat silent and thoughtful.

The more Grace thought about it, the better her scheme appeared. Jordan was going to snarl like a trapped wolf, and Miri no doubt would succumb to an attack of priggishness. But when all the growling and wailing were over, both would realize there was no other road to take. Grace would make sure that they realized it.

The farmhouse door opened and admitted a scowling Jordan, trailed by Margaret and Mary Beth. "What's all this?" he asked, taking in the mood of the gathering with one glance. "Margaret said there was an emergency with Jane. What's wrong?"

Miri halted her pacing in midstride and looked up in surprise. "There's nothing wrong with Jane." Her puzzled look bounced from Jordan to Margaret, then back to Jordan. "What are you doing here?"

"That's what I'd like to know. Margaret . . . ?"

Margaret backed away from the impatient inquiry in his eyes. "It's not my fault. Ma told me to fetch you right away."

"Sit down, Jordan," Grace directed firmly. "I told Margaret to fetch you however she could. Nothing is wrong with little Jane. It's our Miri who has a problem."

Jordan had become an expert over the past weeks at being in the same room with Miriam Sutcliffe without looking at her. Her face and form affected him in a way that he wasn't ready to accept, though if it hadn't been for her keeping Jane, he regularly told himself, he would have forgotten the prim little English girl weeks ago. Now Grace's words forced him to look at her, and once again he felt the familiar quickening of his body. What a shame that all those sweet, womanly curves hid such a staid and priggish soul.

"Whatever Miss Sutcliffe's problem is, Grace, I can't be of much help to you. I'm leaving for winter camp in a few days."

Grace gave him a satisfied smile. "That's just what I wanted to talk to you about."

Grace outlined her proposition, and Jordan felt the jaws of the steel trap slowly closing around him. He glanced across the parlor several times at Miri and saw that this scheme was as much a surprise to her as it was to him. Her face grew even whiter, if that were possible, and she attempted to interrupt more than once, only to be hushed by a firm word from Grace.

"So you see," Grace concluded, looking alternately at Jordan and Miri, "you will both have what you need. You, Jordan, will have a woman to care for your little daughter. And you, Miri, will have a man's protection and a safe place to hide. The British will never think to look for you with the Chippewa. And if they did—well, even I don't know exactly where these folks take themselves to do their winter hunting. And by spring this Michaels fellow might be gone, or your cousin might have been found."

The stunned silence was broken only by a giggle from Mary Beth, which was promptly quelled by a pinch from her older sister. Then both Miri and Jordan spoke at the same time. Miri flushed angrily as Jordan's stronger voice won the battle for ascendancy.

"You've taken leave of your goddamned senses, Grace."

He longed to spit out every foul word he knew to let her know just what he thought of her idea, but a warning flash from Grace's eyes stopped him. Jordan's gaze dropped to Mary Beth, who was watching him in rapt attention, her little ears pricked to catch every word. "Go do your chores," he snapped. "And take your sisters with you."

"Aw, Jordan!" Mary Beth whined. "Are you going to cuss?"

"You do as he says, all of you," Grace agreed, giving Mary Beth a good-natured slap on the behind. "Your Uncle Jordan's going to make a jackass of himself, and he doesn't want you to watch."

Jordan waited until the girls were out of earshot, then regarded Grace with narrow-eyed determination. "If you think I'm going to drag some damned pampered little witch of an English spinster with me to winter camp, you're crazy. You're both goddamned crazy!" He spared an angry glance for Miri, who was looking none too happy herself. "She wouldn't last a week. Or a day, even. She'd be more helpless than that baby, and a hell of a lot bigger pain in the ass!"

Grace waved down Miri's angry retort and merely shrugged. "She'd do all right, Jordan. After all, she is David Sutcliffe's daughter. And he was as tough as they come."

"I don't care if she's Daniel Boone's daughter! Look at her. Not a pound of her is muscle. She hasn't worked a day in her life. She'll whine like a spoiled child the minute the weather turns cold, or the first time she has to sleep on something other than a feather bed. And she'll damn well make my life miserable." Jordan couldn't imagine a winter living in the same small encampment with Miriam Sutcliffe and not either breaking her neck or forcibly quenching his frustrations in her soft flesh. But of course he couldn't tell that to Grace. Women just didn't understand that sometimes a man was ruled by his loins, not by his head.

"That's enough!" Miri had held her peace long enough in the face of these outrageous insults. "I'll have you know I am a very self-reliant person. I am perfectly capable of doing anything your Chippewa ladies can do, *if* I cared to learn. But I have no intention of spending the winter in the middle of the wilderness with this . . . this man.''

"Now, Miriam," Grace cautioned.

"Don't 'now Miriam' me," Miri said, her mouth a prim little line. "I appreciate your trying to help, but surely you can see that I couldn't possibly spend months in the company of an . . . an unattached man with only savages for chaperones. It would be terribly improper." Miri could just imagine what Mrs. Pelham and London society would do with a tidbit like that. The scandal would make her parents' divorce pall in comparison.

"Yes," Jordan parroted sarcastically. "It would be terribly improper."

"And just what do you know about propriety?" Miri sneered.

"I know it's not proper to saddle me with a weak-kneed female who doesn't have the sense God gave a tree. You think you can hold your own in a Chippewa winter camp? Think about it, woman! There are days during the winter when the wind can freeze your tongue to your teeth. And there are no fancy stoves or fireplaces to keep you warm, no hot water to wash in, and only the ground for a bed. You'd be better off in prison."

"I agree with you there, Mr. Scott. Winter in prison would certainly be preferable to a winter in your company, though I'll admit there's little to choose from between the two."

Grace wouldn't give up. She saw the two looking daggers at each other and knew in her motherly heart that each would be bitter medicine for the other. That sort of draught was never easy to swallow, but once you'd drunk it down, it always did some good.

Jordan Scott was one of Grace's favorite people. The white traders and farmers in the area despised him for his way of living, and feared him for his imagined savagery, but Grace knew there was a rare man behind that reserved shell, and a spunky little girl like Miriam Sutcliffe might just bring that man into the open where he could see the right path again. And Miriam—poor little flower who was afraid to bloom. She needed a man to teach her there was more to life than cold propriety—a man brash enough to batter down her defenses and touch her with passion, but wise enough to know where gentleness must take over from strength. A man like Jordan.

There was a fire in Jordan's eyes that was more than anger, and an uncertainty about Miriam that had its roots in something other than outrage. Grace's sharp eyes noted it well, and it hardened her resolve. She couldn't give up now. The two of them would thank her someday for her interference, if they didn't kill each other first.

"What about that little daughter of yours, Jordan Scott?" Grace threw out a sharp reminder. "Who's going to care for her if Miriam is carted back to England? I've got three of my own to look after, and a farm to run. That baby of yours is a sickly little sprite, and she needs watching all the day long. And with just Waves and his folks in your camp, no one will have time for a little baby."

Jordan gave Grace a dark look, but he had no answer.

"And you, Miriam. I'm surprised at you! You cross the sea and half a continent to set things right for yourself and your aunt, and now you're ready to give up in the face of a new little problem. I thought you had more determination than that, girl." Miri was beginning to look properly shamed, and Grace followed up quickly on her advantage. "If you go with Jordan, you might find your cousin by next spring and be able to put yourself in the clear. Gage Delacroix is bound to come in one of these days soon, and I'll be sure to ask him where your cousin is. Not a winter goes by when he doesn't stop by the farm here at least once to have me make him some cranberry pies."

Miri still looked stubborn, so Grace pulled out her last round of ammunition. "And you don't truly want to leave that baby, do you, dear?"

Jordan felt his heart sink as he saw Miri's face soften. Damn Grace and her bright ideas! She had them both trapped, and she full well knew that she'd set a torch to gunpowder. George Peavey had complained more than once that his wife was the biggest busybody ever born, and he'd been right.

He flashed Grace a look that promised vengeance, then turned cold eyes on Miri. "I can see the matter's been decided without regard to a yea or nay from me. I'll give you an hour, Miss Sutcliffe. If you're ready to go, I'll take you. If you're not, you can go to prison and be damned." Without a further word he turned on his heel and strode out of the room.

"Oh, Lord Almighty!" Lucy opened her mouth for the first time. She turned to her mistress with wide eyes. "Ye ain't really goin' off with that . . . that wild-eyed savage, are ye, miss? What would Miss Eliza say?"

"She'd faint dead away, I'm sure," Miri replied in an acid voice. Though in truth she suspected that Aunt Eliza wouldn't be too displeased. She had always sung praises of the childish sort of fellow who is always running around looking virile. No doubt Jordan Scott, half-naked back-woods savage, would be just her cup of tea, as Miri's father had been. "At least with you as companion, Lucy, there will be a modicum of propriety preserved. I daresay we will both manage to muddle through."

"Me?" Lucy squeaked.

"Yes, of course. Did you expect me to go without you?"

Grace frowned at Miri's words. "I don't think Jordan could be persuaded to take both of you, dear. He seemed a trifle upset with the idea of just one, didn't he?"

Miri's daintily pointed chin set at its most stubborn angle. "Lucy is my responsibility. I wouldn't think of leaving her behind. What would she do without me?"

"Oh, miss!" Lucy was quick to volunteer. "I'm sure I'll do just fine!"

"She can stay with me," Grace offered. "There's always the need of an extra pair of hands on a farm, you know. Especially when the only other hands belong to layabout girls." A muffled exclamation carried through the parlor window. "You can come in now, girls," Grace said with a half smile. "And don't think I don't know who's been listening at the window instead of doing their chores."

A moment later the door opened and three guilty faces looked inside.

"And I don't want a word of this conversation to leak to anyone, you hear? There's not one of you too old or too young for a good thrashing if you so much as hint at what was said in this room. Now, go on about your chores and remember what I said."

Only Mary Beth looked unimpressed with the threat. She gave Miri a wink before closing the door behind her and her sisters.

Lucy was still looking hopefully at Miri, and Miri noted a new hint of rebelliousness in her face. These cocky Americans had been filling her maid's head with ideas of independence and democracy, no doubt. The girl had never been so self-willed before. Still, there was no reason to force Lucy to endure this nightmare just because her mistress must.

"Well, I suppose if Grace is willing to have you stay . . ."

"Oh, thank you, miss." Lucy sprang forward and gave Miri an impetuous hug. "I'll make Mrs. Peavey glad she let me stay, and I'll finish those dresses we started on, so when you find Mr. Hamilton, you can sail back to London dressed like a duchess."

With Lucy's eager help, Miri packed a minimum of clothing. But Grace shook her head when she saw the bundle that included a redingote, three pairs of shoes, two cotton dresses, and three woollen dresses, along with chemises, pantalets, stockings, and scarves to last a week without washing.

"These people carry their bundles on their backs, my dear, or if the snow is hard, they pack it on a dogsled. You've got at least three times as much as any Chippewa woman I've ever seen."

"Well," Miri replied sharply. "I'm not a Chippewa

woman. And Jordan himself said there was very little warm water for washing. I don't see how I can get by with less.''

Grace shook her head again, but this time a little smile played around her mouth. "I imagine Jordan might show you how."

Grace left the two girls alone to argue over what should go and what should be left behind, and Lucy took the rare moment away from the widow's hearing to express her secret fears to her mistress.

"You be careful o' that man, miss. I don't like the look 'e gets in those eyes o' 'is when 'e turns 'em on you. 'E's a fellow what civilized ladies shouldn't oughta take up with, that's fer sure.''

Miri sniffed. "I can handle Mr. Scott, Lucy. I'm a woman grown, not some simpering schoolgirl to be mowed under by a man's advances. He'll keep his distance, or our arrogant Mr. Scott will have more trouble than he can handle.''

Her voice had more confidence than she felt, and Miri admitted to herself that she didn't quite know what she would do if Jordan Scott made improper advances. He was a detestable fellow, but he did have a certain animalistic appeal that ignited the baser instincts. Everyone, no matter how refined, had to fight a lower self now and then, but Miri suspected that her lower self might be lower than some others, since she was, after all, an offspring of her father. Perhaps that might explain why Jordan's visits to his infant daughter had never failed to speed the rhythm of Miri's heart, or why she constantly relived in her dreams that first brutal night they had met—not as a nightmare, but as a strange and compelling drama that never failed to leave her awash with feelings that were distressingly unfamiliar and completely unnerving.

Lucy continued in a confidential whisper. "A lady like you wouldn't know about the sneaky things a bloke will do to have his fun with a girl. All men think about is what's in their bloody pants—beggin' yer pardon, miss.''

Miri flushed bright red and opened her mouth to chastise

her maid, but Lucy shook an admonishing finger at her mistress and barged right ahead.

"That Mr. Scott, from the look o' 'im, he wouldn't be one to let a skirt pass 'im by without givin' it a twitch. Ye mark me words, miss. 'E's not like the gentlemen ye've known. Ye put yer foot down at the very first, or 'e'll be kickin' like a randy stud the 'ole winter long."

"Wherever did you learn such language?" Miri asked, aghast.

"On the farm, miss. We didn't mince our words there like the ladies and gents do in the city."

"Well, I appreciate your concern, Lucy. But there will be no tricks. You needn't worry yourself. I can handle myself quite well."

The unbelieving look that Lucy gave her mistress could have been a reflection of Miri's own doubts.

Miri had always hated good-byes, and the leave-taking from the Peavey farm was worse than most. Grace and Margaret sniveled, little Martha looked confused, and even impudent Mary Beth was a bit subdued. Miri herself felt tears close to the surface and wondered how she had become so attached to this family in so short a time. They were not at all the sort of people with whom she usually associated, but they had certainly found a place in her heart. Back in England, Miri realized, she wouldn't have given the family a second glance, and she certainly would not have considered them for friends. And now look what she had come to.

When Miri had boarded ship at the dock in London, she had known exactly who she was and what she wanted out of life. Right and wrong, proper and improper, were set in concrete. Now, walking toward a beach where a canoe would take her to an alien world, where her only companion would be a renegade who despised her as thoroughly as she despised him, Miri felt the foundations of her world turning to mush. She had already changed from the self-assured young woman who had left England. Would she be able to recognize herself at winter's end, or would life with the savages bury Miriam Sutcliffe and put a stranger in her place? It was a frightening thought, but Miri had no time to dwell upon it, for Jordan was impatiently hustling them toward the shore.

The little procession was headed by Jordan and Miri, followed by Lucy, Grace, and her three daughters. Bringing up the rear was Petunia, who was coming along to provide milk for Jane. The goat had left the barn readily enough and had stood placidly while Mary Beth slipped a halter over her head, but now that the lake and canoe were in sight, she was developing her own ideas about the merit of the journey. She let loose a pathetic bleat and dug her cloven hooves into the sand.

"Come on, you stupid ol' goat!" Mary Beth tugged at the tether. Petunia didn't move, merely gave the girl a look of hurt betrayal.

"Kick her butt," Jordan advised. "But hurry it up. I would like to be away from here before the British army arrives looking for Miss Sutcliffe."

"She won't move," Mary Beth grunted, putting all her weight on the rope to drag the goat forward. "She hates water, and she hates boats."

Jordan heaved a sigh of exasperation, went to Petunia's rear end, and pushed. "This goat damn well better learn to behave, or goat steaks are going to be sizzling over the fire."

In answer, Petunia lifted her tail and decorated Jordan's moccasins with what Mary Beth aptly termed goatberries. Mary Beth let go the tether in a fit of giggles, and Petunia stumbled backward and sat, knocking Jordan to the ground.

The string of expletives that Jordan loosed burned Miri's ears and had Grace frowning ominously in disapproval. Still cursing, he heaved the reluctant animal onto one broad shoulder and carried her the rest of the way to the shore, where he dumped her none too gently into the bottom of his canoe.

"Tie her." Jordan handed a length of rope to Miri. "If she kicks a hole in my canoe, I'm not pulling you out of the lake again."

A sharp retort rose to Miri's lips, but the metallic glint in Jordan's eyes forestalled it. The man was obviously as cross as a bear, as Grace was wont to say, and Miri was uncomfortably aware that her very life over the next few months was going to depend on his goodwill. If he had such a thing as goodwill.

The sun was a glowing red ball on the horizon by the time farewells were said and the canoe pulled away from the shore. As they headed across the straits, Miri waved a despondent farewell to the people she was leaving behind. She felt more alone than she had even on the day her ship had sailed from London, and that had been the blackest day in her life up until right now. Worst of all, Miri knew things were going to get worse before they got better.

The pull across the straits was not a good harbinger of things to come. An indignant Petunia bleated and struggled in the bottom of the canoe, and Jane frightened Miri by her very lack of noise. Once Miri even went so far as to press her ear to the listless infant's chest to make sure she was breathing.

Jordan was silent. Even in the fading light Miri could see that the scowl on his face grew darker as Petunia's bleatings grew louder. His lowered brows made dark shadows of his eyes, and his clenched jaw emphasized every harsh angle of his face. For the first time, it occurred to Miri that Jordan Scott might be more than just an insolent, degenerate renegade—he could be a dangerous man, as well as a despicable one. The thought gave her pause. Was she running from the hounds to take shelter with a wolf? She might have been far safer throwing herself on the mercy of Gerald Michaels.

Their canoe was met at the Chippewa village by Rides the Waves, whose greeting elicited only a surly grunt from Jordan. Neither man offered to carry Miri ashore while the goat and baggage were being unloaded, and since the canoe could not be beached while any weight remained to load it down, Miri had no choice but to wade. Giving Jordan's back a venomous look, she settled Jane firmly into the crook of one arm and clambered over the side. The cold water reached to her waist. Her skirt floated around her while her stockings and pantalets quickly became soaked. By the time she reached dry land her skirt was sodden, as well.

As Miri sloshed up onto the shore, Jordan turned his attention toward her for the first time. It did nothing for Miri's temper to see a hint of amusement in his face.

"You've met Ride the Waves," he said.

Waves nodded politely, and Miri made an attempt at a pleasant smile.

"And I see the rest are headed our way," Jordan noted in a chagrined voice.

In a moment it seemed the whole village surrounded them—adults, children, and dogs swarming in curiosity. Miri had been to the village often enough before, but never looking as though she intended to stay. As if sensing her change in status, the onlookers chattered among themselves in speculation. Even Petunia came in for her fair share of attention, especially by the children and dogs. She bleated in distress, and Miri agreed with her wholeheartedly.

The crowd fell silent as a dignified woman with graying hair muttered a question in Jordan's direction. Miri recognized the woman as one of Dancer's attendants on the tragic night of her confinement. Jordan hesitated, scowling, then answered, the Chippewa language sounding natural on his lips. At his answer the crowd fell silent. Then the woman nodded, and every voice exploded in gleeful comment. They chattered happily at Miri and took turns patting her arms and face. Not knowing exactly what was transpiring, Miri's stiff smile grew weaker and weaker. She was tempted to cling to Jordan's strong arm as he led her from the crowd, and only the severest self-discipline prevented her.

The wigwam to which Jordan led Miri was very similar to Lake Dancer's hut, but on the other side of the little village. It was nothing more than a frame of bent saplings tied into a dome shape and draped with bulrush mats. The floor was swept dirt, and in the center, under a smoke hole, a fire burned low within a fire pit outlined by stones. Along the perimeter of the one room were rolls of mats and furs that were used at night for beds. Near the door were shelves and hooks for storing cooking implements. All in all, Miri thought, the place made even Grace's rustic farmhouse look like a palace.

She directed Waves to put her baggage along one wall, then gave him a polite smile as he left. Without a word to Jordan she unrolled one of the bedding bundles and set Jane upon it, then left to milk Petunia for the baby's nighttime feeding. Perhaps if she kept busy enough, Miri thought, she wouldn't worry about spending the winter in a hut similar to this one, among people who hadn't the slightest notion of civilized manners, and "protected" by a man who was no better than a surly brute.

She eyed Jordan with distaste as she stepped back into the hut with a bucket of milk. He sat in cross-legged ease beside the fire and made no move to help with her heavy load.

"It would be easier just to bring the goat in here," he advised.

Miri sniffed. "Bring the goat inside? Don't be ludicrous." She filled a wooden cup with milk and stretched the nipple over the rim.

"She'll have to live inside this winter," he answered, seeming to think there was nothing remarkable about the idea.

Miri settled Jane on her lap, wedged the nipple into her mouth, and regarded Jordan with narrow-eyed disdain. "You can build her a pen. Or she can live in your wigwam. I am certainly not going to live in the same dwelling with a goat."

Jordan smiled maliciously. "This is my wigwam."

For a moment there was silence as Miri digested this news. "Do you mean to tell me that we are to live together in a single-room hut?"

"What did you expect? You'd be little use to me living in

another wigwam. Among the Chippewa, young women do not live alone. They live with their parents or their husbands.''

Miri tried to hold on to her temper, telling herself that she was at the mercy of this beast of a man. ''And just what do the Chippewa think of this arrangement?'' she asked in an acid voice. ''Grace was telling me the Indians are a very moral people. Don't you think they might have some questions about you moving an unmarried lady into your little hut?''

''They did,'' he admitted with a shrug. ''But I soothed their ruffled feathers.''

''And just how did you do that?''

Jordan uncrossed his legs, rose to his feet, and stretched like he hadn't a care in the world. His mouth lifted in a crooked smile as he headed toward the wigwam opening. Over his shoulder, he tossed the answer to her question.

''Congratulations,'' he said. ''In the eyes of the Chippewa, you've just become my wife.''

✳ 8 ✳

Jordan never made it to the doorway. Miriam was on him like a banshee, one arm holding Jane close to her body, the other hand grabbing his arm and tugging him around to face her fury.

''Your wife?'' she repeated incredulously. ''You must be joking!'' When he merely looked down his arrogant nose at her, she self-consciously yanked her hand back from where it held his arm. ''Tell me that you're joking!'' she demanded.

''I wouldn't joke about such a distasteful subject.''

''You told them that we're married?'' she gasped.

''We are married, Miss Sutcliffe. According to Chippewa

tradition, when a man and woman move into a wigwam together, then they are man and wife.'' His mouth twisted in contempt. "But I would hardly expect a civilized lady like you to pay much heed to the customs of savages."

The day had been too much for Miri. She turned abruptly and set Jane on the bedding, then pressed her temples with her fingers and shut her eyes tightly. If she willed it hard enough, perhaps this whole horrible day would prove to be only a nightmare. When she opened her eyes she would be back at Grace's farm, Jane would be sleeping peacefully in her bedroom, Gerald Michaels would be back in England, and Jordan Scott . . . Jordan Scott would be anywhere but where she was—preferably, somewhere on the other side of the globe. But the sound of Jordan's voice reminded her that there was no normal reality to awaken to. The nightmare was real.

"I'm going to bring the goat in," Jordan said calmly. "There's too much chance that one of the children will set her loose, or one of the dogs might have her for a late-night meal."

Miri whirled, her face white with exhaustion and anger. "Don't you dare bring that goat in here! It's bad enough that I have to live in a filthy hut made of . . . of trees and grass mats, and sleep on the dirt, and . . . and live with a naked barbarian. But I will not live in the same hut with a goat!" Her voice was rising to hysteria. She kept her fists balled at her sides trying to resist the urge to bury them in the man's infuriatingly arrogant face. "If you want to sleep with the goat, then sleep with her outside. I hope you'll be very happy together! You suit each other!"

"Not very grateful, are you? Perhaps I should have left you for your friend Captain Michaels."

"This wasn't my idea! And I'll not tolerate . . . !"

"You'll tolerate anything I tell you to tolerate!" Jordan commanded. "You went along with this harebrained scheme, and you'll damned well play by the rules. My rules!"

"I won't . . . !"

"You will! I don't want to hear another word from your

whining mouth! Now unroll the rest of the bedding and get to bed. The Chippewa do not commonly beat their women, but right now I'm tempted.'' With the threat hanging in the air, he brushed aside the doorway covering with an angry swipe of his arm and ducked out the opening.

Miri stumbled back toward the bedding, her hysteria cooled by the sudden, icy realization of her situation. She had no desire to feel Jordan's strong arm lifted against her. And certainly nobody in this wretched village would come to her rescue if she were to scream. She had to endure this unpleasant fellow for an entire winter, and such a man would have no compunctions about beating her soundly if she pushed him too far. But how far was too far? Miri wondered. Playing Miss Meek to his Surly Barbarian was simply too much to ask.

By the time she had unknotted the basswood cord that tied the rolls of bedding, Jordan had led a reluctant Petunia into the wigwam and staked her well away from the opening. Miri lay down, stiff-backed and sullen, ignoring them both. But it was impossible to ignore Jordan when he stretched his long body out beside her.

''What do you think you're doing?'' she gritted through angrily clenched teeth.

''Going to sleep. I suggest that you do the same. There's going to be plenty of work for the women tomorrow in packing the camp, and you'll be expected to help.''

He paused, and Miri could feel his eyes crawling over her body. Here it comes, she thought. Lucy was right. Men think of nothing but their animal lusts.

''How do you expect to sleep like that?'' he finally asked. ''That dress must cut off your breathing even when you stand.'' He yanked at the back fastenings of her snug bodice.

''Don't touch me!'' Miri shot up like a tightly wound spring. ''Get away from me! You can't sleep here!'' Put your foot down. Let him know you won't stand for this sort of behavior. That's what Lucy had advised.

"I'm not going to sleep on the bare ground, and Jane doesn't have nearly the warmth to offer that you do."

"Then *I* will sleep outside!"

Jordan grabbed Miri's arm as she tried to rise to her feet. "Like hell you will. These are my people, and they think that you're my wife. I won't have them think I was shunned on my wedding night, Miss Sutcliffe. So you will stay right where you are."

"I will not!"

"You will, if I have to tie you hand and foot and lie on top of you to keep you down." One brow lifted in devilish glee at her wide-eyed distress. "And though I'll be damned if I'm desperate enough to climb atop a thin-blooded little prig like you, I wouldn't put too much temptation in my path."

Miri was too mortified to speak. Seething, she wrenched her arm out of Jordan's grip and settled herself on the very edge of the bedding with her back toward him. His amused chuckle as he made himself comfortable only added fuel to her anger.

She had lain there only minutes when her whole body started to shiver, both from the effort of holding herself so rigid and the cold seeping into the wigwam. She had neglected to pull up the soft hides and furs that served as blankets, but she would die before crawling under the covers with that detestable subhuman beast. The shivering grew almost convulsive, but Miri refused to move.

"You are a fool, aren't you?" Jordan commented softly. "I can see you'd freeze for the sake of your damned stiff-necked pride."

Miri heard the hides rustle as he moved, then his hands were on her waist as he pulled her into the curve of his body and covered them both.

"Better?" he asked, silent laughter underlining the simple question.

Miri didn't deign to answer. She was trying to decide if she should fight, but the warmth seeping into her body made proper indignation hard to achieve. The hard muscles of Jordan's thighs cradled hers; his big hand was splayed across her ribs, lying suspiciously close to her breasts; and his warm breath sighed through her hair. Miri's own baser instincts were alive and well, she discovered, for her body was softening at his touch, inviting his warmth, and a traitorous pleasure was glowing in the pit of her stomach. As her eyelids drooped in sleep, Miri wondered if she would spend the winter fighting herself, as well as Jordan Scott.

Miri woke to the awareness of cold. Through the smoke hole she could see that the velvet black of night had faded to morning gray. Every muscle in her body ached—those that were not numb, at least—and every bone felt as though it would creak the moment she moved. But she had no intention of moving until the sun was higher in the sky. The bedding beside her was empty—thank heaven. Jordan had gone about his business, Jane was quiet, and there was no reason in the world why Miri couldn't pull the hides more tightly about her and drift back to sleep.

Miri had scarcely shut her eyes before a rude shove at her leg brought them open again. She turned her head to see Petunia's brown slotted eyes gazing an inquiry. The rope that had tied her to a stake trailed behind her with a frayed and broken end.

"Go away," Miri said irritably. "Go eat some grass, or jump in the lake, or whatever goats do at this time of morning."

Petunia bleated a reminder that goats are ordinarily milked at this time of morning. Miri ignored her and settled back into the warm bedding. Several more pathetic bleats failed to get her attention, and it wasn't until she felt goat teeth nibbling at her toes did she finally surrender.

"I'll make you regret this," Miri promised, climbing from her warm cocoon.

She thought of mornings in England, where the household was hushed until the sun was well above the horizon, and Lucy would bring her hot chocolate and freshly baked sweet rolls before she ever had to stir from her bed. That was another world—a dream, Miri decided. And this was a nightmare.

Shivering, she peeled off her gown and underthings and rummaged through her bundle to find clean clothes. As Jordan had promised, there was no warm water in which to wash her face and hands, and no looking glass to help her straighten the tousled disarray of her curls. Petunia continued to bleat, and now Jane was awake and filling the wigwam with her thin cry.

"Just be patient, Petunia. I'll get to you when . . . oh, no! Don't!"

An offering of goatberries rained onto the floor as Petunia regarded Miri with a satisfied gleam in her eye.

"Dammit! You lousy goat!"

Miri managed to get Petunia to do the rest of her business outside, then brought her back inside the wigwam for the milking. Jordan had been right—the morning air was too cold for comfort—but she hoped her hands had retained the icy chill. It would serve the cursed goat right.

Miri thought the morning's work was ended once she had milked the goat, staked her outside in a patch of grass and leaves, fed Jane, swept the goatberries from the wigwam, rolled the bedding, and gathered a few sticks to keep the fire burning. It was going to be a hard life, she acknowledged, but she would learn to survive, if only to show the arrogant Jordan Scott that he was wrong and she was right. But she did certainly wish she could locate a kettle among the items that were stored on the shelves along the wall. She would be willing to pay half her fortune for a cup of tea—even that dreadful cherry twig tea that Lake Dancer used to make.

But there was no kettle, and no food for breakfast except milk, so she wrapped Jane in a blanket, donned a smart little cape that had been one of her first efforts at sewing, and emerged from the wigwam to discover what the morning held in store.

Massed layers of gray clouds hid the sun, making the morning seem more like winter than fall. The tangy odors of wood smoke and wet vegetation scented the air, and newly fallen leaves drifted and tumbled with the light, chilly breeze. A large campfire burned in the center of the rough circle of wigwams. Over the fire several kettles and other containers were suspended from poles driven slantwise into the ground.

Miri had hardly emerged from the wigwam when she was accosted by a tall woman with iron-gray hair and a high-cheeked, straight-nosed profile that made her look like a queen in buckskins. Her brown skin was smooth and fine. Only the gray of her hair and fine lines around her eyes and mouth betrayed the fact that she was not young.

"I am Smiles at Sunrise," she said in a well-modulated voice.

Miri smiled tentatively. It was this woman who had questioned Jordan so sharply on their arrival the evening before. Miri had noticed the deference paid her by the other women, and suddenly felt she was committing a grave breach of etiquette by not curtsying, inappropriate as it seemed.

"I am the mother of Rides the Waves," the woman clarified, "and the wife of Smoke Catcher. My adopted son, Eyes of the Ghost, was rude not to introduce us. I am your husband's mother."

Wonderful. She not only had a bogus husband, but a mother-in-law was included in the package. "I'm happy . . . uh . . . honored to meet you," Miri fibbed.

Smiles at Sunrise glanced down at Jane, who was fast asleep in Miri's arms. Her eyes softened. "You will need a cradle board for Bright Spirit, so you can join the work of the other women without disturbing her sleep."

"Work?" Miri asked.

"I prepared a cradle board for Lake Dancer when I learned she was to have a child. Come with me and I will get it."

Little Jane was stuffed into a contraption made of board with a curved section at one end to hold the infant's feet. Two binding straps held her securely in place, happily naked (Smiles at Sunrise had clucked in disapproval at Jane's nightie) and cradled in dry, sweet-smelling moss that could be periodically changed. A perpendicular hoop at the infant's head held the blanket that kept her warm. Jane seemed perfectly content hanging from a branch where she was out of reach of the rambunctious children and dogs.

With the baby safely stashed away, Miri soon learned that the morning's work was not nearly over, as she had believed. Smiles at Sunrise took her to the central fire, fed her a breakfast of fish broth, rice seasoned with maple sugar, hard bread made from flour and salt, and spruce tea. While she was eating she was obliged to listen to instructions on how to make herself a kettle from freshly cut birch bark, which Smiles at Sunrise insisted was far superior to the kettles one could get from the trading houses.

After breakfast Sunrise took Miri to the wigwam where she had slept with Jordan the night before. Lessons on how to pack all of her belongings and Jordan's into bundles that could be neatly loaded in a canoe, on a dogsled, or carried on the back took the entire morning. A brief noon meal of more fish broth and dried berries mashed with deer tallow made Miri contemplate the merits of fasting. And then there were more lessons—how to dismantle a wigwam, and how to compact the bulrush mats into rolls that would be transported from camp to camp. As the afternoon marched on, Miri learned that most of the day's food was stored on racks outside each wigwam, and more in a central cache out of which the whole village drew rations. She was expected to cook over an open fire using disgusting ingredients such as stored animal tallow, unidentifiable roots dug from the ground, animal entrails, and unsavory-looking dried fish and meats. The seemingly tireless Chippewa matron helped Miri to start an evening meal for when Jordan returned, lending her one of her own birchbark cooking containers and showing her how to combine venison, wild potatoes, bulrush roots, and various herbs for a spicy stew.

By the time Smiles at Sunrise left the wigwam, Miri was so exhausted that the smell of the stew simmering over the fire pit nauseated her. She had spent the entire day learning things she had no desire to learn, eating food that she would not ordinarily have fed to Grace's pigs, putting up with a woman who regarded her as an ignorant and somewhat slow child, and trying not to wonder where Jordan had taken himself for the entire day. Not that she cared where he was. He could drop off the face of the earth and she would give a cheer.

Miri dragged herself over to a roll of bedding, sat down, and wearily leaned back against the grass mats of the walls. How nice it would be simply to close her eyes and sleep until spring was here. But there was still the goat to milk, the baby to clean and feed, and the stew to tend. She wondered if she would survive the winter!

Jordan's lip curled in disgust as his four drinking companions tossed aside the bottle they had been sharing and dared each other to rise to their feet. The four young men—all Chippewa warriors from a village near Sault Ste. Marie— thought themselves riotously funny as they tried to attain an upright position. Their legs were made of rubber, and their arms flapped in the breeze like a woman's wash hung to dry on a tree branch. One staggered around the secluded beach until his legs tangled and he measured his length on the water-washed pebbles. Another simply stood and swayed until gravity claimed him and sat him down hard upon his haunches. The two remaining leaned against a tree and spewed their pickled guts onto the ground.

Jordan remained where he was, not yet willing to risk the feat of standing. He could sneer at his companions all he wanted, but he acknowledged that he was in no better condition than they. The four Chippewa were a wild band of youngsters he most often ignored, but today, when they had greeted him in the Northwest Company's trading house and invited him to join them in consuming a hefty quantity of rum, a bout of good, solid drinking had seemed just the thing he needed. They had found this secluded beach and spent the rest of the day drinking rotgut. Jordan had done himself proud on the amount of rum he had downed and now had cause to regret it. Liquor didn't bury problems, he decided. It simply made the body feel as rotten as the soul.

"More?" one of the youngsters grunted, handing him a new bottle.

"No more," Jordan groaned.

He felt bad enough. Already he was out of control, drunk and dizzy and watching his imagination play havoc with his brain. Images released by the liquor assaulted his mind. The Englishwoman, naked and shivering, her hair a sodden mass hanging down past her waist. Again the Englishwoman, her back stiff and her eyes sparkling with righteous indignation as she chastised him for his lack of morals and lectured him on the responsibilities of a white man in this world of savages. And still there was more—the feel of her, warm and pliant, tucked into the curve of his body as if she belonged there, her crop of curls, sweet-smelling and soft, tickling his nose and lips. Her round little bottom pressed against his groin while she slept, unaware that she was a mere hairbreadth away from being turned on her back and taught just how savage and immoral Jordan Scott could really be. Mercy! Would the drunken visions never stop?

What kind of a monster could feel his blood heat for another woman when his sweet wife was not yet three months dead? It should be Lake Dancer who filled his visions, not that starch-souled Englishwoman who called righteousness and morality down upon his head every time he turned around. The little prig was everything he had run away from ten years ago—judgmental hypocrites with their noses in the air and their feet in the slime. The only thing about her that was not prim and proper was that unruly crop of red-brown hair on her head. Lord, how he wanted to run his fingers through that silken mass of curls. He'd wanted to ever since he had first seen them bouncing with her every energetic stride. Just the night before he had almost done it, but the little vixen probably would have bitten him.

Jordan lay back on the pebbled beach and closed his eyes, trying to bring Lake Dancer to mind. She was there, smiling—no, laughing. She turned, and there was the

Englishwoman beside her. The white woman was laughing, too, with the musical laugh he'd heard only once or twice. They were sharing a private joke, it seemed, no doubt at Jordan's expense.

How was he going to survive a winter in Miriam Sutcliffe's company? How could he keep himself from grabbing the damned little busybody by that crop of sweet-smelling hair, pinning her to the ground, and teaching her what it meant to be a woman? And when he was sated he just might strangle her for that oh-so-superior, civilized attitude. Jordan shut his eyes tighter. Now, there was a vision he welcomed. Temptation just might win out. After all, the gods could only expect so much of a man.

The sun was long down by the time that Jordan stumbled up onto the beach of the mainland and made his slightly unsteady way into the village. He had hoped the paddle across the straits would sober him, and he thought that it had. He felt strong now—strong and powerful. Invincible, even. No pasty-faced, curly-headed little she-cat was going to get the best of him. He could make her pull in those sharp claws and start purring any time he wanted. He just hadn't quite made up his mind what he wanted yet. His brain was still a bit fuzzy on that score.

After several circuits of the quiet village, Jordan managed to locate his wigwam. He had to wrestle with the blanket to push it back from the door opening, but finally he succeeded and stepped through into the dimly lit interior. The smell of venison stew assaulted his nose. Normally, he liked venison, but right at this moment, the odor made his stomach lurch. Maybe he wasn't quite as sober as he thought.

"Where have you been?"

At first Jordan thought the goat had asked the sharp-voiced question, but then he turned and saw the Englishwoman—his own personal thorn in the side. She looked as though she wanted to curse, but of course she wouldn't. Ladies of civilized society would never dream of letting a foul word escape from their foul little minds.

He snickered, then hiccuped.

"You've been drinking!" The voice was even sharper now, and the thought of her irritation made Jordan smile. "You stupid, rum-soaked toad! How dare you leave me here alone all day and come back in this condition!"

Poor thing. She'd been lonely for him. Who would've guessed that the starchy little bitch could get lonely? Maybe now was the time to turn that little spitting cat into a purring kitten. Lonely, was she?

Jordan took a step forward, then another. At the look of horror on the woman's face, he crooned like he would to a frightened child. "You're not alone now. Here I am." His next step took him into the fire pit.

It took the smell of burning rawhide moccasins to make Jordan realize that the little witch had moved the fire pit to where he would step in it. Witch, indeed! He lurched away, hopping on one foot with a grace that almost tumbled him to the floor. The other foot was smoking, and the infuriating woman was actually laughing at him. He would put a stop to that. He was master here, by damn! And that hellcat had better learn not to laugh at a man in his own home!

Jordan gingerly tested his smoking foot. Only the moccasin was burned, and when his examination shifted from the smoking rawhide to the chortling Englishwoman, she changed her tune quickly enough. The little bitch knew she was in trouble now!

With all the grace of a woozy panther, Jordan began to stalk his prey. His arms flashed out to hold her fast, but for all the deftness of his attack, she neatly sidestepped, and he continued on until brought up short by the wigwam wall. When he turned she was laughing again, damn her hide!

"The great white Indian!" she sneered. "It's a good thing you're not out hunting bear in this condition, mighty warrior. The bear wouldn't know whether to pass out from the fumes or die laughing."

That really did it! The woman needed a lesson, and Jordan Scott was just the man to teach it. He marshaled his few remaining faculties for a second attack.

The Englishwoman was overconfident this time. He feinted

to the left and she stepped to the right, but before she could chuckle her derision Jordan was there, his hands pinning her arms to her sides and drawing her body close to his. *This is more like it*, he thought, and after a few tries he found her mouth with his, bringing his lips down upon hers with a punishing savagery.

The jolt that shot though his body almost made him let go of his prey, and it certainly went a long way toward clearing the rum from his brain. For a moment he released the Englishwoman's mouth and looked into those wide blue eyes. They swam with confusion, wonder, and dismay, but the laughter was gone.

No one was more surprised than Miri when she fell for Jordan's little trap and ended up in his grasp. But his kiss was more of a surprise. The blackguard was hurtful, and savage, and he smelled of sweat and stale rum. But it seemed that her troublesome baser instincts didn't mind. The feelings that had always tantalized her at Jordan's touch suddenly washed through her in a scalding flood.

When he released her she scarcely knew it. Miri felt as drunk as Jordan when he had first come into the wigwam, and now his silver-gray eyes looked down at her with crystal lucidity, while hers had gone foggy with unnamed feelings. What was happening to her? She should be screaming, clawing, fighting—not frozen like a rabbit mesmerized by a snake.

Miri didn't struggle when Jordan's mouth came down again. His lips were gentle this time. His tongue flicked softly around the outline of her mouth, finally persuading her lips to open to him. When that insidious tongue pushed past her teeth and into the sweet recesses beyond, she felt the penetration to her very toes. His hands had shifted to her head, holding her still for his invasion. Her arms wrapped themselves around his lean waist, pulling them closer together. Everywhere the renegade's hard body pressed—against her breasts, her hips, her belly—Miri felt the white heat of desire. It spread down her legs and tightened her buttocks, burned in her breasts, and tingled down her arms all the way to the fingers that dug into the hard muscle of his back.

As abruptly as she had been captured, Miri was released. She staggered, reaching out for support. But Jordan had backed out of reach, muttering guttural words in Chippewa that certainly didn't sound like endearments. Her eyes focused slowly, taking in the wigwam, the fire pit, Jane sleeping peacefully on the bedding. Everything was the same, and yet in an instant, everything had changed.

"No," she whispered hoarsely, denying not only her own feelings, but anything else he might care to do to her. She was suddenly desperate for fresh air, frantic to be away from this barbarian who was reaching up from his bed in the muck of the world and trying to drag her down with him. Without a thought to where she was going she turned, brushed past the doorway, and ran out into the night.

The cold air brought Miri at least partially to her senses, but her head was still swimming, her mind reeling. She shivered—from the cold, she told herself—and wrapped her arms around herself.

Without consciously choosing a direction, Miri walked straight away from the wigwam. There was going to be a hard freeze that night, she noted absently. Already the leaves crackled brittly underfoot and her breath clouded the air in front of her. She had nowhere to go to keep warm, and in her haste to get away from Jordan, she had neglected to grab even a light wrap. But she couldn't go back, not now—not even if she froze all through the night. If she went back to the wigwam, then Jordan would look at her with those silver-gray eyes, and touch her with those big, hardened hands. And before the night was out he would take her in whatever way a man took a woman, and Miri would let him, because her lower self had suddenly broken free and was playing havoc with her decency and common sense.

She came up abruptly against a tree and jumped back in alarm. She was at the edge of the village. Behind her the Chippewa were settling in for the night, wrapping themselves in their warm furs and drifting off to sleep, everyone neatly placed with their feet toward the fire pit for warmth. Even the dogs were quiet. Jordan would be sleeping off the remainder of his drunk, or lying back on the furs, laughing at what a fine lesson he had taught her. And Miriam Sutcliffe was left out in the cold and the dark, alone, with the devil waiting for her in Fort Michilimackinac and another devil waiting for her back in the village. She leaned against the rough bark of the tree and surrendered to tears of self-pity, crying until she felt wrung dry and her throat ached from sobbing.

"My daughter," came a voice from the dark, "what are you doing here?"

Miri straightened hastily and wiped at her streaming eyes. "Sunrise?" she sniveled. "Is that you?"

"It is I. I came to see what brings these tears."

"How did you know it was me?" Miri asked.

"Who else would be out in the night crying against a tree? We women of the Anishanabe have better sense."

Tears were beginning to leak from Miri's eyes again.

"Have you quarreled with my son, Eyes of a Ghost? Sometimes he can be very difficult, like all men."

"To say the least," Miri agreed with a sniff.

"And yet you care for him, or you would not be his wife."

Miri was silent. What could she say? Jordan had certainly put her in an impossible position, and no doubt it had been deliberate.

"You should go back to your wigwam, my daughter. Many quarrels between a man and woman can be ended in the furs."

That was precisely what Miri feared.

"I can't go back tonight. Jordan . . . Eyes of a Ghost . . . is being hateful. He needs to be taught a lesson."

Sunrise's white teeth flashed in a grin. "So you must be the one to shiver on the cold ground?" The Indian woman shook her head. "So be it. I will bring you hides and furs, and tomorrow my son will be shamed when he sees that you have had to endure discomfort because of his behavior. Chippewa men do not treat their women so.''

Like hell! Miri thought in a rare indulgence of mental profanity. He would likely laugh his fool head off.

Miri slept not at all that night, even though the bedding that Smiles at Sunrise had brought kept out the cold. Her mind kept drifting back to the incident with Jordan, and try as she might, she could find no excuse for her reaction. Somewhere within her lurked a wanton, and she was going to have the very devil of a time fighting her off for the entire winter.

She rose before the morning's light, slipped silently into the wigwam, milked Petunia, fed the baby, and was out at the central fire breakfasting with Sunrise before Jordan awoke. The rest of the morning she busied herself helping the other women. Sunrise assisted her in dismantling the wigwam, rolling the bulrush mats, and preparing Jordan's and her bundles to be loaded into the canoes.

Miri was happy to note that Jordan's skin had taken on a greenish tinge as he moved about the camp helping the men do the heavy work that the women couldn't manage. They didn't speak, or even look at each other. But when Jordan wasn't looking, Miri couldn't resist following him with her eyes. He scarcely spoke to anyone, and was even surly to Rides the Waves, who seemed to enjoy ribbing him about his lack of vigor this day. She hoped the devil was sick as a dog for a week. He deserved it.

By midday everything was ready to go. The canoes were loaded, and each family unit or allied group of families was ready to depart on the long, slow journey that would end at their individual winter hunting grounds. Jane was packed securely into her cradle board, and as soon as she was settled into the gently rocking canoe, her usual fretfulness stopped. Unfortunately, Petunia's fretfulness began the moment the goat sighted the canoe, but her recalcitrance got her no further than it had before. Jordan was in no mood to be patient with an unhappy goat, and the poor nanny was trussed and wedged in between the bundles with no mercy and very little gentleness.

Daintily lifting her skirts, Miri waded out to the canoe without bothering to ask for Jordan's assistance. Considering the black cloud that hung over the rogue's head, Miri feared he might serve her the same as he had done the goat. She only wished she could ride with Smoke Catcher and Smiles at Sunrise, or even Rides the Waves. She could tolerate being crowded into a small canoe with a whining baby and bleating goat, but being in such close quarters with a surly Jordan Scott was another matter entirely.

The family pointed their canoes toward the west as they paddled out into the straits. The day was gray and gloomy, much suited to Miri's mood. If possible, she felt even lonelier and more frightened than before. The village at least had the comfort of being familiar. From here on out she was breaking new ground.

Up until meeting Jordan Scott, Miri's life had been as smooth as the water over which they were so peacefully gliding. Even the trouble with Hamilton had been a mere ripple. But now her whole world was headed for a cataract. She could feel the rapids rushing her toward it, could hear the roar of the falls. An inescapable current was carrying her toward the precipice with relentless and frightening resolve.

Grace—dear, naive Grace—had thought to make Jordan Miri's life raft, but Miri knew better. Jordan Scott was no savior. He would laugh and push her over the edge.

✳ 9 ✳

"Madam, I know that Miss Sutcliffe was staying at your farm. And I know also that you must be aware of the lady's whereabouts. It would save us all a great deal of trouble if you would simply tell me where she is.'' Captain Gerald Michaels' sharp eyes seemed to miss nothing as he walked slowly through the small farmhouse, Lieutenant Renquist at his heels like a faithful dog. Grace and Margaret looked on resentfully.

The widow fixed Captain Michaels with a stern eye. ''You've got no call to come stomping onto my property making your redcoat threats. Just who do you think you are?''

''You know very well who I am, Widow Peavey. And I assure you that the British army does not make threats. They make promises. And I promise you, madam, that unless you take a more cooperative attitude, we can make a good deal of trouble for you.''

''I am a citizen of the United States,'' Grace declared proudly. She reached out and drew Margaret to her side in a show of solidarity. ''No British tin soldier is going to push me around.''

While Michaels' face was carefully neutral, the lieutenant's showed malicious enjoyment. ''Need we remind you,'' the young officer asked haughtily, ''that your country is at war with ours, and at this moment the British army is in possession of your insignificant little mud hole of an island? I would tread carefully if I were you, madam!''

''I always watch my step around snakes, Lieutenant,'' Grace returned in an equally haughty tone.

Michaels stepped in before Renquist could give vent to his anger. ''Are you saying that Miss Sutcliffe did not stay with you?''

''I'm not saying anything, Captain.'' Grace folded her arms across her generous bosom. ''Except that I don't understand how a gentleman like yourself can figure it's right and honorable to harass an innocent little girl like Miriam Sutcliffe.''

''There!'' Renquist exploded. ''You see? She knows her. I told you the girl was staying here! I'd be surprised if this

lying *American*"—he spit out the word like a foul curse—
"hasn't hidden her somewhere just to spite British authority."

"Not an unlikely surmise, Lieutenant."

The scarlet-coated captain made a second circuit of the
house, casting a curious glance toward the parlor wall where
hung a small painting of the widow's late husband, peeking
into the bedrooms, climbing into the loft where the girls
slept, and finally ending his tour in the kitchen.

"I was raised in a farmhouse very similar to this one."
He sniffed appreciatively at the aroma of baking bread.
"The same smells, the same sort of open loft, the same tiny
parlor opening into a big kitchen. It's a very nice little farm
you have here, Widow Peavey. Such a pity that it's caught
in the middle of a war. Someday you may value the
friendship of the British army."

"I value my friendship with Miriam Sutcliffe more,"
Grace answered.

"Ah. Well, in that case . . ."

Just then the farmhouse door flew open, admitting Mary
Beth, Martha, and Lucy. Michaels' eyes immediately fastened
on Lucy's face. The maid instantly turned red and made a
little *O* with her mouth.

"Miss Sutcliffe's maid, I believe," Michaels ventured.
"Yes, I remember you from London."

Lucy panicked and turned to flee, but was brought up
short by Renquist, who grabbed her arm and yanked her
roughly toward Michaels. Grace opened her mouth to protest, and Michaels himself looked ready to give a sharp
reprimand, when a little demon with blond pigtails tackled
Renquist's knees and sent him crashing to the hard plank
floor. Mary Beth's forward momentum landed her atop her
victim in a tangle of arms and legs.

"Run!" Mary Beth screeched to the abruptly freed Lucy.
"Go fetch Pa's musket!"

Her voice was cut off in a strangled gasp as Renquist
untangled himself from his attacker and grabbed the little
girl's neck. He rose to his feet, his face a furious red, and

carried Mary Beth up with him until her feet dangled a foot off the floor. Then he shook her like a rag doll.

Grace was on him like a she-bear protecting her cub. But it was a sharp command from Michaels that forced the lieutenant to put the little girl back on her feet.

"I'll see you about this in my office, directly after we return. Do you understand?" The captain's voice shook with controlled fury.

"Yes, sir." Renquist eyed the group malevolently. His face was crimson with anger and humiliation.

Mary Beth had run to Grace and buried her face in her mother's skirts. Martha was already there, and the sobs from the two of them were drawing concerned little clucks from the widow. Nevertheless, Michaels didn't miss the fact that one of Mary Beth's eyes surfaced from the folds of Grace's skirts and gave him an assessing once-over in a manner that was anything but cowed. The captain's stern mouth twitched upward in the hint of a smile, and the eye disappeared once again amid renewed wails and sobs.

"I apologize, madam," Michaels said, his clipped military tones carrying even through the girls' wailing. "The British army does not usually attack children, even"—he cocked an eye toward Mary Beth, who had turned to regard him from above an indignantly outthrust lower lip—"even when we are attacked first. And I have no quarrel with Miss Sutcliffe's maid. But her presence here does confirm that Miss Sutcliffe has been in residence at your farm, does it not?"

Grace answered only with silence. She drew her daughters closer into her protective embrace.

"Perhaps you will now tell me where your guest has taken herself."

For a moment the widow gave him a stubborn face, then she allowed it to slowly fall into lines of resignation. "She left for Montreal."

The British commander frowned.

"Her pa was a partner in the Northwest Company. She

got them to smuggle her into a canoe that was headed upriver.''

Michaels' smile revealed nothing of his thoughts. ''As you say,'' he finally conceded. ''Renquist, return to the fort and set men to make inquiries. And if Miss Sutcliffe is apprehended, no one is to question her in any way, or to treat her with anything but courtesy, until she is brought to me. Understand?''

Without a word the lieutenant left. When the door slammed behind him, Mary Beth squirmed out of her mother's arms and ran to the kitchen window. She hailed his departure with a pointed little tongue stuck out in his direction.

''Mary Beth!'' Grace admonished. ''Mind your manners, you saucebox! Here, take Martha. The two of you find out where Lucy ran to, bless her! Margaret, you go with them.''

The girls left, detouring a wary distance around the British captain as they passed him. Michaels watched them go, then turned to their mother. For the first time, he looked something other than entirely composed.

''I am extremely sorry to meet you under such unpleasant circumstances, Widow Peavey. I had hoped to establish a cordial relationship with the people who call this island home.''

''I'd hardly call it cordial to come blustering into a body's home making threats, or to be troubling a harmless girl who's as innocent as a newborn lamb.''

Michaels raised a doubtful brow. ''Come now, madam. Be realistic. Surely, after having hosted Miss Sutcliffe for these past weeks, you must realize that any man who chases after that girl—for whatever reason—is likely to get as good as he gives.''

Grace sent him a warning frown, and he sighed. ''And I can assure you that when Miss Sutcliffe is apprehended, she will be given every courtesy. I have never intended the girl harm, you see.''

The widow didn't debate the point. The captain wasn't about to find his victim, so it mattered very little how he thought he was going to treat her. It did appear, however, that Michaels wasn't quite the ogre that Miriam had painted him. In fact, when his spine wasn't quite so stiff, he almost had a human look about him, with his dignified iron gray hair and snapping hazel eyes. And he had prevented that miserable lieutenant from harming Mary Beth.

"I suppose I do owe you some thanks, Captain. Mary Beth was very naughty. There is never any excuse for that sort of behavior."

"Nor is there an excuse for my lieutenant's response, madam. I feel I must apologize again. What he did was completely against any gentleman's code of honor."

Grace folded her hands, then unfolded them again. Michaels was looking around the kitchen, a smile on his face. Suddenly the widow felt almost sorry for the man, so stiff and formal and correct, so bound by honor and duty. Did the poor fellow never unbend?

She wiped suddenly moist palms on her apron. "I . . . you . . . that is, I have some fresh-made cranberry pie, Captain. If you could stay a moment, you might have a piece. And some coffee—but no, you Britishers drink tea, don't you? I'm not sure I have any tea."

"Coffee would be splendid." Michaels nodded, took off his hat, and took a seat at the kitchen table.

Miri sat on the cold ground, staring into the bonfire, poking irritably at her food and listening to the Indian chatter that floated around her. The day had been a disaster and the night wasn't going to be any better. First there had been the morning, when she'd had to pack everything to Sunrise's exacting standards, carry all the bundles to the canoe, and also manage to care for a fretting baby whose poor color and lack of vitality worried her more each day.

The afternoon had been still worse. At least during the morning Miri had been able to avoid Jordan's surly mood by taking care to be where he was not, but once the canoes were underway, she was forced to sit for hours in his silent, brooding presence. A feeling of rushing toward disaster had hounded her, as did the unnerving sense that she herself was out of control. All through the afternoon her eyes had been drawn against her will to the play of muscles under Jordan's bronzed skin as he paddled in stoic and unbroken rhythm. Early on he had discarded his muskrat chest protector and shirt, displaying a shocking amount of masculine torso. The sight made Miri's stomach tighten and inspired her mind into unwanted but vivid memories of his kiss the night before.

Miri had been kissed before—nervous pecks by suitors who were careful not to offend her delicate sensibilities. But those kisses had been nothing like Jordan's. His had been a primitive attack, an animal gesture of anger and dominance and bestial passion. It had been disgusting, and frightening, and entirely abhorrent.

Then why had that raw kiss sent something in Miri flying joyously out of control? Why had one part of her cringed in horror while another part melted like wax in a hot candle flame. God help her! The longer she remained in this wilderness, the stronger those base instincts became. Thank heaven she had fled the wigwam before her lower self had propelled her back into the renegade's arms. Lord only knew what would have happened!

The afternoon had been long. The weather had cleared, but the sun brought very little warmth with it. Miri's woolen dress and capelet were not equal to the chill, and every hour had brought more discomfort. But Miri had been more uncomfortable with Jordan's proximity than the wintry weather. His brooding silence made her uneasy. Who knew what was going on in that enigmatic male mind of his?

The misery hadn't ended with the day's journey. When the sun dropped below the seemingly endless expanse of water to the west, the three canoes had beached on a sandy shore that sloped up to a village much larger than the one they had left that morning. The inhabitants of the village had flocked to the beach to greet them with welcoming smiles on their faces.

"Where are we?" Miri had asked Smiles at Sunrise once they had both waded ashore.

"This is L'Arbre Croche," the Chippewa woman had told her. "We are now on the northeastern shore of what your people name Lake Michigan. These people are Ottawa. They are good friends. We will spend the night here."

"Thank heaven. I thought we were never going to stop."

But Miri's hopes of rest for her stiff and aching body had been in vain. The Ottawa, it seemed, knew Jordan well, and they all were curious about the white woman who was introduced as his new wife.

Immediately after Miri and Jordan had deposited their bundles in a cedar-bark lean-to, Sunrise had dragged Miri away. In her usual imperious manner, Jordan's adopted mother had deposited Jane with a grandmotherly looking Ottawa who seemed delighted to be charged with the baby's care. Then she had led a protesting Miri from one group of people to another, putting her on display, chattering in rapid-fire heathen, and occasionally interpreting some comment for Miri's benefit. There were many moans and wails when the villagers heard of Lake Dancer's death, but heads nodded in approval at news of Jordan's remarriage. Miri had smiled and tried her best to be properly polite, even though she had no idea what the Indians said as they regarded her with their grins and nods and dark, unreadable eyes. Twice she had caught glimpses of Jordan, once while he was still unloading their canoe, and then again as he stood in animated conversation with an attractive young woman. But he had made no attempt to rescue her from the trials of Ottawa scrutiny, and her patience was wearing dangerously thin by the time the crowds started to disperse.

Even then she'd had no time for respite. After the introductions were done, the entire village had hastened to the central oval of the village, where a feast was laid out to celebrate the arrival of the guests. Sunrise retrieved little Jane from the old woman who had watched her, then led Miri to the spot beside Jordan and motioned her to sit. Settling the baby in Miri's lap, she had smiled approvingly. Then, without another word, she had left to join Smoke

Catcher, her eyes sparkling as she caught a glimpse of the resentful glare Miri gave her back.

Now Miri sat and toyed with her food, too exhausted to eat and wanting only the warmth and privacy of her own bed. Jordan turned toward Miri and seemed to probe her sullen demeanor with silver-metal eyes. Miri felt a frisson travel up her spine as his gaze briefly caught hers. But he said nothing, merely looked. The cad was playing the role of silent savage to the very hilt, she mused resentfully. Well, two could play that game. They had nothing to say to each other anyway.

Miri turned her face away from Jordan's gaze and watched the villagers dip into the food with unleashed appetites. Sweet heaven, how she wished she could simply go to the wigwam and sleep! If there was anything Miri didn't need that evening, it was to sit cross-legged on the cold ground and watch a hundred Indians eat with their hands. She had no appetite to begin with.

The fresh fish, roasted corn, wild potatoes, and dried berries that had been boiled and seasoned with maple sugar continued to sit untouched before her. But Miri did manage to conceal her sullen mood behind a pleasant face. It wouldn't do at all for Jordan to think she was some weak-spirited female who went into a sulk just because he was displeased with her. He was the one who had made a fool of himself the night before. Miri hoped he was still sick from the rum. It would serve him right if all this food he must eat for politeness' sake curdled in his rum-shriveled stomach.

After everyone had eaten their fill, the elders of the Ottawa village rose to speak, one by one. Miri assumed the long speeches were words of welcome, but it was difficult to maintain a look of polite interest when she couldn't understand a single word.

The stars had progressed a good way across the sky by the time they had all spoken. Miri prayed that the primitive social gathering was over, but her hopes were dashed when several men entered the circle with what looked like crude musical instruments. Soon an eerie melody was rising from a flutelike rod constructed of either wood or bone—Miri couldn't tell which, and truly didn't care.

The melody was accompanied by rhythmic drumbeats that soon were vibrating every fiber of Miri's body. Even her heart seemed to be beating in rhythm with the cadence, almost lulling her into a trance. If this went on much longer, Miri was sure she would fall asleep right where she was and probably awaken so stiff that her legs would be permanently crossed. Jane had fallen asleep on her lap long ago, and Miri was tempted to join her. She was so, so tired, and the drums were so hypnotic.

Then Miri came abruptly awake. A sense of something being not quite right broke the spell the drums were weaving. She focused her eyes, and there in front of her was a sight certainly worth staring at. The others in the circle must have agreed, for every pair of eyes was turned upon the woman who had stepped into the circle to dance.

The music had inspired a few others to dance, also. Their movements were playful and accompanied by the laughing encouragement of their friends. But no one laughed at the woman's dancing. It was purposeful, sinuous, intense, and clearly performed for the benefit of one man—Jordan Scott. One by one the other dancers sat down. Even the flutist gave up his playing to watch the spectacle.

The circle grew quiet. Soon the only sounds in the night were the crackling of the fire, the beat of the drums, and the soft scuffing of the woman's feet on the ground. The dancer swayed and dipped, glossy black braids swinging around her slender torso as she moved. She turned and wove, hips undulating, breasts jutting. Nature and earth and ripe female, grace and beauty and sensuousness—the woman was all these things, Miri acknowledged. She was also the damnedest little hussy Miri had ever seen. Miri had no trouble recognizing the tart. She was the woman who had been in such enthusiastic conversation with Jordan that afternoon.

Miri stole a glance at Jordan, who was doing absolutely

nothing to discourage the obscene display from continuing. The jackass couldn't take his eyes off the baggage. And for all her weaving and turning, neither did the dancer allow her gaze to stray from her prey. The two of them might as well be making love right in the crowd of all these people, Miri fumed.

Not that she was jealous. Jordan Scott, Eyes of a Ghost, renegade bastard, could make a fool of himself in any way he pleased and cavort with any female he wanted. But these people thought he was Miri's husband. And she was sitting right beside him, his baby sleeping in her lap. At least the blackguard could show a little discretion where his amours were concerned. After all, she did have her pride. Already the Ottawa villagers were looking at her with pity in their dark eyes.

Now the little Indian tart was pulling at Jordan's hands, urging him to join her obscene little dance. Jordan was actually smiling, curse him. Surely he wouldn't... He would. He was standing and swaying in time to the drums. The girl placed her hands on his broad shoulders and started to draw him into the circle when Miri decided she'd had enough. She tucked Jane into the crook of one arm and stood, picking up the bowl of berries mashed with maple sugar that was sitting uneaten in front of her. Jordan turned to look at her. Surprise! Miri thought. He knew she was alive after all. Without allowing herself a second to consider, Miri emptied the contents of the bowl over Jordan's head, pleased to note that a goodly portion of it spattered onto his dancing partner as well. The drums stopped. Even the crackling of the fire seemed muted as Jordan stared at Miri in stunned surprise. Before his surprise could turn to anger, she stalked out of the circle and into the dark night.

The cedar-bark lean-to did not seem like much of a haven to Miri, but it was the best she had. Someone had built a fire earlier, and now red coals winked at her from the fire pit. They provided a little warmth, and scarcely enough light for Miri to find the bedding that was rolled against one wall. She nearly stumbled into Petunia, who was staked just inside the door. The goat's plaintive bleats echoed Miri's sentiments exactly.

Miri settled Jane on a pile of furs in one corner of the learn-to, then crawled gratefully into her own bedding. Never had she been so grateful to lie down. Never had she anticipated sleep with such pleasure.

But sleep would not come. Jane fussed in the corner. Petunia rustled near the door. But most of all, uneasy visions rattled around in her mind. Miri could shut out the noises of the night, but the whirling of her mind refused to be ignored.

Jordan was going to be furious, Miri's conscience whispered disapprovingly. The wonder was that he hadn't shown up already and shaken her until her teeth shook.

Jordan deserved everything he got, Miri answered sullenly, wishing her conscience would go to sleep and allow her to do the same. *Everything he got and still more.* And to think back a few weeks ago she had begun to like the cad, after seeing his gentleness with little Jane and his faithfulness in helping the Peavey family. How wrong she had been to believe he might have some redeeming qualities. The man was an immoral bounder through and through.

The bounder has put himself out to protect you from Captain Michaels, her conscience persisted.

Grace forced him, Miri explained. Jordan Scott would just as soon see her rot in prison.

Forced him? her conscience asked. Do you really think someone could force Jordan Scott to do something he wasn't willing to do? Be honest now.

He needs me as much as I need him. What about Jane?

Other arrangements could have been made. Don't fool yourself. You've got no right to behave like a brat to a man who not only saved your life, but is rescuing you from prison.

Did he have a right to flaunt that hussy in front of me and the whole village? Even if the man isn't really my husband, everyone thinks he is. What about my feelings?

Feelings aren't important right now. Survival is important.

Go jump in the lake, Miri invited. She buried her face in the furs, hoping to hide from herself. A conscience was a very inconvenient thing to have, and hers had been getting entirely too uppity of late.

At that moment Jordan swept into the lean-to and forestalled any additional conversations between Miri and herself. He carried a sputtering lamp that reeked of some kind of animal fat, and by its light Miri could see that his face was grimmer than usual. A dollop of berry mush still clung to his sculptured cheek. Feigning sleep, she decided, was her only defense, but an ungentle prod from his moccasin-clad toe put an end to that.

"Go away," she complained, turning over to give him her back.

"Like hell." He prodded again. "Stand up, you miserable little brat, and explain just what the hell you thought you were doing out there! It's taken me the last hour to smooth Willow Song's ruffled feathers, and after your little performance, I'll be damned if a few of yours don't deserve to be fluffed up."

"Don't you use that kind of language around me!" She threw off the furs and pushed herself angrily to her feet. With Jordan this near, she felt more confident on her feet than her back.

"I'll damn well use whatever language I please."

"Just like you do everything else you please! Is Willow Song that tart's name? You must have had a good time smoothing her feathers after leering at her all evening long. Damn you, Jordan Scott! You treat me like a slave, get disgustingly drunk and mistake me for a whore, glare at me all day, and now you humiliate me by encouraging that obscene display and leering like a satyr at that Indian Jezebel! The whole village thinks my supposed husband is diddling with another woman in front of my very eyes."

Jordan snorted. "Since when have you ever cared what savages think? And it's none of your business whom I choose to leer at."

"It most certainly is my business." Miri shook her finger

at his broad chest, and suddenly it seemed a very inadequate weapon against the anger she read on his face. "As long as those people think I'm your wife, you owe me some respect. That means you should at least act the part of a loyal husband, if you know what loyalty is."

Jordan continued to glare, then he smiled suddenly. Miri found the smile more frightening than the frown. "And are you prepared to act the part of the loyal wife?"

"What do you mean?"

The smile grew broader, and even less pleasant. "What I mean is, a loyal husband deserves a loyal wife. If I had a warm little Englishwoman in my bed, I might be less inclined to look at other women."

Miri's eyes grew wide. She drew back her hand, itching to slap that arrogantly masculine face, but at the last moment, something in his eyes made her curl that hand into a fist and bring it back to her side. "You are a savage. At least the Indians have an excuse. But you! You're mad!"

"You're right." He looked disdainfully unmoved by her denunciation. "I was mad to listen to Grace, and mad to ever think that you might be something other than a pain in the ass." He lifted the blanket that covered the lean-to doorway and gave Miri a final look of disgust. "You'd better behave yourself from now on, Miss Sutcliffe. Any more sass from you and I'll leave you as a winter feast for the wolves."

The blanket dropped back into place, leaving the lean-to once again dark, and also with a feeling of emptiness that Miri couldn't explain. She collapsed on the bedding, and tears of frustration traced their way down her cheeks. He had gone to be with that woman, of course. What had he said her name was? Willow Song? Not that she cared where the devil went. He could go straight to hell and Miri would be delighted. And if he wanted to lust after some woman who threw herself at him in such a disgusting manner, it just showed how low he had sunk.

Miri pulled the furs up over her head and closed her eyes in determination. She didn't care. Really, she didn't. It was just all . . . so disgusting. That woman and Jordan Scott, rutting like animals on the dirt floor of a wigwam. How could such a bestial act bring pleasure to anyone? Miri envisioned Willow Song's sinuous brown body rolling in the furs with the renegade's harder, larger one. The woman was wrapping herself around him like a snake, and he was kissing her as he had kissed Miri, his legs clamping around her as she writhed beneath him. And suddenly the woman in her vision was no longer Willow Song. It was herself.

Miri buried her face and moaned. Her whole body was flushed with shame. Curse those low urges she had inherited from her father. She was sure her pure-hearted mother had never had thoughts so unholy. A curse on her father, a curse on Willow Song, a curse on Jordan Scott, and a curse on Miri herself. How she wished she had chosen prison!

Jordan took a swipe at a tree as he strode through the darkness. When his knuckles scraped jagged bark and came away bleeding, he didn't regret it one bit. The pain felt good. It was a distraction from the anger and confusion.

"What devil drives you, my brother?" Rides the Waves' voice came out of the night, a sane damper on Jordan's mounting frustration.

Jordan slowed and allowed his friend to come up beside him. "That woman is going to drive me to murder. I should turn back and make a gift of the bitch to the British. It would be a telling blow for the American cause."

"Wives are often a mighty burden to bear." Waves' teeth flashed in a grin. "But what would we do without them?"

"Shit!" Jordan cursed in English. The Chippewa language was sorely inadequate on that score. "The little she-wolf isn't my wife. I told you that."

"And now you have told Willow Song, also. I heard you this afternoon after we arrived. Not a wise thing to do, Eyes of a Ghost. I could have told you that Willow Song has long envied Lake Dancer's place in your bed. If she believed you were truly wed, she might have left you alone. But now she'll be after you like a she-wolf after a rabbit.''

Jordan cursed again. There had been too many things to curse about in the last few months. "It was just an innocent conversation, dammit! The only reason I singled Willow out was to ask her if Miri's cousin had passed through the village last spring."

"And . . . ?"

"She remembered him, all right. He must have impressed her, because she rattled on about him for a good long while. And then, somehow, the conversation got turned around to me and Miriam Sutcliffe. Seeing as how I'd already told her about Miri's cousin, it seemed natural to tell her the whole story. Dammit! How was I to know that Willow Song was leaving her husband? Or that she would think I needed another woman in my bed? And that dance—shit! She was just playing a game. Willow's been a friend—a sister, almost—since I first came to live with you."

Waves chuckled and shook his head. "You are blind, my brother, but the Englishwoman is not. I think your little wife was not pleased at Willow Song's attention."

"That hellcat is not my wife. And no, she was not pleased, as you saw."

Waves shrugged philosophically. "In the traditions of our people, she is your wife. Perhaps you would feel better if you simply took her to your bed. Any woman who sleeps alone is bound to be a shrew. Fill her with a baby and she will be calm."

They stopped in a star-illumined clearing. Jordan sighed and leaned against a pine, his head facedown on his arm. "I'm not in the mood for your jokes."

Rides the Waves refused to be subdued. He knew his adopted brother too well to be cowed by his sour temper. "You are feeling sorry for yourself, my brother. Your soul is full of bile. Come and we will let it spill out on the ground so it will bother you no more." He sprang to a crouch, a clear invitation to wrestle.

A fight, even a friendly contest of strength, suited Jordan's mood very well. He flexed his powerful shoulders to loosen the muscles, and then sprang to attack. Both men crashed to the ground among the brittle grasses and weeds. They grappled, grunted, broke loose, and rose to their feet to attack again.

It took only a few moments for the wrestling match to deteriorate into a free-for-all. Chippewa referees would have stopped the hard-fisted blows that began to fall, but the silent audience of night-shrouded pines didn't care that the two warriors were ignoring the rules, and neither did Jordan. He was losing the match, and he didn't care about that, either. His mind was on matters more painful than a cut cheek or blackened eye. With every blow he landed, he enumerated his frustrations—his desire, his guilt, his confusion, and his helplessness to escape. If both his eyes were swollen shut the next day, at least he would not have to see the graceful lilt in the Englishwoman's stride, or the burnished auburn of her hair, or the velvet line of her throat, or the curve of that stubborn mouth. He wouldn't have to see her cuddle his pathetic little daughter, or widen those impossibly large, improbably blue eyes at some imagined insult or slight from him. Perhaps if he fought until he dropped from exhaustion, then he would be able to sleep without dreaming about her. Then again, maybe not.

Jordan fell to his knees, then to all fours. Waves knelt down beside him, just as scraped and bruised and bloody.

"Are you through?" the Indian asked.

"I'm through," Jordan panted.

He might be through in more ways than one. The damned woman was an angel one moment and a witch the next. But every moment of the day and night she was raw female temptation. And the hell of it was, she didn't seem to know it.

Jordan shivered as a cold wind sighed through the tall pines, making them sway. The stars had ducked behind a veil of clouds, and there was a feel of moisture in the air. The long, cold winter was on its way.

✳ **10** ✳

The next morning, when Miri brushed aside the blanket over the doorway, she was greeted by a dazzling white carpet of snow. The pail of water sitting beside the lean-to was covered with an inch of ice, and her breath condensed to a dense fog in front of her face.

Miri smiled. She had certainly not felt like smiling when she first woke, but now she couldn't help herself. Even in London she had loved the snow, and here it was even more wonderful. In the forest behind the village, each tree, branch, and needle was frosted with pristine white. The pines stood like tall frozen guardians, etched in sharp relief against a brilliant blue sky. Everywhere one looked, the colors of the world seemed fresh and new, the crisp air washed clean of summer's debris.

Still smiling, Miri ducked back into the lean-to, donned fresh underwear and a clean woolen dress, and set about the morning's chores. The smile soon wore thin, and then disappeared altogether.

Petunia had not been in the best of humors since she had first seen the canoe waiting for her the night they had left the Peavey farm. Yesterday's trip hadn't improved matters, and now the newly fallen snow was definitely the goat's last straw. She took one look at the white stuff outside the lean-to and refused to budge. All of Miri's cajoling brought only a look of stubbornness to her slotted eyes, and no amount of pushing or pulling could get her to set one foot in the cold snow. Petunia decided that the lean-to was a fine place to do anything she had to do. And so she did, much to Miri's disgust.

The time Miri and Petunia spent together milking was less than cordial, and by the time Jane awoke, Miri was not in the mood for a fussy baby. Miri cleaned her, fed her, and tried to soothe her crying with as much patience as she could muster. As much as she loved little Jane, she wished just once the baby would give a gurgle of laughter, or even a lusty cry of wrath, like other infants. The thin, plaintive tone of Jane's almost constant wailing was getting under Miri's skin like an irritating splinter.

With Jane cleaned and fed, the goat mess swept out the doorway, and herself dressed, brushed, and washed (the icy water outside the lean-to had tempted her to pass up her morning ablutions just this once, but cleanliness had won out in the end), Miri set her hand to rolling the bedding and tidying the bundle of clothing for repacking into the canoe. Jordan's belongings were untouched—still neatly rolled into a bundle and tied with basswood cord. Miri kicked his bundle out into the snow to wait beside her own. The thought of giving its owner a similar kick momentarily brought a smile back to her face, but it disappeared as she remembered why his belongings were still neatly packed and why his side of the bedding was cold and unrumpled. A simple kick was much less than the man deserved, she decided.

Smiles at Sunrise walked up just as Miri gave Jordan's bundle a final kick. She regarded the younger woman with a knowing eye.

"Eyes of a Ghost is with Smoke Catcher and Rides the Waves. They left very early to go hunting," she explained. "We will have fresh duck for our evening meal."

"I thought we were continuing our journey this morning."

"We will continue. They will meet us when the sun is high."

"How . . .?" Miri looked toward the beach for the first time. Their canoes were unloaded and pulled up onto the sand. The lake stretched out smooth and unruffled under the cold blue sky. The near-shore surface was dulled by a thin scum of ice.

"The cold comes early this year," Sunrise said with a shrug. "We must continue on foot."

"But the ice is so thin. And surely by midday it will melt."

Sunrise shook her head. "The skin of our canoes is thin, also, Eyes of the Sky. And we cannot wait until midday to start our journey."

"What did you call me?" Miri asked with a frown.

"Eyes of the Sky. You are a good woman. It is fitting that you should have a good name."

Miri's frown grew deeper. Now they were changing her name, as well. She thought Miriam Sutcliffe was just fine.

Sunrise motioned for Miri to follow and moved to where the items that had been packed into Jordan's canoe were lying in a neat pile on the ground. With efficient motions she began to tie the food packs and bulrush mats to the bundles of personal belongings until they made one huge pack. Unenthusiastically, Miri helped.

"You must adjust to our ways," Sunrise advised, seeing Miri's frown. "It is only a pet name, my daughter. I meant no insult. It means nothing. Only the spirit name has meaning."

"I have no spirit name."

Sunrise shrugged. "You will someday, I think. When the spirits know you are ready."

Miri didn't comment, since the woman obviously set great store by her superstitions. She continued to work in silence. Then, when they were finished, she asked, "Where do we put all this?"

"On your back," Sunrise answered, one brow arched in amusement.

"What? You mean I have to carry it?"

"And the cradle board, as well, my daughter. You must learn."

"And what about my strong warrior husband?" Miri asked in an acid tone.

Sunrise gave her a stern look. "He and the other men protect us, and provide us with food. The burden is easy once you learn. And when the snow is firm, we will load the heaviest bundles on the dogsleds.''

Miri turned away with a disgusted snort, and the older woman shook her head.

''You are much displeased with Eyes of a Ghost.'' It was a statement, not a question. ''Last night you showed your displeasure and embarrassed him in front of his friends. That is not good, Eyes of the Sky. You are a white woman, so much excuse was given your behavior. But you should learn that a Chippewa wife respects her husband.''

The new name only added to Miri's irritation. ''My behavior?'' she cried. ''What about his behavior? He humiliated me! Is it Chippewa custom for a husband to lust after another woman in front of his wife?''

''When a man looks at another woman, my daughter, there is usually a reason.''

''I'll give him a reason,'' Miri muttered to herself. How could she explain to this woman that she was not really Jordan's wife? If Jordan's adopted mother knew Miri was living with her son under false pretenses, she would most certainly think her a jade of the lowest sort. And Smiles at Sunrise was the closest thing Miri had to a friend in this miserable adventure.

''I will try to learn,'' Miri conceded stiffly. ''But if any man expects respect from me, he has to earn it.''

''Eyes of the Ghost is a man any woman can be proud to call husband.''

Miri kept her skepticism to herself. Smiles at Sunrise, it seemed, was every bit as gullible as Grace Peavey when it came to Jordan Scott's character—or lack thereof. But then all mothers—even adopted ones, it seemed—were blind to their children's faults.

It was still early morning when, having broken their fast and said goodbye to their Chippewa friends, the women prepared to set upon their way. Sunrise had checked the bindings of Miri's pack, then urged her to change her wool dress for a buckskin tunic, leggings, and moccasins that had once belonged to Lake Dancer. Miri refused politely. She might sleep on the dirt floor of a miserable hut, trudge through the wilderness with only savages for company, and permit herself to be loaded like a pack mule, but the refinement of civilized garb was something she absolutely would not abandon. She compromised only by accepting the moccasins, because her leather slippers would not fit onto the bindings of the snowshoes she was required to put upon her feet.

Miri was struggling to settle the enormous pack on her back when she noticed that the sleek-bodied hussy from the night before was similarly laden and walking their way.

"What is *she* doing?" Miri asked Sunrise through tightly clenched teeth.

"That is Willow Song. She will be coming with us."

Miri's jaw dropped. "What? But she's . . . she's . . ."

"Willow Song is my daughter, and sister to Rides the Waves and Lake Dancer. She married an Ottawa man, but now she has decided to leave him. My husband has given her permission to winter with us."

As if the morning hasn't been bad enough already, Miri mused bitterly. How nice for Jordan. Now, at least, he wouldn't lack for entertainment during the long winter.

"My mother," Willow Song greeted Sunrise as she drew even with them. She walked easily under her burden, Miri noted with envy.

"Willow Song. You have met the wife of Eyes of a Ghost. I call her Eyes of the Sky."

Willow Song turned to Miri. "You are the one who has taken my sister's place." The tone was not exactly hostile, but her smile held enough challenge to start a war, had one not already been brewing between them.

"I doubt anyone could take your sister's place." Miri felt her claws flex instinctively. "What a shame you are leaving your husband. How unhappy you must be to be alone."

"He will be alone, not me. The man is a pig. I will soon find another." The twist of her smile made clear just whom she intended to find.

Miri smiled with venomous sweetness. "Then perhaps

your next find will not be a pig.'' *But he will be if he's Jordan*, she continued smugly to herself. On closer examination, she could see Willow Song's resemblance to both Smiles at Sunrise and Lake Dancer. But her mouth had a hard curve where Dancer's had been soft and sweet, and the obsidian glitter of her eyes made her look older than her years could possibly be.

The morning did not get any better once the women were on the trail. Miri's pack felt as though it weighed at least as much as she did herself. It was fortunate that at the last moment Smiles at Sunrise had volunteered to carry Jane. The cradle board rested on the older woman's back alongside her other bundles, secured in place by a broad strap fastened to the top of the cradle board and passing around Sunrise's forehead. Miri didn't understand how the woman could look so comfortable with so much weight on her back.

Miri herself was extremely uncomfortable, even though she was carrying less weight than the other two women. Her back ached miserably, the pack straps cut into her shoulders, her body was sweating in a very unladylike manner, her hands and feet were freezing, and the cursed snowshoes that Sunrise had lashed to her feet were more of a hindrance than a help. To make matters worse, she was leading a recalcitrant goat who balked at every step and crow-hopped when she wasn't balking.

Before an hour was out, Miri was so exhausted that her eyes were crossing, as well as her snowshoes. It seemed she could not progress more than five feet before her feet tangled and she went sprawling into the snow. If she landed on her back, which was often the case, she was trapped as helplessly as an overturned turtle until one of the others backtracked to pull her to her feet. If she landed on her front, she invariably got a faceful of snow. The other women were patient. At least, Smiles at Sunrise was patient, and Willow Song refrained from turning her frowns into words at a sharp look from her mother.

At midday, as Sunrise had promised, the women were

met by the three men, who glided soundlessly out of the forest as if they were part of the foliage.

"You are very slow this morning, woman," Smoke Catcher said, frowning at his wife. "We have tracked three miles back from where we expected to meet you."

Sunrise merely smiled in return. "Are we in a hurry, husband? The winter is long."

Miri staggered to the side of the trail and collapsed onto a log. She didn't understand the Chippewa exchange between Sunrise and Smoke Catcher, but it was obvious the woman was being chastised for their tardiness, and it was all Miri's fault. Exhaustion had brought her almost to the point of crying. This was not going to work. They were simply going to have to turn back, or find her a guide back to Michilimackinac. She would gladly turn herself over to Captain Michaels and spend the winter in a nice, civilized prison. Even hanging was better than this.

"Have you spent a pleasant morning?" Jordan's voice cut through Miri's thoughts and made her heart jump alarmingly. Anger, she told herself. There was no other reason for her pulse to flutter so erratically.

He did not wait for an answer, and she didn't offer one. The villain could see for himself how she fared—her clothes were wet, her shoulders slumped. Her face was probably blue by now, Miri thought. The seeping cold almost made her want to start moving again, but her rapidly stiffening muscles protested. Sweet heaven! Had she once boasted to this man that she could do anything a Chippewa woman could do?

Miri kept her eyes on her snowshoes, too tired to lift her head and meet the cold mockery of Jordan's eyes, so it took her by surprise when a small flock of lifeless ducks dropped at her feet. They were bloodied and limp, and looked almost as bad as she felt.

She summoned the energy to lift her head. Her frowning gaze traveled slowly up the length of Jordan's heavy leather leggings, jumped quickly over the area of his breechclout, moved up the muskrat skin that protected his chest, and rested finally on the chiseled features of his face. She marveled that a man who wore only a strip of hair on his scalp could appear so devilishly handsome, and then wondered further when she had begun to think him so. Handsome is as handsome does, Aunt Eliza was fond of saying. What would she say about this villain?

"What are these?" she asked, pointing to the feathered pile at her feet.

"Ducks."

"I know they're ducks, Mr. Scott. Why are they lying upon my snowshoes?"

"Clean them," he ordered curtly. "We can roast them this evening."

That managed to bring Miri to her feet. Almost ignoring the weight on her back and the fractious pulling of Petunia on the lead rope, she bent down, gingerly lifted the dead fowl, and shoved them into Jordan's broad chest. She was in no mood to play the part of a willing slave, even if she had known what to do with the birds, which she didn't.

"Clean them yourself, mighty hunter." With that she gave a yank on Petunia's rope and trudged off to find a place where she could have some peace.

Smiles at Sunrise intervened quickly, taking the ducks from Jordan's arms before he could go in pursuit of Miri. "I will take the ducks, my son. Eyes of the Sky must feed your daughter."

"What did you call her?"

"It is a good name, is it not? Your wife has eyes that are the color of the sky on a clear, moonlit night." She smiled winningly, trying to cajole him from his evil mood. "Or perhaps men do not notice such things."

Jordan's gaze followed Miri as she tethered Petunia to a tree, then fetched Jane's cradle board from Sunrise's pack and propped it against a log. The look on his face told the Indian woman that he had indeed noticed the color of Miri's eyes, and much more. She nodded in satisfaction.

"Tonight I will show your wife how to boil duck with vegetables, just as you like it. You will be pleased."

Refusing to be discouraged by Jordan's skeptical snort, she fetched a bone knife from her pack and set about gutting and plucking the fowl, eating her noon meal of parched corn and dried venison strips as she worked.

She was shortly joined by Smoke Catcher, who regarded her task with detached interest.

"Eyes of a Ghost is having trouble with his new wife," he finally commented. "He means to teach her our ways, and yet you interfere." He gestured to the ducks.

Sunrise shook her head. "Eyes of the Sky is not of the Anishanabe. It is hard for her. But she is a good woman. She will learn, if Eyes of a Ghost will let her." She frowned at the two of them—Jordan moodily slicing strips off his dried meat while his eyes followed Miri's every move; Miri making a great effort not to meet Jordan's brooding gaze. "Our son is unwise where this woman is concerned. Something about her drives him to foolishness."

Smoke Catcher nodded agreement. "She is a troublesome woman." He looked at his wife, and his eyes crinkled in silent laughter. "In the days when we were first together, my wife, a woman who showed disrespect to her husband was rewarded with a sound beating."

Smiles at Sunrise gave him a loving smile. "Is that so, husband? I think your memory plays tricks on you. If you had ever treated me the way Eyes of a Ghost treats his new wife, you would have had no wigwam to keep you warm, and the part you sit on would have been bruised with the mark of my foot."

"Ho! Perhaps I should warn our son that you are instructing his wife in such unseemly ways."

"Eyes of the Sky will find ways of her own," Sunrise assured him happily. "And as for our son, at first I wondered why he married the girl so soon after our Lake Dancer was taken. But when I see him watching her, then I know. He fights against giving his heart, but he has already given it. Now he acts like a child, but soon he will be a man again."

Smoke Catcher snorted contemptuously. "Women and your matters of the heart. You give men no peace. If you must do your new daughter's chores for her, then do them. We must cover more distance this day."

The Chippewa woman merely smiled at his blustering, for she could see the same affection in his eyes that had been there for thirty years.

The noon rest was only a brief respite, but it was long enough for Miri's muscles to stiffen. When she once again set upon the trail, she found herself more awkward than ever. The snowshoes were impossible to maneuver, Petunia was more stubborn with every step she took through the snow, and the pack on Miri's back seemed balanced precisely to topple her from her feet at the slightest misstep. On top of it all, she was tired, the dried venison and parched corn had done little to appease her hunger, and Jordan—curse the man!—had taken half of Sunrise's pack on his own back but had lightened Miri's not at all.

The pace was faster now that the men had joined them, and only a few minutes passed before Miri's legs throbbed. Her snowshoes crossed, and Miri planted her face in the snow as she had done so many times that morning.

Jordan glanced back, but made no move to help. Miri thought she detected a gleam of amusement in those silver-gray eyes, and she cursed the day she had ever bragged about her ability to take care of herself. Perhaps if she had fluttered her lashes and played the helpless female she would have inspired Jordan to gallantry, or at least to some decent consideration.

Miri struggled to her feet and gave Jordan a venomous look. Someday, she promised herself, she would think of a way to make him as miserable as he was making her.

Five minutes later she fell again, and again ten feet farther on, and then in five feet. This last time she made no attempt to get up. Tears overflowed her eyes and streamed down her windburned cheeks. She would stay rooted to the ground and freeze, she swore, before she would take another step on these cursed snowshoes or haul this pack another foot. Then Jordan's moccasins crunched the snow in front of her face.

"You're just not good for much of anything, are you? You can't cook, you can't sew, you can't handle a canoe, or keep a man warm at night. And now it seems you can't even walk."

"Damn you, Jordan Scott!"

He shook his head. "Indecent language, as well. Who would have thought such a proper English lady would be brought to such straits?"

Fury would have brought Miri to her feet if she'd had the strength. As it was, she struggled to her knees.

"We've got a long walk ahead of us, and we can't always be waiting on your clumsiness. Sunrise has leggings and a tunic that belonged to Dancer. Put them on. You'll find it easier to walk without those ridiculous skirts pulling at your legs."

"I will not!" she declared, her voice trembling. "I am not an Indian woman, to wear such savage attire!" She focused straight ahead. It was much easier, she discovered, to shout at Jordan's knees, which were at her eye level, than to deal with that arrogant face and those mocking silver eyes. She only wished the tears would stop flowing. How satisfied he must be to see her cry. "I am a civilized woman. And civilized women do not clean dead birds, carry packs that would stagger a mule, cook over open fires, or deal with stubborn goats."

"Then civilized women are not much use, are they?"

Miri's fury was gaining ground over her tears. "I suppose that depends on how you intend to use them. I am not a packhorse, or a servant, or some wanton jade to warm your bed at night. I am..."

"A civilized woman," he supplied with lazy amusement. "You are so civilized, Miss Sutcliffe, that you are nearly inhuman."

Miri's eyes finally left Jordan's knees and traveled up to his face. "At least, Mr. Scott, I'm not subhuman."

Jordan stared for a moment at the little vixen, then smiled a smile that would make most men tread with caution if they saw it. He had to give the witch credit. Bedraggled, exhausted, and limp with discouragement, she still could slice a man's gut with her tongue. But he'd had enough of her mulish childishness. Be damned if he hadn't!

Abruptly, he turned on his heel and strode over to where the others were watching with interest. He spoke a few words to Smiles at Sunrise, who nodded, set down her pack, and pulled out the clothing she had earlier offered to Miri. With the look of a man going into battle, Jordan walked back to Miri and threw the buckskin in front of her.

"Put those on."

"Put them on yourself," Miri shot back, ignoring the warning in his eyes. "I always thought you should wear more clothes."

Jordan moved before Miri could defend herself. He ripped off her pack, picked up the buckskin with one hand, and pulled her roughly to her feet with the other.

"Last chance," he warned, holding the Indian attire before her face.

In answer, Miri pulled one foot out of its snowshoe webbing and landed a hefty kick to his shin.

"You asked for it!" He got a good deal of satisfaction out of the look on her face as he lifted her off the ground and tucked her under his arm. With Dancer's clothes under one arm and a struggling, shrieking she-cat under the other, he headed for the concealing foliage. Behind him, Smoke Catcher and Smiles at Sunrise looked at each other in amused understanding.

Miri's snowshoes were left where she had been standing, and her moccasins flew off her furiously kicking feet before Jordan had carried her three strides. But Jordan had a more complete undressing in mind once they had reached the privacy of the thick trees. He had performed this service once before for this brattish hellion, but then it had not given him so much pleasure to hear her shriek.

"Hold still, damn you!"

He dumped her onto the ground, then pinned her by sitting astride her hips. His enjoyment of her struggles must have shown on his face, because the flush of anger on her cheeks turned to a crimson stain of mortification. She promptly became still.

"You are a monster," she snarled, slapping futilely at his hands as he deftly unfastened the tiny buttons of her bodice.

"And you are a brat." He smiled malignantly. "If you refuse to dress yourself in sensible clothes, someone must do it for you."

As her bodice was peeled down, then her chemise, she struggled to cover herself with her arms.

"Don't bother," he said. "I've seen everything you have to offer, if you'll remember. It didn't move me then, and I doubt it's more interesting now." It was a whopping lie, he acknowledged, for the perfect contours of her breasts, the rosy nipples puckered with cold, the silky smoothness of her skin, had started a throbbing in his groin. But the outrage his denial brought to her face was worth the struggle.

He jerked the buckskin tunic over her head, pinning her arms. Then he yanked off the ridiculous lacy pantalets, along with her skirts. His hand landed on a shapely bare thigh, and the throbbing in his groin became a painful ache.

At the feel of Jordan's caldused hand sliding down her leg, Miri screamed. She finally won her struggle to put her arms through the sleeves of the tunic, and promptly attacked her assailant with her nails.

Jordan fended off the attack with ease, ending her struggles by sitting on her once again and pinning her shoulders with his hands.

"Behave yourself, woman, or I'll give you more than your clothes to scream about."

Miri's eyes grew wide. She saw the look in his eyes. The same look had been there the night he had kissed her, but this time he wasn't drunk and foolish. This time he was angry and very, very serious. Tears overflowed her eyes once again, and suddenly, nonsensically, the whole terrible day struck her as funny. She giggled, then laughed outright, and the laughter wouldn't stop. She laughed and cried with the same breath, unable to stop.

"Shut up, dammit!" Jordan shook her, and she only laughed harder. "Damn you, have you gone mad?"

She tossed her head from side to side. Jordan didn't know if she was shaking her head no, or struggling with hysteria. He guessed hysteria, and ended it the best way he knew how, by holding her head and covering her mouth with his own.

Her lips were hot and tasted of salty tears. And they were sweet—so sweet. Her breasts pushed against his chest, her hips ground into his groin. The reason for the kiss, the reason for even sitting there on top of a woman in the middle of a snowy forest, faded away, scorched out of his mind by raw need. When she stopped pushing against him and wound her arms around his waist, he stretched out his full length on top of her, entwined her bare legs with his, and pressed against her until the ache in his groin became a swelling explosion of desire.

Miri's moan brought Jordan to his senses—just barely. Gasping for breath and sanity, he pulled away. The Englishwoman's eyes were filled with both wonder and fear. Lord! The woman didn't know what power she held within her. Beneath that staid exterior a living, breathing siren struggled to break free. Jordan was of a mind to help her break her bonds. He lowered his mouth to the wildly racing pulse in her throat, then moved once again to her lips.

"No." Her mouth formed the word against his.

Her face showed the struggle; the staid and proper prig was beating down the fledgling newcomer. "Get off me. Please."

The sudden vulnerability in her face made Jordan relent. He got up, untangled his legs from hers, and pulled the tunic down over her hips. At this last gesture Miri closed her eyes. When they opened again, the soft, yielding woman that Jordan had glimpsed had been banished. With a quickness that startled him, she brought her hand up and dealt Jordan's face a resounding slap.

Anger doused the last of his passion. He caught her hand as she attempted to repeat her feat. "If you ever do that again, you little witch, I'll teach you just how far a man can be pushed, and what happens when he's pushed too far. Do you understand?''

Miri's eyes were glassy, her lips set in a grim line. He rose to his feet and pulled her up beside him.

''Now put on those leggings, unless you want everyone to be looking at your bare ass for the rest of the trip.''

He didn't stay to see her outrage. He'd had enough of Miriam Sutcliffe for one day. The fact of the matter was, he'd had entirely too much.

Captain Gerald Michaels drummed restless fingers on his desk as he read the reports of the men he had sent to inquire after Miriam Sutcliffe. The results were as he had expected. Along the traders' route to Montreal, no one had seen or heard of a young auburn-haired Englishwoman traveling toward the east. There were a few voyageurs who remembered her journey west at the beginning of the summer, and a few Indians who recalled two white women traveling with a canoe brigade that had stopped in their villages. But no one had seen a white woman traveling east.

It was just as he had thought, Michaels mused. The searchers had so far covered only the area around the North Channel. They would continue on to Montreal, but Michaels suspected they would find nothing.

The captain rose and opened the door into the anteroom that adjoined his office. ''Lieutenant Renquist, may I speak with you a moment, please?''

''Yes, sir.''

Seated once more at his desk, Michaels studied his second in command. The man was far from being an ideal officer. He had a hasty temper and a regrettable lack of judgment. But he was the only officer who could be spared for the mission Michaels had in mind.

''It seems that Miriam Sutcliffe has evaded us once again, Lieutenant. The canoe brigade that came in this morning carried preliminary reports from Jones and Hawkins. No one has seen her, or heard of anyone else seeing her. I think our little dove did not fly off toward the east, as we were told."

"I could have told you that woman was lying, sir."

Michaels fixed the lieutenant with a cold, gray stare. He didn't like hearing Grace Peavey referred to as "that woman," especially in the tone that Renquist used.

"We are not discussing the Widow Peavey, Lieutenant. We are discussing Miriam Sutcliffe, who may or may not herself be an innocent, but who is certainly the key to finding Hamilton Greer. Why else would she be here in America unless she came to meet her betrothed? If we find the girl, then through her we will find the traitor."

"Yes, sir."

"I have given the matter some thought and have decided that if she did not flee to Montreal, then the only other possibility is Jordan Scott."

"Scott? That arrogant fellow who roams with Smoke Catcher and his band?"

"Yes. As you say, the girl was staying with the Widow Peavey, who appears to be quite fond of her. I've been told that the widow is great friends with this white Indian fellow, and it seems logical that she may have convinced the man to offer Miss Sutcliffe his protection. A Chippewa winter hunting camp would be an ideal place to hide a fugitive. Don't you agree?"

Renquist's brows puckered in annoyance. "I doubt the lady would have been so desperate as to put herself in Scott's hands, sir. After all, she is an English gentlewoman."

Michaels cocked a dubious eye at the warmth of Renquist's tone. "Miss Sutcliffe is quite an unusual specimen of English womanhood, Lieutenant. I wouldn't put it past the lady to strike an alliance with the devil himself to spite me."

"I think you do Miss Sutcliffe an injustice, sir."

"Hm," Michaels grunted impatiently. He was not interested in his lieutenant's amours, if that was what was involved here. He was only interested in doing his duty by finding Hamilton Greer. "Whatever, Lieutenant. I am convinced that Miss Sutcliffe is with the Chippewa."

In truth, he had put the question directly to Grace Peavey when he had last called upon the pretty widow—quite amazing, he thought, how calling at the Peavey farm had so rapidly become a habit. The widow, of course, had answered in the negative, but she was an incompetent liar. The truth had been in her eyes.

"You will take three troopers and track Scott and his band to their winter camp. They should only have about a week's start on you, and since they're traveling with women, you should catch them easily enough. I want you to take Miss Sutcliffe without offending our Indian friends, and she is to receive every courtesy on your journey back. As you say, she is an English gentlewoman. Do you understand?"

"I understand, sir."

"And make no mistake about it, Lieutenant. That Scott fellow is a dangerous man. From what I've heard, he's lived with those savages for ten years or more, and he's respected as a cunning fighter even among the Indians. Don't underestimate your foe, man. I want this done quickly and cleanly, without a lot of fuss."

"You'll have it, sir."

Michaels watched skeptically as the lieutenant left. He wished he could undertake the mission himself. But Renquist was a British officer, after all. He would get the job done and bring the girl back safe and sound.

The captain shuffled once more through the reports, then filed them neatly away, leaving his desk as ordered as it always was. He would be glad when this whole affair was over. It went against the grain to pursue a woman in this manner, but Hamilton Greer was important, and those damned names he had copied were even more important. And the girl was the key. Providence—embodied in the British high command—had sent him to the very place the two of them had fled. And Michaels was bound by both duty and honor to pursue the matter to the end.

He wondered how he would explain things to Grace

Peavey once he had Miss Sutcliffe in custody. The widow seemed damnably fond of the chit. Michaels sighed, thinking of the row that was likely to ensue. Now he knew why he had never married. How did a soldier explain duty to a woman?

✳ 11 ✳

Thanks to Miri, the trip to the family's winter hunting grounds, which usually took seven days, took ten. The Chippewa were patient as she stumbled along behind them. Day by day they all watched her struggle. Smoke Catcher and Rides the Waves kept close watch that she was always within range of their protection. Sunrise watched with growing respect, Willow Song with sullen resentment. But no one watched more closely than Jordan.

That first afternoon, Miri stumbled along in her newly donned buckskin garb, her mouth set in a determined scowl and her face coloring crimson every time she glanced at Jordan. Without long skirts to hamper her legs, her stride became more rhythmic and balanced, but she still fell with a regularity that became monotonous.

Halfway through the afternoon Willow Song, with one eye cocked toward Jordan, helped Miri to her feet after a particularly spectacular tumble into the snow. "I will take your pack," the Chippewa girl offered. "I am strong and can carry your load along with mine. Then perhaps you will not go so slowly."

Miri pulled her arm out of Willow Song's solicitous grasp. "No, thank you," she replied in a chilly tone. "I can manage."

Willow Song gave a pitying shake of her head, then

shrugged. Maneuvering her snowshoes with an expert flair and moving as though the burden on her back were a mere feather, she returned to her brother's side.

"You put on a good show," Rides the Waves commented with a wry smile.

Willow Song shrugged. "The woman is a weakling, and she knows nothing about how to please a man. Soon Eyes of a Ghost will send her back to her people and come to my wigwam."

Rides the Waves chuckled. "Do not count the days, my sister." He looked at Jordan and noted that his friend's eyes were fixed firmly on the small figure that struggled at the back of the line. "Sometimes a woman does not have to know how to please a man; she simply does. Our brother is like a trout who has taken the bait and does not yet feel the hook." The stocky Chippewa smiled and shook his head. "But soon he will feel it, Willow. Soon."

Rides the Waves was close to being right, for if Jordan hadn't yet grabbed the bait, at least he was watching it very closely. He was a silent observer as Miri gritted her teeth and accepted her lot. Inch by painful inch she conquered her snowshoes and forced her weary back to straighten under its burden of clothes, food, and bulrush mats. Dragging at the end of each day, she nevertheless helped the other women prepare the evening meal from whatever game the men provided. Her face screwed into a grimace of distaste, she learned from Sunrise how to skin a rabbit and pluck a duck, how to clean a fish and roast it between two platters of bark, and how to construct a crude shelter of branches and saplings to protect her and her "husband" from the cold night. And though Willow Song frequently laughed at her lack of skill, Miri doggedly persisted.

At the same time, she managed somehow to give Jane the care that she needed. Though Sunrise took on the burden of carrying the baby and the cradle board, Miri diligently kept the infant clean, fed, warmed, and loved. No child could have had a more doting mother, and no natural mother could have looked upon a baby with more love. The look on

Miri's face whenever she fed his daughter made Jordan more than a little uncomfortable. The truth was, a number of things about the Englishwoman were beginning to make Jordan feel that he had fallen into a hole and was in so deep he would never dig his way out.

Miriam Sutcliffe was not quite what Jordan had first thought her. After a week on the trail he was ready to admit that Lake Dancer had been right. There was something more to the girl than a stiff-backed English prig. Miriam Sutcliffe might have an uncomfortable obsession with right and proper behavior, but she at least had grit—and the honesty of her convictions. She also possessed a feminine appeal that was impossible to deny—the kind that sets its hooks into a man and won't let go. What Jordan had believed was a piece of irritating fluff was turning out to have the tenacity of a cockleburr.

It miffed Jordan that Miri did not whine, as he had predicted, and scarcely even spoke. And when she did, it certainly wasn't to him. She had given him only monosyllables since that first day when he had physically enforced his will about her clothing. And her rare glances his way were swift and furtive, laden with emotion he couldn't read. At night she lay stiffly on the edge of their bedding, hugging Jane close to her warmth and giving Jordan her back. Her quiet rejection stung. It was Jordan's privilege to reject. He was the one put upon; she was the intruder. What right did she have to suffer in silent martyrdom?

Of course, Jordan admitted, the little twit wouldn't be such a martyr if he himself weren't acting like a bee-stung bear. Tired of their silent battle and willing to admit he had been wrong about some things, at least, Jordan decided to be generous and apologize.

It didn't occur to Jordan that it was not up to him to call off the war. The evening he presented his much-rehearsed apology offering friendship in place of battle, he discovered that Miss Miriam Sutcliffe was in no mood to be friends with anyone, least of all Jordan Scott.

"It's very manful of you to admit you've been acting the

fool,'' Miri replied icily to Jordan's carefully worded peace offering. "Because you certainly have. But I think any friendship between us is straining the limits of possibility."

The tiny fire that glowed in front of the lean-to etched Miri's features in stark relief. There were deep shadows under her eyes, and lines of weariness creased her brow. She seemed almost as listless as the baby she held in her arms.

Jordan was determined to be patient. He folded himself into a cross-legged position by the fire. "I didn't say I acted the fool. I simply admitted that I've been wrong to treat you as I have. I was making you the whipping boy for something that happened a long time ago, and that was unfair. An apology is in order."

"I should say!" Miri seconded. "You've been boorish and childish and . . . and downright brutal, if you must know. I never expected that you would be a gentleman, but your behavior gives new meaning to the word *scoundrel*."

Jordan expelled a long, slow breath. "For a woman who lays such claim to gentility, you are an accomplished shrew, Miss Sutcliffe." Damn the woman! How could she sit there with her sweet Madonna's face and be such a witch? "If my behavior has been so poor, what would you call yours?"

"My behavior has been above reproach," she shot back. "I have done more than anyone could reasonably have expected of me."

"Yes," he agreed sardonically. "And done it like a martyred saint. What do you suppose would happen if your plaster mask of righteousness ever slipped? Is there someone behind it? A real human being, perhaps? Fallible and imperfect and only marginally better than the beasts, just like the rest of us?"

Miri's flinch gave him satisfaction. Jordan had come offering the olive branch of peace, and she had waved a thornbush in his face. He felt justified in being mad.

"Admitting that you are marginally better than a beast may be an insult to the beast, Mr. Scott. At least an animal has an excuse for his lack of decency."

"I don't make excuses for myself, Miss Sutcliffe. I'm a

bastard and a savage, and I'm perfectly comfortable with what I am. What about you? Can you say the same?''

"I certainly don't have to answer to you for what I am!''

"I doubt you can answer! To anyone. Do you even know what you are?''

"I—''

"I'll tell you what you are. You're a narrow-minded, hidebound little prig whose only use is to decorate some man's drawing room. No doubt you'd do very well in Boston, or London, or some other place where females are expected to be of no damned use. But Grace should have known better than to think you could pull your weight in a place like this. And I should have known better than to let you try, dammit!''

So much for apologies and friendship. The woman was as impossible as she was irresistible. Jordan shifted uncomfortably. His groin had started to ache the minute he saw her. Damned if the woman didn't inspire him to lust even when she was being a witch!

Miri raked him with a look of pure contempt, then laid Jane on the bedding and covered her with a thick layer of trade blankets. "I think I have proven my adaptability,'' she said in a cool voice. "I do everything the other women do.''

Jordan's mouth twisted into a mocking smile. "Oh, yes. And you do it so well. You can't plant one foot in front of the other without falling, your attempts at building a shelter have twice collapsed around our ears in the middle of the night, and you have yet to learn that wild onions must be peeled before they can be used in a stew. The only thing you might possibly be good at, Miss Sutcliffe, is warming a man's bed. And I can't imagine you'd be much good at that, either.''

Miri's eyes grew wide with fury. Point scored, Jordan beat a strategic retreat from the lean-to while she still stuttered over a reply. The cold night air didn't cool his anger, and he strode away from the camp to vent his mood upon the forest.

Damn the woman anyway! He had gone to her with an

honest apology and offer of friendship, and she had called him a fool and a beast. He should show her what a beast really was—prove her judgment right by throwing her down and having her again and again until the little bitch was out of his blood. Maybe that was what he should have done so long ago in Boston to a certain prim and proper lady whose coy little invitations and subtle touches had set a bastard to dreaming of marriage and respectability, and all the while she had simply been playing the jealousy game against another suitor of much more impeccable pedigree.

Jordan was itching to hit something, hard and repeatedly, when his ear caught the evidence he was being followed. He slowed, dropped his hand toward the knife at his hip, and poised himself to spring as the pursuer came closer.

"Eyes of a Ghost," a soft voice came from the darkness behind him. "It is I, Willow Song."

Shit and damn! All he needed now was another female to deal with!

"I saw you leave the camp," Willow Song explained. "You looked upset, my brother. I was concerned."

"Go back to camp, Willow Song."

"You are upset," she confirmed, a hint of satisfaction in her voice. "The white woman is wrong to trouble you so."

"She does not trouble me."

Willow Song laid a gentle hand upon Jordan's arm. "She troubles you, my brother. She is weak and ignorant and knows nothing of life—or of men. Why do you bother with her? You must know that I will come to you willingly. I have always held you above all other men in my heart. Did you not know?"

Jordan firmly removed Willow's hand. "You are my sister," he said impatiently. "You have always been my sister, and it can be no other way. Go back to the camp. We will speak no more of this."

The Chippewa girl was not to be put off. "Do not send me away. You cannot know how long I have loved you. While your favor fell upon my sister, I was silent. But now you will hear me. I am a good woman. I am young, and my body is pleasing. I can bear you healthy children, make your clothing, cook your meals, and build a shelter that will stand before the wind. And I can fill your nights with pleasure. You have admitted to me that the white-faced, sharp-tongued weakling is not really your wife. You have not chosen her. Choose me."

If he'd had a choice right at that moment, Jordan would have consigned all females to perdition—Willow Song and Miriam Sutcliffe included. "Go back to camp, Willow Song."

He turned and walked onward, determined to be alone.

"No!" The Chippewa girl leapt in front of him and grasped his shoulders. "You want me. I can feel it. I can smell your lust, Eyes of a Ghost." Her knowledgeable hands swept down his chest and abdomen and found evidence for her words in the swelling at his groin. "She sends you away still wanting. I will give you what you need." Willow Song pressed her body closer and slithered downward until her lips rested at his crotch and her hands clutched at his buttocks.

Her warm breath added fuel to an unwanted fire that had begun in the lean-to, but it wasn't Willow Song that Jordan wanted. With an impatient groan he pushed her away.

"I'm sorry, Willow. I wish it was you that I wanted, but it isn't."

Still on her knees, Willow Song reached out to hold Jordan back, but her hand came away only with the beaded band that gathered his leggings at the knee. As he disappeared into the darkness, she clutched the knee band next to her heart.

Miri spent a sleepless night listening for Jordan's return. Jane's warm little body was snuggled close in her arms. Dry cedar boughs kept them from the cold of the ground, and trade blankets and furs were piled high over the bedding, but still Miri was cold.

She had never been so tired in her life. Every muscle ached; every bone felt as if it were broken, or at least bruised. And to top it all off, she had dirt under her fingernails and embedded in her skin, her closely guarded complexion was raw and chafed from the icy wind, and her scalp itched—actually itched!—from lack of washing.

She felt as if she had been thrown into quicksand and was sinking fast. Every day of this miserable journey the world had grown lonelier, until now that loneliness was a knife cutting into her breast. And that beast of a man had the effrontery to accuse her of being a narrow-minded prig—a useless piece of decoration that no man would want. She had wanted to scream at him, hit him, hurt him—and then prove to him that she was a warm-blooded woman who could have a man begging at her feet if she pleased.

To add to the misery, the loneliness, and the discomfort, Jordan Scott's undeniable attraction was eating into Miri's heart like acid. The man was a renegade, a self-made barbarian, a blackguard of the lowest order. He treated her abominably, despised everything she admired, embodied everything she held in contempt. But something in the arch of his brow, the mystery of his eyes, the generous curve of his lips, the small dimple that dented his chin; something in the way he laughed with Rides the Waves, smiled at Sunrise, and worried over the baby—something in all that tugged irresistibly at her heart. It was not an organ inclined to good sense or reason, it seemed.

Miri shifted restlessly under the pile of covers. Jordan wasn't going to come back this night, she decided. There was no reason why he should. He'd made an attempt at apology and friendship, and she had acted the witch, like the spoiled and pampered female he said she was. He wanted to be friends, he'd said, and that had frightened her into pushing him away. Better to remain foes, and he would never see past the wall of her anger to the vulnerability that lurked below.

No doubt he had run to his Willow Song and was even now finding comfort in her supple brown body. Miri pictured him folding the Chippewa girl in the cage of his strong arms, his beautifully curved mouth meeting hers in raw and desperate passion. Be glad, Miri told herself. If it weren't for Willow Song, the uncouth barbarian might be forcing his attentions elsewhere. Even now, Miri might be the one feeling his weight press her to the ground, feeling his big hands move under her clothing, warming—nay, burning her flesh with his touch. Be glad, she repeated until it became a litany. Be glad he's with Willow Song, not with Miriam Sutcliffe.

Unable to follow her own advice, Miri turned her face into the bedding and wept.

For three more days the little group traveled south along the eastern shore of Lake Michigan. At the sandy hills that marked the mouth of the Aux Sables River they turned inland, and after a day's walk upriver they made permanent camp. The women cut saplings of ironwood, drove them into the ground, and tied them together in arching frameworks for two wigwams—a large one for Smoke Catcher, Sunrise, and family, and a smaller one for Jordan and Miri. Each dwelling was completed by spreading a double layer of bulrush mats over the framework and covering the domed top with sheets of birchbark.

By the time the evening shadows had merged into dusk, two sturdy shelters stood in the little clearing not far from the river. In the middle of the clearing, a large central fire pit had been outlined with stones, and Sunrise and Miri were putting the last touches on a small hut that would be used for food storage.

Miri straightened and stretched the muscles of her back. She was tired, but not as exhausted as when she had first started this journey. Her muscles had hardened, and her hands had sprouted calluses. Most unladylike, but there was a certain satisfaction in the new suppleness and strength. She remembered Jordan's remark that she hadn't a muscle in her entire body. He certainly couldn't say that now. Not that he'd bothered to notice the changes in her. The daylight hours he spent scouting ahead of their little band, and the nights he spent . . . somewhere. Not with Miri. Probably with Willow Song, for whenever the little hussy glanced

Miri's way she had a smirk of triumph on her face. Miri told herself that she didn't care, but she knew that she lied.

By nightfall all the chores were done. Miri sat at the central fire with Smiles at Sunrise, who had been tutoring her for the last week in the Chippewa language. She was learning fast, and could already carry on a stilted conversation, as long as the right subjects were discussed. She was also becoming competent at weaving, beadwork, and recognizing wild herbs. While her wigwam building that afternoon had required considerable assistance from Sunrise, the evening's rabbit stew had been entirely Miri's doing, and everyone had eaten it with gusto.

It wasn't that she wanted Jordan Scott to eat his words, Miri explained to a sympathetic Sunrise. She wouldn't be so childish. But just let the villain say at the end of the winter that she could pull her own weight! Just let him!

Soon after dark Miri retired to the dwelling that she'd built with her own hands. After all that effort, she couldn't have been prouder than if she were laying her bedding out in a palace. Wearily, she milked Petunia, who had been much more cooperative since the second day of the journey, when Jordan had relented and taken the recalcitrant goat up on his shoulders during their treks through the snow. Jane finished off a good portion of her cup of milk, and even though the infant spit out the fish broth that Sunrise had provided, Miri had to be content that at least she was eating something. There had been days during the journey when she wouldn't eat at all.

Miri wrapped the baby in a blanket and crawled with her beneath the blankets and furs of her own bedding. The bed of fragrant cedar boughs was beginning to feel comfortable, and Miri admitted to herself that her buckskin tunic and leggings, so warm and unrestricting, were much more practical than the woolen dresses still packed away in her little bundle. Scandalous attire, of course, but practical all the same.

The night settled in around her as the little fire flickered and faded to a mere glow. Miri fell asleep trying not to think of where Jordan was this night.

Lieutenant George Renquist was enjoying his mission. Following Captain Michaels's orders, he and three men had trailed Jordan Scott's little band of Chippewa until they finally came within sight of the group a day's journey north of the Aux Sables River. They had been easy to track, for they were traveling slowly and making no attempt to cover their trail. The renegade no doubt had thought he'd taken the prize with no one any the wiser. He was about to discover, the lieutenant mused with satisfaction, that the British army had a sharper wit than he believed.

Renquist had been reluctant to believe that Miriam Sutcliffe would lower herself to take such a route of escape. She was a lady through and through. Disgruntled as he had been after having made a fool of himself in front of her, the lieutenant still admitted that she was quality—not like the local colonial upstarts who called themselves Americans and were in reality little better than the savages who had originally inhabited this godforsaken land. Whether or not she was involved in traitorous activities, Miriam Sutcliffe was a breath of refinement straight from civilization.

It had been a bitter blow when he had recognized the lady among the savages. Jordan Scott seemed to have succeeded where George Renquist, heir to a baronetcy and a substantial fortune, had failed. It was a crime, an injustice beyond any excuse, that a baseborn villain like Scott should be able to corrupt an English lady and bring her down to his vulgar level of existence. But the evidence was before his very eyes. It made eventual retribution against Scott an inevitable matter of honor.

Renquist squatted in a prickly spruce thicket and ran his thumb along the edge of his knife.

"That should do," he said, and slid the blade into the sheath at his hip.

"'Scuse me, sir. But you're goin' to take more than that knife, aren't you, sir?"

"I'm not going to shoot anyone, soldier. I'm simply going to abscond with one relatively helpless female, and none of those savages will be the wiser until we're well away from here."

"What about Scott? If I were goin' to tangle with that one, sir, I'd want me more than a knife." The trooper shook his head. He had lived on Michilimackinac for the last five years, serving with the American force before the British had arrived, then pressed into service by the desperately undermanned redcoats. He knew Jordan Scott was not a danger to be dealt with in such a casual fashion.

"I'm not going to deal with Scott tonight, my man. I don't know where the fellow is, but I'm damned sure he's not anywhere near Miss Sutcliffe. He hasn't gone near her for the last two days that we've been watching them. I'll snatch the girl from under his nose, so to speak, and then deal with him in my own good time."

The trooper shrugged. It wasn't his problem if the dimwit officer couldn't tell a wolf from a tame dog. "Suit yourself . . . sir."

"You men stay put," Renquist ordered. "This is a job that calls for a delicate touch. Be ready to move the moment I return with our prisoner. And keep your weapons ready."

Renquist crept toward the encampment with what he thought was admirable stealth. He wished fervently that Scott was in the hut with his prey. It would be a rare satisfaction to demonstrate to the uncouth savage how a real man fought, and an even greater one to feel the steel of his knife slice through the renegade's flesh. Miriam Sutcliffe would be watching, and she would realize what a poor choice she had made in protectors.

Nothing in the encampment moved as Renquist stole silently up to Miri's wigwam. For a moment he lay on his stomach in the crusty snow, listening intently. There was no sound from inside. All evening long he had been able to watch the camp by the light of their central fire, which now glowed in a mound of banked coals. The girl had entered the hut over two hours ago, and no one had followed her. By now she had to be asleep.

With scarcely a rustle the lieutenant drew his knife and cut a long vertical slit in the double layer of bulrush mats that Miri had so painstakingly fastened to her dwelling. Parting the rushes, he slithered through the opening like a noctural snake.

Lying half in and half out of the hut, Renquist oriented himself by the dim red glow of the fire pit coals. By the wigwam door, an animal was folded up in a posture of sleep. Half unpacked bundles were scattered about the mats that covered the dirt floor—obstacles easily avoided. Not ten feet away from where he waited, a heap of blankets and the soft sound of even breathing located the hut's one occupant, the prey that he sought.

It was no great task to creep over to the sleeping figure without waking her. Even when Renquist's hand closed over her mouth and his arm wound around her throat, Miri did not immediately awake. She merely snuggled into the blankets and murmured a softly slurred name. When she finally came to awareness it was much too late. He had her firmly in his grip.

"Mmmmmmph!" was the only objection Miri could get around her attacker's smothering hand.

"Quiet now!" Renquist whispered. "Be a good girl, Miss Sutcliffe, and come without a fuss, or I might have to forget that I'm a gentleman."

Miri struggled like a wild animal as he dragged her from the bed. The wigwam seemed to come alive as Jane woke with a piteous wail and Petunia commented on the action with a string of indignant bleats.

"Christ!" Renquist hissed. "This is a madhouse!"

Miri punctuated his comment by biting down viciously on the hand that covered her mouth.

"You little bitch!" Renquist grunted, but didn't loose his hold. "I'll teach you!"

A stunning blow to the head quieted the lieutenant's uncooperative victim enough for him to drag her through the slit he had made in the wigwam. Praying no one would pay any mind to a fussy baby and noisy goat, he backed away into the dark, still with the weakly struggling girl fast in his grip.

Then a steel band of flesh closed about his throat, and the cold razor steel of a knife pricked at his windpipe.

"Let the girl go," a voice hissed in his ear.

Renquist hastened to obey, and Miri dropped to the ground with a thump.

"Now turn around, friend, so I can get a look at your face."

The lieutenant turned and met the silver steel gaze of Jordan Scott. Even in the dim starlight he could see the menace lurking in those eyes. His hand groped for the hilt of his knife.

"Don't even think it," Jordan warned with a cold smile. In a flash of steel his knife severed Renquist's leather belt, coming within a hairbreadth of slicing flesh, as well. Renquist's weapon plopped into the snow along with the belt, and the lieutenant's breeches sagged halfway down to his crotch.

Renquist's face turned to stone as the renegade's knife paused in front of his face.

"You give your Captain Michaels a message for me, Renquist, old boy."

The lieutenant expelled a cautious breath, his eyes never leaving Jordan's knife.

"You tell him that Miss Miriam Sutcliffe doesn't have what he seeks, and any more of his men I catch within ten miles of her I will personally skin alive and use their hides for moccasins. Understand?"

The knife came closer, lingering in front of Renquist's nose. "I understand," the lieutenant breathed.

Jordan's mouth twisted into an unpleasant smile. "Don't doubt that I mean it, redcoat."

"I don't doubt it a bit." Renquist backed slowly away, holding his hands out from his sides to indicate his lack of weapons. His breeches slipped another inch, and he felt the damned girl's eyes following his every move, probably laughing under her breath. She would pay for this humiliation, and Scott would pay as well, Renquist vowed. He had underestimated the renegade, had mistaken a vicious wolf for a cur dog. Next time he would know better.

"Move!" Jordan twitched the knife, and Renquist jerked. "Before I change my mind."

The lieutenant fled, managing to hold on to his breeches, if not his dignity.

Miri crouched where she had fallen, stunned senses struggling to register what had happened. The feel of Jordan's brooding gaze finally brought her eyes up to meet his. There was a quality in his regard that frightened her more than anything the night had yet brought.

Finally he spoke. His voice was quiet, but his eyes were hot. "Now." The one word vibrated along nerves that were already stretched taut and quivering. Miri flinched as he picked up the British officer's dropped knife and shoved it forcefully back into its sheath. "Now," he repeated in a dark voice. "What am I going to do with you?"

✳ **12** ✳

As Jordan took a step toward her, Miri jerked back. But despite her protest, he scooped her up in his arms and carried her into the wigwam.

"That son of a bitch hurt you," Jordan noted in a tight voice, setting her down upon the bedding. He reached out to gently touch the abrasion where Renquist had hit her.

Miri shivered as his fingers touched her brow. An aura of violence still clung to him. It repelled her, and at the same time appealed to some dark and primitive instinct that tightened her loins in excitement. The wolf with his teeth bared in a snarl was a frightful creature, but she felt a strange fascination at the thought of the teeth being bared in her defense.

She shook her head, driving his fingers away and trying to clear her spinning senses. "He hit me," she answered.

"So I see." His tone gentled once he determined the injury was not serious. "It seems you have lost favor with your suitor, Miss Sutcliffe."

"He's not my suitor, and he never was."

"Is that so? I thought you favored civilized gentlemen."

"Please," Miri begged, dropping her aching head into her hands. "Don't. I'm not in the mood to quarrel."

Jordan gave her a twisted smile. The familiar mocking renegade was back, for the time being, banishing the wolf to the shadows. "Not in the mood to fight, are you? That's a first," he commented approvingly. "Perhaps I should ensure you're hit more often. We would have more peace around here."

Miri refused for once to rise to the bait. She was still quivering with the memory of how Jordan had looked as he had held the unfortunate Renquist in his grip. "You wouldn't really skin anyone alive, would you?"

For a frightening moment, as Jordan's eyes met hers, the wolf returned. Then Jordan chuckled, dispelling the illusion. "I doubt I'd go to the trouble. It would be a messy job, at best."

"What did you mean—asking what should you do with me?"

Jordan turned away, seeming to ignore her question while he stoked the fire pit coals into flame. When he finally turned back, the silver-gray eyes regarded her with unnerving speculation.

"What should I do with you?" he asked. "Now that Michaels knows where you are, Grace's little plan is revealed. Once the winter sets in, you'll be safe enough here, but come spring he'll be waiting for you at the island. No doubt he'll be waiting for both of us."

"Oh." Miri had gotten a different feeling entirely when

the question had first been asked. He had looked ready to pounce, to devour. Her imagination, surely. "Don't concern yourself, Mr. Scott. I begged your protection for the winter only. By the time spring comes I will have thought of a way to help myself, you can be sure."

"Knowing you, Miss Sutcliffe, I have no doubts on that score."

Jane whimpered feebly, and Miri turned her attention from the suddenly too penetrating silver-gray eyes. The intensity of his gaze seemed to press in on her as she adjusted the baby's blanket.

"I'll go now," Jordan told her as she turned toward him again.

"No!" Her hand reached out in a tentative gesture to stop him. "Jordan . . . Mr. Scott. I confess this night has given me a fright. I would rather you stayed."

Before she could draw back her restraining hand, Jordan grasped it in a gentle but unbreakable vise.

"Are you so frightened?" His voice was husky. It had a tautness that unnerved her.

Suddenly Miri was very afraid—of Jordan, of herself, of the queer spasms that were rippling out from her very core. Fear of Renquist and Michaels faded before this new onslaught.

"I'll stay if you ask it, Miss Sutcliffe." Jordan's hand tightened around hers. "But I give fair warning. If you bid me stay, I'll be sleeping beside you on that bed, and no priggishness of yours will keep me from you on this night. You ask too much of any man."

For a moment Miri couldn't breathe. Blood thundered in her ears as the silence stretched. Two people seemed to inhabit her body—the proper lady, horrified at the animal intensity that had suddenly sprung to life between them, and the fascinated wanton, longing to move into Jordan's embrace, press against him, exult in the power and fire she saw waiting in his eyes, his mouth, his tautly poised body.

The wanton had eons of female instinct on her side. But they were not enough to combat the chains that had bound Miri all her life, or to dampen the fear of the frighteningly potent urges that were erupting in her body. The chains held; the fear triumphed.

Jordan saw the sudden shuttering of Miri's eyes. He released her hand, turned, and walked out, leaving Miri with a hollow, aching emptiness in her heart.

The morning light did not disperse Miri's feeling that she was a ship that had slipped its mooring. The values that had anchored her life were wavering, and she no longer knew the person she had become. But the morning soon presented mundane problems that shoved Miri's philosophical struggles to the background.

Jordan and Rides the Waves had left before the sun had risen. They would not return, Sunrise told Miri, until they had set their trap lines and brought down enough game to see the family through the first part of the winter. While they were gone, it was the women's job to set the camp in order—to build the log storehouse for tools and extra clothing, to erect the hut that would contain the common food supply, to reinforce the dwellings against the cold winds soon to come.

There were more than enough chores to keep three women busy. A large rack for drying meat was built and set over the central fire pit, and smaller racks constructed for inside the wigwams. Smiles at Sunrise and Willow Song both set up frames for weaving new rush mats to replace the ones that had become stained and grimy. Miri was sent out to hunt for long thorns that could be used for sewing needles once the men had provided enough hides to replace and refurbish the family's winter clothing.

There were many tasks to learn, many concerns to divert Miri's mind from her own uncertainties—and from nagging thoughts of why Jordan had left without a single word.

Jordan was also well occupied. Together, he and Rides the Waves searched out the best sites to lay their trap lines, carefully assessing the movement and abundance of game. It was going to be a good winter, for already the beaver, muskrat, rabbit, mink, and otter sported heavy fur, and their coats would grow thicker as the weather got colder. Moose, deer, and elk were numerous and fat, and the men spotted two large bears as well, noted their territory, and spied out the most likely lairs for the animals to hibernate.

But Jordan was not so well occupied that his thoughts did not stray back to the camp on the Aux Sables, and the troublesome woman with whom he'd been saddled for the rest of the winter. Even in the refuge of the cold, clean forest the Englishwoman followed him, dogging both his waking and sleeping hours like a persistent nightmare or a dream—he couldn't decide which.

Rides the Waves noticed Jordan's preoccupation and guessed its cause.

"You make your bed at night outside your wigwam on the forest floor," the stocky warrior commented one night as they both sat listening to the forest silence and watching the bright band of stars that girdled the sky. "What is there about this white woman that drives you from your own dwelling?"

The Chippewa's words were sober, but his eyes crinkled with silent amusement. Jordan looked at him with ill-tempered suspicion.

"I leave to have some peace for myself. The woman is a temptation to madness."

Waves smiled and nodded. "Every woman is a temptation to madness."

Miriam Sutcliffe stole into Jordan's mind and smiled that impish smile that occasionally managed to break through her shell of sober propriety. Her cap of auburn curls glistened in the autumn sunlight, and the smooth sheen of her skin put the finest silk to shame.

"This one certainly is," Jordan growled. "And if I spend any more time in that wigwam I'll be on top of her, whether she wants it or not. Then she'll hang my hide out to dry, and Grace Peavey will help her."

Waves poked at the fire with a stick, rearranging the coals in aimless fashion. "I cannot see why it would be so, my brother. Every woman needs a strong man to protect her, give her children, and fill her bed. I have seen Eyes of the

Sky look at you with a woman's needs plain upon her face. She should welcome you into her body."

Jordan snorted. "Proper white women have their own notions about such things."

Especially this white woman, Jordan brooded. How many times had he been the target of blue eyes narrowed in disapproval, glinting with indignation? And how many lectures on morality, responsibility, and decorum had she treated him to since he'd first had the misfortune to cross her path? The woman was a bundle of contradictions. That sweet smile hid a shrewish tongue, and stiff propriety bottled up a jumble of hidden passions. If those passions ever burst free, she would no doubt die of pure fright.

"White women are strange creatures," Waves agreed. "A wise man would stay away from this one." He gave Jordan an all-too-knowing smile. "Yet I think perhaps that you are not a wise man, my brother."

Jordan shook his head. "She's a strange woman, Waves. So damned certain of the rules of life, and a regular spitting cat when someone challenges her ideas of right and proper. Sometimes I almost feel sorry for her." He chuckled. "Almost. Not quite. But I goddamn sure feel sorry for any man who gets too close to that English thistle."

Waves smiled. "It is not wise for a man to feel sorry for himself, Eyes of a Ghost."

The comment brought a cynical smile to Jordan's austere face. How ironic that a straitlaced, hidebound virgin should be the woman to set him afire, to make him doubt the worth of his present life, and to remind him that he was, after all, a white man. Waves was right. Jordan Scott, the stupid ass, had fallen for a piece of female bait that some malicious spirit had tossed in his path. He could rail at himself until Judgment Day that Miriam Sutcliffe was the embodiment of everything he had tried to escape and had come to despise, but it wouldn't do any good. It seemed that the bastard from Boston hadn't learned his lesson after all.

Giving Rides the Waves an ill-humored grunt, Jordan sought the comfort of his bed.

Morning brought the promise of a storm. The sun was veiled by a murky haze, and the wind had a bite that was straight out of winter's lair. Jordan rose, stretched, and padded down to the trickle of a creek where Rides the Waves was washing the sleep from his eyes. Bending down to cup his hands in the icy water, he caught sight of his reflection staring back at him from the glassy surface. His skin was almost as brown as that of Rides the Waves. The aristocratic, lean face could easily have passed for that of a Chippewa, except for the scalp lock—tawny gold with streaks of sun-bleached blond.

Self-consciously, he ran a hand over his shaved scalp, wondering how long it might take if he decided to let it grow. A glance upward and his eyes merged with Rides the Waves's knowing gaze.

"Is it time for you to become a white man once again, my brother?" the Chippewa warrior asked.

Jordan merely shook his head and gave his friend a rueful smile.

Miri sat cross-legged on a mat outside the wigwam door. The sun shot red sparks off her hair as she bent in concentration over the moccasin she was sewing. It was large enough for two of her own feet, but would fit Jordan's perfectly once the tough moose hide was stuffed with rabbit fur to ward off the winter chill. Her needle, the thorn of a thorn-apple tree, dipped rapidly in and out, securing the flaps of hide with a strand of moose sinew.

Smiles at Sunrise sat by Miri's side, busy at the same task. Occasionally one of the women would reach out and give a push to Jane's gently swinging cradle board, which hung from an overhead branch. Across the clearing, Smoke Catcher snowshoed along the riverbank, on his way to his favorite fishing hole a half mile upriver.

"A storm is on its way," Sunrise predicted, looking up at the hazy sky. "Perhaps my sons will smell its coming and return."

Miri smiled. "Smoke Catcher will be glad of their return. I think he grows weary of seeing no one but women."

Sunrise nodded in approval as Miri labored over the Chippewa words. "My husband knows he is needed here to guard against the men who might take you. He will be glad of this storm, for it will mean that the white men will not want to travel, and you will be safe."

"If Jordan thought I needed guarding, why didn't he stay himself?"

"Eyes of a Ghost needed to leave, my daughter." Her statement carried neither reproof nor sympathy, but simply an acceptance of fact.

Miri dropped her eyes, regarding her task with renewed concentration. Sunrise spoke the truth. Over the ten days of their journey, the tension between Miri and Jordan had risen to an unbearable level, and everyone could feel it.

What would she have done, Miri mused, if Jordan had been waiting when she had emerged from her wigwam the next morning? The relationship between them had changed somehow, pushed to the edge of a precipice by the current that had passed between them the night before. Miri could no longer tell herself that Jordan Scott was merely an insufferable toad of a renegade, a man with no redeeming qualities whatsoever, a barbarian who was a disgrace to his countrymen. She had known she was drawn to him in a primitive sort of way, had admitted to herself that when he was close, when she heard his voice, saw his smile, felt his touch, she was plagued by strange feelings. But his ultimatum and her instant and appalling response had brought those strange feelings into focus. She was crazy for the man, as fluttery and moonstruck as any simpering maiden of seventeen.

The very thought of anything between them was impossible, of course. Miri tried to imagine Jordan Scott in a London drawing room. It would be like putting an eagle in a cage, or locking a wolf in a steel trap. And like the wolf, who would chew off his own leg to escape, Jordan would do anything to return to his forests—as Miri's own father had done. Miri wondered what Jordan would destroy in escaping. Her father had destroyed her mother's heart.

The thought caused Miri's hand to jerk, and she jabbed her finger with the needle thorn.

"Ouch! Curses!"

Smiles at Sunrise looked up from her own work. "You are not concentrating, Daughter. How do you expect to improve if you do not pay attention?

Miri sighed and sucked at her pricked finger. How could she concentrate on anything until she had this mess resolved? She was very much her mother's daughter, falling for that unruly savage. Jordan Scott would surely laugh if he knew he'd made such a conquest. But at the moment, Miri couldn't think of a thing to do about it. Her base instincts had proven all but unconquerable.

She was still mulling over her quandary when Willow Song walked up, a load of firewood on her back. She looked at the moccasins in Miri's lap and smiled. It was a smile of contempt that set Miri's hackles standing on end.

"You sew no better than you cook, I see," Willow Song commented. "The stitching along the toe should be tighter, Eyes of the Sky. That seam will not last through one hunting trip, and your husband's feet will freeze." The word *husband* came out with a skeptical twist of tone, as though Willow did not really believe the title applied.

Miri was silent. In a way she felt sorry for the girl. She had decided in the midst of her inner turmoil that Jordan could not be sleeping with the all-too-willing Willow Song. If he was dousing his passions with Willow, then where came that tightly leashed fire that had reached out to burn Miri again and again? The revelation had made her look upon Jordan with a good deal more charity.

"She is learning," Smiles at Sunrise intervened. "Soon she will have all the skills of a good wife."

"Yes," Miri said, her voice a quiet challenge. "I will, soon." She couldn't resist the barb, even though she knew it was cruel. And after all, Willow was the one who had declared war.

Willow Song blinked, then her eyes narrowed as she took Miri's meaning. Her hand reached into the pouch that hung at her waist.

"As long as you are in need of sewing practice, Eyes of the Sky, perhaps you would mend this for me." She held Jordan's beaded knee band out for Miri's inspection. "Men are so careless when they are eager to remove their clothing."

Miri's face blanched. She recognized the band, and could think of only one way it had gotten into Willow Song's hands. She had been wrong, it seemed. The fire she had seen in Jordan's eyes was only an ember left over from the furnace that burned for Willow Song. She took the proffered band and crumpled it in her hand.

"Excuse me, please," she said to Sunrise. "Surely something needs doing in my wigwam."

Sunrise pursed her lips as Miri walked away. Then she turned to her daughter, who was smiling in triumph.

"Did I never teach you manners, or kindness, that you should say such a thing?"

Willow Song appeared unconcerned. "She should have gone with the Englishmen. She does not belong here."

"She is the wife of Eyes of a Ghost. She belongs wherever he is."

"She belongs with her own people. She is like her cousin—brash, not caring that she offends and burdens others who are more worthy."

Sunrise looked at her daughter in surprise. "What do you know of this cousin?"

"He came through L'Arbre Croche in the spring." Willow's face grew shuttered. "Eyes of a Ghost asked about him and told me who he is."

"Why did you not tell Eyes of the Sky? Perhaps she would like to know of this cousin of hers."

Willow sniffed. "She never asked me." She thought of telling her mother of the Englishwoman's true reason for leaving with their family. Only the thought of Jordan's wrath held her back. "Why should I help her? She is a burden to all and a joy to none. The Englishwoman does

Eyes of a Ghost no good. He is unhappy with her, and soon he will send her back where she belongs.''

"And you think he will be happy with you, Daughter, if you lie to bring him to your bed?''

Willow smiled slowly, sensuously. "He will be happy.''

Once out of sight within the wigwam, Miri let her rage surface. It had been one thing to suspect that Jordan had been spending his nights with Willow Song. It was quite another to be confronted with proof by that conniving hussy—especially after Miri had given the blackguard credit where none was due. No doubt he had been anxious to return to his lover's arms the night he had saved her from Renquist. The arousal she had sensed in his taut body had not been for her—it had been for that tart who now paraded the evidence that he could not wait to tear the clothes from his body when he was in her presence. Damn Jordan Scott for a rutting animal! Damn Willow Song for a jade! And damn Miri Sutcliffe for being such a fool!

Miri paced the confines of the wigwam, not knowing whether she was angriest at Jordan, Willow Song, or herself. The thought that she had no right to be jealous only fueled the fire. The more she thought herself a fool, the angrier she became.

"Damn! Damn! Damn!" She kicked the roll of bedding that rested against the wall, then kicked it again. Was she to endure an entire winter of this, her heart turned to mush, her pride ripped to shreds, letting this primitive life mold her and change her until she was no better than a savage herself? Was she going to stay and watch while Jordan Scott indulged in disgusting behavior with that Chippewa tart and while that hussy smirked at her every time they met? She was most certainly not!

Miri grabbed a blanket and started making herself a small pack. Escaping Michaels was not worth the price she was paying. She was being corrupted by association with these savages. Her very surroundings were sucking her slowly but surely down into barbarism. Just look at her—sewing hides, cooking wild game over an open fire, sleeping in a dirt-floored hut, indulging in uncivilized, unladylike, and unacceptable feelings of jealousy and lust. All because of an immoral and irresponsible renegade who hadn't a shred of decency in his entire overmuscled body. She was even beginning to believe in miracles performed by a painted witch doctor, as if little Jane's life owed anything to Smoke Catcher's heathen ceremonies. Miri would be damned if she stayed in this camp one day longer—literally, irrevocably damned.

Smiles at Sunrise shook her head in violent disapproval when Miri told her that Jane and Petunia would be left in her care.

"You must milk the goat twice a day," Miri instructed in a tight voice. "You've watched how I do it. And you must not give Bright Spirit milk that is over a day old, or she will spit it up."

"You are a fool, Eyes of the Sky. And my daughter is a fool also. She set her sights on Eyes of a Ghost even before he took Dancer as his wife. But he would never go to Willow. Neither does he go to her now."

Miri lifted her chin in a fine show of unconcern. "Eyes of a Ghost may go to anyone he pleases. He may go to the devil himself and it would be most appropriate."

"You cannot travel alone, my daughter. Even a woman of the Anishanabe would not think to travel alone back to the island."

Miri picked up her pack, and with a notable lack of her former awkwardness, swung it up to her back and fastened it. "You have taught me enough to make my own way for a few days, and the Englishmen who tried to take me cannot be far ahead."

"They are your enemies," Sunrise objected.

Miri scowled, avoiding the older woman's eyes. "I am a worse enemy to myself than they will ever be."

Smiles at Sunrise crossed her arms in stern determination. "Soon Smoke Catcher will return from where he fishes upriver. I will send him after you."

"No, you won't." Miri abandoned her pose of lofty

indifference and put a gentle hand on Sunrise's arm. "You are a woman, my mother. Think how it would be if you were taken away to England, where strange people and strange ways surrounded you. Think how you would feel as you forgot your Chippewa ways, forgot your visions, forgot the very roots of who you are. And then you come to love a man who despises you—someone who will use you then throw you aside, who has nothing but contempt for what you really are. Think how it would be, my mother, and then let me go."

"You are a fool, my daughter." The older woman's tone was still stern, but there was a hint of compassion in her eyes.

Without a word, Miri turned and walked out of camp, steeling herself not to turn for a last look at the baby and Smiles at Sunrise standing beside the suspended cradle board.

A hollowness invaded Miri's soul as she trudged westward along the Aux Sables River. This same forest had seemed on the trip out to be a haven of peace and beauty. Now it was empty, lonely, and silently hostile. The recesses of the darkly shadowed pine groves harbored unseen dangers. Fallen trees and twisted stumps took on the guise of predators watching her progress with malevolent eyes. Only the thought of Willow Song and Jordan Scott laughing at her kept her from turning around and following her tracks back to the Chippewa camp.

Late in the afternoon she came across the tracks of Renquist and his men. It was as if she suddenly had company on her lonely trek. With bolstered spirits, she followed the trail until darkness forced her to halt.

The skills she had learned from Smiles at Sunrise stood Miri in good stead. She made a little fire, boiled water for tea, and dined on dried corn mixed with deer tallow. By the light of the moon she set a rabbit snare, using the leavings of her dinner for bait. Then she built herself a crude shelter of pine branches, rolled up in her blankets, and went to sleep.

The next morning, breakfasting on the rabbit that was spit over her little fire, she remembered that not too many days ago she had haughtily refused to clean Jordan's ducks. A few days had made a mighty change. She truly was becoming a barbarian.

The second day of travel was better than the first. Shadows were only shadows, and stumps and logs seemed no more than what they really were. Miri had no trouble following the tracks of the slow-moving Englishmen. Accustomed by now to snowshoes, she was traveling faster than they, and she estimated that she would overtake them by sometime the next morning. Then she could revert to the role of the English gentlewoman and let the men do all the hard work. Whatever Michaels might do with her, it would be better than watching Jordan cavort with Willow Song. And it would be better than allowing herself to sink so deeply into barbarism that she might never find her way back to who she really was.

The second night passed much as the first until Miri was awakened by the wind swirling a fine dust of snow into her shelter. The rest of the night Miri shivered in her blankets and listened to the keening of the rising storm. Morning came as only a slight graying of the darkness. The wind continued to howl, and driving snow obliterated sun, sky, and forest alike. The world became a tiny patch of white encompassing Miri's shelter and the few trees that were close enough to not be drowned in the obscurity of the blizzard.

Miri's limited woods skills were not sufficient to deal with a winter storm in the middle of the wilderness. She did her best to improve her shelter, weaving a sturdy framework of pine branches, draping them with the hides she had brought as bedding, then securing the hides with lengths of basswood cord, as Sunrise had taught her. She faced the opening away from the wind and managed to build a tiny fire. But the feeble flames did little to ward off the biting cold, and the supply of dry tinder was very limited. Miri did not dare leave the shelter in search of more wood, so she huddled in her blanket as the fire died, listening to the wind, and wondered if her frozen, lifeless body would ever be found, or if anyone would even care.

Day merged into night, and night into day. The snow continued to fly. Miri figured that two days had passed when her supply of parched corn and dried venison ran out, but she wasn't sure. It made little difference that there was no longer any food. Hunger was just one more misery to add to cold, isolation, and the certainty of death.

For two more days she huddled in her little shelter, venturing out into the snow and wind only to answer the call of nature and to scoop snow to melt into water with her own body's heat. Off and on she slept, and each time sleep claimed her she thought to never wake. And always she woke to find the world was the same white, howling nightmare she had left.

Then came the time she woke and realized it was the silence that had awakened her. She crawled, blanket and all, to the opening of her shelter. Sunlight nearly blinded her. The sky was blue—a brilliant backdrop for a world of pristine, sparkling white.

It took Miri a full hour to decide whether to simply die where she was or try to make her way back to the Chippewa camp. Death seemed an old friend. Miri had become well acquainted with its dark presence over the last few days. It would have been easy to lie down and accept her fate. Only pure bulldog stubbornness made her gather up her hides, blankets, knife, kettle, and snowshoes and stumble off in the direction from which she had come.

Miri didn't get far. She hadn't really thought that she would, but something within her demanded that she at least try. The snow was soft and deep, and the wind had piled shoulder-high drifts across the way she must go. Even if she hadn't fasted for the last few days, Miri would not have had the strength to break a trail along the riverbank.

The sun was sinking toward the horizon when Miri finally gave up. She stumbled against a tree, sank down upon her backside, and stayed there. Cold and hunger had become companions that were too demanding, and exhaustion was numbing Miri's mind as well as her body. Summoning the last of her energy, she unfastened her pack, dug out a blanket, and wrapped it around herself. Her mind was oddly at peace as she settled down to watch the world fade.

Miri sat for a long time, it seemed, and the sun scarcely moved. Somehow the world seemed brighter than before— trees, rocks, and shadows were etched with a cold and unwavering clarity. No longer cold or exhausted, Miri seemed to hover somewhere apart from her own body—a strange feeling that brought no fear, only a sense of waiting, watching, of something to be learned.

It was with this feeling of unnatural complacency that Miri watched a huge gray wolf emerge from the forest and trot toward the riverbank. His great head swung back and forth, nose lifted to scent the breeze. For a moment he paused at the river and lapped at the icy water. When he lifted his dripping muzzle, he stood frozen for a moment. Then the lithe gray body turned. The predator's eyes fastened unerringly on Miri's form propped against the tree.

The wolf trotted toward Miri's resting place at an unhurried pace. He stopped ten feet away from her and stood like a statue. Totally unafraid, Miri watched herself from a distance as she got to her feet and advanced slowly toward the animal. There was a dreamlike quality about the scene, and Miri viewed the wolf from the vantage point of both the Miri who approached the huge animal and the Miri who watched and waited at a distance. It was all very odd, she acknowledged, and yet somehow not odd at all.

There was a waiting stillness about the wolf. His eyes were silver-gray, Miri noted without surprise, and they were human in their intelligence. She reached out to touch him, to run her fingers through his luxurious coat of black-tipped gray, but he moved warily just out of reach. Suddenly it seemed very important to touch him, but the wolf insisted on his distance. With stoic patience he moved away each time she reached out. And yet he made no move to leave. He constantly sniffed the wind and surveyed the wilderness around them with wary vigilance, ever on guard, and ever out of reach. Finally Miri gave up and sat back against her tree. The wolf lay down several feet away, licking his chops and regarding her from out of those unnerving, familiar, ghostly eyes.

Time seemed to hover for a moment. Slowly Miri faded back into herself. Once again she felt the cold. Exhaustion dragged her down. She opened her eyes, noting that the light had faded. The sun had dipped below the horizon.

And Jordan Scott stood where the gray wolf had just lain.

✳ 13 ✳

Jordan was not as calm as Miri's dream wolf. He had been angry when Smoke Catcher had caught up with him and Rides the Waves a day's walk from the winter encampment. Setting out on a course that should have intercepted Miri well before she could catch up to Renquist, Jordan had allowed his mind to dwell on the methods he would use to make a certain senseless English miss sorry she had ever had the misfortune to cross his path.

Then the snow had started to fly. And it had continued, on and on. Fear had washed away anger. For four days Jordan had sat in his shelter, picturing a stubborn, curly-headed sprite defeated by starvation and frozen exhaustion, being buried by the relentless snow. He was haunted by the image of midnight blue eyes gazing sightlessly at the bleak sky, of delicately molded lips frozen into a rictus grin of death, of a mop of auburn curls rigid with a coating of ice. He alternated curses at Miri's foolishness with prayers for a miracle, addressing the white man's God and the Chippewa spirits with equal fervor. Promising any kind of concessions to the spirits if they would grant his petition, Jordan also promised himself that if he should by some chance find his wandering little stubborn prig, he would find a way to never let her go again. There was nothing like the threat of loss to make a man realize what he had, or nearly had, Jordan had realized sadly.

Now, seeing that Miri had somehow managed to survive the storm, Jordan was even angrier than before. Part of him was weak with joy, and another part raged with fury. But all of him was itching to lay his hand on Miri's sweetly rounded posterior, and not in sensuous caress.

"Just what the goddamn hell do you think you are doing, you thickheaded idiot? Are you trying to kill yourself? Or did you really think that a fluff-brained drawing room doily like you could survive alone in this wilderness?"

Miri didn't respond. She couldn't respond, in fact, for when she tried to move her lips, she discovered that they were too numb to form words.

"Answer me, you rabbit-brained little dolt! Do you know how much trouble you've been? I could have died out here if that storm had lasted any longer, and you most certainly would have. Sunrise is probably singing her mourning song for both of us right now. All because of your pigheaded, ignorant foolishness!"

Miri merely stared at him, her eyes clinging to his face in wonder as though she had never seen him before. He wasn't so much angry as he was frantic with worry, she realized with a flash of feminine intuition. He did care about her after all.

"Answer me, dammit!"

But she couldn't answer. She couldn't even move, her body was so stiff. For a moment she wondered if she was dead and just didn't know it yet.

Jordan stepped forward, took her by the shoulders, and shook her. "Answer me, I said." A note of concern had crept into his voice. "What's wrong with you?"

Miri tried to speak, but only a raspy squeak emerged from her mouth. She was alive all right. Even through the thickness of his gloves and her blanket, Jordan's hands were burning her cold flesh where they grasped her shoulders.

"Lord! You're frozen stiff!"

He took off his own beaver-lined, hooded coat and wrapped it around her, threading her stiff arms into the sleeves and stuffing her hands into warm, fur-lined pockets

"Wait here," he ordered, as if she could do anything else.

In a short time Jordan had built two roaring fires. Gently he lifted Miri and sat her down on a log between them. His pack yielded up a block of shredded venison mixed with deer tallow. He cut the venison in slices and ordered her to eat, ignoring her feeble protests that her stomach was as numb as the rest of her. When she finally consented to nibble at the food, he hastened away to cut poles and gather heavy pine branches to make a shelter, all the while muttering a combination of Chippewa and English under his breath.

The fires were doing their work. Miri felt herself thawing, and it wasn't a pleasant sensation at all. Her flesh felt as though it were being pricked with a thousand needles as feeling came back into her body. The sensation brought her close to tears—another weakness for Jordan to chide her about. Drawing room doily indeed! She had survived, hadn't she? To keep her mind away from the pain, Miri concentrated on Jordan, reminding herself that he really did care about her. His anger, his very being here, proved that. She watched him as he worked. He had extinguished one of the fires and was erecting a sturdy shelter over the warmed ground where it had burned, burying some of the coals and covering the heated dirt with a thick hide to serve as a floor.

"I thought only women built shelters," Miri commented in a hoarse voice that was only beginning to work.

Jordan paused and looked her way. "Do you want to build this and let me sit by the fire?"

"If I built it the thing would blow away in the first puff of a breeze, as well you know."

Jordan smiled. His mood seemed to have lightened. "Are you warming up?"

"I hurt," she admitted.

"Serves you right." He fastened the last hide down to his framework of branches, walked over to Miri, and lifted her from her seat.

"Can you stand?" he asked.

Miri's legs seemed to be made of limp string. Knives of pain shot up from her feet as Jordan let her slide gently to the ground.

"No," she gasped. "I can't."

"You're still as cold as an icicle. God only knows why you're still alive."

"The wolf kept me alive," Miri said without really meaning to say it.

"What?"

"I . . . I dreamed about a wolf."

"Did you indeed?" His voice was bland, but there was an underlying tone that sent a shiver down Miri's spine. Hadn't Dancer told her once that Jordan was of the Wolf Clan? Was he offended that she would have the temerity to conjure up a dream wolf?

"I'm still cold," she said, trying to change the subject.

He set her down upon the warmed moose hide that was the floor of the shelter, then pulled a pile of furs over her. She started to shiver and couldn't stop.

"Your clothes are wet. Give them to me. I'll put them by the fire to dry."

Miri modestly pulled the furs up to her shoulders as she peeled the wet leggings and tunic away from her skin. Immediately she felt warmer.

"Better?"

"Yes."

Miri's eyes widened as Jordan started to peel off his own clothes.

"What are you doing?"

"Stripping."

He was down to a brief loincloth now, and Miri averted her eyes, despite a perverse fascination with the play of muscles in his chest and abdomen; the lean, sinewy sculpting of his arms and legs. Her cheeks tingled with a rush of blood. "I can see that. Why are you . . . stripping?"

"Flesh is a good source of heat. Do you want to stay warm tonight?"

"We're staying here tonight?"

"Did you expect to start back to camp in the dark?"

"I—No." Jordan was right. The sun had set, and outside the shelter the world was the dusky blue that precedes full night.

"Make room," he said, lifting the furs and sliding his long lithe body in beside hers. She flinched as his hard thigh touched hers. "This is going to be like sleeping with an icicle," he said, taking one of her hands and starting to chafe gently.

Miri closed her eyes. She was an icicle in more ways than one, God help her. Her mind held no doubts that Jordan planned to generate heat by more than just lying together under the furs.

"You intended this all along," she accused softly as his chafing moved up her arm. "From the moment you started building this shelter."

"Yes." He didn't question what she meant. There was no shame in his voice.

Of course there wouldn't be, Miri thought. Jordan Scott was proud of being a male animal. It showed in his every movement, sounded in his every word, flashed in the shadowed depths of his eyes. And when he touched her as he was doing now, he infected her with the same frightening passions that held his own soul in thrall.

"This has been coming since the first day we met," Jordan said calmly. "We both know it, and I for one am through fighting it. Some jester of a god intended you for me, Miriam Sutcliffe, and I mean to take him up on his offer."

He sat up to give attention to her foot, which still felt like a block of ice.

"And suppose I decline the offer," she asked with a hint

of indignation. "I suppose then you'd rape me, wouldn't you?"

"I wouldn't rape you, woman. I won't have to rape you."

His voice was very confident. Perhaps he had been granted a vision also, Miri mused. She was beginning to feel light-headed. The wolf had not allowed her touch, but now he was touching her, and his touch was doing more than thawing her cold flesh. It was melting her resolve, as well.

"No," she whispered in a sad voice. "You won't have to rape me. How well you know."

His hand had moved from her foot to her calf, and the chafing had become a soft caress.

"Are you getting warmer?"

"Yes." Indeed, her blood had begun to run like a hot river through her veins, and an insidious warmth was spreading out from the pit of her belly. It was a most improper reaction. Ladies did not enjoy a man's touch— they tolerated it. An unmarried lady should be willing to die rather than submit. But then, Miri was beginning to suspect that she was no lady, because she was most certainly about to submit without even a decent struggle, much less a fight to the death.

Jordan lay back down beside her. His hand moved from her calf, slid up her thigh, over her hip, and came to rest on the soft mound of her breast. Miri jumped in alarm, and her heart raced so that surely he could feel it fluttering beneath his hand.

He did feel it. "There's no need to be frightened," he said softly.

Miri tried to catch a breath. A strange excitement galloped through her body, warring with fear for ascendancy. "I . . . I've never done this," she breathed uncertainly.

"I didn't think you had." His hand gently massaged her breast as his head dipped. Miri gasped as she felt his warm, wet tongue stroke her nipple.

"I'm not going to hurt you, little one. Don't be afraid."

"I'm not afraid." It was true, Miri thought with amazement. Not for the whole world would she have him stop. She was awash with sensations she hadn't known existed, and while they had to be very improper, they were also quite lovely.

His hands slid down over her ribs, fanned out over her flat belly, then dived beneath her to gently grasp her buttocks while his mouth continued to pay homage to her breasts. As he kneaded her firm, round bottom, his fingers brushed the down between her thighs. It sent a heart-stopping sensation from her groin to her throat.

"Don't," she gasped, wanting him to stop and longing for him to continue at the same time.

He raised his head. "You don't really want me to stop. Not now." He traced a path with his finger over her abdomen, circled her dainty navel, traveled a line between her perfect breasts, and ended up with a gentle touch on her lips. "You are quite beautiful. Did you know that?"

"No," she answered honestly.

"I've never seen more beautiful breasts." He cupped an object of admiration in one hand. "Or more perfect thighs. Firm and slender. And your skin is like silk. You were made for a man to love."

"No." She laughed nervously. "Now you're just trying to flatter me. You're a complete rogue, you know. There's absolutely no excuse for all of this."

He smiled. "We don't need an excuse." He lowered his mouth to hers. The first contact of his lips was gentle. His tongue flicked between her lips, and slowly, tentatively, her mouth opened beneath his, allowing him entrance to her silky moist softness. With gentle caresses of his tongue he showed his appreciation of her offering, and with every caress her heartbeat stepped up its pace. An urgent throbbing started between her legs and vibrated through every fiber of her body. With only the briefest hesitation, her hands came up and roamed over the masculine torso arched so possessively above her, reveling in the feel of his taut nipples, of the ridges of muscle in his back, shoulders, and abdomen. She felt the hard muscle tense and ripple under her touch, and he groaned into her mouth.

"Lord, but I want you!" His knees urged her legs apart, and a muscle-corded thigh came in intimate contact with the very core of her femininity. She gasped, but her instinctive objection was smothered in a kiss that was savage with need. For the first time she struggled to escape his grasp, but the insistent pressure of his thigh between her legs soon turned her struggles into wriggles of desperate, aching delight. *Was this what it was about?* a still-coherent part of her mind asked. *Was this the brutal male consummation that married women whispered about behind their hands?*

With a hasty movement he rose to his knees and untied the cord that held his loincloth in place.

"What are you doing?" she asked, half afraid, half deliciously curious.

He chuckled—a husky sound from deep in his chest. "This is getting in the way." He tossed the piece of buckskin aside. "It's time to be rid of it."

What sprang forth into Miri's view was truly frightening. Miri had only the vaguest notions of male anatomy, and she certainly had no idea of anything like this. Eerily lit by the firelight that streamed into the shelter, Jordan suddenly seemed huge, menacing, frighteningly strong. The firelight cast ridges of muscle into stark relief, emphasized the breadth of his shoulders, the thick-muscled strength of his thighs, and hid none of the aroused glory of his maleness.

She averted her face from the sight of him, suddenly frightened.

"You are an innocent, aren't you?" he said with a soft laugh. "Did your mother never explain the way of a man with a woman?"

"Such things are not talked about." Her voice shuddered.

Jordan shook his head and smiled. "Look at me, my love." When she refused to comply, he took her chin and forced her head around. "There is nothing here to frighten you. I fit with you, little one, to slide up inside you, to give you pleasure, to take us both to paradise."

That was outrageous. No wonder unmarried women were never told about such things. No female would ever get married. Miri looked doubtfully at the part of him that was new to her, then closed her eyes. "I don't think that's going to work."

"It will work," he assured her in a husky voice. "Time and time again it will work." For a moment his hungry gaze roamed her body. His face was taut with desire, his mouth a tight line of painful restraint. "Touch me, Miriam."

"I don't think so."

He caught her hand and placed it firmly where he wanted it to be. To Miri's surprise, the texture was soft—hard, hot steel under a velvet glove. A shudder traveled through her body, and it was not only from fear.

"Only this first time you will feel a little pain. After that, all the many times we will have together, there will be only pleasure," he promised.

He lay down beside her. Gently he flicked an auburn curl back from her face. "Do you know, Miss Miriam Sutcliffe?" His hand moved to her breast, then slid down to her abdomen. A tingle started once again between her legs. "I want you more than I've ever wanted a woman. God help me, but I do."

Miri released her breath in a long sigh. She scarcely heard his words. What his hand was doing on her belly was driving all understanding from her brain. Then his fingers dripped into the nest of curls between her legs.

"Easy, love, easy." He slipped a finger gently inside her welcoming moistness. Her body was ready for him, even if her mind was not. "Close your eyes," he urged softly. "Relax and come with me, sweet Miriam."

She was aware of his shifting position, of the coarse hair of his chest brushing against the skin of her breasts. And then she felt the hot probe of his shaft poise as his fingers withdrew.

"Open to me."

Her soul seemed to float above her body. His big, callused

hands were on her thighs, spreading them wide for his pleasure.

"Relax, my love."

Miri felt herself spread as he pushed slowly into her flesh. She tightened instinctively, and he stopped. Then his lips were on hers, whispering so gently in Chippewa, words she didn't understand but were soothing all the same.

Jordan was a savage, a renegade, an animal of a man who had no respect for anything other than himself and his own misguided opinions. A desperate condemnation of everything he was flashed through Miri's mind, and suddenly she discovered it didn't make any difference if Jordan Scott was the most ignorant, most savage man on the face of the earth. She loved him.

"Please, " Miri whispered against his lips, hardly aware of what she needed. "Now."

With a merciful thrust, he buried himself deep inside her.

The pain wasn't so bad, Miri decided. But perhaps that was because the insistent throbbing that pulsed through her body was demanding that he fill her to the aching limit, even if pain was an accompaniment. She arched against him in pleading.

"Impatient little witch, aren't you?" he chuckled.

He began to move, gently grasping her buttocks and rocking her in time to his slow, thrusting rhythm. With every sensuous stroke he kissed her eyelids, her nose, her mouth, her breasts. Within a very few moments Miri's world came to be centered entirely on their joining. The pain was gone, replaced by a spiraling ascent of taut pleasure mixed with unbearable tension. The wanton within her had broken through all the barriers Miri had erected to contain her. She wrapped her slender legs around Jordan's waist and urged him deeper, faster, rolling and twisting in desperate counterpoint to his thrusts.

A tortured moan escaped from deep in Jordan's throat as he desperately slowed their cresting ascent. He muttered a guttural phrase in Chippewa, then picked up the rhythm again.

"Say you want me," he demanded hoarsely.

"I want you," she declared without hesitation.

"Again."

"I want you," she breathed, arching up to meet thrusts that were becoming more savage with every stroke. "Again, and again, and again," she said, catching the rhythm. "I want you. Oh, sweet heaven, Jordan! I love you!"

They strained together, trying to merge into one physical being. His battering-ram thrusts caused no pain, only unendurable tension. Miri felt herself rushing into a dark eddy of passion. The currents were tearing her apart. She couldn't breathe. Blood thundered in her ears. Surely she was going to die.

Then a savage cry of victory cut through the darkness. Jordan's hands grasped her buttocks and pressed her to him in desperate ecstasy as he spilled desire's hot offering deep inside her. Like a spring too tightly wound, Miri's body released, sending her soaring, floating on a wave of pleasure so acute it was almost painful. She reached out and clutched at the masculine body that crouched above her, her one anchor in the dizzying world of desire. Jordan's arms went around her and gathered her close to his chest as they slowly floated downward through the flames. Feeling ridiculously safe, Miri let herself go, drifting away from the heat and dazzling explosions of passion, and into warm and welcoming darkness.

Miri woke to the unfamiliar sensation of being wrapped in a man's arms. Drowsy, warm, and content, she let herself drift slowly back toward sleep, until an insistent tickling at her nose made her sneeze.

She opened her eyes to find Jordan's face smiling down into hers. He waved a raggedy wet feather dangerously close to her nose.

"Are you finally awake, lazy woman?"

"No," she said, promptly closing her eyes and turning over in the circle of his arm. Just then the first sliver of the sun rose above the trees and sent a shaft of light directly into her eyes. "How did morning get here so soon?" she asked in a plaintive voice. The night before had taken on the fuzzy outlines of a dream. Miri wasn't sure she wanted to wake up to reality.

"How do you feel?" Jordan asked.

"Mm. Like a woman," Miri answered with a certain sense of proud satisfaction. Then she tried to move, and discovered that being a woman wasn't all wonderful. She was sore, and sticky, and the cold was beginning to seep into the shelter in spite of the fire still burning just outside the entrance.

Jordan laughed at the grimace on her face. "You'll want to wash," he said with a roguish lift of his brows.

For the first time, Miri noticed he was in possession of a handful of snow. Her eyes widened. "You wouldn't!"

"It's the least I can do."

Tangled in the furs and hides of their bed, Miri couldn't escape fast enough to evade the handful of snow that Jordan planted precisely at the spot she was stickiest and tenderest. She shrieked in protest as he thoroughly washed the leavings of passion from her thighs and the intimate folds of her womanhood.

"Cold?" he inquired with a solicitous grin.

"Why, you . . . !" she sputtered, still breathless. "Mr. Scott . . . !"

He put a finger to her quivering lips. "Don't you think, after last night, it would be proper to call me . . . Jordan?"

It was the first time Miri had ever heard him refer to himself by anything but his Chippewa name. He seemed to grope for his Christian name, as though he had almost forgotten it.

"I have no intention of calling you Miss Sutcliffe ever again. And Miriam is much too formal, considering how well we know each other. So I suppose it will have to be Miri."

Miri closed her eyes. Her world had become a merry-go-round. It was whirling much too fast. She couldn't keep up.

"Wake up, Miri, and answer me." There was a thread of

passion in his voice. A new supply of snow had been added to the first, but now she scarcely noticed the cold, for his hand lingered between her legs.

"Jordan," she whispered softly, savoring the sound of his name on her tongue. "What are you doing to me?"

He gave her a knowing smile. "Loving you, my woman." The smile grew broader. "And keeping you warm."

In a quick movement he joined her under the covers and pulled her against him back to front. Her ice-covered buttocks coming into contact with his naked abdomen did not discourage him in the least.

"What are you doing?" The question answered itself as the hungry shaft of Jordan's manhood prodded between her thighs, seeking from behind what it had tasted the night before. Surely this was impossible, Miri thought, even as a frisson of desire quivered through every nerve. "You can't . . .!" she objected in her innocence.

But Jordan could. And he did.

Breaking camp was delayed by another hour.

The walk back to the Chippewa encampment took two days of hard snowshoeing. Reality seeped back into Miri's world, just as the cold had curled its insidious fingers into their cozy shelter. Two days of travel gave her too much time to think. One moment she could find a host of excuses for her behavior with Jordan. The next moment there was no excuse possible. She was a wanton, a slut, and a jade. Her mind swung between believing Jordan had to love her after what they had done together, then chiding herself that not only was it unthinkable that he loved her, but it was equally impossible that she really loved him in spite of what her heart had whispered during their bout of unhallowed passion.

By the end of the first day's travel Miri felt bruised and battered by her own mind. She was tired and sore and confused. She was no longer the gentlewoman who had left London so many months ago, and she felt like a stranger to herself. All the day long she had spent watching Jordan, remembering how it had felt to see him smile at her, joke with her, run his hand across her naked body.

She *was* in love with the rogue, Miri finally decided. Reason had not fled so far out of her grasp that she couldn't tell love from lust. But that knowledge didn't make her situation any easier. She was stranded in the wilderness, pursued by dragoons, in love with an enigmatic savage, and breaking every moral code she had ever been taught. Somehow, that wasn't the future she had pictured for herself as a young lady back in London.

Miri had insisted on helping Jordan build a shelter at the end of that first day. She had also skinned, cleaned, and spitted the rabbit he had brought down with a deftly aimed rock, admitting to herself that she was flaunting abilities he had once chided her for lacking. Jordan's pleased nod of approval was worth the effort—almost.

But Miri could not stay awake long enough to enjoy her small victory, or even eat the rabbit she had cooked. She didn't remember falling asleep while she was still turning the rabbit on the spit, or being lifted and carried to the shelter. In the first gray light of morning she woke and found herself folded against Jordan's bare body, her head pressed against his shoulder, her legs intertwined with his. It seemed a proper and natural position, somehow—safe, secure, wanted, even if not exactly loved. Sighing her contentment, she closed her eyes and drifted back to sleep.

That afternoon the two wanderers were welcomed back to the Chippewa camp with great shouts of joy. Smoke Catcher promptly and vocally offered prayers of thanks to his guardian spirit. Sunrise enfolded Miri in a warm embrace and exclaimed at her loss of weight, and Rides the Waves thumped Jordan on the back until Jordan threatened to thump him back.

Miri allowed herself to be caught up in the enthusiastic greeting until she caught sight of Willow Song staring at her with unconcealed hostility. That stare was like a splash of icy water in the face, reminding her of why she had fled in the first place. Her hand slipped into the pocket on one side of her tunic and closed around the beaded knee band that the Indian girl had dropped with such challenge into her lap. Had Jordan told Willow Song how he wanted her as he had ripped off his clothing in such passionate haste? She had almost forgotten, Miri thought bitterly. The trip to Jordan's paradise, as he had called it, was a very well-trodden path.

"Are you still so tired?" Jordan asked, once they were safely alone in their wigwam. Everything was just as it had been. Jane slept on a blanket by the fire pit and Petunia regarded them curiously out of slotted brown eyes.

"I'm not tired," Miri denied.

"Then why are these lines between your brows," he said, raising a finger to the creases in question, "and why does your mouth pull down so at the corners?"

Miri jerked away from his touch. Before she could escape, he caught her by the shoulders and held her prisoner.

"What is this?" he asked, his voice grown dark.

"Let me go."

"Answer me," he countered. "Then I'll let you go. Perhaps."

Miri's mouth drew into a tight line, then softened. "I've been a fool," she admitted, her voice no longer sharp, but very sad. "Willow Song was very glad to see you."

"Everyone was glad to see us." His voice was sharp with impatience. "Tell me what you mean, Miri. I have little patience with word games."

Miri reached into her pocket and brought out the damaged knee band. "You lost this."

"Yes." His mouth tightened into a harsh line. "I remember."

"I'm sure you do. It must have been an unforgettable experience. Willow Song told me in great detail how it came about."

"I doubt it."

"Are you saying I lie?"

"I'm saying Willow lied. If she had told you the truth, it would not have upset you."

"You didn't sleep with her?"

"No."

Miri twisted out of his grasp and turned away. Tears were close to the surface. She was more tired than she had thought. She wanted to believe him—how she wanted to believe him—but she didn't. He was a self-admitted rogue, and Lucy had warned her that a man's morals resided between his legs.

"You have no obligation to me, Jordan, so you needn't deny it. You can sleep with whomever you please. But don't expect me to join your harem. I behaved like a slut. Don't expect a repetition of such foolishness."

Jordan's hand latched onto her shoulders from behind, tightening with anger. "You did not behave like a slut—you behaved like a woman, for a change. And if you ever again use that term to degrade yourself, I'll make you sorry you ever learned the meaning of the word." His voice gentled, and his hands moved to the tight muscles in her shoulders and started to knead them into relaxation. "You said you loved me, Miri. Don't tarnish the gift you gave me."

"I never said I loved you," she denied in a frightened voice.

"You did. And you remember it well, just as I do."

"I didn't mean it," she lied. "I was . . . distracted."

He chuckled and spun her around to face him. "You meant it," he told her. "I might say something like that in the heat of passion, but you never would. You're wrong about Willow Song, Miri. I have had more than one woman in my lifetime, but never more than one at a time."

"And I am the next in line?" she asked in an acid voice.

"The last in line, I think." He caught her gaze with his, and she wondered how she had ever thought his eyes cold. Now they looked like molten silver, burning her with their heat. "You said you dreamed of a wolf, Miri," Jordan said.

"Yes," she answered, feeling caught in a spell.

"The wolf saved you, kept you alive."

"Yes."

"I am the wolf, Miri. I saved you. I kept you alive, and I made you mine. The wolf mates for a lifetime, and as long as his mate is alive, he will take no other."

Her heart pounded. The molten metal of his eyes seemed to invade her veins. "Are we truly mated, Jordan?"

He released her, and suddenly she felt adrift without an anchor. "That," he answered, turning to leave, "is up to you."

✳ **14** ✳

She had lost all sense of reason, Miri chided herself. Wasn't it enough that she had lost her chastity, her heart, her good sense, without losing her mind, as well?

She stood outside the doorway of the larger of the two wigwams, hesitating. She wanted to enter, and yet she didn't. The dream meant nothing. It had been a hallucination, not a vision. Visions were a superstition—a silly superstition of ignorant savages.

And yet the Chippewa set great store by dreams, thinking them the source of all wisdom. Smoke Catcher had told her that fasting purified the body and mind, allowed it to open to the messages of the manido—spirits that controlled the earth. Nonsense, of course. Pure rubbish. And yet Smoke Catcher had told her of dreams he had been given as a young man, and how his dreams had predicted the events of his future life. Sunrise had confirmed his stories.

Miri was too civilized to believe such things, to be sure. There was no doubt some very good reason that the wolf kept returning to her dreams, and why she remembered with such unearthly clarity the strange vision she'd had in the wilderness—the great silver-gray wolf who had stood guard, watching with unwolflike intelligence and backing away so warily from her every advance. In the dreams that had haunted her for the last few weeks, it was not the wolf who backed away. It was Miri who faded back from his presence, as though afraid that sharp fangs went with those unearthly silver-gray eyes.

The dreams didn't mean anything, of that Miri was certain. It was merely curiosity as to what the Midewiwin— the Wise Man—would say. That was why she was standing before his wigwam, wondering if she should call out for permission to enter.

"Why do you not come in, Daughter?"

Miri felt more than a little silly. Smoke Catcher had known she was there all along. She must have made a noise. Miri pushed aside the blanket and stepped into the wigwam's dim interior.

The old shaman was seated cross-legged beside the fire pit. He was an impressive-looking man, Miri acknowledged. It was no wonder that the uneducated savages believed in his magic. She had almost believed in it herself when Jane had improved after his naming ceremony. And twice in the last three weeks he had cured the baby's persistent colds with his knowledge of herbs, which Sunrise had told her was the central teaching of the Midewiwin.

But herbs were not magic, and Jane's recovery had been mere coincidence.

And visions and dreams had no meaning.

"What brings you here, Eyes of the Sky?"

Miri seated herself across from the Smoke Catcher. "I have brought a question, Father." She labored to find the right Chippewa words, as it seemed only right for this conversation to be conducted in the heathen tongue rather than the king's good English.

The shaman nodded in appreciation.

"I'm really just curious. That's all."

He nodded again.

"When I was in the forest alone, I . . . I had a dream."

For a moment Smoke Catcher was silent. His obsidian eyes swept her with unnerving scrutiny. "That is good," he finally said, seeming satisfied with what he saw. "You have been honored, Eyes of the Sky. Dreams bring wisdom and knowledge to those who are worthy. Our young men—and sometimes young women, also—fast for many days to receive a dream.''

"This was a very strange dream, Father. I can see no meaning to it.''

"Perhaps your eyes are closed to what it tells you.''

Miri could see the wisdom in the old man's face—wisdom, certainty of belief, inner peace. She suddenly longed to have some of that peace for herself.

"I saw a wolf,'' she began, remembering again the strange feeling of being apart from her own body and the out-of-time sensation that had accompanied the whole experience. The whole dream tumbled out, along with the wolf's return in what amounted to nightmares.

When Miri had finished, the old man was silent. All through her recital the shaman had listened carefully, his gaze fastened on her face. Now his eyes shifted to the embers in the fire pit. Finally he spoke.

"Only the dreamer can say what a dream means, my daughter. Dreams give knowledge, wisdom, and sometimes power. You were visited by a spirit wolf. Perhaps this means you have power over the wolf. Perhaps the wolf has power over you. He might be enemy, or friend. Only you can say, for it is you to whom the vision speaks.''

This is ridiculous, Miri thought. And yet it didn't feel ridiculous. It felt important. "This dream says nothing to me, Father. It brings me no wisdom—only sleepless nights.''

A flash of sympathy softened Smoke Catcher's craggy face. "Even for the children of Gitchimanido it is sometimes difficult to understand the wisdom of the spirits. You are not of the Anishanabe, my daughter, so perhaps this dream is not a gift from a manido. Perhaps it is a vision from your own heart. That, too, may bring wisdom, if you listen to what it says.''

"I don't know what it says,'' Miri said, letting her gaze drop to the floor. She didn't know what she had hoped to find in the shaman's wigwam, but whatever it was, she wasn't finding it. Not that it really mattered. The dream was nothing more than a hallucination. She was silly to think it might be more.

"My daughter," Smoke Catcher chided, "you do not listen closely enough. You are white, and whites listen only with their ears, not with their hearts. Wisdom speaks to the heart, and through the heart. You must learn to listen if you are to have peace within you."

Miri sensed that the interview was at an end. She thanked Smoke Catcher and rose to leave. As she reached the door, he called her name, a thoughtful look upon his face.

"Eyes of the Sky, do you know who the wolf is?"

"Yes, Father," she answered quietly. "I know who the wolf is."

The winter weeks settled into a familiar routine, and Miri found herself absorbed more and more into the Chippewa way of life. The world shrank to the snowy clearing beside the Aux Sables River and the white-clad forest that pressed in on every side. For Miri it was easy to let London, Aunt Eliza, Hamilton Greer, and Captain Michaels fade to the back of her mind. They belonged to another world—one that had no meaning in the frozen wilderness. The only things that had meaning were the here and now—the daily task of survival, the kind patience of Smiles at Sunrise and Smoke Catcher, her ever-growing love for the baby, and overshadowing all, her baffling relationship with Jordan Scott.

Where Jordan was concerned, Miri felt her life veering out of control. Their private war was over, it seemed, the hostility burned to ashes by the heat of their sudden passion. At night, in the warm privacy of their wigwam, Jordan would not be denied, and Miri did not attempt to hold herself from him. Indeed, she couldn't. He lit a fire in her blood that burned hotter every time he touched her. He was an addiction, a need coursing through her veins that only his touch could ease.

Her usually active conscience seemed to be asleep, or at least taking a very peculiar view of Miri's fall from grace.

No matter how frequently Miri reminded herself that her behavior was criminally immoral and foolish in the extreme, her conscience failed to respond with appropriate pangs of guilt or remorse. In the world she inhabited, it seemed only right and natural that she and Jordan should be together. Male and female, they were two parts of a natural whole, and it seemed more sinful to deny their union than to revel in their mating. The wintry forest became Miri's own personal Eden. There was nothing evil in the blaze of Jordan's passion, and nothing evil in her eager response. The past didn't matter, the future didn't bear thinking on. All that mattered was the present—the joy of being a part of Jordan Scott and having him as part of her.

What Miri forgot was that even Eden was flawed. Inevitably there came a time when a snake slithered into paradise and brought harsh reality back into the world.

It was the end of a peaceful afternoon, and the sun was just dropping below the line of trees. Jordan and Rides the Waves had returned from a two-day tour of the trap lines just an hour before and were now sitting with Smoke Catcher in front of the big wigwam, deep in conversation about the quality of pelts of the beaver, otter, and marten that they had recovered. While Willow Song and Smiles at Sunrise skinned and butchered the animals, Miri busied herself cutting up wild onions and potatoes to add to the stew that would be the evening meal. Tonight there would be fresh meat, but the rest of the catch would be smoked or dried for use in the weeks to come. No part of the animals would be wasted.

Willow Song brought Miri a slab of beaver tail to add to the pot boiling over the fire.

"Don't add so many onions this time. The last time you made stew I nearly choked."

Miri grimaced at the Indian girl's back as she turned. Usually Willow Song's taunting didn't bother her. She could understand jealousy, knowing how she herself had felt when she'd thought that Jordan was seeking solace in the Chippewa girl's arms. But sometimes it was past bearing, like one mosquito bite too many. Miri was becoming skilled at skinning the beaver, muskrat, otter, marten, and deer that the men brought in from the forest. She could scrape and tan hides almost as well as Willow herself, smoke and dry the meat, and sew the tanned hides into clothes and footgear for herself and Jordan. Nevertheless, she could do nothing to Willow's satisfaction. And the more tenderness Jordan displayed toward Miri, the crueler were the barbs Willow Song sent her way.

But on this afternoon Miri had no time to brood upon Willow's jealousies, for the girl had no sooner turned her back than she stiffened, gazing into the dense forest at the edge of the clearing. The dogs were staring in the same direction, hackles raised in ridges along their spines, and the men had broken off their conversation and risen from their seats on the ground. All three reached for the weapons they always kept close at hand.

Miri stopped her knife in midslice when a deerskin-clad, pack-laden figure appeared at the edge of the clearing and halted. Smoke Catcher raised his rifle, and both Jordan and Waves locked an arrow onto their bowstrings. But the newcomer showed no fear. He raised his hands and clasped them above his head.

"Hola! Smoke Catcher! Eyes of a Ghost, you old son of a bitch!"

The men immediately lowered their weapons.

"Gage Delacroix!" Jordan strode forward and greeted the stranger with a hearty clasping of arms. "You mangy old wolverine! What are you doing out so far this time of year?"

Delacroix dropped his pack to the snowy ground. "*Mon Dieu*! It is good to see a familiar face."

"You were expected back many weeks ago," Jordan said as the newcomer unstrapped the snowshoes from his boots.

"*Oui*! That cursed prancing Britisher I took down to the Mississippi was as slow as sap in winter. Then, when we arrive at our destination, your American compatriots put a lead ball in my britches. Almost, *mon ami*, I was no longer a man. For two months I stayed at Prairie du Chien with an ice pack on my balls.''

Jordan clapped him on the shoulder. ''I trust they are back in shape. Though if not, the women of the Ojibwa and Iroquois will breathe a sigh of relief.''

''No, *mon ami*. They would have wept in their grief.''

Delacroix flashed strong white teeth in a smile. Then he caught sight of Miri staring at him from where she was still standing over the stew pot.

''What have we here?'' He looked at Jordan, saw a sudden flash of possessive caution cross his friend's face, and laughed. ''You old bastard devil, you! Where did you find a *petite fille de joie* like that? She's yours, is she?''

''She's mine.''

''Wife number two? Always knew Dancer was an understanding woman, but I didn't know, *mon ami*, that you had the balls to take care of more than one woman at a time. Eh? Perhaps you could use some help?''

''Lake Dancer is dead, Delacroix.''

The Frenchman promptly sobered and made the sign of the cross. ''Bless her soul. I am sorry, *mon ami*. My mouth is too big for my brain, no?''

Miri's mind was whirling. She had thought she recognized the name, and the newcomer's story about his ''cursed Britisher'' confirmed it. This was the guide Hamilton Greer had hired to take him into the American wilderness to hide from British authority. She abandoned her worktable and crossed to where the men were talking.

''Are you Gage Delacroix?'' she asked breathlessly.

The Canadian half-breed smiled and swept off his hat, revealing a thick mane of cropped hair that caught the sun's last rays like a glossy raven's wing. He was ruggedly handsome, with the high-cheeked bone structure of the Iroquois contrasting with eyes that were the deep green of summer grass. Those eyes raked over Miri's form in frank appraisal. ''At your service, *mademoiselle*. I can see my fame has reached even this remote part of the wilderness.''

Jordan moved to Miri's side and put a proprietary arm

around her shoulders. "Not in the way you mean. That British greenhorn you took to the Mississippi is Miss Sutcliffe's cousin. She's looking for him."

"*Mon Dieu!*" Delacroix exclaimed, unabashed. "Lucky man! If you were looking for me, *ma petite*, I would certainly make sure that you found me."

"Can you tell me where you took Hamilton?" Miri asked eagerly, ignoring his playful leer.

"Hamilton? That is not the name of this man, *cherie*. The Englishman's name was Kenneth Shelby."

"His real name is Hamilton Greer. Please, tell me where he is."

Delacroix shrugged. "But of course. I left him at Prairie du Chien, where even now he is making the western savages very happy by offering outrageous prices for their furs. He has taken a liking to the wilderness, this cousin of yours. But if he were like me, *mademoiselle*, he would leave at the beckoning crook of your smallest finger."

"Enough, Delacroix. Miri isn't interested. She's more particular than to fall for that French flattery."

Delacroix feigned insult, but he took the warning from Jordan's eyes. The talk hastily turned to the unexpected appearance of American forces along the northern stretch of the Mississippi River.

"I tell you, my friend. Your generals are planning to build a fort and bring the war into the West." Delacroix drifted with Jordan toward the fire that was burning in the middle of the campsite, leaving Miri behind. "These were soldiers, not traders. Why else would they fire on one so harmless as I?"

"You're far from harmless in any man's book," Jordan replied. "But if you're right, the British won't like it when they find out."

"They will not find out until too late, I think. I have even less fondness for the redcoat bastards than the American fools, and my companion . . ." He shrugged expressively. "I think right now he prefers the Americans to his own countrymen. After the so-hasty American shot me, my

British friend managed to talk his way into their friendship and saved both our hides from being hung out in the sun to dry.''

Miri's mouth tightened to a stubborn line as she followed the men toward the fire. She wasn't about to be dismissed so lightly.

"Jordan!"

The men's heads turned in her direction. Delacroix's face wore an anticipatory smile. Jordan's was ominous with a frown.

"Jordan, you will take me to find Hamilton, won't you?"

"We'll talk about it later," he said curtly.

"We can't wait, Jordan. He might leave, or..."

"I said, later."

His tone, along with the cold glitter of his eyes, hit Miri like a brick wall. She hadn't felt the cutting edge of his voice in several weeks. It was even sharper than she remembered.

"As you wish," she conceded with deceptive meekness. Returning to the vegetables on her worktable, she resumed her slicing with a savage vigor.

Miri attacked with determination as soon as Jordan entered the wigwam for the night. She was in a proper mood for a war. Jane had been fussing all evening long, and Petunia had stomped and fidgeted during a particularly unfriendly bout of milking. The goat was giving less and less milk every day, and Jane was steadfastly refusing the fish broth that was her only other source of nourishment.

"Why won't you take me to find Hamilton?" she demanded as the heavy hides that covered the doorway dropped in place behind Jordan.

"Because it's winter." His voice was calm and maddeningly patronizing, as if he were talking to an ignorant child. "The ice never melts, even in the sun. The wind is like a knife, and day and night alike, your fingers and toes can freeze before you even know they're cold. Prairie du Chien is two weeks away, even when the weather is warm. Now that the lake is frozen, the trip is impossible."

"You travel during the winter," Miri debated. "It doesn't bother you, or Waves, or that Frenchman."

"I am stronger than you are, Miri. And Jane would certainly never survive the trip if we had to walk, which we would." He lifted the baby from Miri's lap, where she was waving thin arms and emitting a plaintive whine.

Miri gave a guilty grimace. In her excitement over Delacroix's news, she had almost forgotten about Jane. Of course the baby couldn't make the trip. Indeed, sometimes Miri worried that the infant might not survive the winter. Like the wren for which Smoke Catcher had named her, she might be with them for only a short season. The baby had grown, but her arms and legs had no chubby baby fat, and the bluish tinge persisted in her skin. Jordan sat by the fire pit and cradled Jane against his broad chest, and his infant daughter seemed even weaker in contrast to her father's vibrant strength.

"Don't look so troubled, Miri," Jordan said, his face impassive. "I will take you to Prairie du Chien in the spring, after we have returned to the village. If you are still determined to find your cousin, we will find him then."

Miri looked at him doubtfully, not trusting his tone of voice. "Of course I am still determined to find him."

"Why?" Jordan asked.

His silver eyes had become knives, sharp and piercing as they bored into her own. His intensity made her want to shrink back. She was at a loss as to what he sought.

"You know why I must find him, Jordan. Until I find out the location of that cursed list, I can never go back home to London."

"Do you want to go back?"

Miri pulled her eyes away from his and looked at the ground. The future was a huge question mark that she'd not dared to explore in these past weeks. And now Jordan was unequivocally, brutally demanding an answer.

"Why shouldn't I want to go back?" she asked with a hint of belligerence.

"I thought perhaps you'd found something to keep you here."

Miri was silent, refusing to meet his gaze. How nice it would be if such a thing were possible. But in spite of finding friendships here that ran deeper and clearer than any she had in London—Grace and her daughters, Sunrise, Smoke Catcher, Waves, and yes, even Willow Song had her good points at times—and in spite of the knowledge that her heart would always be focused on the man who sat across from her, Miri knew she could never belong in this world. She was as out of place here as Jordan would be in a London drawing room.

"You know I must go back," she told Jordan in a quiet voice. "How many times have you told me I am good only as an ornament for some man's drawing room?"

Jordan regarded her silently for a long moment. Then he rose and placed Jane in her roll of furs beside the fire, giving Miri a broad and unreadable expanse of back. When he finally turned, his eyes were just as unreadable.

"I will take you to find Hamilton in the spring. I promise. I will do it if only not to lose you to this foolish mission of yours."

"Why do you wish to keep me, Jordan?" Miri demanded. Her little Eden had dissolved around her with Delacroix's reminder of who she was and why she was here. But Jordan could restore paradise with a word. Beyond all reason, Miri allowed herself to hope.

"Jane needs you."

Jane needed her. That was all. Paradise was gone, not to be reclaimed.

Miri shoved the hurt to the back of her mind. What had she expected? Jordan had said he wanted her, but he had never claimed to love her. He wanted her fiercely. There could be no doubt of that, for he proved it every night. But want was not enough to make her defy reason and turn her back on everything she was. Not forever, at least. Jordan's love might have been enough to make her so foolish, but now she would not have to make that decision.

"Are you coming to bed, Miri? Or are you going to sit there all night staring at the fire?"

Miri came out of her dark thoughts. Jordan had unrolled the bedding and stripped to the skin. The firelight played across his body. Flickering shadows etched the firm muscles and underlined the smooth strength of his torso. Below the waist he was in shadow, but her mind's eye filled in the missing details—the strong columns of his legs, and what lay between. A rush of desire flooded her veins—a sensation that had become as familiar as breathing, and just as necessary to life, it seemed. But this desire had a wicked feel to it. Reality had returned. Miri's conscience was tapping its proverbial foot in disapproval.

"I'm coming," she murmured, getting up. Reality had returned; reason had not. Miri wondered if it ever would.

The furs were warm. Jordan's muscular body pressed close to hers in familiar comfort, and his heartbeat drummed steadily in her ear. But other than a gentle caress up and down her spine, Jordan showed no awareness that Miri was beside him. He seemed lost in brooding, making her wonder if he was as disturbed by Delacroix's intrusion as she was. The fire burned down to embers, but neither of them slept.

"Why did you come here, Jordan?" Miri's question broke the brooding silence. The quiet mantle of darkness invited intimacy, and gave Miri the courage to probe. She knew almost nothing about this man, other than what Grace had told her, and yet right now he was the mainstay of her life. He had taken her world and turned it upside down, shaken her life to its very foundations. It suddenly seemed very unfair that he could do that and still be a stranger to her. "Surely it was something more than . . . than being illegitimate."

Jordan's hand splayed across the small of her back and pressed her closer to him. For a moment he didn't answer, and Miri thought he might refuse to let her into this closely guarded part of his life. But then he sighed and chuckled, his warm breath gusting through her hair.

"It was a long time ago," he said, his voice contemplative. "Right now it seems a world away and not very important."

Miri rested her cheek against his shoulder. Jordan seemed impervious to hurt, just as he seemed invulnerable to cold, to exhaustion, to fear.

"Grace said there was a woman," she ventured.

Miri could feel his smile in the darkness. "Did she? Trust that busybody to know a man's life history, even when it's none of her damned business."

Was it her damned business? Miri wondered. It didn't matter. She wanted to know. "Who was she?"

Jordan raised himself on one elbow and looked down at her. "Nosy little witch, aren't you? Just like every other woman in the world."

"Yes."

He laughed softly. "All right, my curious lady. Her name was Elizabeth Bowles, daughter of one of the finest families in Boston. She was a prim and proper lady, very much like Miriam Sutcliffe, or so I once thought."

"And you fell in love with her," Miri supplied.

Jordan lay back down, pillowed his head upon his hands, and stared at the black sky beyond the smoke hole. "I was a green kid," he admitted. "Didn't know what love was back then. Maybe I still don't."

Images that Jordan had buried long ago rose to the surface of his mind. They were less painful than before. Perhaps it had taken him until now to realize just how green and foolish he had been during his youth in Boston.

"She loved you?" Miri prompted.

Jordan snorted. "Elizabeth Bowles didn't love anyone but herself. She was society's darling—all sweetness and light, good works, and right causes, and the right friends. There was never a more proper lady than my sweet Elizabeth."

He paused, letting the memories flow. Elizabeth Bowles, green eyes and blond ringlets, laughing at his earnest proposal. Breaking his heart? Perhaps not. But certainly breaking his pride. She had thought it was a joke.

Her father had not, however. He'd not only thrown Jordan

out of his house, he'd set his hirelings on the boy to beat him within an inch of his life. They had broken more than his pride.

"My mother left me quite a lot of money." He smiled bitterly. "She was disowned by my righteous grandparents when she discovered herself pregnant with me. Her sea captain lover had unfortunately neglected to marry her before he was lost at sea, so they forced her to the streets in disgrace, and she bore me in a filthy dockside whorehouse. It took more than that to keep my mother down, though. She became quite a successful courtesan, although Boston prefers to believe such things don't exist. It seems that Boston's finest, under their proper civilized clothes and behind their proper civilized manners, have as much of an animal itch as the rest of humanity."

"Your mother was rich, then?"

"Very. Part of her money bought my way into Harvard. The rest has been managed by a bank for all these years. I suppose it's grown to quite a pile."

"Why did you decide to go to school?"

"To become respectable." He chuckled at the memories. "Harvard is a very respected institution. It didn't work, of course. I was as much an outcast there as anywhere else. But a few fellows were decent to me. Elizabeth's cousin was one of them."

"And he introduced you to her?"

"Yes. He didn't know Elizabeth very well. If he had, he might have done me the favor of keeping us apart. But she took a liking to me right off, or so it seemed. The only other women I'd known were whores. I thought Elizabeth Bowles sat on the clouds, even if she was faster to spread her legs than any woman I ever knew."

"Jordan! Surely she didn't! An unmarried woman . . ." The prig raised her disapproving head, and then promptly subsided. Miri reminded herself that she was certainly not in a position to condemn an unmarried woman lying with her lover—not when she was committing the same sin herself.

Jordan laughed at Miri's resurgent attack of maidenly

virtue. "You're right. She didn't. Elizabeth was a valiant guard of her precious virginity. But she knew other ways to take her pleasure, and she didn't mind leaving a man hard as iron and hot enough to breathe fire while she pleaded the excuse of her maidenhead."

Somehow that seemed to Miri much more depraved than a simple surrender of virginity. She wondered if she would have thought so before she became rather soiled herself.

"We became...quite close," Jordan continued. "Elizabeth dared her father's wrath to invite me to society picnics and parties. We rode in the park, danced in the best ballrooms in Boston. I began to have visions of respectability, and certainly she was spending enough time with me to set society to gossiping. In the end, I managed to reach a new low of stupidity. I proposed to the bitch."

"She turned you down?" Miri asked in an unbelieving voice.

"She laughed in my face. The idea of her marrying a bastard, the son of a whore, was so ridiculous that she was amazed I'd thought of it. She'd simply been having a fling, and at the same time using me to make another suitor jealous. It worked. He proposed a week after I did. Reginald Bartlett. He had a pedigree as long as your arm, and money to go with it."

Jordan stared at the black night sky. How had he let that bitch get to him, and why had he carried the onus of his youthful stupidity all these years? Elizabeth Bowles had done him a favor. By inspiring him to spit upon the whole idea of respectability, she had given him back himself.

"As I said," he continued. "I was a green kid. I took off for the northwest frontier with a sea captain friend of mine who wanted to turn his hand to fur trading. We were neither one as smart as we thought. Silas ended up dead—drowned when our canoe overturned in a sault. I ended up here."

"And you are still bitter, after all this time?"

"No. I'm not bitter." His grim tone belied his words. "I was lucky to find out early that respectability and civilization are havens for small minds. Just the same, I'll not make my parents' mistake. No child of mine will ever bear the label *bastard*."

"What about Jane?" Miri asked.

"Jane will live her life with the Chippewa. Only the white man considers a formal ceremony necessary for a child to have a proper name."

Miri was silent for a moment, pondering a new question his words had provoked. "Then perhaps the problem of bastardy is something you should have considered before . . . before taking a white woman into your bed," Miri said somewhat stiffly.

"I did consider it," Jordan replied quietly, turning to look at her in the dim glow of the embers. "Are you pregnant, Miri?"

"No." Even as she gave her answer, Miri wondered if she wished it were otherwise.

Jordan raised himself on one elbow and looked down upon her. "There will be no bastard born to us, Miriam Sutcliffe. I told you that I mate for life, then stood back for you to make your own decision. If you conceive, you will marry me. Make no mistake about it."

Miri was silent. Marriage would be a solution to her moral dilemma, but she also had vowed not to make her parents' mistake. Her mother had fallen for a rough-cut savage of a man—a man from a world alien to her own. He had destroyed her, even though he had loved her.

But Lord, how she loved Jordan Scott! She loved him more with every passing day, and something in his eyes told her that he might love her, too, for all that he said he didn't know what love was. She couldn't marry him, but she hadn't the strength to hold herself from him, no matter what the consequences. Perhaps she was as venal and shallow as his Elizabeth Bowles.

"Will you ever go back?" Miri brushed her finger against his cheek.

"Miri," he answered with a gentle smile. "I don't want to go back."

"You don't want to go back," she repeated quietly. "Ever."

"No." He took her hand and kissed it. Then he brushed back the furs that covered one breast, lowered his head, and brushed the nipple ever so gently with his lips. "I don't want to go back," he affirmed, shifting his position so that he crouched above her. "Neither do you," he added confidently. "You just don't know it yet."

Miri closed her eyes and arched instinctively against him as Jordan's knee pressed between her thighs. Maybe, she thought, just maybe, he was right.

✳ 15 ✳

Gage Delacroix stayed in camp for three days. His presence was a constant reminder to Miri that she was still not facing up to reality. She had accepted Jordan's lame excuses for not taking her to Hamilton immediately too easily. The winter weather! Bah! And Jane. Smiles at Sunrise could care for Jane while they were gone. The older woman had become every bit as good at milking Petunia as Miri was. Not that the goat gave milk anymore. Poor Jane was having to survive on fish broth and parched corn softened to a mush in water.

Miri chided herself hourly for being too easily diverted from her duty. Jordan had a way of doing that to her. First he had made her doubt every belief she held dear, then he had seduced her into unhallowed passion—with considerable help from herself, Miri admitted—and now he would keep her from proving that Miss Miriam Sutcliffe of London, England, was still alive and kicking.

She would not let him do it. Miri felt as if her back was

against the wall. This was her last chance to prove that she hadn't lost sight of who she was or where she was going. She refused to be defeated. So on the second afternoon of Delacroix's stay she laid down the moccasins she was decorating for Sunrise. The half-breed had just come to the central fire to warm himself, and Miri had a proposition for him.

"Mr. Delacroix," she began, uncertain how to begin.

"Oh, please, *mademoiselle*. To you I am Gage."

"Well then, Gage, I have a favor to ask of you."

"For you, *ma petite*, anything!"

"I want you to take me to Prairie du Chien to find my cousin."

The half-breed cocked a black brow in her direction. "*Mon Dieu, mademoiselle*! You do not ask for much, do you?"

"I can pay you, Mr. Delacroix. I will need to send to my bank in London to obtain the money, but I promise you'll be handsomely paid."

He gave a deep sigh and rubbed his hands in front of the fire. "I'm sure you have plenty of money, *ma petite*, but what good is money to a dead man, eh?"

"Oh, come now!" Miri scoffed. "Surely you're not going to tell me about the weather, and the ice, and the cold, are you?"

"No, *mademoiselle*. But Prairie du Chien is getting to be a dangerous place. I have already been the target for one bullet, and I do not wish another to find me. And even were that not so, who would put me back together after your husband had torn me limb from limb?"

"My husband?"

"Eyes of a Ghost. The one you call Jordan. I know it for a fact, *ma petite*—this is not a man to be trifled with."

Miri felt her face grow hot. Of course Delacroix would believe she was Jordan's wife. They slept in the same wigwam, and Jordan's attitude since the French Canadian had been in camp was overtly possessive.

"Jordan is not my husband." It cost her pride to admit

her lack of virtue, but what was pride where duty was concerned? And her duty right now was to find Ham, pry from him the information that would free her, and resume her sane and normal life.

Delacroix shot her a knowing look. "That is what you think. Perhaps Eyes of a Ghost thinks differently. No, *mademoiselle*. It grieves me sorely to refuse a beautiful woman anything her heart desires. But I will not take you to Prairie du Chien."

And that was the end of that rebellion. A day later, Miri watched the half-breed guide strap on his pack and snow-shoes and wave a last greeting to the Chippewa camp. As he disappeared behind the snowdrifts piled along the riverbank, Miri felt abandoned—not to the wilderness, or even to Jordan Scott, but to the strange newcomer known as Eyes of the Sky, who was slowly but surely taking the place of Miriam Sutcliffe.

Miri was not the only one watching her transformation with distress. Willow Song reluctantly acknowledged that Eyes of a Ghost's white woman was not quite the useless thing she had appeared. If the woman had not been truly his wife, as Eyes of a Ghost had told Willow at the village of L'Arbre Croche, then she certainly was his wife now. The Indian girl recognized the way he looked at the white woman, saw the tenderness in his touch, the desire in his eyes even when the two of them exchanged sharp words. Willow Song saw her dreams of many years fading to nothing, and her jealousy grew apace.

Willow Song had been with her sister Lake Dancer on that day long ago when the canoe of Eyes of a Ghost and his white companion had overturned. She had been as instrumental as her sister in saving his life, and, like her sister, had grown to love the white man as he adopted Chippewa ways and was accepted as one of their family.

But Eyes of a Ghost had chosen Dancer, and Willow Song had buried her love deep in the back of her mind. She would not dishonor her sister, even should the opportunity present itself, which it never did. She might have accepted the humbler position of second wife, but Eyes of a Ghost had never asked. So Willow had married elsewhere. First a Chippewa, then, dissatisfied with her first mating, she took an Ottawa warrior. He also had been unable to hold her. Always Eyes of a Ghost was held up as comparison, and all other men were found lacking.

When Dancer had died, Willow Song had been genuinely desolate, for she had loved her sister. But such things happen when a woman tries to give her man a child. Dancer had had her joy, and Willow Song was positive that her sister would have wanted Eyes of a Ghost to turn to Willow for comfort.

But the white woman had intruded. She had refused to be driven off. And now, every night, Eyes of a Ghost filled her pale, insipid body with his, giving her the passion and pleasure and the living seed that should by rights belong to Willow Song. Every night Willow lay awake and imagined that just across the clearing, Jordan's strong body was plunging into the white woman. She imagined the little moans of pleasure that must fill their wigwam, the straining and quiet groaning and sighs of bliss that must come from their union. And all the while, Willow was unfairly condemned to a chaste life in the wigwam of her parents and brother.

Willow Song had comforted herself these last weeks by making the white woman's life as miserable as possible. But since Eyes of a Ghost had truly taken her as his wife, the woman seemed immune to her barbs. Now the Indian girl had decided on a more effective course of action. If Eyes of a Ghost should become dissatisfied with this white wife of his. . . .

Willow smiled and scraped furiously at the hide she was cleaning. Her eyes followed Miri as she emerged from her wigwam and took strips of venison and flavoring herbs off the rack outside the doorway. Such a diligent little wife the milk-faced intruder had become. Willow hoped Jordan would enjoy that evening's meal.

Jordan did indeed enjoy the stew that Miri had been simmering all afternoon long. He enjoyed it even more because he knew that Miri had skinned and butchered the deer herself. Part of the hide had gone to mend the soles of his moccasins. Another part had gone to make a blanket for Jane, and the rest adorned Miri's lithe body as soft tunic and leggings. Miri had smoked the meat in the stew, along with most of the rest of the deer, on racks over the fire. Not even the bones had been wasted. The split bones had become fine needles for sewing, and the long bones of the legs had been set aside for Smoke Catcher's carving.

Every day Jordan was more amazed at the transformation in his little English prig. When he had first laid a hand upon her, so long ago when he had pulled her half-drowned and frozen out of Lake Huron, he had sensed a woman of fire and passion somewhere behind the facade of society claptrap. But what he had not known was that a siren lurked deep in her soul who would lure him from his safe haven and make a white man of him again. With a smile here, a soft word there, she was stripping him of his defenses. Unconsciously she was laying a trap as wicked as any he had ever set for the marten and beaver of the forest. And he had taken the bait, knowing what it would mean. But it would be worth the price. If he had to once again become a white man, the bastard son of a Boston whore, he would do it in order to have Miriam Sutcliffe for the rest of his days.

Self-consciously, Jordan ran his hand over his head, which now boasted an inch of tawny, sun-streaked hair. Miri noticed the gesture and smiled. When she had first noticed his growing hair, he had told her he always let it grow during the winter. She didn't quite believe him.

"You look good with hair on your head," she said, putting a sleeping Jane down on her pallet. They spoke Chippewa between them now almost exclusively, even though Miri still sometimes had to struggle for words. "I don't understand why the other men don't let theirs grow, too. It would be warmer."

"I'm the only one with any sense," Jordan replied, then hastily changed the subject. "This stew is good."

"It must be. You've had two helpings already." Miri dished herself out a bowlful.

"You tried a different seasoning," Jordan guessed.

"I didn't try anything different. Sunrise is the one who knows every herb in the woods, not me." She took a mouthful, then another. "It is a bit different, though, isn't it?"

Jordan finished off his last bowl and scraped the leavings into Petunia's corn bucket. The goat gave him a cautious look, sniffed at his offering, and whiffed in disgust.

"Goats don't eat meat," Miri admonished Jordan.

"That wasn't meat—just a few vegetables and herbs."

Miri frowned. "She's usually eager for those. I hope she isn't getting sick."

Petunia gave them both a look of unperturbed superiority.

"That damned goat's as strong as I am. She's not getting sick, she's just peculiar."

"You look a bit peculiar yourself, Jordan. Are you all right?"

"I'm fine." His voice had an edge that the innocent question didn't merit. "It's late. Are you coming to bed?"

"As soon as I get these dishes clean."

Water had been warming over the fire. Miri poured it into a bucket and began scrubbing the wooden platters that had served as dinner plates. Jordan occupied himself with rolling out the bedding and stripping down to breechclout and leggings. By the time Miri joined him, he already had a familiar gleam in his eye.

"Let me do that," he offered as Miri started to loosen her clothing.

In a very short time Miri was divested of everything but her moccasins. Gently, Jordan pushed her down onto the bedding and joined her there. He laced his fingers into the silky mass of her hair, now grown almost to shoulder length, and gave each eyelid and the tip of her nose a playful kiss while his leg worked a subtle magic between hers.

Then he stopped. Drawing back, he propped himself on

one arm and stared at a point over her shoulder, an uncertain look on his face.

"What's wrong?" she said.

The uncertain look was replaced with a grimace. "What was in that stew, dammit? Is this your idea of a joke?"

Miri was becoming alarmed. "Are you ill?"

The sudden pallor of his skin was her answer. He had closed his eyes, and beads of sweat were popping out on his brow and upper lips, despite the chill.

"Lord!" Jordan staggered to his feet and made for the exit, both hands clutching his stomach. His doubled-over, crablike motion bore no resemblance to his usually proud demeanor.

Miri's eyes widened in dismay as she listened to the sounds of his agony, which was distressingly audible through the wigwam walls. But she did not have many minutes to listen until she felt a twinge in her own stomach. The twinge rapidly became a cramp, and the cramp a twisting agony. Suddenly her stomach was crowding up into her throat and her bowels were seeking similar exit at the other end of her. Miri dashed for the doorway in a manner every bit as undignified as Jordan's had been.

The night became a dark pit of misery. Even after the stew was emptied from their bellies and bowels, the purgative continued to squeeze fluid from their bodies in a most uncomfortable and undignified manner. The night was punctuated by mad dashes out of the wigwam and into the freezing cold, and equally mad scrambles for the warmth of the shelter. Periods between were spent curled on the bedding in tight, cramped balls of discomfort.

"I didn't do this," Miri ground out during one such period of quiescence.

"I know," Jordan answered, his voice hoarse.

Miri made the effort to turn and look at him. "You believe me?"

"God knows you've the temperament to do it," Jordan sighed. "And there are times when I've deserved something like this. But you wouldn't be fool enough to eat it yourself."

The conversation was ended by an urgent visit to the frozen outdoors.

It wasn't until midmorning, when the spasms and cramps had abated, leaving only soreness and exhaustion in their wake, that Miri had a chance to think. Most of the members of the camp had an excellent knowledge of herbs—Smoke Catcher most of all, for he was a member of the Midewiwin, which had herbology as one of its primary teachings. Smiles at Sunrise also knew every plant in the forest—what could be used to cure a cough, to aid in childbirth, to spice a stew. But Sunrise had no reason for the vicious prank that had laid them low. And Rides the Waves was innocent beyond question. That left only Willow Song. Her motives were easily guessed. She must have imagined that Jordan would be furious at Miri's incompetence. Or even worse, he might think Miri had dosed him deliberately. Willow might believe that in his anger Jordan would turn to her for comfort. Well, the little tart had a surprise coming to her—and quite a bit more, as well.

Case closed, Miri thought. She shut her eyes and let sleep claim her, thinking as she sank into exhausted slumber of just how she would take her pound of flesh from Willow Song's hide.

An entire day passed before either Miri or Jordan could stir from their bed. A concerned Sunrise took Jane into the big wigwam and took over Miri's chores of milking the goat and caring for the baby. Every two hours she dosed both Jordan and Miri with a vile-tasting tea. Shame clouded the older woman's eyes, and Miri knew she had guessed what must have happened. Sunrise had probably already given her daughter a severe tongue-lashing, but it didn't matter. Miri intended to deal with the bitch in her own way.

It was a full week before Miri felt strong enough to issue her challenge. Jordan had left the day before with Rides the Waves to check the trap lines and also try to locate one of the bears they had seen in the autumn. He would be gone a long time—maybe as much as two weeks, leaving a perfect opportunity for Miri to take care of her little problem.

Jordan would never have allowed her to carry out her plan, but she was determined to settle things with Willow Song once and for all.

"What do you want?" Willow Song frowned as Miri approached the spot where she was stretching a moose hide in the sun.

"I wish to have an understanding between us, Willow Song."

"We understand each other well enough."

"Not quite," Miri denied. "I know it was you who dosed my stew to make us sick. What I want you to understand is that I won't tolerate any more of your viciousness."

Willow Song gave her a level look full of hostility. "If you were a proper Chippewa woman, you would have recognized the herbs I mixed in with the flavorings on your food rack. Then you would not have used them, and Eyes of a Ghost would not have been ill. It is you who are at fault, white woman, not I."

"I will not argue about who was at fault," Miri said in a calm voice. "We both know the answer to that. I simply wish to discover how good a Chippewa woman you really are, Willow."

"Chippewa or white, I am a better woman than you. Someday Eyes of a Ghost will come to realize that, and he will send you back to your people." Willow Song turned her back and continued her work. But the white woman refused to leave.

"If you are such a splendid woman, Willow Song, I suppose you would not mind proving to everyone just how much better you are than me. A bout of the woman's game should do the job. This afternoon on the riverbank?"

Willow Song turned to look at her. Her face was impassive, but deep in her eyes there glinted a spark of joy. "You are foolish to suggest such a contest," she warned. "I am Anishanabe. You"—her lips curled in a sneer—"are white."

"You shouldn't worry, then, should you? Here's your chance to properly humiliate me."

Miri smiled to herself as she walked away.

Along the riverbank was a clear area about three hundred feet long where the daily traffic of moccasined feet had packed the snow to a hard surface. It made an ideal spot for the contest that Miri had proposed. Smoke Catcher, delighted at the prospect of entertainment, had set two poles in the snow, one on each end of what would be the playing field. Smiles at Sunrise scolded her husband for permitting the game to take place; nevertheless, she busied herself cutting and smoothing long, slender sticks for the two rivals to use. Even she was curious as to what would happen when Miri confronted her adversary.

Miri watched the preparations with a smile on her face. Two months ago she would never have thought of such a thing. It would have been beneath her dignity, and well beyond her strength and agility. But now her arms and legs were firm with supple muscle. If anything could get Willow out of her hair, it would be beating her at her own game. By whatever method necessary, Miri intended to be the winner. Justice, she thought, was on her side.

Justice might have been on Miri's side, but skill was not. She had often watched the woman's game being played when she had visited Lake Dancer in the village. It had looked simple. Players each held two long, slender sticks. With these sticks they attempted to catch and carry two small balls that were tied together with basswood twine. The poles set at the end of the playing field were goals, and the player who carried the balls to the goal most often was the winner.

It was not simple, however, as Miri discovered, to her dismay. Only an exceedingly deft touch could keep the balls from slipping out from between the carrying sticks, and picking them up and catching them were almost impossible feats. Impossible for Miri—not so for Willow Song.

Only sheer determination got Miri through the first part of the game. Willow Song was far ahead in the scoring by the time she began to get the hang of carrying the balls without dropping them. The Chippewa girl, smirking with the certainty of victory, began to grow overconfident. Visions of her rival's humiliation kept her from realizing that Miri's score was slowly but surely gaining on her own. With the game three-quarters over, Smoke Catcher's proclamation of a tied score caught her by surprise.

It was then that Willow Song began to get angry. Things were not going quite as she had planned. Where was the milk-faced weakling who had not been able to carry a pack five steps without tumbling into the snow? Miri's face gleamed with sweat and her hands shook as they held the sticks, but she was still strong. The looks she gave Willow were still full of challenge, and her mouth was a tight line of determination.

Willow Song renewed the play with a vengeance. When Miri lost the balls, her sticks flipping them high up into the air, both women scrambled in for the catch. Willow charged in with her eyes more on Miri than the balls. Her shoulder crashed into Miri's midsection. Both women went down, and the balls dropped unheeded into the snow.

Miri felt as if her eyes were swimming in her head, and at least a ton of snow had found its way down her tunic. As she pushed her way to her feet, she saw that Willow was already up, a triumphant smile stretched across her face. If that was the way the bitch wanted it, Miri thought, two could play that game.

From then on the balls and goals were a scarcely heeded part of the game. The object became to see who could deliver the hardest body blocks, who could trip without being tripped, who could best survive having her face plowed into the snow, and who could still walk and run after having a stick broken over her head. This was a game that Miri knew well, for when Hamilton and she had roamed the Kentish countryside in the golden days of her childhood, she had been no stranger to the tussles and scrapes that all children indulge in, especially when away from watchful parental eyes. She'd had a rare talent for brawling, long forgotten since propriety had taken its hold upon her. But Miri was no longer a proper lady, and the hoydenish talent returned with a vengeance.

Smoke Catcher's eyes widened in dismay as the playing field became the site of a free-for-all. He rose to his feet, intending to put a halt to this breach of rules, but Smiles at Sunrise restrained him with a hand on his arm.

"They will not kill each other, Husband. The surest way to put out a fire is to let it burn until it is done."

The old shaman shook his head in bemusement. For all the wisdom that the spirits had seen fit to give him, he would never understand the female half of mankind.

The women on the playing field had stopped keeping score of goals made or blows delivered. Their moves had slowed, and both had given up the pretense of playing a game. Carrying sticks and balls lay unheeded in the snow. Willow Song's braids had loosened and her glossy black hair flew in snarled disarray around her head. Her lip was swollen, and one eye was beginning to color a livid purple.

Miri was little better off. Her hair curled against her neck and cheeks in strands of wet auburn, glinting a coppery fire from the dying rays of the sun. The knuckles of one hand were scraped and swollen, and a split in her lower lip had smeared a crimson stain across her cheek. But she was still on her feet, and Willow was swaying like a sapling in a strong wind.

Finally the Chippewa girl gave in and let herself collapse onto the snow in exhaustion. She gave her rival a rueful smile.

"You have won, Eyes of the Sky. My mother should have named you Head Like a Rock, for you truly have one."

Miri felt the glow of victory flow like heated wine through her veins, banishing weariness. She had won. No matter that she had behaved in a monstrously barbarian manner. It felt good. It felt wonderful. A primitive victory cry rose into her throat, and it was all she could do to keep from shouting it out upon the wind. Lord! What a savage she had become!

Miri looked down at the defeated and bedraggled Chippewa girl. "If you ever play your dirty tricks again, or lay a single finger on Eyes of a Ghost while I'm here to see it, the next thrashing won't be in a game, Willow Song.''

Willow Song got wearily to her feet. Her face, for all its black eye and swollen lip, had a strange dignity. "I am not without honor. You have bested me. In my eyes you are now Anishanabe, and your honor is mine.''

"Friends, then?" Miri asked suspiciously.

"Not friends," Willow replied stiffly. "I do not think we will ever be friends, Eyes of the Sky. But now we are sisters. That is more binding than friendship.''

With this statement she turned and walked back toward the wigwams, her posture bent, her stride stiff and sore, but with a fair amount of poise nonetheless.

April was named by the Chippewa as the moon of putting away snowshoes. It was a month of changes. The snow still flew, but between the days of gloomy cold the sun shone bright and warm. The forest tinkled with the sound of dripping, and everywhere little rivulets of mud and water tumbled down to join the streams and rivers, which in their turn became torrents rushing toward the lake.

When the first patches of bare ground and rock peeked through the snow, Smoke Catcher announced that it was time for the family to move. It had been a good winter season. The log storage hut was overflowing with tightly wrapped bundles of prime-quality peltries, and all winter the women had worked hard to dry and smoke the meat of the deer, elk, and moose that the forest—and the deadly arrows of Eyes of a Ghost and Rides the Waves—had provided. A fat bear had also given its life for the sustenance of their family, and the carcass had yielded enough meat to burden three women. The fat, when boiled down to oil, filled six large porcupine skins, and Eyes of a Ghost was decorated with an impressive bear-claw necklace.

The winter had indeed been a profitable one, and as Smoke Catcher's family broke camp and loaded the dogsleds, spirits were high. They looked forward to the coming weeks in the sugar bush—the maple grove that had been worked by the family for generations to obtain the maple syrup and sugar that was the universal seasoning among the Chippewa. Even more did they look forward to a summer of fishing and gardening in the village on the Straits of Mackinac.

Spring brought changes to Miri, as well. Helping Sunrise and Willow set up temporary cedar-bark lodges and clean the big boiling kettles that had been stored in the maple grove since the last spring, she struggled to hide her exhaustion. She was grateful that when winter camp had been broken, the snow was still sufficiently crusted for the dogsleds to be used in transporting the households. In spite of her new strength and suppleness, she would have faltered had she been required to carry a heavy pack. Jordan would have seen, and it would not have taken him long to figure out what was wrong.

It would be the end of April before she would know for certain, but Miri was reasonably sure that Jane had a sister or brother on the way. She had missed her monthly courses at the end of March, and a new lassitude had come upon her. She was tired from the moment she rose in the morning to the time when she gratefully crawled under the furs at night. Her breasts were tender and bloated, and a growing disinterest in food was accompanied by a nausea that struck erratically at any time of the day.

This was a complication that Miri definitely didn't need. But in spite of the inconvenience, the moral dilemma, and the queasiness that dogged her every waking hour, she couldn't help but hug herself with joy at the thought of bearing Jordan's child. It seemed so right that the feelings she bore him, the passion that marked their every coming together, should be consummated in a new life that was part of both of them.

But if her pregnancy seemed right in the natural order of things, it made Miri's moral dilemma staggering. For the time being, she didn't feel up to facing it. Her emotions the last week had been riding a seesaw, with the ups sending her into clouds of euphoria and the downs into a sea of tears. This was no time to be wondering whether Jordan truly loved her, if she loved him, or if a marriage between them, with all their differences, would have the least chance of working. The most important thing right now was to make sure that Jordan didn't find out about her pregnancy, for if he did, all decisions would be swiftly taken out of her hands.

Hiding her secret from Jordan was more easily thought about than accomplished, however. Miri quickly discovered that a Chippewa sugar camp was a difficult place to hide a queasy stomach, for the sap kettles were kept boiling all day and all night, and the air was always heavy with the sticky-sweet odor of cooking sugar. To make matters worse, once the syrup had been boiled, strained, and reheated, it was then transferred to granulating troughs where it was worked by hand. And this job fell to Miri and Willow.

On the second afternoon squatting before a trough of redolent warm sugar, Miri knew she couldn't last. All day long she had been choking on the cloying odor of the air, and the very sight of the sugar in the trough made her stomach crowd into her throat. With a hasty word of excuse to Willow Song, Miri bolted for the clean air of the forest.

More than a little curious, Willow Song promptly left her task and followed. She found Miri leaning against a tall spruce, emptying the contents of her stomach onto the needle-carpeted ground.

"You are ill?" Willow asked.

The guilty look that flashed across Miri's features told the story well enough.

"You are with child."

Miri nodded, knowing there was no use in denying it. Then she groaned and retched again.

Willow's face was shuttered. "You must have great joy. And Eyes of a Ghost, also. Perhaps you will give him the healthy child that my sister was unable to bear."

Miri shook her head miserably. "Please, Willow. Jordan . . . Eyes of a Ghost . . . doesn't know." She sat down upon a nearby rock and let her head sink into her hands. Willow came to hover over her.

"What kind of fools are white women? Why do you not tell Eyes of a Ghost that his seed is growing within you? And why do you cry? Are you afraid of the birth, Eyes of the Sky? I did not think you were such a coward."

"I'm not afraid," Miri sniveled. She wrapped her arms around herself, as though embracing the child within her. "I want this child. I love it already. But...you don't understand."

How was she to tell Willow Song that Jordan would take all choices from her if he learned about the baby? No child of his would bear the bastard's onus, he had said. And Jordan Scott had the strength of will and the strength of arm to enforce his decision. In all the jumble of hostility, love, desire, and confusion she held in her heart for the renegade, she had never really been afraid of him. Until now. Now she was afraid of his power over her body and her heart. She had to make the decisions herself about what was best for her child. What Jordan wanted, and what Miri wanted for herself, would have to come second.

Willow Song sat down beside her and regarded her with a puzzled frown. "You're right, Eyes of the Sky, I do not understand. Your husband will be grateful that you give him this child. It will bind him to you for the rest of your days. What do you fear?"

"I do not fear anything," Miri lied. The fountain of tears had stopped. "I will tell him when the time is right. I'm not yet sure of anything. Only six weeks has passed since my last monthly flow."

Willow shook her head. "You are a woman, just as I am. I would know if a child grows within me. You know also. I can see it in your eyes, my sister."

Miri sighed. "Please respect my wishes in this, Willow Song. I wish Eyes of a Ghost to hear the news from me, when the time is right."

Willow rose from their seat and dusted off her trim behind. When she turned to Miri her face was thoughtful. "I will do as you ask," she conceded. "But I think you are a fool, my sister. You say you are not afraid, but I smell fear in the air around you. I do not know why it is, but you are afraid.''

Miri watched her go, then hugged herself tightly, as though she could provide herself the comfort that she needed. There were so many uncertainties, so many things to set right before she could be her own woman again. And now this. Perhaps she would never be her own woman again.

But one thing was certain. No matter what Miri said to herself or others, Willow Song spoke the truth about her.

She was afraid.

✳ 16 ✳

June was the month of homecoming. The strawberry moon, as the Chippewa named it, was a time of reconvening the whole village, greeting friends, catching up on news, and sharing the exploits of the winter. While men counted peltries and readied them to be taken to the trading house, women broke ground for gardens of squash and corn and repaired fishing seines in preparation to reap the bounty of Lake Huron. Others busied themselves opening the village food caches of vegetables and rice, storing the winter's bounty of meat, and repairing wigwams. Warriors and women smiled and talked as they worked, happy to be finished with winter's isolation. A herd of children and winter-scrawny dogs raced around the village in a heedless current of laughter and barking. Summer had finally returned, with all its boisterous energy.

Smoke Catcher's family was one of the last to arrive at the reawakened village. They were greeted by the news that had spread like wildfire among the returned Chippewa. A senior war chief of the British had come to the island across the straits, and the Americans were finally on the march to regain what had been taken from them.

The morning after the family arrived, the rumors were confirmed by Margaret Peavey. Miri welcomed her with a joyous bear hug that took the girl's breath away, then quickly escorted her into the wigwam that Miri had just completed with a bit of help from Sunrise and Willow.

"Miri!"

Margaret looked her up and down, obviously taken aback by her appearance. Miri's face was golden from the sun's kiss. Freckles dotted her nose, and her hair, now grown past her shoulders, was plaited into two stubby braids. She was dressed in a lightweight buckskin tunic that fell to her knees and was split along the sides for easy movement. Fringed leggings, moccasins, and an elaborately beaded headband completed her attire.

"You've . . . you've changed so!" Margaret exclaimed.

Miri smiled. "Did you expect me to be gowned, coiffed, plucked, and painted after spending the winter with the Chippewa?"

"Well, no. I guess not. I just didn't think . . . that is . . ."

"You didn't think what?" Jordan said as he entered the hut.

Margaret's head spun around toward Jordan, and her cheeks warmed to a rosy pink. He was naked but for breechclout and leggings, and the work he had just quit had put a glistening sheen of sweat over his torso, emphasizing every ridge of muscle. His hair had grown to an even length of two inches and framed his face with a tousled mass of tawny gold.

"Jordan!" Margaret was rapt. Always before, the masculine austerity of his face had been almost frightening. But now, though the features were the same, the cold austerity had softened. *It must be the hair,* Margaret thought. Though there was something different in his eyes, as well. "Jordan! Is that you?"

"Who else would it be, puss?"

He reached out a hand and teasingly tweaked her chin, making the girl's face flame even brighter. *Poor Margaret,*

Miri thought, smiling. Jordan didn't realize that the very maleness of him could send any woman's heart into arrest, and would certainly devastate the tentatively budding sensibilities of a girl Margaret's age.

"Leave off, Jordan," Miri said, a lilt of laughter in her voice. "Let Margaret be. I want to know if these rumors we hear are true—about the Americans, and the new commander."

Margaret cleared her throat, her eyes following Jordan as he sat cross-legged beside Miri. She had no more thought for Miri's outrageous appearance. As of that moment, she had only envy for the fortunate woman who could so casually sit by Jordan Scott's side. And was his hand stealing around her waist? It was, by George! How utterly, sinfully delicious! She could hardly wait to tell her mother.

"Margaret?" Miri prompted.

"What? Oh, yes." Her voice lowered, as though she had a secret to impart that no one else should hear. "I've been coming to the village every day since the Chippewa started drifting in, hoping to find you. It's all true, Miri. Captain Michaels has been replaced by another fellow, a man named McDouall. He's a lieutenant colonel, I think. And everyone on the island says the Americans are going to attack soon, though no one knows quite where they are or what they're up to."

"Michaels has gone back to England?" Miri asked anxiously.

"Well, I suppose he will soon, though he's not too happy about it, and neither is Ma."

Miri's face puckered in a puzzled frown. "What has your mother got to do with Captain Michaels?"

"Just wait till you hear!" Margaret practically giggled.

"Michaels is still here, then?" Jordan interrupted impatiently.

"Oh, yes. He's second in command, for now. And he's at the farm all the time, it seems, talking to Ma. So you'd better not come home just yet, Miri."

Jordan cursed under his breath. "I'm surprised he wasn't here to meet us."

Margaret shrugged. "All those Britishers are busy figuring out when the Americans are going to come. Ma says Captain Michaels doesn't have time to go chasing after you any longer, Miri. But she says to be sure to stay away from the farm. If he were to see you, he'd likely make the time.''

"You can be sure I'll stay away, then," Miri assured her.

Margaret's visit was brief, though she promised to convey Miri's love to her mother and sisters and come often to visit. When she had gone, Jordan gave Miri a thorough kiss, speculated jovially that she might escape hanging after all, and left to rejoin Smoke Catcher, who had recruited him to the task of constructing several new canoes.

Left to her own thoughts, Miri smiled with contentment. Perhaps the jagged pieces of her life were falling into place at last. She'd spent weeks puzzling out a solution to her problems with only partial success. Her queasiness had passed quickly, and the rest of the season had seen Miri's happiness blooming alongside spring's new verdant growth. She had not taken long to decide that Jordan had a right to know of the unborn child who curled so sweetly within her, and that she, Miriam Sutcliffe, Eyes of the Sky, or whomever she had become, had a right to happiness. Though Miri had delayed again and again telling Jordan of her decision, she could not return to a barren life of social calls, petty gossip, and sedate rides through the park—not when she knew that across the sea there lived a man with tawny gold hair and ghostly gray eyes who had managed to interweave himself with every cell of her body.

Miri had not delayed telling Jordan because of uncertainty, she told herself. It was just that the time had never been right. But Jordan would have his new child, and its mother, if he truly wanted her, and be damned with the voices of reason that shrieked to her of disaster.

But there had remained the problem of Michaels. Miri might be willing to give up her quest for Hamilton, to live the rest of her life in primitive obscurity, but she very much doubted that the cursed, hidebound captain would see it her way. There was a war on, after all, and Hamilton had sold his country out in a most disgraceful way. Michaels wanted

Hamilton, and he wanted that list of names. To find them both, he would probably plague Miri from America to England and back again if he had to.

But that particular problem had solved itself, it seemed. If Michaels soon returned to England, he could not very well keep up his pursuit, and with any luck at all, this silly war would soon be over and the good captain would lose interest. She and Jordan could go their way without fear, and Hamilton, the fool, could stay in his little trading post on the Mississippi River for all Miri cared. And if she ever saw her blackguard cousin again, she would . . .

Miri let the thought hang. It was worth pondering another day, perhaps, but right now she wanted to savor the feeling of having reached her decision, once and for all, and to think of a good way to tell Jordan that he was going to be a father again. She looked forward to seeing the expression on his face, or perhaps she didn't. God help her—and him, too—if he weren't happy about the coming event.

Miri spent the rest of the day in busy preparation. This was going to be a special night for her, and for Jordan. The evening meal would be just right—wild rice and vegetables, venison, baked freshly caught fish, and Juneberries topped with maple sugar. When Jordan was full and content, she would break the news. There would be no more delays.

But the special night did not go precisely as Miri had envisioned it. Jordan did not enter the wigwam until well after dark, and when he did, his features were taut with weariness. Still dripping with cold lake water from his evening swim, he sat down and started to eat, scarcely even noticing that all his favorite dishes were laid out before him. The smile he gave Miri was a stiff excuse for a greeting. His heart wasn't in it, she could tell, and rather than fastening on her with their customary warmth, his eyes slid past her gaze as if in avoidance. It was all very puzzling—unless he had learned from Willow Song of her pregnancy and was displeased.

Miri's heart was in her throat as she sat down beside him. After a few strained moments, she could stand the silence no longer. "Who were the men I saw talking with you and Smoke Catcher this afternoon by the lake?"

Her question had merely been an attempt at conversation, and surely did not merit the scowl he turned her way.

"They were military men," he answered slowly, seeming to choose his words with care. "Americans."

"American military men? Then it's true? The Americans really are planning an attack upon the fort?"

"I do not know their plans," Jordan hedged.

"What did they want?" Miri felt a glimmer of British conscience. The upstart Americans were planning to attack her countrymen, after all. No matter that she and the British authorities hadn't quite seen eye to eye in the last months, she was still a loyal subject of the king. The British garrison should be warned if mischief was afoot.

"These fellows are just scouts," Jordan told her. "They had nothing much to say. Food is what they were looking for."

"Oh." That took the newborn wind out of her patriotic sails. She supposed that in any case the Americans weren't really much of a threat, though she would never have said so to Grace or her daughters, patriotic Americans that they were. But one could not expect the rabble of Americans to be effective against a fortress being held by the British army—a fortress that had originally been wrested from them without so much as a shot being fired.

She raised her eyes to find Jordan regarding her with a speculative gaze that sent a little chill shivering down her spine. Had he learned that she was carrying his child? If he was this displeased about it then surely it was best to know the truth of the matter. And since he was being so close-- mouthed, she would bring up the subject herself.

"Jordan, I have something to talk to you about."

"And I also want to speak with you."

Sweet heaven! He *had* learned of her pregnancy! And he didn't sound pleased at all. "What about?" she asked with a stiff smile.

"I'm going away for a while."

Miri's relief was short-lived. This wasn't good news at all. "Where are you going?"

"I'm going to act as guide for the troops that are coming into this area. That is what those scouts were talking to me about."

"American troops?"

"Would you expect me to be leading British reinforcements?"

"I don't know. No, I suppose not."

Miri got up and turned away, ostensibly to check on little Jane. Suddenly she felt very vulnerable to those eyes that were regarding her so closely. It had been easy to forget that Jordan was an American. The Great Lakes Indians were for the most part pro-British, and Jordan had always seemed much more Chippewa than white. Miri had simply assumed that if Jordan took sides at all in the current struggle, he would side with the British, as his Chippewa friends had done.

"I don't suppose you're going to wish me Godspeed." Jordan's hands landed on Miri's shoulders from behind, making her jump.

"I don't know what to wish you," she answered quietly. "Except perhaps to wish you would change your mind."

With gentle but irresistible strength he turned her around to face him. "Were you not the one always lecturing me on responsibility and duty?"

"And were you not the one who said he wanted no part of the white man's world?"

"I met a little sprite who lit a fire under my conscience." He smiled ruefully. "Did you really think I could side with the British?"

"I didn't think you would take sides at all. Or I suppose I thought you might side with me, not against me. It's my cousin who's the traitor, Jordan, not me. I am British to my very marrow."

"You were not British enough to give yourself over to Captain Michaels."

"That little misunderstanding has nothing at all to do with my patriotism. I am British. I will always be British."

Halfheartedly she tried to pull herself from his grasp. "What did you expect me to say?"

Jordan frowned. His hands tightened on her shoulders to keep her close. "I expect you to say that you'll be here when I get back."

Miri met his frown with a glare of her own. She was not at all pleased with this new wrinkle appearing in her life just when she thought she had her problems solved. "I'm not going to make any promises, Jordan. I'll have to think about it."

"Be here, Miri. If you're not, I'll find you. That's a promise you can count on."

Miri's retort was cut short by the sudden assault of Jordan's mouth. His hands shifted to either side of her head, holding her still. His lips moved sensuously against her resisting mouth, both a demand and a supplication.

Finally he released her, then moved to nibble at her ear. "We have unfinished business between us, woman. Don't leave me now."

Miri could think of a dozen sarcastic retorts to put him in his place, but Jordan reappropriated her lips before she could give them voice. By the time he released her again, every objection to him or what he was doing had fled before his assault.

"I'm going to miss you." Silver eyes raked her face and form as though memorizing every detail. "I'm going to miss your fire, your stubbornness, even the damned razor edge of your tongue." His voice dropped to a husky whisper. "And most surely I'm going to miss this."

His hands grasped her buttocks and pulled her hard against him, pressing the swollen length of his desire against her belly. It was the completion of Miri's undoing. The fire that had begun deep in the pit of her stomach flashed outward to burn along every nerve. She strained against him, and he answered with a kiss savage enough to rob her of any remnants of her tattered will. Ruthlessly his lips ground upon hers, his tongue plunging in and out of her softness in passionate rehearsal of what was still to come.

"You're not playing fair." Her voice was breathless as Jordan eased her down upon their pallet.

He grinned wickedly, reaching for the lacings of her tunic. "When have you ever known me to play fair, my love?"

"Never."

There was no more breath for words. Miri's heart did a dance in her chest as Jordan slowly undressed her and then, with his gaze never leaving her naked body, stripped himself to the skin. He didn't have to lay a hand on her to have her panting for him, Miri realized without shame. His eyes alone, raking her with such possessive satisfaction, were enough to make her blood boil within her veins. When he finally had looked his fill and lowered himself upon her, Miri clutched him with desperate need. Coarse male body hair brushed her heated skin, setting it afire. Lean muscles rolled and bunched beneath her roaming hands. Her sigh of pleasure merged with his as Jordan's weight pressed her down into the bedding.

"Every time I touch you I want you more," he whispered hoarsely. "Lord, woman! You set me on fire. I'm burning alive."

They burned together. Miri squirmed beneath him in unladylike urgency, knowing she would surely die if he didn't ease her desperate need with the gift of his body. When he grasped her thighs and plunged between them with a savage, heart-stopping thrust, she welcomed him with a moan of ecstasy. She wrapped her slender legs around his waist, and urged him on. Never had she felt such desperation in herself, or such savage passion in him as he thrust again and again, each stroke harder and deeper.

The bout was short and violent, climaxing in a spasm almost painful in its intensity. Miri held to Jordan as her only anchor in a maelstrom that threatened to sweep her away. For a moment she thought she might lose consciousness, so overwhelming was her release. Jordan's rock-solid hardness above her and within her was the only thing that kept the world from swirling away.

When ecstasy had finally burned down to mere contentedness, Miri opened her eyes. Jordan loomed above her. His hands brushed tenderly at the curls that stuck to her sweat-dampened brow. She closed her eyes again, enjoying the feel of him still within her, reveling in the gentleness of his strong hands touching her brow, stroking her hair.

"There's your paradise again," she said, her hand lifting to caress his cheek.

He caught her hand in his. Their fingers intertwined. "You are my paradise."

He was hardening once again within her. Miri closed her eyes in dreamy delight.

"Promise me you will be here," he demanded. Slowly he lowered his head until their mouths met. "Promise," he whispered against her lips.

One of his hands slipped beneath her and arched her against him. He was once again huge, hungry, and throbbing inside her.

"You're a part of me," he breathed, his mouth curling into a wicked smile. "And I'm very much a part of you. You *will* be here when I return."

"Yes," she sighed, opening her eyes to meet the gaze that riveted her beneath him.

Slowly he withdrew and then pressed his hard length inside her once again. "Swear it."

Miri felt the trembling of his arms as he held himself above her, keeping himself from moving as nature demanded. He was torturing himself, as well as her. Her eyes smiled up into his, a hint of mischief in their depths. She twisted her hips and was gratified to see sweat break out on his brow. "Go to your damned Americans, Jordan Scott. I will be here when you return." Closing her eyes as his mouth descended toward hers, Miri gave herself over to his desire, and to hers.

The morning sun peeked into the wigwam to find Miri still sleeping. It was Jane's crying that finally woke her. Still weary from a night spent in activities that were anything but restful, Miri groaned and rolled over, seeking to snuggle against the hard body that should have been lying next to hers. Her hand groped aimlessly up and down, finding only furs cold with the morning chill. Her eyes popped open beneath puckered brows, and she muttered a colorful exclamation that would have curled her Aunt Eliza's hair.

Jane wailed again, and a plaintive bleat from Petunia reminded Miri that unless she bestirred herself, the whole village was likely to be treated to a concert from both of her charges.

While Jane's fish broth and corn mush was warming over the fire pit, Miri's stomach rebelled for the first time in weeks, reminding her that she was still pregnant, still unmarried, and now faced with a complication she hadn't foreseen. It was one thing to give up her personal standards for the sake of love. It was quite something else to consort with a man who was actively engaged in warfare against one's king and country, even if he was doing no more than acting as a local guide. Neither was she happy about the way Jordan had manipulated her the night before. He had shamelessly and expertly played upon her passions to extract her promise to stay, and then left in the early morning hours without a word of farewell, and without the declaration of love that might have made everything more acceptable, if not all right. As it was she was left merely with the assurance of his passion, with the presence of his child inside her, and with the knowledge that he had left her to consort with Britain's enemies. She'd not even had the chance to tell him of the new life they had created, and right at that moment, with her stomach rebelling and her pride stinging, Miri was glad.

By midmorning she was thoroughly depressed. She needed to talk to someone who understood the complexities of her position, Miri decided. Someone like Grace. Smiles at Sunrise had become almost like a mother to her, but Sunrise was a Chippewa, after all, and in her eyes Miri was Jordan's wife. British and American soldiers and unborn bastard babies did not figure into the Chippewa matron's viewpoint.

So Miri dug down into her belongings and pulled out a muslin gown that had been packed away all winter. Shaking out the gown's wrinkles as best she could, she pulled off tunic, leggings, and moccasins, and replaced them with chemise, pantalets, and the high-waisted, tightly sashed, narrow-sleeved dress that had been the height of fashion in Montreal when she had passed through the summer before. Had she gained weight over the winter, Miri wondered in distress, or had tight bodices and narrow sleeves always been so uncomfortable? As the last step in her transformation, she shook out her stubby auburn braids and confined the resulting riot of curls with a ribbon.

Though she had no mirror, Miri suspected that her sun-browned face and freckles were anything but ladylike. But her appearance would have to do. After all, she was going to Grace's farm, not to Almack's.

The paddle across the straits took the rest of the morning, though Miri noted with pleasure that the labor which had exhausted her last autumn now merely left her feeling exhilarated—a tribute to a winter of hard work and exercise. But her stomach definitely knew it was dinnertime. Miri remembered the delicious aroma of freshly baked bread that usually filled Grace's kitchen and the wonderful preserves and pies that had earned the widow a reputation all over Michilimackinac Island. Her stomach rumbled as she followed the path from the beach up to the farmhouse.

The house looked just as Miri had remembered it. Nothing had changed. Miri could almost imagine she was the innocent English girl who had spent the last summer learning to milk goats and sew her own clothes—the girl who hadn't the faintest idea of the joy, sorrow, passion, and hurt that could exist between a man and a woman. Almost, Miri could imagine it. But not quite.

The girls were not in evidence as Miri approached the house. Likely they were in the kitchen eating a hearty dinner, she surmised. Or, if this was Wednesday—how long since she had heeded the days of the week!—they might be in town doing the marketing. But Grace would be home, and it was Grace who could help Miri thread her way through the complexities of her problems.

Grace was indeed home, and she had a visitor. As Miri knocked briefly and swung open the door that led from the porch into the big combination kitchen-parlor, two heads swiveled in her direction. One belonged to Grace, the other to Gerald Michaels.

Too late Miri remembered Margaret's warning. For a moment she merely stared. Grace and Michaels stared back. They all three wore identical expressions of surprise. Michaels was the first to recover.

"Welcome back, Miss Sutcliffe. I trust you spent a safe winter with your Chippewa friends."

Miri stood frozen in her tracks, unable to think, poised to flee.

Michaels rose and put his teacup on the table beside the sofa. His expression was bland, cool, and matter-of-fact.

"I wouldn't turn and run, if I were you. It would grieve me to offer a lady violence, but I can assure you that I would not hesitate to do my duty if you tried to escape."

Miri shot a desperate look toward Grace, who responded valiantly.

"Gerald, now don't be getting on that high horse of yours. You've got no business treating this girl like some criminal. You know as well as I that she's innocent as a babe."

"Grace, my dear. Why don't you bring Miss Sutcliffe a cup of tea. And put a dram of rum in it. She looks as though she might need a bit of bracing, doesn't she?"

The captain had the right of it there, Miri thought. But the bracing she would rather have had was a pistol in her hand.

Grace came forward and gave Miri's shoulder a comforting squeeze, then moved into the kitchen area.

"Sit down, Miss Sutcliffe," Michaels offered.

Miri sat, regarding him warily all the while.

"I don't suppose you brought your stalwart protector along with you, eh? I have a thing or two to take up with that fellow." When Miri's only answer was hostile silence, the captain continued in an affable tone. "Lieutenant Renquist tells an interesting tale about his adventures on your behalf, my dear. He was most upset that he had to leave you in the possession of that savage renegade. But I see you've come to no apparent harm."

A bitter smile curled the corners of Miri's lips. "Your Lieutenant Renquist was the only one who did me violence this past winter, Captain. When you speak of savages, perhaps you should consider your own officers."

Michaels sighed. "I'm sorry to hear it. That was not the story he told, and since none of his troops survived—I understand there was quite a storm out there—his story was accepted by one and all. He was quite a hero upon his return." Michaels gave her a not-unfriendly smile. "I'm sure if the record needs to be set straight, you will quite enjoy doing it."

Grace returned and gave Michaels a stern look. "Here's a hot cup of tea, Miriam. When you drink that down I've got a nice pot of stew warming on the stove."

"Yes, well, I suppose we have time to let Miss Sutcliffe dine," Michaels said. "After all, I've waited this long."

Grace placed herself between the captain and Miri, as if she would protect her friend with her own body. "Gerald! Now don't you be getting ideas. Miri is my guest, and . . ."

"And she is my prisoner," Michaels finished for her. "Do you expect me to forget my duty as a favor to you, Grace? I fear that's quite impossible."

"She's innocent as a lamb!"

"She's a traitor to the British empire. Or at least she knows where a traitor is hiding. As much as it pains me to disoblige you, my dear, my country and this wretched war must take precedence over personal considerations."

Grace snorted. "You men and your silly war. I tell you, Gerald Michaels! You let Miriam walk out of here a free woman or you needn't show your face in this house ever again."

Michaels's face became shuttered. "I would be only too happy to let Miss Sutcliffe leave whenever she wishes, as long as she first tells me what she knows of her cousin and his traitorous list of names."

They both turned to look at Miri. "I gave you my answer back in London," she told him, her chin set at a stubborn angle. "My wretched cousin can go hang, as far as I'm concerned. And so can you."

Michaels could not help but admire the picture she presented, just as he had in her London drawing room. If anything, the winter in the wilderness had given her a glow. Her skin was a golden brown, decorated by a faint sprinking of freckles that gave her a girlish charm. The sun had brought a wealth of red highlights alive in her hair. Such a shame, Michaels thought, that all that spirit, fire, and beauty was marred by such a stubbornness.

"I'm bound that your cousin will indeed hang," he replied calmly. "And you may either tell me where he is, or you may tell Lieutenant Colonel McDouall, who's likely to send you back home to meet a rather unpleasant fate reserved for traitors."

Miri met his confident gaze with one just as confident— she hoped. When all was said and done, Hamilton Greer was still family. She'd been willing to find the damning list for the authorities, but she wasn't about to hand over a family member who'd been her closest childhood friend.

Michaels sighed, reading the answer in her eyes. "Have it as you will, then. I expect the lieutenant colonel will have something to say about your stubbornness." With the look of regret at a furious Grace, Michaels shook his head at the inexplicability of female behavior.

Lieutenant Colonel Robert McDouall looked up from his desk as the captain escorted Miri into the commander's office. "What's this?" he asked gruffly, a cigar clamped firmly between his teeth. His desk was covered with reports. One neat stack was held down by a cup of cold coffee. Another littered the desk in front of him.

"This," Michaels said with dour satisfaction, "is Miss Miriam Sutcliffe."

"Who?"

"Miriam Sutcliffe," Michaels prompted. "I told you about her. She's cousin—and fiancée—to Hamilton Greer."

"Oh." The commander ground the stub of his cigar into

an overflowing ashtray. "Yes. Now I remember. Found the chit, did ye?"

"I'm afraid she has refused to cooperate."

McDouall glanced at Miri with suddenly sharp eyes. She had the uncomfortable impression that this burly Scotsman was no man's fool, and no woman's fool, either. "What do ye know of this cousin of yours?" he snapped.

Miri lifted her head higher. "My cousin came to my home to break our engagement one night a year ago last spring. The morning after, Captain Michaels barged into my parlor to demand his whereabouts." She shot Michaels a venomous look. "I've not seen Hamilton since."

McDouall was not to be put off by evasion. "Do ye know where he is? If ye do, lass, ye'd best be telling us."

"I don't know where he is." It wasn't quite a lie, Miri comforted her conscience. In truth, she had no idea where on this wild continent Prairie du Chien was, and no notion at all if Hamilton was still there after the long winter. He might be anywhere.

"Then why are *you* here?" Michaels demanded impatiently. "Don't tell me you don't have some connection with the traitor."

"I came to visit my father," she said frostily. "When I learned of his death, I stayed on with Mrs. Peavey because we had become friends. And if it had not been for your harassment, sir, I would have returned to London last fall."

"And you just conveniently decided to take off for your visit to America the night after I threatened you with prison," Michaels added dryly.

"The visit had been planned well in advance, Captain. I saw no reason to delay because of your ludicrous charges."

"Enough!" McDouall growled. "Michaels, do ye think I have time for this, with Indians flocking in from all over the country to swell our ranks—hungry Indians, I might add— and rumors of Americans everywhere we look? Get her out of here, man. Ye've nothing but empty suppositions to go on, and even if her cousin stole the crown jewels, dammit, I'm more concerned with the Americans than with any popinjay Foreign Office twit and his little list. Send her back to Widow Peavey.''

Michaels's face turned gray. ''Yes, sir!''

Miri couldn't resist giving him a satisfied smirk as they left the commander's office.

''Don't look so satisfied, Miss Sutcliffe,'' Michaels warned darkly. ''You may have won this battle, my dear. But I will win the war. You can be sure that I will.''

✳ 17 ✳

''Well, what do you think, Scott? Can we come at them from the north?''

Jordan braced his hands on the table and set his legs against the choppy roll of the *Niagara*'s deck. The map spread out in front of him showed Michilimackinac Island. The town along the involute southern shore, with its distillery, churches, and merchant outlets was clearly marked; the fort crowning the highlands north of town; the high table-land in the center of the island; and two prominent farms— the Peaveys' to the west of the town, and the Dousmans' close to the northern tip of the island.

''That route has been closed,'' Jordan said. ''From what I hear, Michaels started building some kind of blockhouse on that high ground as soon as the snow melted in the spring, just so the Americans wouldn't be able to repeat the British tactics that took the fort.''

Jordan looked at the officer who stood across the table from him. George Croghan was young—not more than twenty-two or twenty-three, Jordan guessed. But the youthful Kentuckian was already a war hero, having distinguished himself in the defense of Fort Stephenson, Ohio. The

American high command had entrusted Croghan with the more than seven hundred soldiers who rode aboard the brigs *Niagara* and *Lawrence*—made famous by the heroic Commodore Perry—and the schooners *Tigress, Scorpion,* and *Caledonia.*

"Aye, trust the British to take care of the easiest attack route," Croghan said with a grimace. His finger traced a route on the map from the northwestern tip of the island to the high tableland in the center, from where the British had positioned their artillery to take over the American-held fort in 1812. "I still think this is the best route, though we'll have to figure a way to take the cannon they've positioned on the highland. I'll have to consult with Captain Sinclair to see what damage he can do with his carronades before we land."

"You do that," Jordan said.

As he climbed abovedecks, leaving Croghan to his plotting, Jordan gratefully turned his face into the fresh breeze that was blowing off the lake. Damn but how he wished he weren't here! The American squadron under the command of Captain Arthur Sinclair had left Detroit on July 3, four days after Jordan had joined the force as guide and scout. Since then nothing had gone right. Half the time, it seemed, they were lost, and the other half, they were confused. They had wreaked some small havoc on a British fortification on St. Joseph's Island, but victory had been an empty one as the post had been deserted long before the Americans had arrived. Now, at the end of July, they were finally within striking distance of the British on Michilimackinac, the key to the entire northwest trading lands, and Croghan was vacillating on plans of attack and bleating about the superiority of the British forces. The young Kentuckian seemed to have lost interest in victory, and Jordan had lost interest in fighting at all.

Jordan leaned on the brig's railing and looked across to where the forested shore was a dark smudge on the horizon. He had been a Chippewa too long, owing allegiance only to his adopted family, and the forests and lakes that provided them sustenance. Sharing quarters with a crowd of foul-smelling white men didn't suit him, and neither did bearing

with the senseless maneuverings of Sinclair and Croghan.
Jordan missed the sharp, musty scent of the forest; he
missed the solid companionship of Rides the Waves; but
most of all he missed Miriam Sutcliffe. She was always at
the front of his mind, distracting his waking thoughts and
dancing through his dreams to make him wake hard and hot
and grinding his teeth in male frustration. How the little
British hellcat would crow to see what fools the Americans
were making of themselves. Jordan smiled at the thought of
her laughter, his heart lifting as he pictured the shine in her
deep sapphire eyes, the curve of that stubborn, delicious mouth.

"You Jordan Scott?"

The rasping voice cut into Jordan's daydreams. Two men
had approached silently from behind, making Jordan wonder if he were already losing his Chippewa-trained alertness.
They were dressed in trousers and homespun shirts, as was
Jordan. One was tall, lean, and dark-haired, with sallow
skin that was darkened by the beginnings of a beard. The
other was built like a bear, powerful and thick-muscled.
Their eyes were as bland as their expressionless faces.

"I'm Scott," Jordan replied.

"Thought you might be," said the tall one. He ran an
assessing eye over Jordan's muscular frame. "You the
fellow who's been living with the Chippewa these past years?"

"I might be."

"My name's Keller. This is Westin." He indicated his
stout companion. "We're working for the American command to find a fellow by the name of Hamilton Greer."

"So?" Jordan asked, his face stony.

"We heard up in Montreal that a British officer sent some
reports to London saying that Greer's cousin is on Michilimackinac. Said she was hiding out from the Brits with a
fellow by the name of Jordan Scott. Captain Sinclair mentioned
your name. I thought you might be the same fellow."

"I see. And you want me to tell you what I know about
Greer?"

"That's about it."

"Greer's not my business," Jordan said curtly. "His

cousin is my wife, and she doesn't know anything about him. Let it ride at that."

Keller sighed. "That Greer fellow sold us some information he didn't deliver. You'd be helping the American cause if you told us what you knew, or at least told us how to find this wife of yours."

Jordan scowled. "I don't like your kind of war, gentlemen. If I kill a man, I do it with an honest knife or a gun, not with documents slipped under some table and sold to the highest bidder. Leave me out of this. I have nothing to say. And neither does my wife."

As Jordan walked away, two pairs of determined eyes followed him.

"Stubborn bastard, isn't he?" Westin grunted.

"Don't worry about it," Keller said, thoughtfully stroking his stubble of a beard. "I have an idea that wife of his won't be nearly so stubborn. Women seldom are."

It was late July when British sentinels first sighted the American fleet. The news spread like a flash fire to the town, then the whole island, and then the Chippewa village across the straits on the mainland.

Miri heard the news with a quickening of her heart as she was sewing with Sunrise and Willow in front of her wigwam. Even the baby inside her jumped, and Miri thought that it must be a reaction to its father being so near. She placed a hand on her slightly mounded abdomen and crooned silently to her unborn child. Soon, soon, she told it in silent comforting. Soon your father will be back and everything will be all right.

Or everything will be much worse, she thought glumly. Miri had spent the summer weeks bouncing between the Chippewa village and Grace's farm. The widow had urged her to return to the farm to live, but Miri chose to remain in the village, instead. Grace clucking over her like a mother hen and Lucy treating her like a fragile porcelain doll simply made Miri uncomfortable. The widow's sharp eyes hadn't missed the signs of Miri's pregnancy, and she'd had a few choice words to say about the behavior of "that scoundrel,'' Jordan Scott. And poor Lucy was horrified. Miri had a hard time convincing her defenders that Jordan hadn't done anything to her that she'd not wanted him to do, and that Grace was not to blame for what Miri had brought upon herself.

When it came down to it, Miri realized that for all of Grace's and Lucy's friendship, she was alone with her problems. No one else knew how she felt. No one else would understand the pain that ripped through her heart every time she pitted her love for Jordan against her inbred loyalty to everything British.

And soon Jordan would walk up the beach and into her life once again. Miri's decision was still unmade. At one moment she knew she could never give Jordan up—not if he still wanted her near; not if there was any chance he might, somewhere in his soul, have some love for her. Then, in the next moment, she was certain she could never forgive him for taking the American side against the British.

"Are you not feeling well, Eyes of the Sky?" Sunrise put down the leggings she was repairing and gave Miri a penetrating look. "Is the child within you restless this night?"

It had been impossible to keep her pregnancy a secret from Sunrise's knowing eyes. Miri could only hope that Jordan was not so discerning when he returned. She was only showing a slight bit, in spite of being more than four months along, and her loose tunic concealed more than it showed.

"I'm fine, my mother." She patted her stomach. "The child has started to move is all. He takes me by surprise."

The older woman smiled indulgently. "Eyes of a Ghost will be pleased."

"Eyes of a Ghost still does not know, my mother," Willow added disapprovingly.

"Doesn't know what?"

The deep voice took Miri by surprise. Her heart gave a lurch as Jordan stepped into view. He seemed bigger than she remembered, and his garb—buckskin trousers and home-spun shirt, with a musket slung across his back—made him seem for once more white than Indian. His hair curled around his neck and ears in tawny profusion. But the smile that curved those sculpted lips was still the same, and the warmth that glinted in his eyes when he looked at Miri made her want to launch herself into his arms in delight.

Miri took a deep breath. No matter that her heart was doing great leaps of joy, there were things to be settled between them.

"Doesn't know what?" he repeated.

"Doesn't know how lucky he is to have Eyes of the Sky as a wife," Sunrise answered smoothly. She rose and scrutinized him as only a mother—even an adopted mother—can scrutinize a son. "Welcome home, Eyes of a Ghost. You have been gone too long."

"Too long, indeed," Jordan agreed. "And if you think I don't properly appreciate my wife, perhaps I should demonstrate how wrong you are."

He pulled Miri to her feet and promptly claimed her mouth in a kiss. Sunrise looked on in satisfaction. Willow's mouth grew tight. Her eyes quickly dropped to study her hands.

Miri quickly forgot the resolves she had made. All the summer long her body had hungered for Jordan's touch. The wigwam had been so lonely with only Jane and Petunia for company, her pallet so cold and sterile. When Jordan's lips touched hers, when his tongue unhesitatingly thrust between her lips in intimate, savage possession, her soul leaped once again to life. She strained against him and felt his instant response. Sweet urgency flooded through her veins.

Released as suddenly as she had been attacked, Miri staggered. Only Jordan's supporting arm held her erect. He smiled a smile of wicked satisfaction.

"Sunrise, Willow, permit me to kidnap my wife. I have things to . . . to say to her."

Sunrise chuckled as Jordan guided Miri toward their wigwam. "I think he has things to do to her, not things to say to her." She chuckled again.

Willow was silent.

Miri preceded Jordan into the wigwam, pumping up her determination to voice the concerns that had haunted her mind since the night he had left. If she didn't speak now, then she might never get the chance. Taut need radiated from Jordan like heat from a white-hot fire, and if she let that need overwhelm her. . . .

She turned right into his arms. Her mouth, ready to speak words of sense and caution, was captured in a kiss that was at once savage and tender. Jordan's hands descended to her buttocks and pressed her close against him. His aroused manhood, already huge and straining the seams of his trousers, ground into her belly.

"Lord!" he groaned, finally coming up for air. "It's been such a long time. There's not been a single hour when I haven't wanted you. You're like a fire in my blood."

Things were fast getting out of hand. Miri made one more valiant attempt as Jordan pushed her down upon the matted floor. "Jordan! Wait! Don't you even want to see Jane, or . . . ?"

"Jane—bless her heart—can wait. This can't."

He literally tore the clothes from both of them. His mouth was everywhere—her lips, her throat, suckling at her tender breasts. His hand dipped between her legs and stroked the softness that was already wet for him. The thought of caution, of good sense, of waiting, left Miri's mind completely.

"Later we'll do this slow and sweet," Jordan murmured against her ear. "But not now." His hot breath tickled, sending a delicious quiver the whole supple length of her. Miri arched up to meet him as he delved intimately with a finger. "You're ready for me now, aren't you, Miri?"

"Yes, Jordan. Oh, yes."

Miri was lost. She had known she would be if she let Jordan so much as touch her.

He positioned himself between her legs and thrust quickly, savagely, into her very depths. A low growl rumbled from his throat as he plunged again and again, Miri meeting his every thrust with one of her own. Her every fiber seemed to coil in unbearable, agonizing, beautiful tension as Jordan paid homage with every movement of his body. She twisted beneath him, wrapped her legs around him, and called his name again and again, until finally the tension burst in an explosion that seared them both. Jordan voiced an oath of savage satisfaction into the nest of her hair, but Miri heard only dimly. She was astride her own personal volcano. Tremors shook the foundations of the earth and fountains of fire flooded through her veins. She wanted never to get off, never to let Jordan from between her legs—never to fall down to the safe, solid, cold earth again.

But of course she did. The fiery fountains burned down to a mere glow that echoed the heat in Jordan's eyes as he crouched above her.

"Welcome home," she said with a lopsided smile.

He kissed her, tenderly now that his passion was temporarily slaked. His tongue traced the delicate line of her lips while his fingers wound themselves in her hair. "Sorceress," he whispered. "I came here to talk. Not to do . . . this." His mouth found her ear, sending little shivers of delight down her spine. Very soon she was going to be lost all over again.

"Jordan." Very gently she pushed him away. "You're right. We need to talk."

Reluctantly, he rolled off her and sat up. "Cover yourself, woman, or I'll never accomplish my task."

Miri caught the blanket he tossed her way. "What task is that?"

"I came to make sure that you'll not be traipsing across to the island in the next few days. There's going to be an American attack, Miri, and I want you well out of the way."

"An attack!" She clasped the blanket around her as in defense. "But surely . . . we've heard the cannon from the ships and the fort. Surely it will just be a naval action."

"There will be a landing," Jordan told her, watching her changing expressions with sharp eyes. "Those shithead Americans can't elevate the ship's cannon high enough to hit the fort, or they'd blow the British to pieces. So they've decided to take the fort by land."

"And you'll go with them," Miri said, her voice a soft but bitter accusation.

"You wanted me to become a white man," he returned, eyes never leaving her face.

Miri was silent. How could she tell him that all her expostulation on the advantages of civilization had been on British civilization, not American? Americans could hardly be called civilized, in any case.

"I want you to stay here, right here"—his finger stabbed toward the floor of the wigwam—"for as long as this action takes. When I come back, Miri, then we'll hammer out this thing between us."

Her silence filled the wigwam.

"I know how you feel," he offered.

"Do you?"

"Yes, Miri, I do."

"Then, why are you going to fight my countrymen?" Her voice became a plea as she looked up into his grim face. "England is my home, and those British soldiers in the fort are good men. McDouall—you would like him. Even Michaels! Did you know that he's been courting Grace? Mary Beth and Martha were all giggles when they told me about it."

He let her babble until she ran down. "I'm sorry, Miri. We can fight about it later. But for the next few days I want your promise that you won't leave the village."

"Jordan. Please don't do this. If the Americans must attack, at least stay here with me."

His silence was her answer.

"If you go, I won't be here when you get back. I don't consort with enemies of my country."

Jordan reached out and pulled her close. His arms went about her, and of their own volition her arms wound about his lean waist. The blanket dropped, and she could feel the heat of his skin burn into her.

"You'll be here," he whispered. "You love me, Miri, so you'll be here."

"I never said I loved you," she denied, her voice quivering.

"I can feel it in your body, see it in your eyes."

"They lie."

"No, they don't, my love. I recognize the symptoms

because I have them myself. I love you, Miri. Lord, how I love you."

Miri took a shuddering breath. She had waited so long for this declaration. Why did it have to come now, when he was denying her?

"Our child was conceived in love as well as lust, woman. By now I've learned the difference."

Miri pulled back abruptly. "You know?"

Jordan laughed softly. "I've known for a long time."

"Willow told you!" Miri accused, eyes narrowed.

"No. I've been a father before, my love. I know the signs. And even if I didn't"—his hand splayed intimately across her belly—"I wasn't so blinded with lust that I didn't remember that this used to be flat."

Miri pulled the blanket around her once again. "And still you're leaving."

"I'll be back," he promised. "And you'll be here waiting. If you're not, I'll find you."

"Why?"

"Because we belong together."

Miri turned her face away. Jordan touched her cheek with one finger.

"We don't have time to argue, my love. I only have a few hours, and there's something else I'd much rather do—this time, slowly." He grinned. "And with more finesse." His finger drifted down from her cheek to her throat, and then traced a fiery path under the blanket to one shapely breast. "Come to me," he demanded softly, his voice husky.

Miri dropped the blanket and came.

She was wakened the next morning by thunder. At first she thought a storm had rolled in from the lake, but when her eyes opened groggily, they were dazzled by sunlight streaming into the wigwam through the smoke hole. The sky was clear and the sun was high, streaming into the hut in yellow-white brilliance and illuminating the empty bedding beside her. Jordan was gone, and the noise was not the rumbling of a thunderstorm, it was the blast of cannon.

Suddenly and unpleasantly pulled from her grogginess, Miri sprang up from the pallet and pulled on a fresh tunic, leggings, and moccasins. Automatically she went about the morning's chores, but all through coaxing a sparse half cup of milk from Petunia, all through the battle with Jane over fish broth and corn mush, all through the shaking out the bedding and forcing down a breakfast of cold baked fish and rice, she cursed Jordan Scott up one side and down the other.

Inside and out, from head to toes, did she curse him. How dare he do this to her! How dare he seduce her, declare his love, then leave to kill her countrymen! It was bad enough when he was scouting for the damned Americans. Fighting for them was infinitely worse. How could he do such a thing if he truly loved her, if he truly cared what she felt?

For a moment a smile touched her lips, smoothing out the lines of her scowl. He had said he loved her. At long last, Jordan had admitted that there was more than lust between them. The admission had cost him, Miri knew. Jordan the wolf, always silently guarding but untouchable, like the wolf in her dream. She had finally touched him.

Or—Miri's fragile smile became a scowl once again—had it been the child inside her that had touched him? Was it his unborn child he loved or its mother? He had declared that no child of his would bear the onus of bastard. If she conceived, he had promised he would marry her. Was a declaration of love Jordan's way of keeping her from running?

Miri kicked the roll of bedding that she'd just brought in from outside, half wishing it were Jordan. Damn the man! Damn all men! How had the good Lord ever created such stubborn, arrogant, irascible, and totally unreasonable creatures to rule the earth? If Jordan thought he was fighting a battle now, just wait until the damned renegade returned! Then he was really going to have a fight on his hands!

The cannon fire continued. When Miri could no longer use chores as an excuse to keep her away, she joined the rest of the village on the beach to peer over the water. The American squadron was anchored off the west side of the island—Miri could not discern just exactly where. Glaring blasts from the ship's guns were clearly visible over the almost glassily calm lake. The roar was endless. Whatever those cannon were aimed at, Miri thought uneasily, would surely be nothing but splinters by the time they quieted. A cold frisson of fear shivered through her as she thought of the Peavey farm. Were Grace and her daughters in the line of that vicious fire?

When the barrage halted, the world seemed unnaturally quiet. Miri was too far away to see the boats that carried the Americans toward the battered shore, but she could imagine what was happening. The troops would land and try to take the island by storm, she was sure. Was Jordan with them? Would a British musket ball find him before the day was out? Or the razor edge of a sword?

For a moment Miri thought she was going to be sick at the very thought. If Jordan got himself hurt or killed, she would never forgive the blackguard. Likewise, if the American troops harmed one hair on the heads of Grace and her daughters, or Lucy, she would . . .

She would what? Miri couldn't help Jordan, curse his stubborn hide! But she could remove the Peavey family from danger. The thought dissolved the knot of sick helplessness that clutched her innards. She would not stand meekly by while her friends were in danger. Indeed she would not!

The American troops landed on the very beach where Captain Roberts and his British troops had landed two years before. Jordan came in with the first boatload; Croghan was with him. When the entire force had landed, the Kentuckian ordered two companies of men to stay behind as a reserve force. The others he signaled forward.

"Well, Scott," Croghan said to his guide, "let's be off to this open field you told me about. It will be as good as anyplace to dig in."

Jordan scanned the troops on the beach. As far as he could see, Keller and Westin were not with them. That bothered him, but there was no time to ponder what the two might be up to. Croghan was anxious to be off.

Taking advantage of the natural cover offered by the thick forest, the Americans made their way south along the same route that the British had followed in their conquest. Jordan was the first to break into the open of the clearing that was Michael Dousman's farm. The troops were close behind him. Jordan waved them back, wanting to scout the open area before exposing their position. But a blast of artillery fire from the south end of the field answered any questions he had. The British were here waiting for them. The American line promptly broke for the cover of the woods.

"Damn!" Croghan exclaimed. "What are those bastards doing so far from the fort?"

"No one seems to be hit," Jordan said, scanning the crowd of men that had taken cover in the brush.

"I'm sure their aim will improve if we give them a chance." Croghan called to the rear, all need for quiet now gone. "Bring up the six-pounders. Be quick about it, lads!"

Jordan scoured the south end of Dousman's field with his eyes. "They seem to be dug in on that ridge on the other side of the farm buildings. I can see one cannon—it looks to be a three-pounder. From that blast we got I'd say they have a six-pounder hidden somewhere in the brush."

"Any idea of their strength?" Croghan had to yell over the blast as the American six-pounders started returning the British fire.

"Even if he's brought every man in the fort, it can't be much over a hundred fifty," Jordan yelled back. "But he'll have plenty of Indian allies, probably posted along the flanks."

The American cannon fell silent. From what Jordan could see, they hadn't made a dent in the British position.

"Shit!" Croghan spat, then stared toward the ridge where the British waited. "This is going to be harder than I thought." He yelled a command over his shoulder. "Form up! Two lines! Artillerymen, ready your cannon!"

The lines moved forward into British artillery and musket fire as the American cannon attempted to clear the way. A musket ball shot by Jordan's head, so close he could feel the wind of it on his temple. An image of Miri flashed into his mind as he pushed forward. She was going to be mad as hell. Returning to her with British blood on his hands was going to make this battle look like a picnic. But both battles were ones he intended to win. From that moment on, he thought only of survival.

A scant mile to the southwest, Miri listened to the thunder of British and American cannon pound against her ears.

"Hurry!" she urged Mary Beth. "No, Martha, we don't have room for any livestock."

Martha looked at her out of frightened, pleading eyes and held up a small piglet for inspection.

"All right," Miri said with an impatient sigh. "I suppose one baby pig won't take up too much room. We can't have the blasted Americans turning Daffodil into pork chops, can we?"

"Miri!" Grace warned. "You forget, dear. We are Americans!"

"I'm sorry, Grace. I'm getting carried away, I guess."

"I still can't think that we're in any danger here," the widow objected as she helped Miri and Lucy bustle the three girls down the path toward the beach, where the canoe Miri had begged from Smoke Catcher waited to take them across the straits. "After all, we are Americans!"

"When has an invading army every stopped to inquire about nationality once it gets the scent of blood?" Miri scoffed.

Miri settled little Martha and her piglet in the canoe, then Margaret and Mary Beth, both of whom had begged to stay and watch the Americans "whip the British," as Mary Beth assured Miri they would. She handed a paddle to both of the older girls.

"You'll have to help paddle," she instructed. "Grace, get in the middle with Martha. Lucy, you can sit in the prow with me." A renewed roar of cannon almost drowned out her words.

"I can't go," Grace shouted above the clamor.

"What?"

"I can't go, Miriam!"

Miri grabbed her hand and urged her toward the canoe.

"You can't stay! God knows what's happening up there, or what will happen when the battle's over!"

Grace looked to the northeast where the cannons were roaring. Now they could hear musket fire, as well. "Gerald will be up there," she said. "I can't leave."

Miri looked at Grace as though the widow had gone mad.

"Take the girls and Lucy. I'll come fetch them when things have settled down."

"I'm staying with you!" Lucy objected. She moved to stand with Grace and slipped an arm around the widow's waist.

"Lucy!" Miri cried. "For God's sake!"

"I'm staying with Grace." The little maid tilted her chin in recently acquired defiance. The widow had taught the girl more than ladylike deportment and proper speech during her stay. She had infected her with damned American independence, as well.

Miri sighed, tight-lipped. "Well, then, at least load that old musket that hangs in the parlor. And don't trust any soldiers—British or American!"

"We'll be careful," Grace assured her. "You girls be good. Do what Miriam tells you to do."

"If you see Jordan . . ." Miri started. Then, for some reason her throat closed, and she couldn't finish.

"Don't worry about Jordan, dear. There's not a man alive better equipped to take care of himself." The widow patted Miri's arm. "If I do see him, I'll give him your love."

Miri's eyes were suspiciously bright as she turned to wade to the canoe.

Keller and Westin stepped out of their canoe, onto the beach below the Chippewa village.

"You sure this is the place?" Westin asked his companion.

"It's the only village close enough," Keller answered.

"Goddamn!" Westin stepped back as the pack of village dogs galloped down to the beach and swirled around them in a canine eddy, barking and howling a vociferous greeting. "I hope these curs are friendly! Shit! I hope the goddamn Indians are friendly!"

The villagers had gone back to their separate pursuits as the excitement of the white man's battle wore thin. But the arrival of newcomers brought Smoke Catcher from where he was stripping bark for a canoe.

"I give you greeting," he said to the two white men.

"Yeah," Keller said. "Likewise. We're looking for an English lady by the name of Miriam Sutcliffe. Or she might be calling herself Miriam Scott. We were told she lives here with you people." He looked around at the milling children and dogs, and the wigwams interspersed with bark lodges. His lips twitched in disgust.

"You seek the woman who is named among us Eyes of the Sky. She is wife to Eyes of a Ghost."

"Right," Keller conceded. "Whatever you say. Is she here?"

"No," Smoke Catcher answered, his face impassive. He looked the two men up and down, not liking them any better than they liked the village.

"Where is she?"

"I do not know." Lying was dishonorable, Smoke Catcher agreed with his conscience, but sometimes it had to be done.

"Is that so?" Westin chimed in. "Mind if we take a look around?"

"You may look if you wish," Smoke Catcher said coldly. "You will not find her."

Smoke Catcher accompanied the two as they strolled through the village. Disapproval was apparent in his eyes, and as a result, the agents' questions were met with blank stares by Chippewa men and women who were very capable of pretending they didn't understand English, even though they did. Finally they stopped before Smiles at Sunrise, who was coaxing a spoonful of corn mush into Jane's reluctant mouth.

"Cute baby," Keller commented, thinking all the while that the kid was one of the puniest looking infants he'd ever seen. "Yours?" he asked Sunrise.

"My granddaughter," she supplied curtly.

Keller bent down and chucked the baby's chin with a

thick forefinger. It was then he noticed Jane's light blue eyes. Smiling, he straightened.

"That baby never slipped out of any squaw woman," he whispered to Westin. "Its eyes are blue as the sky." He hesitated. "They call that English bitch Eyes of the Sky."

Fast as the thought occurred to him, Keller took a pistol from his belt and pointed it toward Sunrise. "Give me the baby, Grandma."

Smoke Catcher was quick to move to Jane's defense, but not quick enough. Westin put him out of action with a solid fist to the face.

"Now give me the baby."

A hostile circle of Chippewa was closing around the scene.

"Anyone makes a move," Keller threatened, sweat beading his upper lip, "I shoot the kid. And the woman, too."

Westin bent down and pried Jane out of Sunrise's arms.

"Why do you do this?" she asked, her voice a hiss of hatred.

"Eyes of the Sky. Blue-eyed baby. Not hard to put the two together, is it?"

Jane screamed in protest as the two agents backed toward the beach, Keller's gun trained on her tiny head.

"You tell Miriam Sutcliffe that if she wants her baby back, she'll meet us at Bois Blanc Island. We'll wait three days. Then the kid goes in the lake."

In the stunned silence that followed the two men to their canoe, Jane's thin wails for once seemed very loud.

✳ 18 ✳

Miri sat on the ground before her wigwam, cross-legged, her head in her hands. Desperately, she held back the tears.

Now was the time for courage and cool thinking. If she could only reach down past her devastation and find some of those qualities in her soul.

"Americans," she whispered, her voice dark with despair. "You're sure they were American?"

Smoke Catcher nodded gravely.

Margaret promptly knelt beside Miri and put an arm around her shoulders. "Americans would never do something like this!" She opened her mouth to say more, but a stern look from Smoke Catcher silenced her.

"Bois Blanc Island." Miri spoke as though to herself. "It will take me the rest of the day to get over there, so I'd better start now."

"I'll go with you," Mary Beth offered, a fierce scowl on her elfin face. "We'll show those baby snatchers a thing or two!"

"I'll go, too," Margaret added.

"Silence!" Smoke Catcher growled. "Eyes of the Sky does not need the help of children. Every warrior in the village is ready to go with her to rescue my granddaughter."

Miri stood. "I go alone."

Smoke Catcher scowled.

"The minute those villains see a war party of Indians on their trail, they will kill Jane. I know what they want, Father, and I will give it to them."

Smoke Catcher glanced toward his wife, who stood with a stoic, gray-tinged face. Smiles at Sunrise hadn't spoken since Jane had been pried from her arms.

His eyes grew fierce as he turned back to Miri. "Do as you think best. But if my granddaughter is harmed, the men who took her are dead, my daughter."

"And you're welcome to their scalps," Miri said, her mouth a hard line of anger. "Margaret, Mary Beth—I expect you to keep good watch over Martha while I'm gone. Stay with Smiles at Sunrise and do as she says."

The girls nodded, in awe of this new, fierce Miri.

Miri picked up the pouch of food that Sunrise had prepared for her and started toward the beach, only to have her way blocked by the broad form of Rides the Waves. Willow Song was at his side.

"You cannot go alone," Waves said sternly. "If I paddle the canoe we will get to Bright Spirit before the night has fallen. If you go alone, the night will be well gone before you reach the island."

Miri shook her head. "The Americans won't like it. We can't take the risk."

"I will stay in the canoe while you fetch my sister's child. And I will be there if you need me."

"Listen to him, Eyes of the Sky!" Willow urged. "These men are wolves. Their eyes are like stone, with nothing in them of honor. You cannot go alone. Take my brother with you."

Miri looked from one to the other. Willow wore a face of genuine concern, and Miri's own helpless frustration, anger, and determination were reflected in the warrior's eyes. "Come, then," she said in a bleak voice. "We will do this together, Rides the Waves."

She walked with the warrior to the waiting canoe. As Waves pushed the boat out into the water, Miri turned to give Willow a shaky smile. "Thank you, my sister."

"Go with care, my sister," Willow returned.

Bois Blanc was a densely forested island that lay just south of the island of Michilimackinac. Along its twenty-two-mile stretch it offered few easy landing spots, which limited the possibilities of where the kidnappers might have brought Jane. Still, the sun was well down toward the horizon when Waves spotted a canoe pulled up a narrow, rocky beach. A thread of smoke rose from the trees beyond the beach. The Americans had made themselves easy to find.

As Miri stepped out of the canoe, a tall man in buckskins emerged from the forest. Even at a distance Miri could see the scowl on his bearded face. "You were told to come alone, Miss Sutcliffe."

"Did you expect me to paddle myself all this way?" she asked in a guileless voice.

"We said you were to come alone."

Miri glanced back at Rides the Waves, who sat with stoic

passivity in the canoe. "He'll behave. I promise. We don't want any trouble. Just give us the baby."

"First we need to talk, little lady. Come with me."

Miri heard Jane's wailing before she saw the baby. The Americans' camp was in a clearing a hundred yards from the beach. A crude bark lean-to sheltered a thickset man who sat cross-legged on the ground. Jane, wrapped in a thin, dirty blanket, was cradled in his lap.

Miri rushed forward, but Keller caught her arm. "Not so fast, little mother. There's a price attached to the kid."

"You bastard!"

"If I were an English slut who's been spreading her legs for an Indian-loving renegade, I wouldn't be tossing names about. *Ma'am.*" The last was uttered with a twisted sneer.

"Let me have the baby."

"First we talk about Hamilton Greer. He your cousin?"

"Yes. Distant cousin." Miri didn't take her eyes off Jane. The villains hadn't bothered to keep the baby clean. Even from ten feet away she could smell the filth. Likely they hadn't fed her, either. "What do you want with him?"

"He sold us something, then didn't deliver. We'd like to talk to him about it. You being his cousin, it stands to reason that you're involved in his little scheme."

"Well, I'm not." Any remnant loyalty Miri had to Hamilton dissolved. "But I know where he is. Give me the baby and I'll tell you."

Keller grinned. "Tell me, Miss Sutcliffe. Then I'll give you the baby."

Miri didn't hesitate. "Prairie du Chien. He's at Prairie du Chien on a river called the Mississippi."

"Glad to see you're so cooperative. Does he have the list with him?"

"I don't know anything about a list. Now, give me the baby."

Keller looked at Westin, who shrugged. "If she's telling the truth, we might be too late. General Clark took Prairie du Chien last spring, and he may have dealt with Greer himself if he realized who he was. The British have it back, though. Devil only knows where the fellow is now.''

''I've told you all that I know. Believe me. Please.'' It went against her grain to beg, but for Jane, Miri would get down on her knees to the villains, if need be.

''Give her the kid,'' Keller told Westin. ''We've got a long trip ahead of us.''

Miri didn't watch the Americans' departure. She had eyes only for baby Jane, whose listlessness and color alarmed her even more than the excrement and urine that soiled the rough blanket swaddling. She rushed the infant to the canoe, discarded the soiled blanket, and wrapped her warmly in the clean ones she had brought. As Rides the Waves started the long pull home, Miri urged Jane to take some of the broth that Sunrise had sent along, but the baby would have none of it. Kisses and entreaties were to no avail. The light in Jane's blue eyes, dim as it always had been, had gotten dimmer still. By the time they were halfway home she scarcely had the strength to cry. All Miri could do was hold the baby close and cry herself.

Jordan's homecoming when he returned to the Chippewa village the next morning was not what he had expected. The village was deathly quiet. Women went about their chores without their usual chatter. Men who sat in front of their wigwams tending to their weapons or smoking their pipes were strangely silent. Even the constantly noisy herd of children and dogs felt the pall.

The blanket that covered the opening of Miri's wigwam was pinned aside, leaving the doorway agape. When Jordan ducked through, he saw Smoke Catcher, Sunrise, and Miri. None of them looked happy.

''What's going on here?'' he asked, premonition making his voice sharp.

Three pairs of eyes looked up in unison. Miri's were the first to drop. She couldn't force herself to meet Jordan's questioning gaze.

''You have returned,'' Smoke Catcher said. ''The greeting we have for you is not good, my son. Bright Spirit is very ill.''

Jordan's lips tightened. He crossed to the bedding where Jane lay. For once the infant wasn't whining. She lay still as death; only an occasional lift of her tiny chest showed that life still resided within.

"I have done all within my power to placate the body and petition the spirits."

The shaman did not need to say more. It was apparent to everyone in the wigwam that little Jane clung feebly to the last fragile threads of her life.

Jordan knelt beside the pallet, taking the baby's miniature hand in his. "When I left she was as well as she's ever been."

Smoke Catcher nodded. "Your daughter has been murdered, Eyes of a Ghost. Blood vengeance is necessary. I would tell you the story of how this came to pass, but Eyes of the Sky has said that the words must come from her." The old man nodded to his wife. "We will leave you now."

When they were alone, Jordan turned iron-hard eyes on Miri, whose gaze was still fastened upon the floor. "What is this story you have to tell me?"

In a quiet monotone Miri told him everything that had led up to this disaster, sparing herself nothing. Not once during the recital did she lift her eyes to meet his. The responsibility for Jane's illness was hers, she knew. If she had obeyed Jordan and stayed in the village, none of this would have happened.

"Keller and Westin," Jordan whispered when her story was finished. "Smoke Catcher is right. Blood vengeance is due."

Miri looked up for the first time, drawn unwillingly but irresistibly by the grim promise in Jordan's voice. The look on his face cast her back to another time, when she had seen the wolf in his eyes—the time when he had held George Renquist in his grip and threatened to skin him alive. Her voice froze in her throat.

Jane lived through the day and into the night. Neither Jordan nor Miri left her side. Miri grew hollow-eyed at Jordan's continued silence, but she hadn't the courage to try to break it. As the hours passed, his taut features seemed to harden into granite. Grief swelled the wigwam's interior in tangible waves. But that wasn't what frightened Miri. Grief was natural, but the black hatred that colored Jordan's grief made her want to run, to hide, to be anywhere but within range of those razor-sharp, silver-metal eyes.

When the dawn came, a small grave was carved out of the rocky ground. Little Bright Spirit was laid to rest beside her mother with the entire saddened village gathered around to wish her on her way. Jordan stood like a grim statue as the tiny body was lowered into the birchbark-lined grave. An ashen-faced Sunrise, her hair tangled and unbound as befitted a woman in mourning, reverently laid a string of beads in the grave. They had hung on Jane's cradle board— the only toy that had every really caught the infant's eye. Miri, tears running a river down her cheeks, stepped forward and added a small kettle of broth. Willow followed with a small blanket, and several other women lovingly donated small toys to entertain the baby on her four-day journey to the hereafter. Grace's three daughters each added a small offering, then returned to their place beside Miri and clung to her and each other, eyes reddened from crying.

Last of all, Smoke Catcher stepped forward and looked with melancholy eyes at the lifeless husk of his only granddaughter. "You are well-named, little Wren," he said softly. "Now your soul flies free of its bonds. May you find joy and strength in the land where the ghosts dance. And may you carry a message of love to your mother, who took this road before you."

The women started to wail as the contents of the grave were covered with a sheet of birchbark and dirt was thrown on top. The only dry-eyed observer was Jordan. He stood like a silent, grim statue, refusing all words of comfort, his gray eyes glinting like steel knives honed to a razor edge. Miri watched him through the cloud of her own grief. He should be shouting accusations at her, flailing her with the whip of his anger, castigating her for leaving Jane while she flaunted his orders. She wished he would rage, weep, or beat her until she lost her senses and could no longer feel the terrible weight of guilt that burdened her heart.

But he just stood there and watched with ice-cold silver eyes as dirt was piled atop his infant child. He was not to be consoled. He was not to be moved from his hatred of the men who had so carelessly caused Jane's death. Miri was sure that at least a splinter of that hatred was directed her way. How could it not be, after what she had done?

When Miri could bear it no longer she returned to her wigwam, followed gloomily by Grace's daughters. Margaret silently started a kettle brewing for tea, and Miri sat down on a roll of bedding, hugged her knees tightly to her chest, and peered inside her soul. There was no comfort to be found there, but there was resolve. She knew what her course must be.

The fragile bonds that had tied her to Jordan were severed now. She had needed him for protection against Michaels. Michaels was no longer a threat. He had needed her to care for Jane. Jane was dead, thanks to Miri's careless disobedience. Their needs for each other no longer existed, and the love that had sprung to life between them would surely die in the morass of Miri's guilt and Jordan's hatred. If Miri stayed, she would only witness the cold and dismal ashes of extinguished love. Better for their child to be born a bastard than be raised in the midst of such unhappiness.

"Can we go home now?" little Martha pleaded. "I want to see Ma and Lucy."

Miri looked up, her eyes bleak. "Yes, Martha. We'll go home now—as soon as you girls can get your things together." She had overheard Jordan tell Rides the Waves that the American attack had ended in a rout. There was no more need for the girls to stay. And now there was no need for Miri to stay, either.

Miri drank a cup of Margaret's raspberry tea to wash the ache from her throat. Then she steeled her spine and went in search of Jordan.

"He is gone," Sunrise told her when Miri asked. The old woman sat alone in her darkened wigwam. All trace of the

queenliness that had impressed Miri on their first meeting
was gone. The unbound hair that signified mourning was limp
from neglect and trailed down her back to hang in the dirt.

"Gone where?"

"Into the forest to soak in his grief. He would talk to no
one. Neither would he listen to any words that were offered."

Miri gave a dispirited sigh. Perhaps it was better this way.

"Then I will tell you good-bye now, my mother. I am
returning the girls to the island."

Sunrise gave her a shrewd look. "You will not return?"

"No. My place is no longer here."

"You are his wife, Eyes of the Sky. You must let him deal
with his grief, as we must deal with ours. He will return."

"When he returns, I will not be here. Jane's death is my
fault, Sunrise. No longer am I the wife of Eyes of a Ghost."

Sunrise shook her head. Miri had never seen her look so
old and worn. "The death of Bright Spirit is not your fault,
my daughter. She was only given to us for a short time. We
all knew she would never grow to run and play with the
other children of the village."

"I can't believe that," Miri said in a voice laced with
guilt and bitterness. "She would have gotten well someday."

"The fault in her death lies with the evil men who took
her," Sunrise insisted. "And they will die by a Chippewa
hand. Revenge has been promised."

"Revenge will not chase away my guilt. I can't look into
Jordan's eyes without crying inside for what I have done."

"And what of the child inside you?"

"It is mine." Miri got up, abruptly ending the conversation. "Please, Sunrise, tell Eyes of a Ghost . . . just tell him
I'm sorry."

Resolving that she would endure no more good-byes,
Miri firmly turned her mind toward the future. She was her
own woman again, albeit sadder and wiser than the one who
had begun this adventure. If she were lucky she could
complete her aborted mission to find Hamilton—this time to
serve her country rather than clear herself—and then return
to England before time for her confinement. Once back on

that cradle, looking at his daughter with eyes at first cautious and hard, then accepting, then loving. The memories hurt, but Miri couldn't stop the replay in her mind.

"If Jordan comes looking for you, what will I say?" Grace complained. "How am I supposed to tell him that I let you take off with that womanizing Frenchie?"

"Don't tell him anything," Miri advised quietly. "Besides, Jordan won't come looking."

Grace lifted her brows smugly. "If that's what you really think, Miriam Sutcliffe, then you're a bigger fool than I thought."

Five days after Miri left the Chippewa village she settled herself in Gage Delacroix's big canoe. The boat was very like the one that had carried her from Montreal to Michilimackinac—somewhat over thirty feet in length and four feet in width at the widest point. As in that first disastrous journey, the canoe was loaded to the gunwales with trade goods. Mid-August was late in the season for trading, but Delacroix was not a man to pass up any opportunity for profit.

The boat and trade goods were where the similarity of the two journeys ended. The woman who seated herself among the packages of kettles, knives, coats, blankets, beads, gunpowder, and brandy bore little resemblance to the young English gentlewoman who had journeyed down the Ottawa River more than a year before. She had left her fashionable gowns with Grace, choosing to take with her only her three sets of Chippewa buckskins and a roll of blankets and hides to use for bedding. At her hip was a long-bladed knife, and slung across her back was the bow that Jordan had taught her to use. A quiver of arrows lay at her feet, and one of Grace Peavey's muskets, along with powder and shot, was close by her right hand. If she was not especially proficient with any of these weapons, at least they gave her a feeling of confidence.

"Good journey," Grace had wished Miri when they'd said good-bye on the beach. Now the widow, hands balled on her hips and lips pursed with disapproval, stood watching as Delacroix paddled the canoe out into the lake. Miri waved and smiled, but Grace simply shook her head. *Good journey, indeed!* Grace thought. She expected them to have anything but.

The rising sun sent its rays slanting through the forest, chasing away the night's shadows. One spear of light hit Jordan full in the face as he sat cross-legged before a crude bark lean-to. Five days of fasting had made his face hollow-cheeked and pale, giving him the gaunt, dangerous look of a hungry wolf. For five days he had sat there, denying himself both food and water, seldom moving, always searching for a vision that would cleanse both his mind and soul of the grayness that had settled upon them. But no vision had come. It was not Eyes of a Ghost who sat before the lean-to, but Jordan Scott, the white man. The manidos did not speak to white men, and Jordan was left alone to wrestle with his soul.

But Jordan's fasting was at an end, and so was his wrestling. Meditation and solitude had combined to give him some measure of peace. Lake Dancer and Jane were both laid to rest. The searing grief that had possessed him was becoming a dull ache. The hatred that had boiled in his blood was settling into a mere simmer. Slowly Jordan's mind came back into focus, remembering, among other things, that he had left Miri alone to deal with her grief.

Miri—she had loved his invalid child, had given Jordan the gift of herself, and would soon give him a gift of new life, as well. He had scarcely spoken to her since that morning when he had returned from losing one battle to find his daughter on the verge of losing another. He had blocked out everyone and everything that might divert him from his guilt and pain, selfishly wallowing in his own grief and refusing to reach out to those who loved him.

Jordan remembered Miri as he had last seen her. She had looked ashen when little Jane was lowered into the grave. The only color in her face had been the red in her eyes. So clearly he could see her, hair disheveled and dull, cheeks hollow and glistening with tears. She had looked up at him once or twice, but each time her glance had bounced away with a haunted skittishness.

Jordan suddenly realized that he had been given his vision after all. Miri—his future. Somehow he had to convince the stubborn little vixen that she belonged with him. The past was buried. Together they could mold the future into a place where both of them could fit. Together.

Jordan returned to the village with the carcass of a fat deer draped across his shoulders—a peace offering of sorts to the people he had slighted. Children and dogs were once again making a noisy ruckus; women chatted and laughed as they went about their chores; old men sat together exchanging stories of battles long past, or smoked their pipes and drowsed in the sun. It was a great improvement on his last homecoming, Jordan thought as he slung the deer to the ground beside the doorway to his wigwam.

"Miri is gone." Jordan turned at the soft sound of Willow Song's voice. She was staring at him from about ten feet away, as though frightened of coming closer. "She took the widow's daughters and the widow's goat and left the morning that Bright Spirit was buried."

Jordan scowled and ducked into the wigwam. What he saw there weighted his heart like lead. Everything of Miri's was gone—her buckskin garments, the birchback kettle she had been so proud of making, the bundle of cotton, muslin, and woolen gowns that she had never used after that violent afternoon when Jordan had forcibly dressed her in buckskins. Even the bundle of her bedding was gone.

Jordan stepped out of the wigwam looking like a storm cloud ready to spit lightning. "Where did she go?"

Willow flinched at his tone. "I don't know."

"Who does?"

"She talked to my mother right before she left."

Jordan strode off in the direction of Sunrise's wigwam. Willow ran to catch up with him.

"Eyes of a Ghost! Wait!" The Indian girl grabbed at his arm. "The winter is over, Eyes of a Ghost. Eyes of the Sky is safe now from the men who pursued her. She told me so herself. Now she has returned to her people, where she belongs.''

"She may be safe from Michaels," Jordan stormed, not bothering to shorten his stride to accommodate his smaller companion. "But she isn't safe from me, dammit!"

"Let her go." With the energy of desperation, Willow trotted out in front of Jordan and made him stop, staying with his every move as he attempted to go around.

"Get out of my way, Willow!"

"Let her go," she repeated. "She belongs to the white world. You belong here."

"She carries my child."

"I can give you children." The plea in Willow's voice gave Jordan pause. Of late he had become too familiar with anguish not to recognize its like. He placed firm hands on the Indian girl's shoulders.

"Willow Song, I love my wife. I no longer belong with the Chippewa. I, too, belong to the white world."

"That's not true!"

"I will always love you, for you are my sister. And when you find a man worthy of you, I will rejoice."

Willow Song recognized the finality in his voice. Lifting her chin and gathering her tattered dignity around her, she stepped aside to let him pass.

When Jordan reached the wigwam of Sunrise and Smoke Catcher, his heart was beating as though he had run a mile. Sunrise nodded gravely at his sharp question, confirming his worst fears.

"She has left you, Eyes of a Ghost." She looked sadly at the man she had considered her son for almost eleven years. Now, wearing the same homespun shirt and buckskin breeches that he'd worn into battle, with his tawny gold hair falling in disarray over his brow and curling around his ears, he looked far more white than Chippewa. "This time, my son, I cannot blame her."

"Neither do I," Jordan agreed. "But I sure as hell am going to get her back."

He turned and looked out over the straits to the island

beyond, his face settling into grim lines of determination. Wherever the little fool had gone, and however long it might take him to find her, sure as the devil rules in hell, he most certainly was going to get Miri Sutcliffe back.

✳ **19** ✳

The August weather was beautiful. Days of blue skies and warm sunshine followed one upon the other. Afternoon skies were decorated with tall piles of cottony clouds that sailed majestically by without troubling the earth below with either wind or rain. The lake remained pleasantly calm, with just enough of a breeze to allow Delacroix occasionally to hoist a sail to relieve him from paddling.

Miri's mood did not match the lovely weather. She was wise enough to know that time would eventually heal the wound of Jane's death, but now the hurt was fresh and raw, pouring forth guilt and grief like pus from an open sore. The memory of Jordan's silent condemnation opened the gash even further.

Miri refused to let herself think of Jordan, but his image haunted her. Everywhere she looked, there he was. The blazing noon sky held the brightness of his eyes. A curling wisp of cloud took the shape of his mouth. The warm breeze brought to mind his breath in her hair. Jordan was in everything she saw, but still her mind veered away from any thought of the months they'd had together, of the tenderness that had somehow grown out of their private war. Miri could not yet bear the thought that soon she would return to gentle England, there to birth a child who might every day look more and more like its father, and that every day she would see Jordan looking at her through his child's eyes. She couldn't bear it, so she refused to think of it. The problems at hand were sufficient without borrowing misery from the future.

Gage Delacroix was an amiable companion. At first he laughed at Miri's private armory of weapons and her determination to fend for herself. But when he saw she was serious, he patiently instructed her on the use of the old musket and even offered a few tips on the bow that Jordan had made especially for her. Miri was surprised that the French Canadian half-breed was almost as skilled with the bow as he was with a musket. He laughed off her compliments, saying that he was not as good with a bow as his Iroquois father, nor as good with a musket as his French whore of a mother. For a moment his carefree facade slipped, revealing a bitter streak that he usually hid under facile words and easy laughter. Miri didn't pry any further.

But their relationship was not all amicability. Delacroix was irritated by Miri's stubbornness when she refused to stop and enjoy the hospitality of L'Arbre Croche. The Ottawa village held too many hurtful memories—Willow's seductive dance, Jordan's avid appreciation, the bitter words that had followed. And Jane. Always memories of Jane. Miri could hardly have explained all that to her guide, so she simply fell back on the fact that she was employer and he employee. The hackles of his pride rose a bit, but his anger soon blew over. Miri hadn't worried much about his pique. Delacroix was much too busy trying to charm her off her feet and onto her back to stay mad for long. But less than a week into the journey, that got to be a problem.

"*Ma petite,* why so glum?" Delacroix smiled coaxingly at Miri, who had folded herself into a tight little ball of introspection as she gazed into their campfire. "Come have a drink with me, *ma belle*. It will make your world warmer and brighter." By way of demonstration, he tilted his bottle of rum once more toward his mouth.

"No, thank you," Miri said primly. No doubt the warmth he had in mind was a lusty tumble in the bedding, and though the woman part of her ached for a man, this man didn't have the qualifications. He didn't have silver-gray eyes, tawny hair, or a smile that could one moment freeze a woman with disdain and the next warm her to the very cockles of her heart. Gage Delacroix was a charming rougue, but he wasn't Jordan Scott.

"Such a sad smile upon your face, *cherie*. Do you not know that life is meant to be happy?"

Miri gave him a look that might have quelled a hungry cougar, but Delacroix was not a man easily discouraged. He put aside his bottle and moved around the fire to sit beside his prey.

"I would make you happy, *ma petite triste*. A woman like you should be worshiped by a man, a man who is strong"—he flexed broad shoulders—"who will fill you with joy and leave you with happy memories, eh?"

Miri almost laughed. Were all men such pathetic little boys? All men but Jordan? "Shame on you, Delacroix," she said in a light voice. "Are you trying to seduce a pregnant woman?"

The guide gave an elaborate shrug. "You are not yet so round, *cherie*. And the little one would not mind me paying a visit, I do not think."

He looked at her through smoldering eyes as Miri tried to decide what to do. Lord knew she couldn't afford to offend the man who was her only guide in the middle of the wilderness, but she certainly had to put him back in his place.

"You are so very beautiful, *petite*." Delacroix's voice grew husky and quiet. "So beautiful. From the moment I saw you I knew you were a very special woman."

He reached out and grasped her thigh in a gesture that he surely thought sensuous. To Miri it was repugnant. All reluctance to offend him evaporated in the heat of her sudden revulsion.

"Get your hand off me!"

"So coy you are!" Delacroix whispered. Far from removing his hand, he let it slide toward the juncture of Miri's legs while his other arm closed around her to hold her still. "No need to be afraid, *cherie*. I will be gentle."

"Well, I won't!"

Before Delacroix knew what had happened, he felt the prick of Miri's long-bladed knife at his throat. His eyes widened, and when he looked down into the face he had thought so engagingly piquant, he saw a mask of fury.

"Take your hands off me!" Miri demanded in a menacing voice. The blade pressed a bit harder and a droplet of crimson blossomed and started to run down the polished blade.

"Oui, madame!" Delacroix promptly loosed his hold, but the knife was still poised at his windpipe. He attempted a sheepish laugh that came out a squeak. "You are upset?"

Miri warily removed the knife. "You're the one who's going to be upset if you ever, ever try anything like that again. Understand?"

Delacroix rubbed a cautious hand across his throat as if to assure himself it was still in one piece. He grimaced as his hand came away smeared with blood. "You can be sure I will be the perfect gentleman from this day forward!" His voice paid her a grudging respect. *"Ma petite,* I had no idea . . ."

"No idea of what?" Miri demanded, still feeling pugnacious.

"No idea that you were such a little savage." He grinned good-naturedly, flashing white teeth. From the half-breed's tone, Miri guessed he had just paid her a compliment.

"Well," she sighed. "I am, aren't I?"

It was the first time she truly realized that the English lady was as dead and buried as Lake Dancer and Jane.

Willow Song waited in the commanding officer's ante-room under the contemptuous eyes of Lieutenant Renquist. Her dark eyes stared straight ahead at the blank wall, refusing to acknowledge the white officer's rude stare. But behind the calm facade of her face, she took her private revenge by remembering the tale that Eyes of the Sky had told about this particular white man. How unmanned he must have been, retreating from Eyes of a Ghost with his ridiculous white man's breeches around his bony knees.

A private in faded scarlet cutaway and gray trousers

paused in the doorway. "Captain Michaels will see you now, uh . . . miss."

Willow rose and, with a knowing glance at Renquist's knees that brought a flush to the lieutenant's face, followed the soldier out of the room.

Now that he was no longer the commanding officer, Captain Michaels was crowded into an office the size of a closet. His desk took nearly the entire floor space. There was no chair for visitors, so Willow Song had to stand.

"What can I do for you, Miss . . . uh . . . ?"

"I am Willow Song, daughter of Smoke Catcher and Smiles at Sunrise."

"Ah . . . yes." Michaels eyed the Indian girl with interest. "You told the guard that you wished to speak to me, Willow Song."

"I have come to give you information on Miriam Sutcliffe. And her cousin, whose name is Greer."

Michaels arched one graying brow. The girl had captured his interest.

"What is this information you would give?"

"First you must give a promise."

"Which is?"

"You must give your word to let Eyes of a Ghost go free. He is the one you name Jordan Scott. You must also free the English woman Miriam Sutcliffe, who is his wife."

Willow's mouth tightened into a determined line. For three days she had wrestled with her fears. Her brief glimpse of the evil Americans who had kidnapped Bright Spirit had convinced her that they were men with black hearts and no honor, and she feared for Eyes of a Ghost stalking them alone, which he surely would do once he had caught up to Eyes of the Sky. How could any man, even one as formidable as Eyes of a Ghost, defeat two evil men and defend his wife at the same time?

Michaels looked at Willow curiously. He had assumed her offer was made from malicious jealousy, which was known to be rampant among young unmarried women of the Chippewa. Apparently he'd been wrong, for the girl was demanding protection for the very woman she was betraying. Might this be a hoax—a mischievous prank played on the gullible white men?

"Why do you offer me this information, Willow Song?"

"Eyes of a Ghost is my brother." Willow flushed. The words came from her mouth with difficulty, but she had finally come to realize that there would never be anything more between them. "His wife is my sister. I fear that they march to a battle they cannot win."

Michaels sighed and folded his hands neatly in front of him on the desk. Perhaps the girl was telling the truth. Perhaps not. In either case, her offer was not something he could ignore.

"I cannot guarantee the safety of Jordan Scott," Michaels admitted. "He was known to have participated in an American attack on the island several days ago, and my chief has put a price on his head. But I will give you my word to do the best I can for him. As for the Englishwoman, I can assure you that if I find her cousin, the British authorities will have no more interest in her." He met Willow's suspicious eyes with a level gaze. "That is the best I can do, young woman."

Willow hesitated. It wasn't the promise she wanted, but it was all she would get. This man was no weak fool like the young officer down the hall. She raised her eyes to Michaels and nodded.

"The elders of my village say that Michaels is a man of honor, even though he is white. I will trust you to keep your word."

"I am honored," Michaels said with a slight smile. Oddly enough, he was.

For the next few minutes Willow Song recounted the story of how in the spring of the year before, Gage Delacroix had brought an Englishman named Shelby—who Willow Song later learned was Hamilton Greer—to spend the night at L'Arbre Croche, where Willow had been living with her Ottawa husband. When she said that the pair had been heading for Prairie du Chien, a bright gleam started in Michaels's eye.

When Willow saw plans forming in the captain's eyes, she knew a moment of regret. The tall Englishman Greer was still bright in her memory, as was the strange elation she had known the night he had broken every rule of honor and seduced her. She had watched him leave the village with mixed emotions, and at times during the last year she had found herself wondering when and if he would ever return. It was a sad thing to have to give the tall English stranger over to his enemies, but if that was necessary to save Eyes of a Ghost, then she was determined to do it.

Willow went on to describe how Miri had wanted to go after her cousin right after Gage Delacroix had returned with news of his whereabouts. But Eyes of a Ghost had prevented her. And then the evil Americans had come while their brothers were fighting the British on the island, and Miri had told them where her cousin was hiding in an attempt to save little Bright Spirit.

"Miriam Sutcliffe has hired Gage Delacroix to guide her to Prairie du Chien," Willow concluded. "And now my brother, Eyes of a Ghost, pursues them. When he finds them, he will go on to fight these evil Americans, who are also looking for the man named Greer. Unless he has help, I fear Eyes of a Ghost will die, and Miriam Sutcliffe also. The evil medicine of these Americans is very strong."

Michaels's eyes glittered as Willow ended her recital. "Your Eyes of a Ghost will have help," he assured her. "I will see to that. My thanks to you, Willow Song. You have done the right thing." A triumphant smile suddenly stripped years off his face.

"You will keep your word," Willow reminded him.

"I will keep my word."

Michaels watched as the Indian girl left. For a few moments he simply sat, enjoying the sweet glow of victory. Then he sent for Renquist.

It took a full week for Delacroix and Miri to work their way down the northeastern shore of Lake Michigan and reach the tip of the narrow finger of water that was Green

Bay. There Delacroix stopped at a Northwest Company trading post and distributed the last of his trade goods upon promise of collecting their price in furs on the return trip. Business transactions completed, they paddled the lightened canoe into the swampy Fox River, stopping only when there wasn't enough water for the hull to clear the bottom.

"Cherie, now we walk for a few miles," the guide told her as they sat and watched three spitted rabbits sizzle over the fire. "A few days and we will reach the beautiful Wisconsin, and it will carry us to our goal. And then we will find this famous cousin of yours, no?"

"Yes." Miri hoped she sounded more confident than she really felt. Would Ham still be at Prairie du Chien after all this time? And if he wasn't, what would she do? "How long will it take us to get there?"

"That depends, *ma petite*, on how fast you can walk. If it was myself alone—two days to the river, another week, and I would be there."

Miri smiled. "I can keep up. You should know that by now."

A camaraderie had sprung up between the two of them since Miri had so forcibly shown Delacroix that she was forbidden fruit. Her fiesty defense had earned his grudging respect, but when she had proven that she could indeed fend for herself in the wilderness, his respect was no longer grudging. The easy conversations and the laughter they had shared during the long days of paddling toward their destination in large part diverted Miri's mind from the ties that still tugged in the direction of Jordan and a tiny grave beside Lake Huron.

But on this evening, Delacroix was not laughing at Miri's lighthearted sallies. "Before we start our walk, it may be that we must make a short delay."

Miri frowned. "What sort of delay?"

"For the past day we have been followed." Delacroix fastened his eyes upon Miri's face, as though seeking her reaction. "Whoever they are, they are very clever. If I were not so clever myself I would not know that they are there."

Miri's breath caught. "Indians?"

"*Peut-être*. Or not. Do you know who else it might be?" The French-Canadian cocked a questioning brow, his voice ripe with accusation.

"No," she denied. The British? Could Michaels have gotten wind of what she was about? Or. . . . Miri's mind drew a tight rein upon her galloping thoughts. Jordan wouldn't follow. He would still be immersed in his own grief. It wasn't Jordan.

"Very well, *ma petite*. If you wish to play games. . . . But remember, eh? You pay me to guide, not to fight."

"That's good to hear." Jordan's voice took them both by surprise. "After working myself down to the bone to catch up to you two, I'm not in the mood for a fight."

Miri stared, too stunned to speak, as Jordan walked, bold as brass, into the clearing. In a homespun shirt and buckskin trousers, he looked as formidable as he had in Indian attire. Or maybe it was the glint in those silver-gray eyes that gave him a look of menace that belied his evenly voiced words.

Delacroix rose from his seat, his hand going toward the musket that was propped against the tree beside him.

"No need for that, friend. As I said, I'm not in the mood for a fight."

The guide hesitated, then shrugged and sat down again, still eyeing Jordan with wary caution.

"Looks as though you have enough rabbit to share." Jordan sat himself on the log beside Miri, took one of the rabbits from over the fire, and tasted it gingerly. "Good," he commented. "Hot."

Delacroix cleared his throat uneasily. "*Mon ami*, your wife assured me that you did not care that she made this journey."

Jordan regarded the half-breed amiably while he tore a bite off the rabbit. Delacroix had seen that particular look before, and it frightened him. "Nice of you to remember that the lady is my wife."

"The lady reminded me," the guide said. His mouth jerked upward in an attempt at a smile. "Not that she had any reason to defend herself, but she is very quick with a knife."

"Fortunate for you that she is," Jordan said in an easy voice. "Because I'm quicker. And nastier, no doubt."

"Stop it!" Miri demanded. "Both of you! It is none of your business what I do or with whom I do it, Jordan Scott! So you can just leave and take yourself back where you came from!"

Jordan ignored her. "Eat one of those rabbits, Delacroix. Then gather your things and leave. I don't think my wife will need your services from here on out."

"Don't you dare leave, Gage! *I* hired you, and . . . !"

"And I fired you," Jordan supplied. "Eat and get out of here, my friend. I have some things to say to my wife in private."

"Dammit! I am not your wife!"

"Tch!" Jordan shook his head sadly, a hint of a smile curving his beautifully molded lips. "Reduced to profanity! How you've changed, Miss Miriam!"

"Gage! You don't have to go."

Delacroix shrugged expressively. "I am so sorry, *cherie*. But as I told you once before, your husband is not a man to be crossed."

The guide slung his bedroll over his shoulder and cautiously reached out for his musket, making sure that Jordan did not misinterpret the move as a threat. Delacroix was a fighter of some repute, but he saw no future in tempting fate. He had seen Jordan in action against the Sioux in the incessant Sioux–Chippewa wars, and he had been very glad that he and the renegade had been on the same side. "I will catch some fish for my supper," he said. "Till we meet again, *mon ami*." He touched his brow in brief salute. "*Cherie*."

And then she was alone with Jordan. Miri promptly hopped up from the log on which they were sitting and took Delacroix's place across the fire, facing him. "What are you doing here, Jordan? And what do you think you're doing, sending my guide away?"

Jordan merely smiled. "You have a guide. Me."

"Awfully sure of yourself, aren't you?"

"Sure enough."

"I don't want you as a guide. Your... your services come at too great a price." Her composure broke and she wrested her gaze from his face. "God, Jordan! Why did you come after me?"

"Why did you run away?"

"I didn't run away," she told him in a clipped, angry voice. "I left. We no longer have a need for each other. Michaels is no longer a danger. And... and Jane is..." Miri sucked in a deep, quivering breath. All the hurt that she had almost pushed to the back of her mind was coming back.

"You ran away," Jordan insisted quietly. "I want to know why."

Miri got up from her log seat and began to pace, as if by keeping in motion she could dodge the silver gaze that seemed to impale her very soul. "You know very well why I left. I couldn't stay. Not after my carelessness caused... caused Jane's death. How could I stay and face you? I knew you hated me, and you had every right."

Jordan was still for a moment, his face cold and blank. Then he lifted his eyes and followed Miri's agitated pacing. "Sit," he commanded. When she warily obeyed, he took another rabbit from its place over the fire, and shoved the stick on which the meat was spitted into Miri's hand. "Eat."

"I don't feel like eating."

"Eat anyway, you stubborn woman. It will give you something to do with your mouth while you listen to me."

Daunted by his tone, Miri took a halfhearted nibble.

"You can't blame Jane's death on yourself. The men responsible are going to pay with their lives. It was not your fault."

"But I..."

"Eat! And listen. You belong with me, Miri. We are going to have a child, and you are my wife in the eyes of God and the Chippewa. Even Grace thinks that, under the circumstances, you should consider yourself well and thoroughly married. You are the only one who disputes the fact."

Miri swallowed a mouthful of rabbit and sputtered. "Did Grace tell you where I was?"

"Of course she did. Grace is a woman with some sense in her head. Not like some others I might mention."

Miri was silent, but her mouth had taken on a mutinous slant. Jordan was tempted to press the point, to tell her again and again that he loved her. For once in his life the words of love and commitment came easily to his lips. But he sensed that her emotions were still raw and hurting. She was like a frightened doe that senses the hunter, ready to run in startled flight at the first hint of danger. Jordan's hunter's instincts told him that if he wanted to have this particular doe, he would have to move with caution.

"Miri," he continued cautiously. "I'm not going to force you to do anything you don't want to do. Right now we have a common goal. You want to find your cousin. And I want to find the men who kidnapped Jane. They are likely to be together. After all this is over, we can discuss what to do with the future. Can you go along with that?"

Miri hesitated while she finished the last bit of rabbit. She could admit now that, somewhere in the bottom of her heart, she had known that Jordan would pursue her, if only for the child she carried within her. But this was not the raging Jordan she had expected and feared. When last she had seen him, his eyes had been so cold they had burned. Now they held a certain wariness, but the hate and anger were gone. He did not blame her for Jane's death, he said. If only she did not blame herself.

"I can go along with that," Miri answered quietly. The future hurt too much to think about right then, and the past was best forgotten. Today, Miri vowed, she would think only of today's problems. Perhaps the future would take care of itself.

At Miri's insistence, they bedded down on separate pallets. Miri was exhausted, but the chaos churning in her mind kept sleep at bay. The past year unrolled itself in her memory—the fear and hardship, the joy, the passion, the pain of all the changes that had made her a stranger to herself. All the people she had met seemed to be painted in colors much deeper and more vivid than the friends she remembered from London. Lake Dancer, Willow, Sunrise, Smoke Catcher, Grace and her brood of daughters—how much more a part of her life they were than her socially proper and civilized friends in England. And Jane, poor Jane—sweet baby with one little foot constantly in the grave. Miri's carelessness had finally pushed her over the brink. All the hours Miri had spent coaxing her to eat, wishing she would smile and gurgle like a healthy child! When she had placed the baby in Sunrise's arms, the last time Miri had seen her alive, the child had actually reached out for her. She had stretched out her arms as if not wanting her to leave.

A choked sob escaped Miri's throat, followed by another. She pressed her face against the blanket, trying to muffle the sounds of her misery. Within a few seconds the coarse material was wet from her tears. She had not cried since the funeral, damming all her grief and anger inside as some kind of punishment for her guilt. But now the dam broke. The tears flooded forth, accompanied by choking, uncontrollable sobs. Miri's whole body convulsed with the power of her anguish.

"Miri."

She became aware of Jordan crouched beside her. His hand on her shoulder was a lifeline pulling her back from an abyss of black, weltering grief. He pried her from the wet blankets and drew her into the safety of his strong arms. She didn't resist. She couldn't resist.

"Miri, love, what is it?"

Miri pressed her face against the fortress of his chest. "Jane!" she wailed. "Sweet Jane!"

Jordan rocked her as he might have rocked a child. Great wracking sobs shook her body as though they would never stop. "It's all right," he crooned, burying his face in her hair. "Jane is happy with Lake Dancer. Do you think either of them would like to see you carry on this way?"

"No," Miri sniveled.

As the sobs turned to liquid hiccups, Jordan used his discarded shirt to wipe her face. Miri sniffed, fought against the awful pressure of sorrow that was once again welling up inside her, and allowed herself to be cradled against Jordan's chest. His soothing voice cut through the pain, assuring her that the sadness would pass, telling her that Jane was safe in Lake Dancer's ghostly arms, just as she was safe in his.

"Are you all right?" Jordan finally asked.

"Yes," Miri whispered, but she made no attempt to move. It felt so good to lie against him, her cheek against his bare chest, her nostrils filled with the warm man scent of him. "Do you want me to move?"

Jordan chuckled and leaned against the smooth birch tree at his back, carrying her with him in the circle of his arms. "What do you think?"

His hand started to wander, and Miri shut her eyes in pleasure as it closed gently around her breast. There he lingered, softly caressing, gently brushing across the taut nipple until Miri felt a familiar ache start between her legs. She had vowed that Jordan would no longer do this to her, but she had been wrong. She wanted him to take her, to sweep away her grief and guilt, if only for a moment, with the force of his loving.

Miri shifted herself from where she was cradled on his lap. Already he was hard for her. She could feel his turgid shaft straining against the confines of his trousers. The hard bulge pressed against her and flooded her with a feeling of feminine power as old as time. She brushed her hand lightly over his furred chest and heard the sharp intake of his breath. Then her hand strayed lower, below his waist, to the bulge that strained the seams at his crotch. When her fingers reached their destination, his breathing seemed to stop entirely.

"Do you know what you're asking for?" Jordan asked in a hoarse rasp of a voice.

"Oh, yes," Miri crooned. "I do. I know exactly what I'm asking for." She laved one hard male nipple with her tongue while her hand between his legs continued to stroke.

"There are buttons down there, you know," Jordan gasped, scarcely able to breathe.

"Are there?" Miri asked innocently, one brow slanting upward in a wicked arch. She flicked one button open, then another. Finally, at his groan of male desperation, she unfastened the last two, freeing his erection into her tender grasp, a captive for the pleasure of both of them. Before she could think of any more games to play, he grabbed her hand.

"Lord, woman! You drive me crazy!"

Miri smiled sweetly. "I know."

"You're a wicked wench!"

"I know that, too." She sobered, and her eyes grew dark as midnight. "But I do love you, Jordan. Whatever comes between us in the future, I'll never forget you."

He laughed shakily, his eyes full of her, full of passion. "I don't intend to let you forget me."

Taking her head in his hands, he leaned forward and kissed her. Miri closed her eyes and gave herself up to the feel of his lips opening over hers, the delight of his tongue ravaging her mouth, the delicious prodding of the hard, hot root of his manhood at her hip.

"Come here, woman!" he breathed as he released her mouth. Slowly he leaned back against the tree, bringing her with him. Her leggings had already been loosened for sleeping, so it was with no difficulty that his seeking erection found the warm, wet cleft of her woman's core. His slightly bent knees and half-erect torso made a perfect saddle as she came astride his lap.

With a twist of her hips Miri sought to impale herself, to cool the burning ache that seared her every nerve, but Jordan captured her slender hips in restraint.

"Patience, wicked wench." With jaw clenched against his own exploding needs, Jordan watched the interplay of emotions that crossed her face as he teased her into desperation, then slowly, sensuously lowered her onto him until every inch of his shaft was throbbing inside her. "Feel how much I love you, Miri. Damn well right you're not going to forget me."

When he allowed her to move, the molten eddy of their passion could not long be denied. Jordan's hips thrust against hers in a white-hot rhythm of need as Miri arched sensuously back, filled with the glory of his savage desire and the sweet fulfillment of her own. She collapsed against his chest in limp abandonment, just as he exploded within her.

Jordan's senses had scarcely come back to earth when he realized that Miri was fast asleep against his chest. Carefully he lifted her and carried her to his own bedroll, then stretched out beside her limp form and caressed her with his eyes. That he should lose her was an impossible thought. She loved him, and he adored her. Neither her pride nor his would keep them apart. He vowed it solemnly.

A wicked smile curved his lips as his eyes found the maternal swell of her belly. Reverently he placed a hand above where his child curled within her. A lusty kick thumped against his palm, and Miri stirred restlessly.

"Go to sleep, little mite," Jordan whispered. "You and your mother both need some rest, I think."

His advice was answered by another, harder kick. Jordan chuckled, then lowered his head to kiss the rounded stomach that cradled their child.

"Just like your mother, no doubt. Stubborn and contentious and never listening to reason. Now I'll have two pigheaded mules to deal with."

The thought of his own history brought a rueful smile to Jordan's face.

"All right," he whispered to the unborn child. "Three of us, then. Three stubborn mules. And your mother is about to find out that I'm the stubbornest of all."

✳ 20 ✳

For the next days Miri basked in an ever-increasing glow of contentment. It seemed that the worst of this wilderness adventure was behind her, and the open sores of guilt, grief, and unhappiness were at last beginning to heal. As she and Jordan portaged southwest toward the Wisconsin River, then rode the waters toward Prairie du Chien and the conclusion of her long quest, her mind hummed with plans for a future in which Jordan and she could somehow be together and provide the child they had created with the best from both of their worlds. With every passing day she grew more certain that Jordan loved her. He had said the requisite words and she'd doubted their truth, but she couldn't continue to deny the eloquent message that his body conveyed each night.

Miri cast her thoughts back to that first morning after he'd sent Delacroix packing. She had awakened when the sun was a mere glow below the horizon, but she'd been loath to move. So sweet it was to lie once again in Jordan's strong arms, warmed by memories of the night's passion. The soft kiss she had pressed to his naked chest had brought Jordan awake. His arms had gathered her even closer, and his breath was warm in her tousled hair. For a long time they had lain together, listening to each other's quiet breathing and two hearts beating in near unison. There had been no time for passion, for the dawn was steadily pushing back the night. But the silent togetherness they had shared was something that Miri had never before experienced. There was a mutual bond between her and Jordan that had nothing to do with their bodies' desire. That realization bolstered her hope for their future against all the knives and arrows of doubt.

On the eighth day Jordan and Miri ended their travel at a small lake that was within half a day's journey from their goal. As Miri gathered dry wood for a fire, Jordan stared off across the water of the lake, motionless as a hunting wolf who has sighted prey.

"What is it?" Miri whispered, not knowing quite why she was whispering.

A wave of his hand motioned her to silence. "We have company at this lake, it appears."

Miri moved to his side and squinted in the direction of his gaze, but she could see nothing. Then a movement caught her attention.

"I see them," she said quietly. Three men moved in the trees across the lake.

"They're making camp. I don't think they've seen us." Jordan took her arm and backed them both into the shelter of the trees. "Hide the canoe in the brush, then stay here. I'm going to pay them a visit."

"No. I'm going with you."

"The hell you are. Stay here."

Confident of obedience, Jordan slung the musket across his back and disappeared silently into the forest.

"Damn!" Miri pulled the canoe into the brush, then sat down on a log and frowned in the direction of the strangers' camp. What were the chances that the men across the lake were dangerous? Very slight, she decided. Traders traveled back and forth from Prairie du Chien all summer long, and these men might have valuable information about Hamilton. In his preoccupation with finding Keller and Westin, would Jordan remember to question the travelers about her cousin?

"We'll see about that!" she said softly.

Slinging Grace's old musket across her back, she dived into the forest where Jordan had disappeared.

* * *

Jordan crouched amid the concealing undergrowth, watching, silent, feeling his recently regained white identity flounder in the flood of old Chippewa instincts. He had no difficulty recognizing the sallow-faced, stubble-bearded Keller or his thickset companion Westin. The third man he guessed to be Miri's infamous cousin—a thin man of medium height and refined features. Greer's hands were tied in front of him, and a swollen lip bore witness to his captors' displeasure.

The two American agents were going to be sorry to see him, Jordan imagined with satisfaction. And rightly so, for he fully intended to take them apart piece by piece for what they had done to his little daughter. The Chippewa demand for blood vengeance was roaring through his veins.

Jordan faded back into the forest where his movements would be concealed. There he checked the loading of his musket and let his fingers caress the familiar hilt of the long-bladed knife at his hip. With a wolfish smile curling the corners of his mouth he went forward, not bothering to move with his customary stealth. Boldly he walked into the agents' camp.

"Howdy, gents," he greeted them quietly.

"What?" Keller spun around from where he was trying to light a fire. Westin jumped up from the log he'd been warming with his backside. Open as it had been, Jordan's final approach had gone unnoticed.

"I see you finally cornered your quarry."

Keller eyed a musket that was propped against a nearby tree. "So we did," he admitted cautiously.

"The information you pried from my wife must have helped."

"We didn't mean no harm," Westin said, his scowl giving him the look of an offended gorilla. "We gave the kid back to its mother."

"The baby wasn't Miri's," Jordan told them in a cold voice. "The baby was mine. And now, thanks to you bastards, she's dead." He grinned a death's-head grin. "I want you to think for a moment on your fate."

Keller snickered. Two against one were odds that gave

him confidence, no matter that the glint in Jordan's eyes sent a chill down his spine. "Kind of big for your britches, aren't you, Scott? There's two of us."

"Both of you cowards who prey on infants and women."

"Cowards like hell!" Westin joined his voice to the fray. He followed up his oath by pulling a pistol from his belt, but before he could thumb the hammer, a well-aimed kick from Jordan sent the weapon flying from his grasp. Jordan's fist exploded in his face with bone-crunching force. Westin flew backward, hit the ground, bounced once, then lay still.

The ruckus with Westin took only a moment, but it gave Keller time to reach his musket. Jordan turned to find himself staring down the business end of the long barrel of death. He didn't hesitate, but dived at Keller's legs in an unexpected move that toppled the tall man from his feet. The moment the agent hit the ground Jordan was atop him, grasping his wrist and squeezing until his fingers went numb and released the musket. Impatiently Jordan kicked the weapon away and proceeded to pummel the cursing man into oblivion.

When the two American agents came to pain-filled awareness, they were both tied securely to a tree. "Goddamn!" Westin mumbled through swollen lips. "What hit us?"

"I did," Jordan said.

The Americans' eyes lifted blearily to where he stood above them, calmly testing the edge of his knife. His cruel intent was immediately understood, and both prisoners' battered faces grew grim.

"How much pain do you think a child's life is worth, Keller? Westin?"

"Shit!" Westin hawked and spat blood.

Keller maintained a tense silence, his sallow face gone paler than even before.

"Jordan, don't."

Miri's strained voice took Jordan by surprise, so intent was he upon his vengeance. She looked at the agents' battered faces, at the fear in their eyes, and her own face turned pale. "They've had enough, Jordan."

Jordan snorted. "You want me to simply let them go after what they did?"

"No." She moved up to place a hand on his arm and felt the tension that ran like a current through his muscles. "We can take them with us and turn them over to the British. They'll get what they deserve."

His mouth lifted in a cynical smile. "I suppose you'll want me to turn myself over, as well."

"Don't be ridiculous." For the first time her eyes strayed from Jordan and noticed the third prisoner, who hunched against a log, fearful eyes turned upon the cruel drama before him. "Hamilton!" As though she were afraid to release him, she kept her hold on Jordan, but her attention was all for the man who looked up at her in amazed recognition.

"Miri? My God! Miri? Is that really you?"

Jordan released pent-up breath from between clenched teeth. Whatever he would have liked to do to the Americans, he couldn't do it before Miri's gentle eyes. One part of him damned her for an interfering nuisance, while another part, the part that every day since he'd first met her had been growing stronger, breathed a sigh of relief that he had not been able to carry out the savage ritual that Chippewa honor demanded.

Having felt some of the tension leave Jordan's arm, Miri released her hold and hurried toward her cousin, who was looking at her in mixed horror and amazement. He cringed when she took her knife from its sheath and moved to cut his bonds.

"Hold still, you silly twit," she said as he jerked away. "Do you want me to cut your wrists?"

"Lord, Miri! Look at you!" He eyed her uneasily as she worked on the ropes that tied his ankles. The Miri he knew did not wear savage Indian garb, did not move with such unfeminine confidence, and certainly would not be so comfortable with a wicked-looking knife in her hand. "You look like a bloodthirsty savage! What's happened to you? And what in God's name are you doing here?"

Jordan had turned from his fearful prisoners and was

regarding Hamilton with unconcealed dislike. "I'd say you need to be answering questions instead of asking them, Greer."

"Please, Jordan!" Miri jumped to Ham's defense. "Let me talk to him." She pressed fingers to her temple, trying to order her jumbled thoughts. "Can't we set up camp and have something to eat? We've got all night to straighten things out."

Hamilton and Jordan continued to eye each other like two duelists waiting for the last of the count.

"Go back across the lake and get the canoe," Miri suggested to Jordan. "We can make camp here." She saw the look of distrust he threw at Ham. "I'll be all right. Truly I will. Just let me talk to him."

Jordan reluctantly nodded. He checked the agents' bonds, then the loading of Miri's musket, and handed her the weapon. "If he tries to escape, shoot him."

"Jordan!" Miri chided.

He turned a chilling gaze on Hamilton. "If you're not here when I get back, I'll do a deal more than shoot you when I find you. And I'll find you."

With that parting shot, he turned and disappeared into the dusk-shrouded woods.

"Lord, Miri!" Hamilton clambered to his feet, shaking his arms and stomping his feet to get his blood circulating again. "Where did you find that?"

"That," Miri returned sharply, "is the man who saved me from the hounds that you set on my trail, you piece of slime. What am I doing here, you ask!" She punctuated each word with a vicious jab of her finger, and Hamilton looked warily at the knife she still held in her other hand. "I had to flee London to save myself from being thrown into prison for *your* crimes! I've been in America for over a year looking for my miserable cousin who sold out his country, then turned tail and ran, leaving me to face the authorities. That's what I'm doing here!"

"Now, Miri! Calm down." Ham took a step back and held up a hand as though to fend her off.

"Don't you 'now Miri' me, you miserable toad! Do you know what I've been through this last year because of you?"

Hamilton arched a brow. "I can see."

Miri felt his disapproving eyes roam over her practical Chippewa buckskins, her sunburned nose with its dotting of freckles, and the two stubby braids that had replaced her fashionable coiffure. She smiled as she realized that she didn't care what he thought of her. She didn't care what anyone thought except Jordan.

"So you can," she said in a calmer tone. She poked her finger into his chest, pushing him back. "Suppose you just sit down on that log and answer a few questions for me? I think you'd rather tell me what you've been up to than wait for Jordan to persuade you."

Hamilton sighed. "Is Jordan the big fellow who left?"

"That's him," Miri said with satisfaction.

"Yes, well, you're right. I wouldn't want to see that one get upset."

Hamilton sat down on the log and dropped his head into his hands. After a moment he began to talk. His tone more befitted the confession of a mischievous prank than the story of traitorous activities in the British Foreign Office.

It had all been for money, he explained. His gambling habits and life-style couldn't be supported on the money he'd inherited from his father, so he'd found an easy way to make money—sell confidential information to the highest bidder. After two years of successful enterprise, he'd been found out.

Miri watched her cousin thoughtfully as he spun out his tale. This was the same Hamilton she remembered—a bit thinner and more ragged, perhaps, but still the man she had decided to take for a husband. How had she thought him so charming, so attractive? She had believed Hamilton the height of fashion, the epitome of civilized manhood. Now he seemed soft and ineffectual. His classically handsome features were bland compared to Jordan's, his affected speech and mannerisms grating irritations. Had she truly changed so much, Miri wondered, or had he?

He had hoped to start a new life in America with the help of Miri's father, Hamilton assured her, but by the time he had arrived at Michilimackinac, David Sutcliffe was dead.

In desperation, he had hired Delacroix and headed for the deepest part of the wilderness he could find. He'd had quite a nice business at Prairie du Chien after the Americans under General Clark had taken the trading post there and started building a fortress. Even when the British had retaken the post, no one in the new contigent had connected Kenneth Shelby with Hamilton Greer the traitor. So he had felt safe—until two American agents masquerading as traders had demanded he produce the information he had sold the Americans so many months ago, and he hadn't been able to deliver.

"And that brings us to the most important question of all."

Miri and Hamilton both jumped at the sound of Jordan's voice. In the darkness, neither of them had seen him return.

"Where is that damned list of names that everyone is looking for?"

"I'll tell you the same thing I told those two jackasses over there." Ham nodded toward the bound agents, who were avidly listening. "I don't have it."

"But you know where it is," Miri prompted.

Hamilton hesitated, his face set in stubbornness. Then he caught sight of the expression on Jordan's face.

"I hid it," he confessed. "That last night I came to your house, when you left to fetch Eliza, I hid the list in the map pocket of your Bible. It was lying on the table beside your chair. As much as you read that damned Bible, I was sure you'd find the list and give it to the authorities. They might still look for me after they got their list back, but I figured they wouldn't look nearly as hard."

"Oh, no!" Miri looked at him in consternation. Hamilton misinterpreted her distress.

"There was really no need for you to come running over here like a bloody idiot, you know. Michaels would never have touched you, no matter what he threatened. He's not the type to put a female in prison on such a flimsy charge."

"No, not that," Miri said with a sigh. "I'm afraid your precious list is beyond anyone's retrieving."

"What do you mean?" Keller demanded, then dropped back into silence under Jordan's glare.

"My Bible is at the bottom of Lake Huron. I had it with me when the canoe overturned."

For a moment the camp was silent. Then Hamilton started to laugh. Not caring that the others were staring at him, he laughed until tears ran down his cheeks.

"What's so funny?" Miri asked in a dark voice.

"Don't you see, Miri?" Hamilton said, choking back the laughter. "The damn British can't put me in prison with no evidence, now, can they? You see, fellows!" he yelled to the American agents. "You wouldn't believe me when I said you wouldn't find the bloody thing no matter how hard you searched. There you have it!"

"So there you have it," Jordan said calmly, sounding as if he didn't believe a word.

Miri turned her head to look at him. She was glad he had never given her the kind of stare he was giving Hamilton. She turned back to her cousin, whose glee was undaunted by Jordan's coldly suspicious regard.

"Stop that snickering, Ham," Miri snapped, "or if Jordan doesn't shoot you, I will."

Hamilton's brows shot upward in offended surprise. His laughter stopped as though it had been cut off with a sharp knife.

Miri got up from her seat and turned a contemptuous back to her cousin. "I'll make a fire," she said to Jordan in a weary voice, "if you'll get us something to eat."

Jordan reached out and circled her shoulders with a comforting arm.

"Journey's end," she said, trying to make her voice light. "I guess it's all over."

Jordan didn't answer. He continued to look at Hamilton, a thoughtful expression on his face.

The next morning dawned in misty gray gloom, a foretaste of autumn that perfectly fit Miri's mood. She had slept apart from Jordan the night before, not relishing the knowing glances of the two American agents and the accusatory glares that came from Hamilton. A night of tossing sleeplessness had resulted, and an early morning bout with nausea. Her miserable retching awakened Jordan just as the sky was turning gray, and he joined her in the bushes to hold her weary head and murmur comforting words.

"Are you sure you're all right?"

Miri took the comfort of leaning her head against his chest. Her face was as gray as the morning sky. "I'm fine," she said quietly. "Although I can't imagine why pregnancy is called a delicate condition. There's nothing delicate about spewing up every time one gets overtired."

Jordan gently kneaded tense muscles in the back of her neck. "Do you want to rest a day? We could wait until tomorrow to start back."

She shook her head. "I'll be much better when all this is over and done with—when we're rid of those wretched agents and . . . Lord! I suppose there's not much we can do with Hamilton, is there? I'll just have to tell Michaels that his precious list is safe at the bottom of the lake. I know Hamilton won't volunteer to face him."

"Mm," Jordan grunted. "We need to have a talk about your cousin, Miri. There's something about him that doesn't ring true."

Miri chuckled bitterly. "There seems to be a lot about my cousin that doesn't ring true, like a piece of flawed pottery—or, in his case, I suppose it would be flawed Dresden china. Lord! To think I only narrowly missed marrying that man!"

"Is our child through bouncing your innards around?"

"I think so," Miri replied with a smile. "I see the sun is coming up, so it's time for me to pull myself together."

Jordan still looked worried as Miri pulled herself out of his embrace. "We'll talk about Hamilton tonight."

Miri prepared a breakfast of leftover fish from the catch that Jordan had landed for the previous night's supper. While she was busy at the campfire, Jordan took the trussed Americans into the woods to take care of their personal needs. Hamilton shuffled aimlessly around the camp, watching Miri work.

"I hope he brings them back in one piece," Ham remarked after Jordan had disappeared with his prisoners.

"What do you care?" Miri asked curtly. "You've never before shown concern for anyone other than yourself."

Ham shrugged. "They seem to be decent enough fellows. When you're in a war, you can't very well regard the other side as personal enemies, now, can you? Your friend there seems overly contentious, if you ask me."

"Those two 'decent fellows' killed his baby daughter. Or at least they kidnapped her, and that resulted in her death. If he tore them apart limb by limb, it would be no more than what they deserve."

"I say! They are miscreants, then! Still, can't say as I like the gleam in that fellow's eye. Looks like he could run a man through with that knife of his and laugh about it."

"Then you'd best be careful, hadn't you? Jordan doesn't like you much better than he likes them."

"You don't say?" Hamilton watched her curiously as she filleted five fish, encased the tender meat between two pieces of green bark, then secured the bark to a stick that was driven into the ground at one end and slanted out over the fire. "I suppose he taught you all these little skills that you're demonstrating?"

"His adopted mother, Smiles at Sunrise, taught me to cook." She smiled with impish wickedness, enjoying his obvious jealousy. "Jordan taught me other things."

"Do tell." One of Hamilton's thin black brows inched upward. "Just what do you see in a fellow like him, Miri? He's worse than a backwoods savage—not civilized at all. Lord! If it weren't for those odd light eyes and the yellow hair, I'd think he was an Indian himself."

His condescending tone struck Miri as an echo of her own of just a year ago. Lord above! Was that how she had sounded? "Jordan Scott is a more civilized man than you'll ever be, Hamilton Greer. He knows the meaning of honor and caring. And he would never run like a frightened rabbit and leave another person in trouble for something he had done."

"My goodness! Aren't we touchy!"

"Yes," Miri agreed fiercely. "We are!"

For the rest of the day, paddling upriver, Miri thought

about her declaration to Hamilton. She had said the words mostly to spite her cousin, but later she wondered if she hadn't unintentionally uttered a significant truth. Perhaps all her life she'd had the wrong notion of just what constituted civilization—polish, gentle manners, knowing the rules of society and following them to the letter. If civilization was actually honor, courage, tolerance, and honesty, then which of them was truly the civilized one, she or Jordan?

Miri was still pondering the question when Jordan raised his arm in a signal to stop paddling. It was midafternoon, but low, heavy clouds joined with wisps of fog to create an illusion of dusk. Just ahead the river valley narrowed to a steep-walled gorge. Light scarcely penetrated the dense weave of trees that choked the canyon, although the trail along its floor was kept clear by the traders who were forced to portage around the rapids.

The look on Jordan's face made Miri uneasy. "What is it?" she asked.

"I thought I saw a movement up ahead."

"Maybe a deer, or a bear?" She had learned not to argue with Jordan's sixth sense, but in this case she desperately wanted to believe that no further complications awaited them on the way back home.

"I don't think so." He looked suspiciously at the two American agents. "You two have reinforcements coming along behind you?"

Westin spat. "If we did, would we tell you?"

"You might, if you realized that you're going to be the first casualty of any battle. Come on, gentlemen. I think we'll do a little survey of this area." He steered the canoe toward the muddy riverbank and motioned with his musket for the Americans to get out. "Miri, stay here, and keep your cousin with you."

Jordan prodded his victims into the forest. For a few moments Miri listened to the sounds of their movement—something she would not have heard had Jordan been alone. Then there was nothing. It was as if she and Hamilton were alone in the silent gray wilderness.

"Miri, I don't like this at all. Suppose Michaels . . . ?"

"Michaels has probably been sent back to London by now. And even if he's still on the island, Grace would never tell him where I've gone, and Jordan certainly didn't fill him in on his plans. It couldn't be the British." She hopped out of the canoe and carefully pulled it up onto the bank.

"Not the British, eh? Ah, well. Don't worry. If it is the Americans, I'm sure I can talk our way out of trouble."

Miri gave him a black scowl. "What do you have up your sleeve, Hamilton?"

Ham never got a chance to answer. The sound of musket fire erupted from the gorge ahead, accompanied by a man's scream.

"Oh my God!" Miri swung her musket from her back, checked the loading, and ran in the direction of the shots. In only a few seconds Hamilton caught up with her and grabbed her arm, stopping her headlong rush.

"Your hero said to stay put! Remember?"

"Let me go, you toad!"

Another fusillade echoed around the valley, diverting Hamilton's attention long enough for Miri to break free. He uttered a curse and followed on her heels as she plunged into the forest.

Miri raced through the dense woods. Sharp-needled pine branches whipped her face, but she paid no heed. Hamilton crashed through the brush behind her, but though he was taller and had longer legs, Miri was swifter. She was the first to reach the mouth of the gorge.

Eyes wide in horror, she plunged to a stop. On the portage trail just below her vantage point in the trees, Keller and Westin lay sprawled in a bloody heap, their wrists still bound together by ropes. Westin had been hit in the chest with more than one musket ball, and Keller's face was a raw and bloody shambles. Miri gagged at the sight.

"Get down, dammit!" Jordan's words were drowned out by another volley of musket fire from the brush across the narrow gorge. He appeared from nowhere, reached out, and yanked Miri to the ground as lead balls whizzed all around them. They were immediately joined by Hamilton, who dived for cover beside them. "I told you to stay put!"

Miri buried her face against Jordan's shoulder as more shots exploded from across the trail, then covered her ears as he returned the fire.

"Who are they?" she gasped. "Americans?"

"That's what those two thought." Jordan nodded toward the bodies sprawled across the trail. "They ran for it, yelling that they were Americans, and got shot for their efforts."

Miri tried to get the breath back into her lungs. Her heart was thundering in her chest.

"Can't we just back off and find another trail? They would never find us."

"There is no other trail through here—or at least no trail that I would take you over. And we can't shoot the rapids— especially with them up there waiting to pick us off. We'll have to drive them off."

"How many are there?"

"I'm not sure. Five—maybe six."

Thirty minutes passed. Each one seemed an eternity to Miri. Jordan continued to exchange shots with the men who had intended to ambush them as they walked unsuspectingly along the trail. The battle was a stalemate. Neither side seemed able to score. Then one of Jordan's carefully placed shots brought a shriek from across the gorge. Amid a crashing of brush and branches, a man catapulted forward onto the trail, clutching at his chest. The chest was covered by a scarlet cutaway uniform coat.

"British," Miri breathed. "Michaels. How in the world . . . ?"

"Miri." Hamilton left his cover and slithered over to Miri on his stomach. She thought his snakelike locomotion very appropriate to his nature. "Who is it out there?"

"Captain Michaels and his men, I'd wager," Jordan answered for her. "I should have known such a bulldog wouldn't give up so easily."

"Michaels! Lord! We've got to get out of here!"

"Thought you weren't afraid of the Brits any longer,

Greer." Jordan's eyes had frozen to ice. "As you said, the evidence against you is at the bottom of Lake Huron."

Hamilton flinched before the assault of Jordan's cutting glare. "You think that fellow out there would heed the niceties of the law? He'd have my head on a pike. I've run into him before!"

Jordan smiled, enjoying the man's richly deserved panic. "It appears you're about to run into him again very shortly."

"Not I!" Hamilton squawked. "I'm getting out of here!"

"Hamilton, no!" Miri pleaded. "You'll make a target of yourself!"

Hamilton crawled a few feet into the brush, then rose and broke into a run. A musket ball caught him in the shoulder before he had gone ten yards.

"Ham! Oh, God! Ham!"

Instinctive reaction propelled Miri toward her cousin as he cursed and stumbled. Once again Hamilton was the boy she'd played with in her happy childhood, a symbol of the bright and golden days of her life before scandal had overtaken her family. The guns on the other side of the gorge were forgotten. Hamilton was hurt.

"Miri! Get down, dammit!"

Jordan's warning was accompanied by the whine of a musket ball. Jerked back to the present, confused, Miri turned. As another shot exploded, she dived for cover. Cursing, Jordan rose to help her. The next round of musket fire caught him and slammed his body back into a thicket. Limp as a puppet whose strings have been severed, he crumpled slowly to the ground.

✳ **21** ✳

While Miri watched from the restraining grasp of George Renquist, a British trooper dragged Jordan from the brush to lie beside the two Americans. Hamilton, sitting nearby under guard of another scarlet-clad soldier, clutched his crimson-stained shoulder and rocked back and forth in pain. Miri had no sympathy to give him.

The trooper stretched Jordan's body out beside Keller and Westin, then bent to examine the Americans. "These two are dead," he called to the lieutenant. A cursory look at Jordan's blood-covered chest and head brought a grimace to his face. "This one, too," he concluded.

Though they had been expected, the trooper's words hit Miri like a hammer.

Dead.

The word tunneled into her mind, ripping the fragile fabric of dreams that had been building since Jordan had first laid his hand upon her so many months ago. It was a monstrous cruel fate that had struck Jordan down and left her alive to endure the agony of his death. If it hadn't been for Jordan's child inside her, she would have sought to join him, no matter that self-inflicted death was mortal sin. The pain tearing at her soul was worse than any torment hell could provide.

"Shall I bury them?" the trooper asked.

"Leave them," Renquist ordered. "Let the vultures have a feast. American agents and a renegade savage—none of them deserves a Christian burial."

Miri struggled in his grasp. "You bastard!" She looked

over to where Michaels, downed by a well-placed ball from Jordan's musket, lay with his right arm and the right half of his chest covered in blood. She had thought the man tending him was a friend of sorts, even though he was in this foul company. But though Gage Delacroix looked uncomfortable with what was happening, he refused to acknowledge her entreaty. She turned back to her captor. "I hope someone serves you the same one day, you miserable piece of slime."

"Hold your tongue, Miss Sutcliffe," Renquist advised. "Your savage lover isn't here to defend you this time."

Miri spat at him. He dodged adroitly and shook his head in disgust. "And to think I once thought you a refined lady."

Miri and Hamilton were bound together by their wrists and shoved down to the beach while Delacroix and a soldier named Peters carefully carried Michaels to a waiting canoe. The captain briefly regained consciousness and questioned his lieutenant. Miri heard angry words pass between the two officers. She couldn't make out what was said, but Renquist came away from the verbal battle with daggers shooting from his eyes.

He strode up to Hamilton and pulled him roughly from his seat on the sand. "Devlin! Get over here! Search this man!" The trooper obeyed with alacrity. "His gear as well," Renquist ordered. "And every bit of clothing on his body. Turn everything inside out." Then the lieutenant turned to Miri with a malicious gleam in his eye.

"Not her." The quiet command came from the bloodied figure in the canoe. "Leave her alone, Renquist." The glance the captain gave Miri was almost apologetic.

Renquist's thin, aristocratic lips drew into an angry line. For a moment he looked as though he might strike her, but Miri didn't really care. Her soul was numb, and she didn't care what harm befell her body. As long as the child within her was safe, Renquist could do anything he pleased. He couldn't hurt her more than she was hurt already.

"Sir?" Private Peters stepped up next to Miri. He had heard the captain's orders, and it looked very much as though Renquist was about to disobey.

"Check her bonds," the lieutenant growled. "Make sure they're tight. If she escapes, I'll hold you personally responsible."

"Yes, sir." The soldier grimaced as Renquist turned away.

With only the three inexpert troopers to paddle, it was a five-day trip up the Wisconsin. After long days spent sitting in the crowded canoe, the three days of portaging across to the Fox were a trial to stiff muscles. Two of the troopers carried the canoe on their shoulders and the third dragged Michaels on a travois. Delacroix kept to the lead, pointedly avoiding Renquist, who grumbled every step of the way. The hot days, cold nights, insects, and primitive food all combined to irritate the lieutenant, and he made sure that all within hearing range knew how he felt about the American wilderness and anyone misguided enough to live there.

Miri stumbled along beside Hamilton, stopping when she was told, moving when she was told. She didn't feel the warmth of the late-August sun, or smell the sharp, musty scent of the damp forest. She didn't hear Hamilton's awkward words of comfort, see Delacroix's surreptitious looks in her direction, or notice Renquist's complaints. While her body was walking along the trail back to Green Bay, her mind was traversing all the days she'd had with Jordan since he'd first pulled her, like a half-drowned mouse, from the churning waters of Lake Huron. She couldn't believe he was dead—all that strength, courage, tenderness; the beautiful mouth that could daze a woman with its smile; the eyes that could burn like white-hot charcoal or freeze to slivers of ice; the dimple in his strong, rock-stubborn chin—all that was rare and beautiful about him was now merely food for vultures. Miri could understand why Chippewa women sometimes did themselves injury in grief over the loss of a beloved. The physical pain could be borne more easily than the grief that was tearing her apart inside.

On the evening of the third day of portaging, all footsore and weary from the pace Delacroix had set, they reached the swampy Fox River. Peters and Devlin set the canoe in a safe spot at the edge of the water and returned to make camp.

Two hours later the canoe was gone. The troopers swore they had set it well away from the water. Renquist answered their pleas of innocence with a series of expletives that made even the hardened Delacroix sit up and take notice.

A day was wasted in futile search. Renquist and Devlin covered the northern riverbank while Delacroix and a trooper named Hayes searched along the southern. Private Peters was left to guard Miri and Hamilton.

With Renquist gone, Peters untied Miri's wrists and, upon her promise to behave, let her have the freedom of the camp. Hamilton, however, was not accorded similar kindness. Miri used her freedom to see to the treatment of Captain Michaels. The captain was, after all, a fellow human being, and for some reason, Grace seemed to think he was an exceptional man. Besides, Miri found herself in need of something to do other than brood. One could soak in grief only so long, she discovered. The pain of loss didn't ease, but the very act of living demanded that she regather her strength and become once again aware of what was going on around her.

Michaels had been lucid for most of the trip up the Wisconsin, but on the three-day portage had drifted in and out of consciousness. The jolting ride on the travois hadn't done his mutilated chest any good. When Miri knelt beside him with fresh bandages and water heated over the fire, he was awake and alert, though the flush of fever burned upon his cheeks and his eyes were dark, burning holes in a face that had become gaunt.

He looked at her skeptically as she began to unwind the bandage from his chest.

"Do you have a knife hidden in the folds of that Indian garb you wear?" he rasped weakly.

"Unfortunately, no." She looked at the gory hole where Jordan's musket ball had ripped open the muscles of his chest. "It looks as though you may live to see Michilimackinac again, though I, for one, won't rejoice in the fact."

Michaels sucked in a shaky breath as Miri bathed the

wound with clean water. He closed his eyes and tried to gather the strength to speak.

"I don't blame you, Miss Sutcliffe," he finally managed to say. "This was not what I intended."

Miri raised a skeptical brow. "Just what did you intend?"

"I wanted to take your cousin from you. And the American agents. That's all. I swear. But a musket ball knocked me flat, and Renquist took over command." He paused for breath. Sweat had broken out on his brow. "I'll see he's punished when we get back. I swear it upon my honor."

Miri gave him a cold look. "Your damned honor won't do Jordan Scott any good now, will it, Captain?"

He closed his eyes, unable to find the strength to meet her accusing glare.

The search parties returned to camp shortly after sunset. Renquist ordered the amiable Peters to retie Miri to a tree at the edge of the camp. With an apologetic smile to his prisoner, the soldier reluctantly complied.

"Captain Michaels wouldn't allow this if he were awake, miss," Peters said as checked her bonds. "He's an honorable man. And I can see Mr. Delacroix isn't too happy about it, either."

"I know all about Michaels' honor." Miri snorted. "And Gage Delacroix's loyalties apparently stay with the highest bidder."

The private turned a shamefaced red, and Miri took sympathy on the boy. "It's not your fault," she said. "Just do what you're told. Don't get yourself into trouble."

He gave her a boyish smile. "I'll see you get a good supper, and before we bed down, I'll come over and make sure these ropes are loose enough so that you can sleep."

She'd better get her share of supper, Miri thought bitterly. It was she who had set the snares for the four rabbits and two squirrels that were the meal. None of the Brits—when had she started thinking of her countrymen by that denigrating term? she wondered—knew the slightest thing about wilderness survival. If they'd not met Delacroix along the trail and engaged him as guide, they never would have come this far.

Miri spent an uncomfortable night feeling the cold bark of the birch tree at her back suck all the warmth from her body. By morning she was so stiff she could scarcely move. When Peters came to release her bonds and convey an order from Renquist that she prepare breakfast, the soldier had to help her to her feet. She stumbled off into the brush to deal with a bout of nausea. Peters waited, diligently guarding as Renquist had ordered. but he shook his head sympathetically, vowing that he would find a way to speak to Michaels about the situation.

Renquist's sharp eyes had noted Miri's absence, and he strode angrily toward the private.

"Soldier, where's your prisoner?"

"She's in the woods right over there, sir. She's uh . . ."

A series of sounds from the brush made it very clear what Miri was doing. Renquist grimaced sourly and turned away.

"Where's Corporal Hayes?" he asked abruptly. "He should already have a fire built, dammit."

"I think Hayes is still in his bedroll, sir."

"Goddamned lazy shirker."

Corporal Hayes had laid out his blankets at the edge of the clearing to be away from the smoke of the smoldering fire. He had not stirred when the camp had started to awaken. The lieutenant meant to put a quick end to that as he marched to the corporal's bedding and gave it a hearty kick.

"What the bloody hell?" Renquist tossed the blankets aside. They were rumpled enough to give the impression that a man lay under them, but no one was there. What was there riveted everyone's eyes. The missing corporal's knife pinned the blankets to the damp ground. Dulling the blade's sheen was an ugly, dark brown stain—a smear of dried blood.

The camp was suddenly still, as though everyone had drawn a breath and held it.

Gage Delacroix strolled into camp from his private sleeping spot in the woods, tucking his homespun shirt into his trousers. He stopped when he saw the group staring at the corporal's blankets.

"I am missing something?" he inquired, stepping up to

get a view. When he saw the knife, his expression went blank, then a slow smile curved his mouth. He stole a glance at Miri.

"Indians?" Renquist ventured. "It must be Indians." He turned on Delacroix. "How could a pack of savages sneak up to our camp like this? We engaged you to be our scout and guide, man! And now it seems we're easy pickings for any red-skinned bastard who happens along and wants to add to his scalp collection."

The French-Canadian shrugged. "You could have set a guard, Lieutenant."

"You could have warned me there were hostile savages in this area!"

"There are savages all over this land, my friend. and they are all hostile to someone or another." He chuckled, chillingly unconcerned, and turned to walk away.

Renquist shot another angry look at the bloodstained knife, then started shouting orders for his two remaining troopers and Delacroix to break camp. Delacroix cut him short.

"Where do you go, Lieutenant? We have no boat."

"We will go by land, of course."

Delacroix lifted a heavy black brow. "If that is what you wish. But you will not reach your fort before the snow comes. It is a very long walk, my friend."

Renquist drew himself up to his full slender height. "And just what do you suggest?"

"We must make a boat, no? One large enough to carry seven people. It will take a few days. No longer."

Renquist pressed his narrow lips into a tight line. "Very well," he conceded. "You are the wilderness expert. Make us a boat."

Renquist set Peters and Devlin as guard around the campsite while he helped Delacroix strip bark, cut cedar staves, and collect pine gum to construct a canoe that would carry them up the Fox River, along the shores of Lake Michigan, and into the Straits of Mackinac. Miri sat beside Hamilton, who was securely bound to a tree, and watched the work progress. They both enjoyed the meticulous officer's discomfiture as the French-Canadian half-breed set him to the dirtiest, most menial tasks—ones that in a Chippewa village would have been delegated to children. Renquist came to a slow boil, knowing he was being insulted but not knowing quite how. He had very little choice but to treat Delacroix with the utmost courtesy, though, as the guide was the only one who could get them home before the snow flew.

When dusk came, the canoe was well started. Two more days, Delacroix promised—three at the most—and they would be on their way. He grinned and winked at Miri across the fire she was feeding. She returned his familiarity with a face of frozen scorn.

"Isn't supper ready yet?" Renquist grumbled, a sour scowl upon his face.

"Go clean the rabbits yourself if you're in such a hurry," Miri invited.

"Don't you know how to cook anything besides bloody rabbit stew?"

"If you're hungry for something else, send one of your men out to hunt. I can't catch a deer in a rabbit snare."

"You'd like that, wouldn't you? No doubt you'd enjoy sending us out of camp one by one to be picked off by the filthy savages who make their home in these godforsaken woods. Don't you think . . . ?"

He was interrupted by a thrashing from the brush and a yelp of fear. Seconds later Private Devlin catapulted himself into the clearing, his attention riveted behind him as his legs worked frantically to propel him toward the fire.

"What the bloody hell?" Renquist stepped forward and caught the fearful trooper while Delacroix and Peters both grabbed their muskets and pointed them toward the brush from which he'd emerged. "What is wrong, man?"

Devlin's mouth fell open in wordless appeal. His eyes seemed to pop out of his bloodless face as Renquist gave him an angry shake.

"Answer me!" the lieutenant demanded.

"Ghost!" Devlin sputtered. "Oh, Lord! Save us all!"

Delacroix chuckled and lowered his musket. "Ghosts?"

His gaze flicked over to Miri. There was a sparkle of humor in his eyes.

Renquist gave Devlin another shake. "Don't talk nonsense! Did you see someone?"

The private's head bobbed up and down in desperate speed. "A dead man," he choked out. "Scott."

The name struck Miri in a ringing blow of hope. The man had seen Jordan. Could he possibly be alive? Was it he who had taken their canoe? Impossible.

Devlin gasped for breath. "I was washing up at the lake. I turned around and there he was. His face was all painted—with blood! And he laughed. Such a sound as you never heard! Lord! He'll kill us all!"

Renquist released the man with a vicious shove. "Scott's dead! You're seeing things."

"It's his ghost! I swear!"

"Shut up!"

Miri's heart wanted to soar, but caution held it in check. Impossible, reason scolded. It was impossible that he was alive and stalking them. Jordan had been struck down before Miri's very eyes. There had been so much blood. And yet. . . . Face painted with blood, Devlin said. That sounded like something Jordan might do to scare the pants off a troop of Brits.

Delacroix's chuckle sliced through the strained silence that followed. "So, we are being haunted by ghosts now." He shook his head, eyes twinkling. "I think I shall take myself elsewhere, Lieutenant." He gave Renquist a flippant wave and started to gather his things.

"What do you mean?" Renquist followed and grabbed his arm. "Don't tell me you believe in ghosts!"

"No, *monsieur*. But I know when something is sour, eh? First you and your commander"—he gestured to Michaels, who had lapsed into unconsciousness in midafternoon and was only now beginning to rouse—"tell me that no one will be hurt on this mission of yours. Then you take it upon yourself, Lieutenant, to kill Jordan Scott." He grinned wickedly into Renquist's angry face. "It appears that you did not do the deed thoroughly. And I know just how dangerous a man this Jordan Scott can be. I would not like to stand in your shoes, *monsieur.* And I do not think that anywhere near you is a safe place to be."

"But we cannot proceed without a canoe! And only you know how to make the damned thing!"

The French-Canadian shrugged. "Walk," he suggested. With a parting grin and a wink at Miri, he hefted his pack and disappeared into the brush.

Renquist's hands clenched at his sides as he stared after Delacroix. For a moment he stood unmoving, scarcely even breathing. Then he turned slowly around, surveying them all, one by one, pinning them with a gaze of rancorous contempt. His eyes came to Miri last of all. She flinched from the fury that twisted his face, but before she could dodge away he grabbed her and pinned her backward against his chest. She struggled, clawing at his face, but he merely slapped her hands away and clamped her arms against her sides.

"Jordan Scott!" he yelled into the night. His voice was swallowed by the darkness. "Show yourself, you bastard! Show yourself, or I'll slit the bitch's throat!"

His only answer was the wind rattling through the trees.

"I know you're watching, dammit!" His voice rose to near hysteria. Pinning Miri securely with one arm, he unsheathed his knife with his free hand and brought the blade to rest against her throat. "I'll do it! I swear I will, you son of a bitch!"

Miri stopped struggling. She, too, could feel the watching eyes, as though the forest itself was alive. The camp held its collective breath, then released it when Hamilton's angry cry broke the silence.

"Leave off, you brute! I'm the criminal here, remember? Not her." He struggled with his bonds, but Renquist ignored him.

"Let her go, Lieutenant," Michaels seconded. "That's an order."

"Like hell!" Renquist swung around in a circle, dragging

Miri with him as he scanned the forest with too-bright eyes. "You're incapacitated, Captain. I'm in command here."

"You're the one who's incapacitated, Renquist. Let her go."

"Scott!" Renquist screamed again. "I'll count to ten, Scott. Then I'm going to start cutting on this slut of yours!"

"Dammit! No!" Ham renewed his struggles and cast Miri a desperate look.

Renquist started the count, shouting each number into the watching night. Miri felt herself go numb as the knife blade pressed more tightly against her vulnerable throat. Thoughts of herself, of Jordan, and of their unborn child whirled around her head in a confused eddy of fear, anger, and sorrow. She didn't know what to pray for, except that God should take them all into His hands.

"Eight!" Renquist shouted.

Silence. More silence. No one so much as breathed.

"Nine!" Renquist gripped the knife in a spasm that whitened his knuckles.

Michaels's quiet voice cut off the final count. "Think, Renquist. With Delacroix gone, that girl is the only one with wilderness skills sufficient to guide us back to the island. If you cut her throat, you kill us all."

Renquist hesitated, his mouth forming around the word *ten*.

"If he's out there, Scott's not going to show himself." The captain's voice was a calm counterpoint to the madness that seemed to have Renquist in its grip. "The man's more savage than white, Lieutenant. He'll let you kill the girl and take his revenge later. You could torture the chit until Judgment Day and he'd not budge an inch. You're not dealing with a civilized man, Renquist."

Michaels's calm, persistent voice finally seemed to break through the younger officer's rigid anger. The lieutenant slumped, as though some inner support had melted. Miri twisted out of his suddenly loosened hold.

"Fix us something to eat," Michaels directed her quietly.

Miri hurried to where the ensnared rabbits waited to be cleaned, hopefully scanning the dark wall of the forest as she did so. Nothing moved. Nothing sounded. But something watched. Miri could feel it.

As the night grew deeper, the darkness seemed to press in upon the camp until the heaviness in the air was a palpable thing. Miri cooked the rabbits, cleaned up after the meal, and tried to ignore the sullen gaze from Renquist that dogged her every move. Last thing before the camp retired she tended Michaels. The wound in his chest looked less angry than it had the past few days, and he seemed to be regaining some of his strength. Miri thought she would never see the day that she prayed for Gerald Michaels' recovery, but now she did.

When she had finished rebandaging Michaels' side, Renquist ordered Peters to haul her bedding to the edge of the clearing and secure her there with an ankle tied to one tree and a wrist tied to another, allowing her to stretch out to sleep but preventing her from escaping her bonds. Then he set Devlin on guard.

"We'll see if our 'ghost' takes the bait," he said. "If you hear anything at all over in this direction"—he nodded toward Miri's bed—"shoot. You might nail yourself a skunk—or two." He gave Miri a chilling smile and walked off toward his own bed.

Miri refused to be cowed. Soon she would be out of this mess. Jordan was alive. She could feel his near presence vibrating her very soul. It was no vengeful ghost who walked the forest—who had made off with the canoe and eliminated the unfortunate Corporal Hayes; it was Jordan himself. And Renquist was no match for him. Only the vivid memory of Renquist's knife pressed against her throat gave her pause. The lieutenant had been about to slice her throat when Michaels had interceded. Had Jordan been watching? Would he have let her die, and their child along with her? She squeezed her eyes shut and tried to chase the thought from her mind. Jordan loved her. He would not have let Renquist harm her. And soon he would come to the rescue. She was determined to hold that hope in her mind. Otherwise, she would not have the courage to face another day.

She drifted into a sleep filled with dreams of Jordan. He walked across her uneasy slumber in images of contempt, anger, love—every way she had ever seen him. One image was so real she could almost reach out and touch the face that hovered above hers. She longed to smooth the anxious lines from that face and coax the familiar warmth back into those silver-gray eyes. His name formed on her lips, and she opened her mouth to call to him, not wanting the vision to fade. It was then that the image frowned and a hard-callused hand clamped over her mouth.

"Quiet," Jordan whispered.

Miri realized with a jolt that her eyes were wide open. The hovering face was not a dream at all. Jordan crouched beside her, clad only in loincloth and moccasins. His face was war-painted with what looked to be blood—his own, no doubt. Bloodstained bandages—the remnants of his homespun shirt—swathed his chest and banded his head. His hand smothered her exclamation of surprise.

He shook his head, cautioning her to silence. Miri gave a little nod, and he released her.

"Shh!" he murmured as she tried to rise into his arms. The ropes restrained her, and he made no move to untie them. Instead, he stretched out beside her, covered them both with her blankets, and pulled her body close to his bare flesh. His mouth closed over hers in a hungry kiss. For a moment she allowed herself the luxury of letting her senses drown in the scent and the feel of him. It took all her determination to pull away.

"The guard!" she whispered.

"Taken care of."

Miri didn't ask how poor Devlin had been disposed of. She had liked the little private. He and Peters had both treated her kindly. But the most important thing was that Jordan was alive and was this very moment holding her against him as if he would never let her go. Her life was restored.

"He and Corporal Hayes are making a little detour with some Indian friends of mine," Jordan elaborated. "The Brits aren't too pleased, but they'll be all right."

Miri smiled and whispered against his shoulder. "Thank you."

"For what?"

"For not killing them."

He brushed a tendril of hair from her cheek, caressing her skin as his finger trailed across her face. "They are not my enemy."

Miri could almost physically feel his mind turn to Renquist. Renquist—who even now could be waking to the quiet sound of their voices.

"Take me out of here before someone wakes," she pleaded.

"Not quite yet, my love. I think there's a good reason to play out this game to the very end." He felt her grip tighten in dismay. "It's all right," he whispered, gently pressing his lips to her forehead, then the very tip of her nose. "They'll not hurt you. I won't let them."

Miri didn't answer, thinking once again of Renquist's sharp knife lying against her throat. As if sensing her thoughts, he tilted her head up so his eyes caught hers.

"My arrow would have pierced his skull before he could have used that knife, Miri. I would not have let him hurt you." He caressed her cheek with his thumb. "Do you believe me?"

"Yes. I believe you." If she had still doubted his love, the look in his eyes and the gentle message of his touch would have convinced her of its strength.

"I won't let anything happen to you."

"I know."

"Good girl," he whispered in her ear. "Are you up for a little more adventure?"

"What do you want, you damned renegade?"

He smiled at her teasing tone. "There's a little ridge just north of here, not too much of a detour off the route you'll be taking tomorrow. It's called Rabbit Ridge, and you can tell it from the formation on top—looks like a pair of short rabbit ears. Lead them that way and take them through the ears. The land gets swampy by the river. You can use that as an excuse for a detour."

"What happens then?"

"Then these damned Brits will find out that ghosts aren't merely stories to scare children."

"You'll be careful?"

Jordan chuckled, a low rumble that was more a vibration of his broad chest than an actual sound. "They're the ones who should be careful." He kissed her, a brief promise of passion—and more. Then he slipped out of the blankets and was gone as silently as he'd come.

Miri almost felt sorry for her captors. Almost, but not quite.

✳ 22 ✳

Rabbit Ridge was just as Jordan had described it. Two rabbit ears of stone loomed above them as Miri led her little party up the gentle incline toward the pass that threaded between the ears.

"I'm beginning to think the swamp would have been easier," Renquist complained.

Peters grunted in agreement. He was the only man left to pull Michaels's travois, for when morning had awakened the camp, Devlin had not been at his guard post. Renquist and Peters had searched diligently, almost desperately, but they had not located him or any tracks to indicate what had become of him. The Brits were genuinely spooked by now. Miri suspected that even the lieutenant was beginning to believe in ghosts. She took a most unchristian delight in the frightened glances he directed toward the surrounding forest as they made their way forward.

"Cheer up, Lieutenant," Michaels said from the travois. "Miss Sutcliffe wouldn't lead us astray, now, would she? After all, she's in this with the rest of us."

He knows, Miri thought, catching the carefully bland look he threw her way. He had to know, the way he had been regarding her all morning since they'd left the riverbank, which had indeed grown uncomfortably swampy. What was his game? Was he so anxious for Jordan's hide that he was willing to walk into a trap on the chance that he might turn the tables and be victor? Or did he despise Renquist enough to let him get his just deserts, even if it would mean his own fall? Miri felt sorry for Michaels, and she felt sorry for Peters. For Renquist she had no pity at all.

They wound their way through the pass. Two columns of stone jutted above them. Miri stopped and surveyed the terrain ahead. They had emerged into a bowl-shaped valley with a grassy bottom rimmed by pine-studded rocky hills. The only way out was the way they had come in. Renquist and Peters might be too inexperienced to recognize a natural trap when they walked into one, but after spending the winter with the wily Chippewa, Miri wasn't. She doubted very much if Michaels was, either. But the captain said nothing— just gave her a shrewd look as he was carried past her.

"About bloody time this trail turned downhill." Hamilton shot Miri an injured look as he stumbled along behind Michaels. Miri shook her head. There was another for whom she could feel no sympathy. Hamilton's shoulder wound was little more than a scratch, yet for all the drama he gave the injury, it might have been a mortal blow. And to think she had almost married that man!

She shook her head in bemusement and broke into a trot to catch up to the front of the line. "There's water down here, I think. Perhaps we should stop and eat something."

"I see a stream," Peters agreed. "Maybe I can catch some fish for dinner."

"Hold fast, there!" came a shout. "Or you won't be needing any dinner."

Jordan's voice came from behind them. Miri whirled. Renquist jerked a pistol from his belt and did the same. Jordan was nowhere in sight, but his challenge had come from the trees on one side of the narrow pass they had just negotiated.

The voice came again. "Surrender, Renquist. You've lost."

"Like hell, you goddamned savage!" The lieutenant raised his pistol, but before he could thumb the hammer an arrow streaked from the trees and buried itself a scant two inches from his boots. He looked at the deadly shaft quivering near his toes and laughed.

"You missed, Scott!"

"No. I didn't. The next one will split your skull."

Miri sidled over to Hamilton. While everyone's attention was riveted on Jordan's voice, she worked hurriedly at the bonds that tied his hands.

"Surrender, Lieutenant!" Jordan called again. "You can move neither forward nor back, and I can sit up here and kill you at my leisure."

"Offer to bargain," Michaels ordered quietly. "He can take Miss Sutcliffe if we keep Greer."

Renquist ignored the captain's suggestion. There was a bargaining chip in this encounter that Michaels might be loath to use, but Renquist wasn't. He glanced around to find Miri, then snarled when he saw her working frantically on Hamilton's bonds. "What do you think you're doing?" He yanked her away, then gave Hamilton's wrists a yank. The ropes were still secure. "You led us into this trap, bitch. You'll get us out." He pushed her in front of him.

"If you shoot, renegade, your arrow will go through her before it gets to me." He brought the muzzle of his pistol up to Miri's temple. "Now come out and surrender yourself, or I'll blow her brains all over this miserable valley."

"No you won't, dammit!" Hamilton took Renquist by surprise as he launched himself forward. But his attempt at rescue was hampered by his still-bound hands. Renquist easily brushed him aside and sent him stumbling to the ground.

"Do you doubt what I say, renegade? Watch."

The lieutenant raised the pistol and fired. Hamilton screamed as a lead ball plowed through his shoulder, leaving not a scratch this time but a gaping, bloody hole.

There was no answer as the pistol's explosion bounced off the valley walls. Then Jordan called in an unperturbed voice, "I should have known you'd hide behind a woman and choose to fight helpless men."

With Miri clasped securely in front of him, Renquist handed the pistol to Peters to be reloaded. He ignored Michaels' urgent order to cease.

"You're a coward, Renquist. You're afraid to stand and fight, man to man."

"I'm a gentleman, Scott! I don't play your savage games."

"Pick any game you want, Lieutenant. I can beat you at it."

Renquist was silent, then a smile stretched his narrow lips. He reached out his hand. "Peters, hand me Captain Michaels' sword."

Peters blinked in confusion, then did as he was ordered.

Renquist raised the weapon above his head. "Let's see how a savage does with a gentleman's weapon, Scott."

There was a pause, and Miri felt Renquist's fingers dig into her arm.

"Meet me halfway," came the call from the trees.

Renquist laughed, then ordered Peters to stay behind. "I can take care of this now." He pushed Miri in front of him, using her as a shield while he advanced toward the pass. At the base of the stone rabbit ears, a tall figure detached itself from a tree and moved forward to meet them.

Miri's heart contracted. Did Jordan have any idea what he was doing? Fencing required years of training and practice. She had no doubt that an aristocrat such as the lieutenant had studied for years.

"Do you still need to hide behind a woman?" Jordan asked contemptuously as they met on the grassy meadow below the pass.

Renquist shoved Miri aside. "You're the one who should hide, Scott. I'm going to show you how a gentleman fights." He threw him Michaels' sword as he drew his own. Jordan's deft catch and the easy way the renegade hefted the sword in his hand sent a twitch of surprise across the lieutenant's face.

"En garde!" Jordan said, raising his sword in traditional salute.

Renquist followed suit.

Miri thought she had never seen anything quite so strange as the scene before her—a scarlet-coated British aristocrat dueling a half-naked, blood-painted savage in the remote wilds of America. But her heart was caught up so in the deadly contest that she failed to appreciate the incongruity.

Jordan parried Renquist's first attack and pressed forward with one of his own. Forced into a strategic retreat, the lieutenant cursed in surprise.

"Boston does have fencing masters for those who can afford them," Jordan explained with a wicked grin. "And my mother was very rich."

Renquist slashed forward, only to be met with a neat parry, followed by a series of thrusts that were just as vicious as his. His mouth compressed into a tight line. For the first time, he looked worried.

Jordan wasted no time in pressing his attack. He was skilled enough for a student who had been only mildly interested in the art of fencing, but he knew that his skill was no match for Renquist's polished style. His advantage lay in speed, strength, agility, and determination.

The contest went back and forth, carrying the duelists toward the spot where Michaels and Peters waited. Miri followed, watching with terrified eyes. Jordan was holding his own, but Renquist's eyes gleamed with rabid hatred. She feared that the very force of his madness would carry him through Jordan's defense. Once she had faced Jordan's death, and it had torn her apart. Nothing was worth losing him again. Absolutely nothing.

Dragging her attention away from the combatants, Miri glanced desperately around the clearing in an attempt to find a weapon that she could use to aid Jordan. Fair play and honor be damned! She wanted this absurd duel finished and Jordan safe. Her gaze fell upon the pistol that Renquist had discarded when he had gone forward to meet Jordan. It lay close by the travois, but Michaels appeared not to have noticed it. She moved closer to the coveted weapon in what she hoped was a deceptively casual manner. The pistol was almost within her reach when a harsh exclamation jolted her awareness back toward the fight.

Renquist had stumbled over a patch of uneven ground. He grabbed a fistful of dirt and flung it into Jordan's face. Jordan managed to dodge the blinding debris, but he was thrown off balance long enough for Renquist to regain his feet and lunge forward with a thrust that grazed Jordan's ribs. Miri gasped and instinctively moved forward, only to find that she was held back by Michaels' hand, locked upon her ankle.

"Leave them be, Miss Sutcliffe. If they manage to kill each other, we'll both be better off."

"Is that the way a gentleman plays the game?" Jordan asked Renquist contemptuously. He ignored the new blood spreading in a crimson blossom across his bandages.

Like a predator who scents blood, Renquist pressed incautiously forward. "When one fights a cur dog, one uses a dog's rules."

Jordan refused to be baited. He let Renquist come, retreating as the lieutenant's thrusts grew wilder and more vicious.

"Cur dog, is it?" Jordan asked in a deceptively mild voice.

Renquist leaped forward again. Jordan retreated, but saw his opening. In a deft movement his sword slipped past the lieutenant's careless guard and buried itself in Renquist's right shoulder. Renquist twisted away as Jordan freed his blade from bloodied flesh. With a pained gasp the officer clutched at his wound. His sword dropped from fingers gone numb.

"You might do well to learn the difference between a dog and a wolf," Jordan advised calmly. He brought his crimson-stained blade to rest at the helpless man's throat. "What's it to be, my gentleman friend? Will you surrender, or are you anxious to make the devil's acquaintance?"

"Surrender," Renquist choked out.

"Then go over to the lady and apologize," Jordan ordered. "Very prettily, as a gentleman should."

The lieutenant stumbled toward Miri. "I apologize." His eyes clung to the ground at her feet.

"You can do better than that," Jordan prompted, prodding with the blade in the small of his victim's back.

Renquist jumped, then dropped hastily down upon his knees. This time his gaze entreated her pity. "Miss Sutcliffe, please forgive me my... my abominable behavior toward you. I offer my humblest apologies. My very humblest apologies."

"I don't want his apologies." Miri had once thought that Renquist on his knees would be quite a satisfying sight. Instead, it turned her stomach. "I don't want him near me, Jordan. End this. Please."

"Yes, do end this."

Michaels' voice took them by surprise. The captain had finally noticed the pistol lying close to his hand and brought it up to point at Jordan's chest. "Take Miss Sutcliffe and be gone, Scott. I want no part of you. But I do want Mr. Greer over there."

A groan from Hamilton reminded Miri that her cousin still lay among the weeds, clutching the shoulder that had been shattered by Renquist's pistol ball. Michaels' attention was diverted, as well—only for a second, but that was enough. Jordan struck out with his foot. The pistol went flying from the captain's hand and bounced on the ground behind him. Peters jumped toward it, but he halted when Jordan brought his bloody blade to rest at the captain's throat.

"Tell your man to leave it, Michaels. Grace would have my hide if I brought you home in more than one piece."

Michaels waved the private back. He managed a rueful smile. "We wouldn't want to rile the widow, would we?"

While Jordan retrieved the pistol and set a confused Peters to tending Renquist's wound, Miri ran to Hamilton, whose moans had been growing in volume. She knelt beside him and pulled his bloody shirt back to expose the hole in his shoulder.

"Ouch! Oooo! Be careful, Miri!"

"Oh, stop your moaning, Ham. It isn't so bad. You'll be

good as new in no time.'' She started to rip bandages from the cleaner part of his shirt.

''Ow! Dammit! Have some sympathy, girl! I got this trying to save your life.''

''After you did your best to ruin it!'' At her cousin's hurt look, Miri relented. ''All right. I'm grateful. That was very brave of you.''

His face brightened like that of a little boy receiving praise. ''You know, Miri, I do love you. I always have, in my own way.''

''You had a fine way of showing it, Ham.''

''I never meant any harm. Ouch! Dammit! Watch what you're doing there!''

''Just be grateful I'm not *really* mad. Then you would have something to complain about!''

Hamilton gave a martyred sigh. ''You never understood that some men just aren't meant to be upright and virtuous. You tried to push me into a mold I couldn't fit.''

''I guess I did.'' Miri glanced up at Jordan, who was testing the bonds that secured Renquist and Peters. There was a man whose mold she certainly wouldn't tamper with, even if she could. She had tried in the past. She knew better now. At last, her mother's love for David Sutcliffe was understandable, and her grief when she lost him. Her mother hadn't made a mistake in falling in love with a backwoods savage. Her mistake had been in trying to keep her savage in a gilded cage. It was an error that Miri didn't intend to make.

As if he felt Miri's eyes upon him, Jordan looked up. ''Is he going to live?'' Face grim, he came to stand by Hamilton.

''The wound isn't as bad as it appears,'' Miri answered. ''He'll be all right.''

''Good.'' Jordan squatted down beside the wounded man. The humorless smile that stretched his mouth made Miri uneasy. It terrified Hamilton. ''I wouldn't want Mr. Greer to die—yet. He and I have some business to take care of.''

Miri had heard that tone of voice before and knew that it boded ill for her cousin. ''Jordan . . . he's my cousin.''

"So he is," Jordan agreed in the same ominous tone. "And I won't harm a hair on his head, my love. Not as long as he tells me what I want to know."

Hamilton was past the point of being stubborn. The glint in those silver-gray eyes made a British prison seem like a haven of safety.

"Where is that cursed list, Greer?"

Miri glanced from her cousin to Jordan in confusion. "The list is at the bottom of Lake Huron."

"One of them is," Jordan agreed. "Where's the other one, Greer?"

Hamilton grimaced. "It was in my left boot—sewn into the sole. But the lieutenant found it when he searched me. His men were very thorough."

"I thought they might be," Jordan said grimly, "or I wouldn't have gone to all this trouble." He turned back to Renquist. "Are you going to tell me where it is, friend? You don't have to. I'm sure I could find it by searching your dead body."

Renquist blanched. "In my coat. Left side."

Jordan pulled the lieutenant's coat open. "You may live another day yet, Renquist." He pulled the soiled and crumpled piece of paper from its hiding place. Michaels's mouth drew into a tight line as Jordan opened the paper, scanned the list, then put it in the small leather pouch that hung from his neck. Renquist only sighed in relief.

"How did you know he would have two?" Miri demanded.

"Human nature, my love. A man who sells out his country for money isn't going to let his hopes for a fortune be buried in your Bible. I would guess he intended for Michaels to find that list and be satisfied in having his information back. Your gentleman cousin could then close his deal with the Americans and the Brits would be none the wiser."

"Hamilton!" Miri turned and gave her cousin a disgusted glare. "You're a toad!"

Ham shrugged ruefully, then grimaced at the pain.

"The list," Michaels demanded. "What are you going to do with the damned list?"

Jordan grinned at the British officer. "Give me time. I'll think of something."

Fall was a beautiful time of year on Grace's farm, Miri decided. The maples, elms, and oaks were all dressed in their autumn reds and golds, and the air was cool and scented with the tang of wood smoke.

Mary Beth skipped out of the farmhouse, waking Miri from her dreamy somnolence where she sat in the porch rocker, looking out onto the garden. "Ma's yelling at the captain again." She giggled.

Miri heard Grace's voice scolding inside the house. "You climb back into that bed right now, Gerald Michaels. Behave yourself, or I'll turn you back over to that butcher you call an army surgeon. Lordy! You'd think with two holes in him, a man would have the sense to stay in bed!"

Miri smiled. Gerald Michaels had supplanted her in the little bedroom facing the lake, and she had moved her things into the loft with Lucy. As soon as they had returned to the island and Grace had heard that Michaels was hurt, she gave none of them a minute's peace until the British officer had consented to recuperate at the farm.

"I like Gerald," Mary Beth said in a worldly-wise tone. "He's nice, even if he does frown a lot. I'll bet he marries Ma."

Miri laughed at the grown-up expression on the girl's face. "I'll bet he does, too, Mary Beth."

There must be something about that bedroom, Miri thought. She had awakened there one day and found herself with one foot on the road to becoming an American. Now the same was happening to the terribly proper, terribly British Captain Michaels. It served him right.

Not that she hadn't learned some respect for the man. He had told her and Jordan about his promise to Willow Song and, as far as he was able, he had honored the Chippewa girl's request. McDouall wouldn't learn of Jordan's whereabouts from Michaels. The British captain owed them that much aside from his promise. After all, they could have left him in the wilderness to die, but instead they had dressed his wound and transported him home. There were times, Michaels had asserted, that personal indebtedness came before duty to one's country, and this was one of them.

"Are you feeling all right, Miri?" Mary Beth asked. "You're not saying much. Is the baby making you sick?"

"No," Miri said with a gentle smile. Mary Beth's own mouth worked so constantly that she couldn't understand the meaning of a quiet mood. "I'm feeling fine, Mary Beth. In fact, I feel better than I have in a long, long time."

"Well, then, if you're not sick, I'm going off to help Margaret in the garden. I saw her sparking with Gavin MacFee in town yesterday, and I'll just bet she's looking for someone to tell about it."

Miri leaned back in the rocker and watched Mary Beth trot toward the garden, where Margaret was gathering the last of the squash. This farm, this whole land, felt so much like home now that she had the peace to enjoy them. All her problems had fallen neatly into place: she was a free woman; Renquist—the treacherous toad—was confined in the fort waiting to face the court martial charges that Michaels had filed; and Cousin Ham was getting exactly what he deserved.

Miri nearly laughed aloud, remembering Hamilton's face when the Ottawa at L'Arbre Croche—prompted by Willow Song—had extended an invitation for him to stay. He had the choice of facing British justice or hiding with the Indians for the rest of the war. With ill grace he had chosen the Indians. Miri hadn't missed the gleam in Willow Song's eye. She doubted that Hamilton Greer—traitor, gentleman gambler, and fop—would recognize himself when Willow was through with him. Miri had walked that road herself, and she knew what it was like.

That took care of all of her problems but one. And the last of her problems was walking up the beach trail toward the house.

When Jordan saw Miri sitting on the porch he quickened his stride. In the week since they had returned he had left her alone with her thoughts, knowing she needed to sort them through. There had been a time when he might have tried to force her to stay, confident that he could make her happy, that he could make her love him as much as she loved England and her home across the sea. But now he was better acquainted with love and realized that it could never be forced, even with the best of intentions.

"Hello, stranger," Miri said as he climbed the steps to the porch. "I thought we'd seen the last of you for a while." Her eyes traveled over the Chippewa garb that had replaced his homespun shirt and buckskin trousers. The only thing about him that still looked white was the wealth of tawny hair that curled about his ears and neck.

"You're a long way from seeing the last of me." He sat down on the porch rail in front of her, trying to read her mood from her face. He wondered at the twinkle in her eye. Was it there because she was free at last to return to England, or was it there for him? For the first time, he allowed himself to consider the possibility that her love for him was not great enough to keep her from going home.

"I thought perhaps you'd gone chasing after the American commanders to give them that precious list of yours," she said.

"I burned the list," he told her, watching for her reaction. "Under-the-table deals are not how I fight. There's been enough misery because of that damned list of names."

Miri lowered her eyes, then peeked up from under her eyelashes in uncharacteristic coyness. "Not all misery, Jordan."

"No," he agreed, his voice dropping to a husky whisper. "Not all misery." Her words and her look gave him courage. "It's time for the family to move, Miri. I'm going with them to winter camp. The British still have a price on my head for my part in the American attack. I'll have to continue to be Chippewa until this war is over."

"And then?" she asked, her voice quiet.

"Then I'll see about becoming a white man again. There's a fortune still waiting for me in Boston, and I'm thinking that with that much money I could have a nice farm or ranch, maybe farther west. It's a big country. There's a lot of opportunity for someone who's willing to work hard—even the bastard son of a rich whore.''

Miri was silent for a moment. Then she smiled.

''You're a free woman, now, Miri. You can go home if you want. The last brigade upriver will be leaving in about a week. You could get to Montreal before the baby is due.''

There. It was out. The decision was laid before her.

''Are you trying to rid yourself of me, Jordan Scott? Mercy me, it seems that every time I latch on to a man, he throws me over to go adventuring.''

''You know that's not true.'' He was unable to smile at her lightheartedness. All week he had feared this moment. He had the courage to face it, but not to smile while she dangled his heart above a fire.

''It's a good thing. You'd have to use a crowbar to pry me away from you.''

Jordan's face went blank with surprise. Then he slowly smiled. ''Is that so?''

''That's so,'' she teased. Then she was suddenly serious. ''In truth, Jordan, even if it's only your child that you want, I'll eventually make you love me, as well.''

He laughed out loud. ''Miriam Sutcliffe! Do you think I would put up with you—stubborn, high-handed, hardheaded witch that you are—for the sake of a baby? No fatherly devotion is so great.''

For a moment Miri was nonplussed. Then her brows puckered in an irritated frown. ''Stubborn, high-handed, hardheaded witch?''

''You are. But I love you, little witch. More than life itself. If you take into that hard head of yours to leave, as soon as this goddamned war is over I'll come looking for you. And when I find you, I'll dog your heels until you love me enough to come home with me.''

She arched a brow in skeptical question. ''You said once that if I carried your child I would come with you whether I willed it or not.''

''Lord, woman. That was when I was still a fool. After

spending the last year with you, I'd rather try to make a she-bear stand up and dance than to force you to do something you don't fancy doing!"

A gentle look came into her eyes. She leaned forward and touched his cheek. "What I want to do is stay with you forever, Jordan. Life with you might be hard, but life without you would be impossible. I learned that lesson when I thought I'd lost you."

A shriek broke the peace of the moment, followed by a flood of girlish giggles. While they had been intent upon each other, Margaret and Mary Beth had eased silently from the garden to a spot just below the porch. Now they jumped up and down in glee, hugging each other and improvising a little ditty about Miri being in love.

"You bratty snoops!" Miri half laughed, half scolded. "What do you think you're doing?"

Margaret had the grace to look shamefaced. Not Mary Beth. She bounded onto the porch and through the farmhouse door, yellow pigtails flying straight out behind her. "Ma! Lucy! Guess what?"

Miri let out an exasperated sigh, but came willingly into Jordan's outstretched arms. Face crimson, Margaret headed back to the garden.

"Shall we send Mary Beth for Father Carroll?" Jordan asked. "It might keep the brat out of our hair for a while."

"You want to get married today?" Miri almost giggled. "We're leaving tomorrow."

"Then today it is."

Jordan's mouth came down to cover Miri's in a kiss that promised a passion scarcely held in check. It had been a long, long time, Miri mused, since they had been alone together. She burrowed her head into the hollow of his throat. From the open door came Mary Beth's exclamations and Grace's clucks of satisfaction, but even louder was the drumming of Jordan's heart under her ear as he pulled her more closely against him.

It seemed hardly possible that the loving man who held her in his arms was the same savage who had bound his own wounds, painted himself in his own blood and stalked Renquist's little troop until they had one by one dissolved in terror. And she herself seemed very little like the priggish and proper spinster who had journeyed from England over a year before.

But people didn't really change much, Miri mused, warm and content against Jordan's chest. At least, not deep down inside they didn't. The savage was still there, and so was the prig. It was going to be an interesting marriage. But then, wasn't that the best kind?